Sasha Blake leads an amazing double life. She sp
every morning with her characters, wafting around the
pool of a Hollywood mansion or sunbathing on a private
beach in the Maldives. The afternoons she spends in
London, chasing a ball around a field with three small
boys, changing nappies and refereeing fights. She is also
the author of *Betrayal*.

D1375283

Also by Sasha Blake

BETRAYAL

and published by Bantam Books

THE WISH

Sasha Blake

BANTAM BOOKS

LONDON • TORONTO • SYDNEY • AUCKLAND • JOHANNESBURG

TRANSWORLD PUBLISHERS
61–63 Uxbridge Road, London W5 5SA
A Random House Group Company
www.rbooks.co.uk

THE WISH
A BANTAM BOOK: 9780553819168

First publication in Great Britain
Bantam edition published 2010

Copyright © The Parallax Corporation 2010

Addresses for Random House Group Ltd companies outside the UK
can be found at: www.randomhouse.co.uk
The Random House Group Ltd Reg. No. 954009

The Random House Group Limited supports The Forest Stewardship
Council (FSC), the leading international forest certification organisation. All
our titles that are printed on Greenpeace approved FSC certified paper carry
the FSC logo. Our paper procurement policy can be found at
www.rbooks.co.uk/environment

Typeset in 11/14pt Palatino by Falcon Oast Graphic Art Ltd.
Printed in the UK by CPI Cox & Wyman, Reading, RG1 8EX.

2 4 6 8 10 9 7 5 3 1

To Mary, with love

Acknowledgements

Thank you to all the very kind generous people who answered my endless questions. I am so grateful for your time and patience. Infuriatingly, towards the end of writing, my laptop died, taking with it a number of names and numbers. So if I mention only first names, please forgive me.

So, thank you, to the one and only Steve Cyr at the Hard Rock. Thank you to LVMPD officers Virginia Griffin, Bill Cassell, and Jack Owen. I am in awe of your courage and dedication – and your sense of humour! Any errors relating to police procedure or policy (and personality) are of course mine. Emily and Dr Jack K were also fantastic – Dr Jack was kind enough to detail 'Bessie's escape' for me, and advised on pharmaceutical matters.

Thank you to Sharyn Rosenblum, my dear friend and LV partner in crime. We must return! Danny Amster, expert on all things LV, and Mike – Ben owes his safe flight from the Bahamas to you! Of the many excellent non-fiction books I read on Las Vegas, the following were particularly enthralling: *Whale Hunt in the Desert* by Deke Castleman, and *Winner Takes All* by Christina Binkley. Senior Lead officer Ralph Sanchez of LAPD helped me again – it is always humbling to speak to those who do a proper job . . . Mary Maxted painted a vivid picture of life in Israel – note to family: Sofia and her opinions hail from my imagination!! Thank you to Harry and Dina Smith for the wonderful depiction of life in Africa.

Lastly, thank you to all the wonderful people at Transworld who have worked so hard to make this book a success.

THE WISH

Prologue

Lulu

It was the tiniest thing that made her realize she might fall in love with him. Or maybe she was so starved of feeling special that when a man praised her, she gravitated towards him like a hungry plant reaching for the sun.

All that had happened was this: Lulu's boss had written an article for the *Las Vegas Review-Journal* and passed it on to her to check. She'd highlighted six errors, marking them in red type. That same evening, giving Joe his bath, she'd had a flash of horror. Had Ben required her nitpicking list of corrections, or had he expected her to say: 'My God, it's genius!'? She'd hauled an indignant Joe out of his bath and tapped out a message to Ben, apologizing for being 'bossy'.

Blip, said her phone a minute later. His response: 'Don't be silly. You are a joy to work with. Ben x'.

Lulu gazed at the word 'joy' – and at the 'x', and then she imagined Ben bending to softly kiss her cheek. And a silly grin lit her face. You idiot, she thought. She was like Miss Moneypenny mooning over James Bond. She was

1

Ben's PA and a single mother, although she took issue with that phrase; she was a double mother, doing the job of two parents. She had no money, no glamour; she was merely a business perk.

Meanwhile, Ben Arlington was a rising star in the sparkling constellation that was the Nevada gaming industry. He was the son and heir of one of the most powerful casino operators in the United States, and, allegedly, the brains of the family. He was also twenty-four, handsome, single, with approximately a million rich, successful, beautiful women fighting like sewer rats for his affections. Why ever would he choose her? Lulu was in urgent need of a fairy godmother but, sadly, they didn't exist.

And yet, staring out of her window at the darkly glittering night sky, she allowed herself to wish. Because everyone has a wish, don't they? And however impossible that wish might seem, is it so wrong to wonder and hope that, one far-off, magical day, it might be granted?

BOOK 1

The Big Bear Cat Hotel & Casino, Las Vegas, Grand Opening, 26 January 2009, Chinese New Year, 9 p.m.

Sofia

Sofia Arlington had spent her life trying to avoid this moment. But it had found her.

She stood still; there was nowhere to run. The diamonds at her neck captured the harsh casino light and changed it to rainbows. All around her was frenetic noise; laughter, coins, the *whoop, whoop, whoop* of a win on the slots – or rather, the computerized recording of an imaginary win, because these days nothing was as it seemed. She was surrounded by smoke, warm bodies, the heat and tension of sex and fear.

Her bodyguard was waiting to go. She couldn't move. Her mind spiralled. It was as if she was seeing her life as frames in a movie; all the important parts picked out.

She saw Ben, placed in her arms for the first time, his newborn face all scrunched up. She had held him and whispered, 'God owes me a boy.' She saw Frank, cradling the baby, a tear rolling down his cheek. He had

5

proposed that evening. She had delivered; marriage was her reward. Together they had built an empire.

Now it would be torn from her. Everything, gone. This woman had the power to take it all.

Surveillance had called her to observe a cheat, amused that some fool would try to hustle the house on its opening night. Seventeen high-def cameras zoomed in on the woman's hand sliding smoothly over the thousand-dollar chips, focusing on a witchy ring with rubies set high and precarious around a frog-green stone on antique gold, long nails painted scarlet like blood pumped fresh from a broken heart, and fingers stained with the tell-tale nicotine of a person failing to smoke out bad memories.

Without seeing the face, Sofia recognized the hand and she knew. It was *Bessie*. After twenty-five years, the enemy had tracked her down.

Terror drained through her slender body, right down to her spiky bespoke stilettos. As her men prepared to remove the woman from the floor, Sofia knew that the joke was on her. She had not trapped a cheat. It was the other way round.

Her brain buzzed. Sofia closed her eyes; the squat square glass holding the mint julep slipped from her grasp and shattered.

Stiffly, she moved away, struggling for air, as underlings dived to clear up the mess of shards. Chief of Security, 'Manhattan' Karl, awaited her instructions, his sharp grey eyes fixed on her.

'Take her downstairs but don't start the questioning. I'll meet you there in five minutes.' Sofia stopped. 'My husband is busy with guests. He doesn't need to know about this.'

She managed to walk out of the surveillance room, but once she reached the casino itself – that beguiling fairy grotto for grown-ups, set amid pretty twinkling lights and lush fake foliage, encircled by the most exclusive expensive stores and restaurants in the world – fear paralysed her.

Twenty-five years ago she had made a pact with the devil so that she could live her dream. She could not accept that her time was up.

This woman would not destroy her. Sofia would fight, and win.

She began the slow walk to face her nemesis. Her progress was slowed by the players, high rollers, famous faces who swirled around her like snowflakes in a blizzard. 'Amazing,' they cooed, 'spectacular . . . a triumph', but she was barely able to nod and smile.

On she strode towards fate, with her silent guard, out of the protective walls of the emerald city and into the long cold tube-lit corridors that snaked down to the vault and the holding cells.

Sofia reached the thick reinforced steel door. Then, quick, sharp, she signalled to the guard to let her through. 'I'll handle this,' she said.

The woman lolled in the metal chair, insolent. Her complexion was red and scuffed. It was the drink and the cigarettes; once you hit forty, time sped to a gallop. If you were careless you could age a decade in one year.

'Hello, Bessie,' said Sofia.

Slowly, Bessie locked eyes with Sofia. And then she spat.

Her men tensed; Sofia raised a hand. As she did so, an imperfection caught her eye; a diamond was missing from her nail polish. There was a tiny pock mark in the pale pink varnish on her ring finger.

The jewel was lost. The ugly absence of perfection was like a curse.

'You', she addressed the woman, her voice clear and taut and unafraid, 'have made a mistake coming here.'

'No, no,' replied the woman. 'I have facts. I have evidence.' The woman paused. 'I have the truth. There are no mistakes except *yours*, Mrs Arlington.'

The brazen tone robbed Sofia of speech.

She turned and swept from the room. She fumbled for her cell phone and spoke urgently into it, then she ran to her private office, pressing the combination lock, fingers clumsy, slipping.

Inside, she sank to her knees and screamed, and as she screamed, she scratched the nail polish, peeling it off in curls, popping off the diamonds. She watched them jump like suicides into the air.

There was a sharp knock. She stood up, and smoothed her hair as Sterling, her PA (or 'henchman' as Frank called him), slid into the room. His long, pale face looked untroubled. He wore his trademark black suit. She had never seen him wear colour.

'Sterling,' she whispered. 'She's found me. Is this the end?'

Sterling smiled – like a crack in a glacier. 'For her, yes,' he said. 'One merely has to conceive *how*. I suggest you start with a friendly drink, and then we'll work out the rest.'

Sofia nodded. Then she snatched a pair of white silk gloves from a desk drawer, marched back to the cell, and dismissed the guards. 'Turn everything off,' she told Karl. 'I don't want this on record.'

The men left and she stood and faced the woman. She forced a smile, placed a bottle of Grey Goose on the metal table and opened it. She poured the vodka slowly into two black lead-crystal goblets filled with crushed ice. 'I see no reason we can't be civilized about this.'

A muscle twitched under the woman's eye. She grabbed a goblet and drained it. Sofia refilled the goblet. This time, the woman took a sip, closed her eyes and shoved it away. 'Just take it,' she said. 'I don't want any more.'

Carefully, Sofia took the goblet, smudged with Bessie's sticky fingerprints, in her silk gloved hands, and placed it to one side. She was desperate.

The woman gazed at her sullenly from under a mess of hair.

'I gave you everything you asked for,' shouted Sofia. 'Everything!'

How did you find me?

The woman gazed at her, unblinking. 'It turned out everything wasn't enough.'

'We had a deal,' said Sofia. 'You already know the consequences of breaking it. I believe your husband died at the hands of, oh, what was it, a drug cartel?'

The woman shrugged and Sofia stared, helpless. She should be in control, but it didn't feel that way. It was incredible to her that this nobody, this *carrier monkey*, had all the power.

9

Bessie licked her dry, cracked lips. 'I don't care,' she said, with a cold finality that squeezed Sofia's heart in its fist.

'I'll make you disappear,' said Sofia. She picked up a chair and smashed it into the table. 'Don't you *see*?'

The woman didn't flinch.

'It doesn't matter to me,' said the woman. The most frightening thing was her lack of emotion. 'Nothing matters. You know what I want, and I don't care what you do with me after. You can threaten anything but it won't change what *is*. Nothing you can do is more powerful than what is in *here*.' Bessie pressed her hand to her chest with some kind of forgotten dignity. 'In here is the wish. Oh God, I was crazy back then. I wish . . .' For the first time her voice faltered. 'I wish I had said no.'

The Cat, that same evening, 10 p.m.

Frank

Yeah, yeah, yeah, here we go, baby!

Frank clapped his hands as a million dollars' worth of fireworks deafened the neighbours for miles around.

All Frank's mistakes were behind him. Frank was half genius, half idiot, so they said, but tonight, he was solid gold; he ruled Las Vegas!

No one talked about the blue-whale episode and the year-long delay it had caused the project, but you had to applaud ambition, even if it had turned out that a marine mammal the length of three buses would never survive in a tank off the Strip. Shame really, it would have been cool.

Now Frank could laugh, and so could his investors. Everything was going great. He looked around; he saw Ben: handsome, charming, smart; surrounded. He winked and raised his glass. Wonderful thing, procreation; he was a lucky guy.

Hard to believe the kid was twenty-four, hard to imagine he'd saved everyone's ass. Thanks to Ben, Frank's crazy-assed whale project the 'Pacific' was dead. The 'Big Bear Cat' (Chinese for 'panda'!) had hastily replaced it, *boom!* Yes, Frank could now admit his plans for a desert ocean had been way off. Thank Christ Ben had stopped him. Instead, after his son had kindly put the thought in his head, Frank had built Nevada's first retreat for giant pandas behind his new casino hotel.

Who the fuck could resist a panda?

Frank loved the idea. The second the kid spoke up, Frank was all over it; it was done. He'd flown to the Sichuan Province for a course in panda handling; he'd written that cheque to the Chinese government for two million dollars so fast he'd left scorch marks on the paper.

It had taken one year of frenzied tweaks – Frank didn't like to overstate the drama and expense of correction – but it was worth it. Ben's theme was catnip to every high roller out of Asia! The pandas made for an easy front page, but the Cat was more of a slick, classy operation. Luke's new venture (Frank's lip curled) the Taj was vast, soulless, trashy – the Walmart of casinos! Frank was not only a businessman, he was an artist. He created wonder.

Rich, young, fun addicts were already fighting to stay and play in the Cat's 1,999 luxury suites in the main building, with its sixteen fabulous restaurants, intimate bars, minimalist spas and exquisite designer stores (dresses, jewels – all the *stuff*). There were concert halls, exclusive clubs; a Maserati showroom; a cabana with waterbed overlooking the dance floor; gorgeous grounds with lush gardens, heated pools, waterfalls, DJs, live music, and wet-bars . . . *day life*, baby!

And for the real big boys – the whales – the players who gambled millions without too much of a care, there were the space villas at Nine. There was the Cat's regular luxury, and then there was the Cat's exclusive hotel.

Nine, the luckiest number in ancient China, signified superiority, which was kind of perfect considering each space villa had its own Imperial Garden, with 2,200-year-old jade phoenix sculptures from the Han Dynasty, not to mention the gold-leaf hot tub for nine that bubbled with Cristal (or hot chocolate if you preferred), the butlers, waterbeds, and bowling alley. 'Hey, want to go bowling?' you'd say to a girl (no mention of the word 'coffee') and you'd lead her back to yours like a little lamb via the express elevator from the high-limit room.

Gambling was the beating heart of Las Vegas, pumping money out of endless willing volunteers. Man, everyone was a donor: it was a communal blood transfusion; but Frank made it look pretty. You had to spoil people. He liked that; it was a thrill to be the gracious host and show people a good time. Frank had heart. He was not an illusionist; that would have made him a liar. Frank was an entertainer.

As he strode along the sumptuous avenue of spanking new designer stores, he winked at his reflection in the Gucci window. A not *very* tall, trim figure in an exquisitely tailored suit winked back. He smoothed his dark hair and admired his profile: 'Roman', his wife said, and he quite agreed.

Frank made gaming glamorous; he took away the guilt. He regretted Las Vegas's sordid reputation; it irked him that his predecessors had been such careless owners of this jewel in the sand. His lavish poker lounge was so beautiful, his hostesses so hot, that you wouldn't care how much cash was choked out of you. You were a superstar, baby, even if you went home without a dime!

No one needed to know it was his son's idea.

The Cat impressed the hell out of everyone; and it was a red carpet laid out for their venture into Macau. The markets knew it; stock had shot up like the forest of bamboo in the Cat's back yard.

This evening was a triumph. He had posed with a panda and his wife – the press had loved it. Chop, chop; through the casino now; everyone, already dressed up nice, crowding the tables. What a beautiful thing. The noise, the lights, the colours, the people, the *effort*; the floor looked classy, expensive, which made him happy. He'd stepped in Harrah's once, and the smell of smoke, the endless slots, and the cheap drabness of it: what a downer. They worked their database, got a lot of freebies off the Strip, but Frank had more of a plan. He gave his clients a buzz; he gave them excitement, a sense of privilege.

He nodded to security, swept down a curling staircase, through small velvet rooms, to the nightclub: 'Brash'. The light effect cascaded pink-and-purple-striped water down the walls. It kept the place cool and added a psychedelic feel. The stripper poles would get their play after midnight. The DJs were graduates from LA's coolest clubs. The waitresses were twenty-three, max, and super sexy. According to their contracts, if they became pregnant, they'd exchange their gold lamé shorts, halter tops and Dior booties for a panda bear costume, complete with ears and furry tail. Frank wasn't totally sold, but Sofia was boss woman.

A young couple swirled past, kissing, giggling; he was tall, gorgeous; she was breathtaking in a silver sequinned sliver of a dress and a necklace of fat diamonds. Frank smiled. Money and power hooking up with sex appeal: a potent combination that always led to more frenzied gambling. When you had a stunning girl to impress, the bets you laid were that bit bigger . . . how he loved romance!

Oh, but just hang on . . . Man, that was Ariel, his baby girl! Ariel swishing her long blond hair, tickling the appreciative nose of Trey Millington, a billionaire Texan businessman. (Now, how'd that kid made his money? Ah, who cared!) Maybe they were just talking. He worried about Ariel, his Little Red Riding Hood in the arms of a wolf, but Trey would behave: Frank owned the forest.

Ariel was too sweet for this town. She didn't have the guile to operate here, but he'd look after his baby; he'd see her right. He saluted Trey, blew Ariel a kiss, and on he strode. Keep that positive energy flowing; always keep moving, baby, onwards and up!

Now here was something: food, glorious food! The one Chinese chef in the world with three Michelin stars now ran their flagship restaurant, Xiqing – 'happiness', baby, and it was! Tonight, even the supermodels had put away as much Peking duck with Beluga caviar as a bunch of Russian businessmen. So what if they recycled in the pink marble toilets? People did what they had to do.

Frank moved swiftly on, past fifteen further restaurants providing whatever his customers craved: macaroni cheese with fried chicken; calamari; crab cakes; burgers; foie gras . . . Frank trotted past, surveying the delights of his kingdom. He didn't want anyone to be forced to leave the premises to satisfy their appetites. (If a high roller wanted a girl, or two, it would be discreetly arranged. God forbid they tried to sort out their own entertainment. They might not lay a bet the whole weekend.)

Whistling, not a bit out of breath, Frank slipped backstage behind the concert hall. The shows were going to suck them in like a tornado in Kansas. If her form tonight was anything to go by, Madonna was going to be as much of a draw as that really huge star, Faye Wong. Truth was, Frank hadn't exactly heard of Faye Wong, but he trusted Ben. The kid had completed his MBA in business at Tsinghua University, Beijing, and swore that Wong would finish what the pandas had started. Her tickets were already sold out for the next twelve months.

Frank sauntered back into the VIP lounge and accepted a lobster wonton canapé from a man dressed as a terracotta warrior. Fifteen minutes until midnight, when he'd give his speech and set the world on a new axis. His Head of PR was ushering in selected media. Where was Ben? Ah, there, still surrounded, by men and women, all laughing. Ben was the son, the sun, the light of Frank's life.

Frank was not a great thinker, he was a doer, but Ben was both.

As a parent, Frank felt a swirl of bewilderment and pride at the realization that he had created a human being whose capabilities, whose brain power surpassed his own. Frank had managed, through dogged persistence, to grasp success; in the greed of the eighties, with the mass of cheap money available, he had opened a casino and become rich.

And yet he had an embarrassing habit of losing his wealth. A rival had told the *Review*: 'Frank is the kind of man who makes money, then loses it, then makes it again.' Twice he had stumbled around and recorrected. But in lean, mean 2009, there was no longer tolerance for business error. He needed the quiet genius of his son to guide him.

And, to ensure that the light of their lives stayed put, Frank and Sofia had made a decision.

Sofia. She looked . . . *ruffled*. She caught his eye; all trace of concern vanished and she smiled, but it looked like a smile of doom. He raised an eyebrow. *Problem?* She tried again. This time her smile was genuine. He guessed it was nothing, some tiny imperfection: a dealer chewing gum, a popped light bulb.

'Hey, Frank, this is some party, but where's the scandal?'

As one of the biggest movie directors in Hollywood engaged Frank in some quite disgusting gossip about a rival studio's most bankable star, he tried to relax and enjoy it. He had nothing to worry about. He was the Creator, and it was a perfect world.

Brash nightclub, the Cat, 11 p.m.

Ariel

Ariel glared at the Pussy Magnate. Trey Millington was young and hot, and had made his money in cat food. Being in Vegas only exaggerated his faults; he saw the trip as a morality holiday. He had just grabbed her and kissed her – in front of Daddy. Now his gaze was riveted to her chest.

'Trey,' she said. 'My eyes are up here.'

With effort, Trey shifted focus. 'Forgive me, sugar,' he drawled. 'I was looking at your baubles.'

She laughed as her fingers flew to her diamond necklace. Her mind scrambled for a quick answer and came up blank.

He watched her discomfort, laughing also. 'Must feel good to be a daddy's girl,' he murmured.

She felt his touch cool and smooth on her skin. He lifted the chain and squinted, as if the jewels were hard to see.

'Actually I bought this piece myself,' she said. She looked away.

Daddy *had* bought the necklace for her, just as he bought everything for her. But she couldn't stand one more jibe about being a spoilt little rich girl. Being spoilt and rich might have been bearable had Ariel felt that her parents saw her as a person rather than a doll. She wanted to be normal, like the other employees of Arlington Corp.

Those people had purpose; they achieved. Ariel watched her co-workers, with their fifty-buck haircuts, chatting and laughing in the breaks, sucking down their Starbucks coffees, wearing their high-street clothes and store-bought shoes. They had come to Vegas from Kentucky, Chicago and Wyoming and she knew that their parents believed in them; their parents had *let them go*. She envied them. Academically, she was a failure; and she wasn't street smart – she had been too cosseted. No one had given her the chance to be clever.

Ariel had been smothered by wealth. She had been given everything but choice.

Her vast inheritance did not come into play until she hit thirty – in case, as her mother had warned the *New Yorker*, she made a foolish marriage (implying she was a fool) – but it seemed to Ariel that no one ever stopped talking about the Trust Fund. The towering shadow of the Trust Fund negated every worthwhile thing Ariel ever did.

And yet, unlike her brother, Ariel couldn't quite bring herself to *pass* on the Trust Fund. She didn't have the confidence.

Meanwhile, Ariel received an annual salary of eighty thousand dollars for her current position in Arlington

Corp. as Junior Associate of Nothing in Particular.

It was exactly the right amount to earn her the resentment, rather than the respect, of the people she worked with. But she wasn't as useless as people supposed. A year back she had tried to persuade Lulu to come out one night to a club. Lulu's baby was eight months old at the time. 'Oh, I couldn't,' she'd said. 'My parents would have to babysit and they go to bed around nine. I need a nightclub that starts at lunchtime!' It had given Ariel an idea; *she* had created the concept of a nightclub that began at 10 a.m. poolside on Sundays. 'Vice' had tested at Ace Harry's, their smaller Vegas property, and seventeen parties had raked in eighteen million dollars. And yet she was still the spoilt little rich girl.

The diamond necklace was not love, it was a dog collar: it proved ownership. And yet you had to look a million dollars to be valued as such. Looking shabby wouldn't help, not in this town. She was lucky that she had decent boobs and long legs ('the right raw materials' as one douche-bag boyfriend had remarked) but she worked hard to keep her figure. She was pretty and she knew it: blonde hair, dark eyes and dimples when she smiled.

But lately, she didn't smile much. She kept on working and working and hoping that one day soon, Daddy would open his eyes and promote her to where she deserved to be. After all, it wasn't always the cleverest people who got to the top – look at George Dubya!

'Trey, there's a private table waiting for you in the Chameleon Lounge,' she said. 'I'll walk you over.' She attempted a grin. 'But I won't gamble. I like to hold on to what I got.'

'I'd like to hold on to what you got.'

She giggled, despite herself, as they walked. 'Trey, honey, work your lines, get back to me.'

He sighed, with not too much disappointment. They had reached the blackjack table in the Members-Only VIP Lounge, where the average bet was ten thousand dollars. Patrons were invited to become members based on their level of play. If they wished to remain members, they would rack up thirty to forty hours of play per month. As the dealer placed the cards, Trey spun her to face him. 'Ariel?'

She kissed the tip of his nose and murmured that his host would take care of him until her return – just so he kept those dice rolling. Then she walked back to where she hoped her father would note that she was doing her best. Trey would return to the Cat again and again, lured by the free jets, suites, dinners, shows, and his gambler's belief that one day he'd get lucky, that she, the curiously chaste Ariel 'Airhead' Arlington, would override not only her principles but her personality, and fall into bed with him for a filthy, no-strings, one-night stand.

'Hey, Daddy,' she said. 'Trey's firing it up big back there.'

Daddy smiled absently, and kissed her. 'You're a good girl,' he said. 'And good girls get rewards. I have a surprise for you, Ariel. Stick around.'

Oh my *God*. He had called her 'Ariel'. Not 'sweetie' or 'darling', not 'honey' or 'angel'. He *was* paying attention. He finally took her seriously as a business prospect. She could feel her heart speeding. Tonight, she would get what she had been waiting for all her adult life – and that *wasn't* Trey Millington.

The Cat, 11.50 p.m.

Sofia

Sofia stood up as both her children walked into her office. She glanced at the clock. It was ten to midnight.

'Thank you for coming,' she said, hoping her voice didn't contain that sharp edge of panic.

'Mom, is everything all right?' asked Ben. 'Dad's making his speech at twelve.'

He looked like a modern-day member of the Rat Pack. She imagined that the feral-looking young women surrounding him like dingoes were furious that their prey had been snatched away. She felt a twitch of triumph: *she* had that power – *she* was Ben's mother. It was the ultimate status.

Ariel just beamed. Her daughter was in a good mood. Sofia sighed. The girl was so dumb: she trotted happily behind each emotion that wafted across her path like a dog following smells on a lead. She was doomed to be forever disappointed.

Sofia smiled and said, 'Why do you assume there's a problem? This is a very special day, and yet we haven't taken a moment to celebrate together. So, on your

21

father's behalf, I just wanted to toast *all* of us, privately.' She paused. With a gloved hand, she pushed the bottle of vodka towards Ariel and smiled. *'You* be mother.'

Ariel tilted her head, shrugged and slowly poured the vodka into the three black lead goblets. Sofia remembered that Ariel hated vodka. All the same, the girl raised her glass, clanked it against Ben's and Sofia's and took a tiny sip.

'L'Chaim,' said Sofia, noting her children's fingerprints on the glasses and hoping that God wouldn't strike her down.

'To life,' murmured Ben.

'L'Chaim,' said Ariel, repeating the Hebrew phrase.

At that moment, Sofia felt awful. But when the clouds gathered, you prepared for rain. And truly, she hadn't done anything bad. At least, not yet.

The Medici Casino, Las Vegas, a week earlier, 20 January 2009

Luke

'The girl with the biggest tits is not always the best lay,' said Luke Castillo, interrupting his chief accountant's earnest speech about 'investigating other revenue streams'.

The Confucius of Sin City watched with disappointment as Mr Schmidt pressed his spectacles further up his nose and sighed. The man was spooked because the Big

Bear Cat Casino & Hotel opened for business in seven days and he was terrified that the Medici – and his job – would pay.

It made no odds that the Medici wasn't the biggest, flashiest property on the Strip, but the Chief Geek didn't get that. Nor, from the gormless looks on their pale, bean-counting faces, did all the Lesser Geeks. The whole row sat in dumb silence, heads swivelling from Luke to Schmidt, as if they were at a tennis match. But Luke knew what mattered.

So what if the Medici did not cater to the players who could blow a million and pay up whistling? It catered to Luke Castillo and the men who'd lent him the money to make his fortune. All the old boys came to Luke because they always had. They wouldn't dare go any-where else.

'Mr Castillo, the recession is . . . If you'll excuse the personal anecdote: last week I took my wife to lunch at the California Pizza Kitchen in Town Square and – not a soul! I look at our figures and I compare them to . . . and I think we would increase profits if we considered the introduction of' – Mr Schmidt blushed to the roots of his comb over – 'European-style sunbathing, an elephant or two, and perhaps a Thai restaurant?'

Luke Castillo pressed his hands together in front of his face, as if in prayer, and took a deep breath. He stood up, and turned his back on the Chief Geek. He could sense the man's fear. Pity that the doc had had a fit about his blood pressure; Luke enjoyed being big. He was a real man, large and hairy. He would have hated to go bald; thank God he was blessed with thick, shiny hair. He cut it short like Steve McQueen; he didn't trust men with flowing locks.

Luke stared out of the boardroom window until he felt sure of remaining composed. The boardroom had red walls and a pool table and a bar – because why not? It was on the second floor, and had an excellent view of the pool area and all the female guests lined up on recliners in string bikinis. It was a pity that most of these women were fat and fifty.

Luke knew what the Geek's panic was about. He was sick of hearing about Frank Arlington, and how every tycoon with a fat ego and a fat wallet was desperate to stay and play at the Cat. He was unimpressed by tales of the élite restaurants, exclusive club nights, sexy waitresses, pool parties, and hot tubs for five.

He returned to his red leather chair and, with slight difficulty, swung his feet on to the table top. 'Maurice, get a grip! This is Vegas, it's about fucking gambling! Everything else is bullshit!'

'But, sir—'

Luke Castillo was doing *them* a favour by permitting them to piss away their family's future on his property. He kept his dignity. He hated how the city had changed and how everyone had believed it. 'Maurice. We will always make money from our core business. That is what I know. But right now, the world is gone to shit. And you know what happens in a recession? *Tourism* suffers. I don't make my money out of people who look; I make my money out of gamblers. Tourists will decide to stay home and save their money. Gamblers are addicted; they can't fucking help but turn up!'

'Mr Castillo, I realize that, but tourists still eat, and sleep—'

'And this year they will be eating and sleeping in their *homes*! The Medici does not have three thousand rooms and you know what? – I'm proud of that. Because at a time like now that is the shit that is going to get you hammered. The other week, I stepped in the Venetian and I fucking gagged. I realize they're piping in some *perfume* shit through the air con! It smells like an old lady's restroom. I mean, what the fuck?'

'Mr Castillo, of course gaming does and will remain our primary source of income, but if you imagine a range of attractions, for instance—'

'Dolphins, acrobats, Elton John is not entertainment, it's bric-à-brac! Maurice, forget the tourists, and as for our *loyal* clients, those losers are going to gamble whatever we do! You can't put them off! Why pretend that Vegas is something other than it is? It's not Manhattan! It's a town built on death, hand jobs and addiction, Maurice. You got to be proud of that, embrace it!'

'Sir, I hear you, but if we are to concentrate on gaming, we still need to compete effectively in an open market place. We need to use all the resources at our disposal. Arling— I mean, other casinos research their players, check their details with Central Credit – they find out everything about them before—'

'Yeah, I know. A high roller comes in; Arlington makes him wait three days before he can play a hand of fucking blackjack!' Luke raked a hand through his hair. He was losing patience. He had hired the Geek because the guy had qualifications and opinions and

Luke found that helpful. But maybe he was too obstinate.

'Maurice, how did you seduce your wife?'

'I'm sorry, sir?'

The row of accountants, a string of paper men, looked at their laps.

'How did you get inside the panties of the woman you are married to from the point of first setting eyes on her?'

'I, er, well . . . it wasn't quite . . . I mean . . . Bruce Springsteen . . . Mahler . . . she has a wide-ranging taste in—'

'Drewry!' Luke snapped his fingers at the most junior associate. 'What about *you*?'

'My wife was a bridesmaid at my cousin's wedding, Mr Castillo. We did it by the dumpster round the back of the church.'

'Thank you, Paul. Maurice, there is more than one route to the same destination. I say, if a guy wants to stick five hundred grand on the table, split aces four times, put up his Rolex, by all means, be my guest! My customers are good for their losses. Fuck that Central Credit shit: if they have to sell Grandma to the Arabs they'll pay up because they owe Luke Castillo – and you don't want to owe Luke Castillo *shit*.' Maurice was looking googly-eyed. 'Maurice?'

'Yes, sir,' said Maurice miserably.

Luke strode around the boardroom as energetically as he could. He needed to inject some optimism into the bean-counting department. The money world had crumbled and these guys were scared: they needed to believe that it would all be OK.

There was a *trip-trap*, *trip-trap* along the path outside

and all heads turned. As if a shower of money had just started jangling from the ceiling, all the men perked up. And Luke realized, goddamn it, that here was his answer. Here was the miracle that would boost morale – and profits, even during a time when all the money seemed to have been sucked out of the world by a tornado of idiocy and greed.

Luke had made one concession to the new Las Vegas. And that was Sunshine Beam.

All his other hosts were over fifty. They wore fucking shirts and ties. Sunshine was twenty-four and she wore what she liked. His other hosts hated her, but Luke didn't care. It was good to stir things up.

Luke watched the row of accountants stare unashamedly out of the window as Sunshine wiggled past in tight jeans and some corset-type top. As they drooled, he nodded happily: she was like a free perk. A guy in red swimming trunks threw himself down on her path, and lay on the ground at her feet. She had that effect on men – any man. Sunshine laughed and stepped daintily over him, her stiletto heel playfully close to his crotch.

The kid was off to play for a few days, travelling to LA to shop and be shallow. Luke was happy to call it a work trip; Sunshine deserved a break. Sunshine was a winner; she was the ace in his pack.

Luke cleared his throat and reluctantly, seven heads swivelled towards him. 'There you go, Maurice. The Medici and the Taj, we are all about personal relationships. And Sunshine is the fucking Princess Diana of Vegas. She doesn't have to reel in her whales. They *love* her. You know what she says to me? "My players would stay in a tent for me and play in a parking lot!" Maurice, you got to focus on what we *got* – and we have got the Queen of Hearts!'

The paper men bowed their balding heads in reverence, but now they were smiling. There it was. Sunshine was his magic ingredient. She would lead them through the rain. The fact of her extreme success made her almost spooky. In this town, you see a hot chick on her own on the casino floor, you're assuming she's a hooker. But Sunshine worked it right.

And her brilliance reflected well on Luke.

Luke had employed her after her father's death; he'd always been fond of the kid. Right from when she was a teenager, he'd seen she had spirit. She was smart, and unafraid. He liked that. She was nothing like her loser of a father. He'd started her out as a waitress. It was ironic, considering, and he'd heard the rumours. Not that he gave a fuck. He was clean.

'Maurice, take your inspiration and optimism from this kid. Sunshine is a hustler. Three years back, I tell her if she wants a job as a host, she's got to bring in ten new clients, each willing to bet two hundred and fifty thousand dollars a pop. I don't think she can do it. So here's what she's done. She's gone through Byzantium's dumpster, each week same thing; taking home stinking bags of trash and sifting through them in her back yard, until, one week, she finds what she's looking for: a list of their best gamblers in California. Seventeen hundred names.

'Then she does a little homework on each one of them.

She makes nice with limo drivers, cocktail waitresses, security guards in every property. For information that helps her secure a high roller, she'll give them free tickets to a show, a dinner for two – and of course I'm fucking hating it, all the free stuff. But you know what, once she got that information, she made it pay. She's cancelling every reservation they got at the rival hotel, meeting them on the tarmac herself with a big bag of swag to damp down any resistance: their first bet for free, or – my worst nightmare – a discount on their losses. And you know what? I grumble and fight her every step of the way but' – Luke shook his head – 'she does phenomenal business.'

Luke grinned. Just talking about that kid lifted everyone's mood. 'And the best bit? These guys have had such a ball, she's treated them so good, that even if they lose a million, it doesn't hurt so bad.'

Luke paused. 'Of course, these jerks sometimes *win*.'

The row of accountants laughed nervously. If you opened a casino tomorrow, and only allowed people to play slots, you'd pretty much know what kind of profit you'd turn by the end of the year. Short of an earthquake or a waitress dropping a pot of coffee in someone's lap, the biggest risk to a casino's bottom line was a whale, gambling a hundred million in the space of a few hours, cleaning them out and pissing off home before the house had the chance to claw the money back.

'But Sunshine doesn't let that get her down. She knows that all you got to do to recoup your losses is to get these schmucks to keep on playing, to keep coming back. And she does that!'

Above and beyond the girls, rooms, and meals,

Sunshine and her tight little ass took Mr X's mind off the fact that while the house had chucked him a hundred thou, he'd lost five times that (and if he hadn't yet, he was going to). Even the wives liked Sunshine – a miracle considering that face, that body. But she'd take them on a fifteen-thousand-dollar shopping spree – Prada shoes, Chanel bags – while their idiot husband lost three hundred thousand at the tables.

Luke was on a roll. 'Maurice,' he cried. 'My girl Sunshine has had men in tears, trying to bribe her with a solid gold diamond-encrusted watch, or stock options worth a million dollars, begging her on their knees to extend their credit line at three a.m. Now I'd have said "yes", straight up. *She* tells them "no", orders them to go to bed, and they go, like puppies. Then, in the hot light of a new Vegas day, those sons of bitches see Sunshine as their *saviour*. On that losing streak, they'd have blown another five hundred grand if she hadn't drawn the line. Now, when I hear this, it's killing me, but Sunshine says I got to be patient. And the truth is, she's right. It's a win-win situation. The whale hasn't bet himself to ruin, and he'll be back, and back, and back, to lose a little more, a little more . . . and a little more: which over time adds up to a lot for the Medici – far more than if Sunshine had let him burn out in one night.'

Luke beamed at his accountants and they beamed back as one. 'You got to admit, gentlemen, she is one classy piece of ass. Now. I am not saying be complacent. I am saying be inspired. Learn from her. Have faith. This kid works here because we are the *best*.'

The bean counters gave him a standing ovation. Luke

bowed, lit a cigar and waved them out of the boardroom. They skipped out like little girls at playtime.

The Medici, twenty minutes later

Luke

His cell phone rang. It was Vince, his Chief of Security. Luke listened, and tasted bile in his throat. He summoned some moisture and managed to speak. His voice was hoarse with shock. 'She wouldn't do that, Vince. I've known her since she was a fucking kid. We are like *family*.'

All the positive energy from the meeting had evaporated. His head felt as if it were bolted to his neck. But it was a rumour. He couldn't believe it was true. Sunshine was the jewel in his crown – he loved her like a fucking *daughter*. There was no way that Ben Arlington would have the nerve to try and poach her. Stealing was a *crime*.

In Saudia Arabia they'd got it right: they chopped off your hand. Luke wondered how much Ben Arlington knew about Saudi Arabian law.

Sunshine was his property. He'd transformed her from zero to a big deal, real Cinderella-type shit. It hurt Luke that Sunshine was ungrateful, but, to be honest, she'd never go through with it, work for his rival's son. She wouldn't leave him, and Luke knew why. He was her one link to her dead father. Ben was after her, and she must have been flattered. Women were vain like that.

Ben Arlington was the true culprit. He had disrespected Luke and he was going to pay.

The Medici, a week later, 26 January 2009, night of the Grand Opening of the Cat, 11 p.m.

Luke

'Tell me some good news!' said Luke, opening his arms wide as if in welcome.

To be honest, there was a fucking cloud hanging over Sunshine. She'd returned from the sneaky meeting with Ben in LA. Well, whatever that prick had tried, it hadn't worked. Here she still was, in the flesh. The Cat had been in business for a whole three hours.

'Don't tell me,' said Luke. 'You've dug up Elvis, stuck on the *Greatest Hits*, and reanimated the guy with electrodes.'

'It's a cute idea,' replied Sunshine, unsmiling. 'I think it will work.'

'Yeah,' Luke sighed. 'We've been fucking raped.'

He hated parties. All the cash and pussy in the world would not erase the shitty memories he had of parties at the age of thirteen, when he was spotty and gangly, a fucking leopard crossed with a giraffe. All the parties he had ever gone to had been crap, full of pretty girls ignoring him. He'd transformed, around seventeen: tall, clear skin, nice bones, but it was too late. He felt ugly inside and just . . . stone cold. Now he could get the girls but they were just skin; everything felt dispensable. It was like eating a Big Mac and throwing away the wrapper. The only thing that turned him on was power. Beating everyone, being able to look down on them and *spit*.

He chewed on a piece of feta from his Greek salad. It tasted like plastic. The Italian chef at the Medici did a wild boar ragù you would kill for. His vegetarian dishes, not so much. Luke had been on this diet for two weeks now, on the order of his doctor ('diet or die'), and he was probably going to expire of boredom.

Sunshine lit up a cigarette, a quick, sharp movement. She was a streak of barely suppressed energy, always moving. Luke would have liked to pin her down with his dick (purely out of habit) but you didn't fuck the golden goose.

'Mr Castillo,' she said, and his heart sank. 'Working for you has been special. You took a chance with me, and I fulfilled my part of the deal. We've made each other a bunch of money. I've always had offers, and I've always rejected them, no matter how lucrative. But this latest offer – I imagine you're aware – it's a chance for me and I've decided to take it. I think it's time.' She paused. 'I like to think there is respect between us. I hope I have your blessing. But I understand if not.'

Luke nearly choked on his food.

He couldn't believe she was making out it was business . . . when it was personal! Fuck that corporate shit: at the Medici everyone was *a friend of his*.

Sunshine was not only leaving him for another man; she was stabbing him in the back with a knife.

She knew it. He saw a tremor in the hand holding the smoke. Despite the big mouth, she was scared and damn right. Ben Arlington.

Youth, ugh, Luke hated it. He hated its vigour, its raw sexiness, its power, its stupid confidence and irrepressible optimism, and its clear smooth skin, sparkling eyes and white teeth. Youth was wasted on everyone except hookers.

'Get out,' he said. He couldn't speak any more, and he held his body still; if he even moved he was scared of what he might do.

She opened her mouth, shut it, and left.

The Cat, midnight

Ben

'Hey, Ben.' As the girl stood on tiptoe and whispered hotly in his ear, he recognized her from billboards. She must be an actress, model or felon. 'How about you and me go check out the presidential suite?'

The red Chinese lanterns floated like bubbles in the air, and as the Big Bear Cat Hotel & Casino opened to the public for the first time, the shrieks of excitement shot through him with an electric energy.

The queues had backed up beyond the gardens and lake on to the Strip. The moon hung yellow in the sky like a slice of lemon in a cocktail glass. There had to be three hundred thousand people out there. A property hadn't caused so much hysteria since the Mirage had opened in 1989.

Ben felt bad. His parents didn't want him to quit the family firm. And his mother was determined to open in Macau. He wondered if she knew that he had received a business offer from the son of Arnold Ping, unofficial ruler of Macau, to open a casino hotel on the island. While Ben saw no reason that this should affect his mother's ambitions, he didn't think she'd see it the same way. His parents wanted him as an employee, not a competitor.

Ben decided that Sofia didn't know; she would have throttled him then and there. Her odd behaviour was probably nervous tension; a grand opening never saw her at her best.

The launch of the first super casino in Vegas almost twenty years ago was memorable because his parents had nearly killed each other. Five-year-old Ben had loved Steve Wynn's volcano. Everyone had. Meanwhile, Frank had shouted and cursed, and Sofia had eaten a whole pack of mint chocolates in eight minutes. She'd twisted each green foil wrapper into a spike.

His father's casinos were successful in the Bahamas and in Atlantic City, yet he had failed to conquer Vegas. Now, at last, it looked as if he might.

Crazy, then, that Ben couldn't enjoy it. The most beautiful women in America were vying for his attention but, God, they were boring.

'The presidential suite is reserved for a player,' he said to the girl finally.

He'd introduced the Beautiful Women of America to Lulu, his PA, and they looked down their noses.

It annoyed him, though Lulu didn't care. As they narrowed their eyes, she told them about going to Whole Foods to pick up some groceries with her year-and-a-half-old kid. 'The cashier was a teenager, and sullen. But Baby Joe took a shine, kept waving and saying, "Hi!" On the first "hi" the cashier ignored him. On the second "hi", the cashier muttered, "hi." On the third "hi" the cashier actually looked Baby in the eye, gave him a great big smile, and said, "*Hi!*"'

As the Beautiful Women of America stood mute and mystified as to why the hell this person was speaking, Ben laughed for the first time that night. 'Joe is *such* a smart kid! He knows if you never quit, you'll get what you want.'

Lulu looked at him narrow-eyed, as if she suspected he was talking crap.

He wasn't, although he was a hypocrite: he had quit with Sunshine Beam. Ben sighed, clanked his glass against Lulu's and kissed her on the cheek. The Beautiful Women of America froze in horror. Ben raised his glass in the direction of Frank. 'Dad finally got what he wanted.'

It was true. This was Dad's big moment. Frank was still smarting from the 1984 misfire, Bijou, on Fremont. Frank had fancied the idea of an elegant Monte-Carlo-type arrangement, but it was too small and no one knew what *bijou* meant. The place was jammed with Baccarat crystal chandeliers and Gobelin tapestries and Van Goghs. The wife of Frank's rival, Luke Castillo, had walked in and burst out laughing. 'Pearls before swine, Frank,' she'd cackled, 'pearls before swine!'

Ben had not yet been born or he could have saved his father millions. Vegas had no time for a poky European-style casino; Sin City was not about making a few rich people happy, it was mass market. Ben had been born in the city; but his father was an import.

Anyway, they'd fixed the problem but it had cost.

Undeterred, Frank had bought his first place on the Strip. It was called Crash and featured a Concorde diving into the roof. The plane's interior had been redesigned as a Japanese restaurant and no one seemed to mind eating sushi at a tilt. The waitresses dressed as super-sexy air hostesses and the most superior suite in the 45-storey hotel was a mile high. The property had enjoyed five years of uproarious success, until 11 September 2001.

In the end, Frank had removed the plane and sold the property. Even after a whopping charity donation, the profit put Frank in a position to build something spectacular and restore pride. Ben had nearly fainted when he'd heard Frank's terrible idea of shipping in a blue whale as the new casino's name attraction. Sometimes, Ben was convinced that his father's mental development had ceased at the age of eleven.

Another of America's Beautiful Women placed a soft hand on his bicep. 'So I *hear*,' she purred, 'that the Cat is *your* kitten.'

Ben hadn't said a word to Frank about the concept of Big Bear Cat until his research was done. The Luxor had been forced to backtrack when a diplomat had objected over their plan to stick a real Egyptian mummy next to a roulette wheel. Ben had liaised with the Chinese authorities over delicate issues. Only then had he asked for a meeting with his father. As with a child, Ben had figured the only way to snap Frank out of his impractical obsession was to distract him with a more attractive (and workable) toy. But that was no one's business but his and Frank's.

Ben arched an eyebrow. 'Dad always says what's his is mine.'

Lulu broke in: 'Hey, did you hear?' she said, as she did when wishing to change subject without being challenged. 'Mr Arlington loves to tell about the time when Ben was six. Ben overheard Frank discuss the purchase of a plot of land with Sofia. They could have built a hotel with the most fabulous views of Red Rock, but Steve Wynn had just bought the Desert Inn Hotel and the golf course across the street, and all those private homes – you know, to create his ultimate Vegas casino dream. Any hotel Frank built would have spoilt Steve's view of the mountains.'

Lulu paused, pushing her spectacles up as they slipped down her nose. Reluctantly eager, the Beautiful Women of America leaned close.

'So Ben pipes up, "Daddy. It will cost too much money and it will make Steve cross so don't do it!"'

Charmed laughter, then: 'Are Frank and Steve *very* friendly?'

'O-o-o-oh,' said Lulu, crossing her eyes. 'What do *you* think?'

'What about Frank and Luke? Frank hates Luke Castillo, right? Is it true, Ben, that your mother used to date him?'

His father hated Luke Castillo and Luke Castillo hated his father. Everyone in this town hated each other!

Ben grinned. 'Frank and Luke are close, as a matter of fact. They share—' He stopped. 'I can't tell you. OK, I will. They're like gym buddies. Except they are . . . ballet buddies. They take a private class. Luke won't wear pink tights, though; his are burgundy. They—'

Lulu made a kind of strangled squeak. Yeah, he should probably shut up.

Truth was, he didn't care about the Beautiful Women of America. He cared about Sunshine, the one who had got away.

She was everything these women were not. Their sharp, angular beauty, without wit or charm, was empty. Sunshine was smart, and gorgeous, and the finest Executive Host in Las Vegas, and yet she was still working for Luke Castillo – and it was all Ben's fault. He had messed up. He had pursued Sunshine until she had finally agreed to see him – and he had blown it.

A Beautiful Woman tapped his arm. 'This place is so wild! Like, no expense spared. You're going to have to make, like, two million a day to break even, right? Is that, like, even possible?'

Ben had flown to LA, to beg and cajole Sunshine, a week earlier. They had ended up in bed. To him, at least, it meant that the possibility of a business alliance was ruined.

Tonight was perfect, but for her absence.

Ben smiled and shrugged. 'You're the expert.'

He checked his watch: a gift from his father. It was an 18-carat white-gold Piaget pendant watch shaped like a casino chip and studded with 158 diamonds, on an 18-carat white-gold chain. It was hideous but he liked it, because it was from his dad. All the same, Ben kept it in his pocket.

Frank was approaching the podium. He looked . . . *cool* . . . in his sixties-style suit and trademark purple tie. The fluorescent white teeth were maybe a cosmetic bridge too far, but he was certainly Vegas.

Frank had invited Ben to stand beside him on the stage, but Ben had declined. The last thing he wanted was public praise from his father when he was planning to quit the company. Ben would retain a nominal affiliation – it was naive to expect otherwise; the Chinese required the brand – but in every other way, there would be autonomy. His mother would freak. It would be like John Lennon leaving the Beatles. And he hated the idea of hurting his father.

'Oh my God, it's midnight,' squealed one of the Beautiful Women of America, 'he's, like, going to speak. Is it true that your dad's going to resign? There was a rumour . . . Has he said anything? Are you, like, going to take over the company?'

A cold sweat rippled across his back at the thought – but it was unfounded gossip.

'Honey, I'm twenty-four. It wasn't so long ago that I took over my sister's room.'

Ben was Vice-President, Research & Development, of Arlington Corporation. It was an honour, and it was great experience. But he craved independence. The worst word in the world was 'nepotism'.

Without meaning to, his father had taught him the

value of independence. Independence was the finest legacy, more than a fat trust fund. Hell, you could fritter ten million dollars in one night: a few bad bets, a few nights of chasing your losses, and an idiot could dispose of a king's ransom in a weekend.

Good sense was the gift that kept on giving.

'Oh, look at your mom. She's so gorgeous! I adore her dress! That orange red is dynamite on her and I love that *fabulous* crystal beading – it has an Asian feel. Oh my God, are they *diamonds*? You look just like her! I mean, obviously, you're six foot, right, you're a lot taller than her, and OK, you are totally *cut*, I mean, you work out, right? But, well, I guess she's fair and you are dark and, like, maybe your eyes are a different colour – hers are green and yours are blue – oh boy, are they blue – but, like, with the cheekbones, oh my God, you are identical!'

The BWA was liquored up to the point of incoherence, but she was right that Sofia was breathtaking. Her blond hair, swept up in severe elegance, framed her exquisite face. Yet, to Ben, she actually looked ill. She'd once said that Vegas disagreed with her worse than red peppers. She was insulted by the city's refusal to lie down and worship her. But now, ascendancy was in sight, so why would his mother look so agitated? And what was she up to, dragging him and Ariel to her office for that *L'Chaim* bullshit?

There was his sister now, stepping shyly up the steps to join Frank. Now, standing before a worshipful crowd, Frank placed a finger to his lips, and there was instant quiet.

Frank began to speak.

Everyone was most joyfully welcome to the Cat, the latest and most exciting addition to the family, because he thought of his casinos – in Vegas, Atlantic City and the Bahamas – and all the people who played in them as part of his family, and his family was the most precious thing to him in this world. That was why he wanted to share his good fortune with not only you, his clients, but also with his son and daughter – sure, his wife too – and so Ariel, my darling, this is for you, to thank you for all you've done to help make the Cat such a special place—

Ben watched as their father took a silver key and pressed it in to his daughter's hand. Ah ha, immediately he knew. Dad had bought Ariel her own place. Ben didn't think that was quite what Ariel was after. She looked dumbstruck – and not with joy.

Ben sighed.

Frank smiled and carried right on talking.

His beloved son made such a contribution to this fabulous outfit, and Nevada's first Giant Panda Reserve – God love those creatures, those big beautiful fur balls! What a gift to the city, what an honour to contribute to the conservation of such fantastic animals. But, ladies, gentlemen, I must be honest, this was Ben's idea [*furious clapping, raucous cheers*] yet he wanted to give me the credit. [*Aaaaah!*] However, I don't like to take what isn't mine. I'm so impressed with his modesty, as well as his ingenuity, his relentless hard work and devotion, his refusal to accept so much as a dime that he didn't earn, that I'm going to let him show me what else he can do.

I'd like to take this moment to officially appoint, or whatever it is they do in those big, grown-up, serious sort of businesses [*laughs*]: the new Senior Vice-President of Arlington Corporation – my only son, Benjamin Franklin Arlington!

He had not expected this. It was a compliment in professional terms, but a personal disaster. It would make his resignation even harder. *Shit*.

'Congratulations, Mr Senior Vice-President,' said a husky voice beside him. The tone was a dry sarcasm atypical of the Beautiful Women of America; Ben looked at the speaker in surprise.

Sunshine Beam, the hottest super host in Las Vegas, grinned. 'You're lucky I've got such a high opinion of myself. All this talk about the Cat about to become the best hotel in the city – it just wasn't going to be possible unless you had *me*. So I quit the Medici. I left Luke Castillo – for *you*. That kind of obliges you to employ me.'

A great smile lit his face and he took her hand and kissed it. He was vaguely aware of Lulu and assorted Beautiful Women fading away into the shadows. Everyone began to clap.

And then Ben became aware of a shrill, discordant sound piercing the applause. It took him a second to register that it was human. He looked towards the noise and his eyes widened in horror. Ariel, his sweet little big sister, was clawing at their father's face and screaming with rage.

The Medici, just after midnight

Luke

Luke stood up and hurled a paperweight through a window.

He pressed a button on his desk. 'Josie-Jo,' he wheezed. 'I need a window fixed.'

'Yes, sir,' replied his busty under-secretary (he had given her this job title himself and thought it very amusing). Josie-Jo was used to broken windows and had the glazier on speed dial.

Then he walked into his study and lay down on the couch. He lay there for an hour, deep breathing. Then he buzzed Josie-Jo again, and said, 'I need answers.'

'Yes, sir.'

'What are you wearing, Josie-Jo?'

Her high squeaky voice rose with excitement. 'I'm wearing a, like, *totally* micro-tube skirt and—'

'Get in here.'

Afterwards, he lay on the couch and choked down some beta-blockers. He turned on the television and then turned it off. The fawning over Arlington's latest venture on 13 was grotesque. The footage of those fucking pandas: what was the guy running here, a casino or a zoo?

Frank's energy was tiresome; he was always hosting some ball, match or race to benefit the Nevada Cancer Institute or the wild donkeys or the kids' playground. Luke did his share of kissing babies and writing cheques, but Frank outgunned the entire Scout movement in community spirit.

Luke didn't give a toss about his image. He knew who he was and that was enough. As long as he made money for himself and his investors, the rest of the world could take a running jump. The trouble was, Frank didn't give a toss about his image – he actually liked doing this stuff. Now that was just weird.

One of tonight's scenes that made his lip curl was footage of Ben Arlington joking around with Matt Damon. You could bet that Matt Damon got the presidential fucking suite every time he showed his face. Matt Damon! Matt Damon wasn't a serious gambler, he was a family man! Matt Damon could wait in line!

Now Luke was sweating, and he hated to sweat. He was obsessed with not sweating. Sweating was for tourists. He was about to bleep Josie-Jo, tell her to turn up the air con, bring in a fresh shirt, when her squeaky voice came through the intercom. She sounded pissed.

'Sir, there's a young lady to see you.'

Luke frowned. Had he ordered a girl? He shrugged. 'Send her in.'

He sat up. The door opened, and in staggered a tall, blonde chick in black hot pants, a kind of spangly scarf thing around her tits, and stilettos with laces up to her ankles. Her hair was a mess and her mascara was streaked; either she was a hooker who didn't know that hookers didn't dress like that any more, or she was an unknown member of Kiss.

Luke looked closer and felt as if he might cardiac arrest right there on the couch. He struggled to his feet, failing to control the great shark-like grin spreading over his face.

Ariel Arlington raised an eyebrow and stuck her nose in the air. 'Hello, Mr Castillo. I'd like to audition for a job.'

Near Lake Geneva, Switzerland, two days later, 28 January 2009

Bessie

Bessie shrugged off the masseuse and glanced across the aisle of the Hawker. Sofia Arlington was hunched in her vast cream leather seat, biting her manicured fingernails. She was frightened and that was good. Bessie felt calm and in control. It was curious to have lived so long in fear. Now Sofia was being forced to placate *her*.

It had taken Bessie a surprisingly short time to discover the identity of the anonymous person who, twenty-five years earlier, had offered her the deal that had changed her life. Bessie had hired a private detective with a fine reputation and he had proven very efficient. But having found out, it had taken Bessie six further years to build up the courage to approach Sofia and tell her that she wanted out. But Bessie had been worrying about nothing! Now Sofia was panicking! It felt glorious to have power, to command respect at last.

Possibly, thought Bessie, draining her Kir royale, it would have been moral to reject all Sofia's bribes. But Bessie missed the good life; if you were offered a free ride in a private jet, of course you should take it! No one deserved a little stroking more than her.

They landed minutes later at a private airfield; it was like fairyland, with all those lights twinkling in the darkness. Sofia's manservant, a tall thin guy in a black suit, helped her from the plane. It was freezing; so cold the air hurt her throat. She felt disorientated but jubilant. Las Vegas was far, far away. A grey Bentley waited on the icy tarmac. Bessie smoothed her skirt – new, all new, Sofia's man had snatched her an entire wardrobe from the Cat's designer shopping mall and she was now clad in Gucci and Prada; hello again, old friends!

'Do you ski?' murmured Sofia as she held open the car door for Bessie. 'The spa is located at the foot of the pistes.'

Bessie shook her head dismissively as the car started up with barely a sound. It was like riding on air. Inside, she was laughing. Let Sofia try to spoil her into submission. The threats had failed and so would this. Bessie would luxuriate in this spa hotel for a week at Sofia's expense and watch her sweat. At the end of their stay, she would return to Las Vegas, no doubt with a final, staggering seven-figure bribe tugging at her conscience. She would accept it. And then she would go straight to Frank Arlington with her evidence against his wife. Some things in life were worth more than money or morals, and it was a shame, thought Bessie, it had taken her so long to figure this out.

The Bentley rolled slowly through pristine grounds, all covered in snow. Bessie sighed at the snow-capped pine trees. Here it was forever Christmas. The spa hotel, the

Mont Blanc, was a severe white symmetrical building; the muted light from its windows was too soft to break the darkness of the night.

'I hope they have a decent chef,' she said to Sofia. 'I abhor health food, or hotel kitchens that close for the night.'

Sofia smiled. 'Bessie,' she said, 'you are their guest, and they will give you everything you need. Here comes the manager now.'

A tall, tanned man in an elegant suit approached the car. He was holding a bouquet of white roses. Sofia slid out of the car and motioned for Bessie to do the same. Bessie shivered in the icy evening air. She hoped Sofia didn't think those white roses were for *her*.

'Dr Erich,' purred Sofia. 'This is Bessie Edwards. I know you will make her feel welcome.'

Bessie fluttered her eyelashes. He was as handsome as hell. His hair was thick, streaked with grey, and perfectly coiffed. His dark eyes gazed down at her, and his thin lips broke into a smile. 'Ms Edwards,' he said. 'It will be my pleasure to be your host.' Gallantly, he kissed her hand and thrust the flowers under her nose. 'Their perfume is intoxicating,' he murmured. His look said: *As are you.*

Obligingly, she took a deep sniff. The faintness was immediate. 'Help me,' she gasped as she fell. The man stepped smoothly forward to catch her.

'How *dare* you,' said Sofia in her ear as everything turned black. The last thing Bessie saw were the white roses, crushed and broken underfoot in the melting snow.

Mont Blanc Sanatorium & Research Facility, Lake Geneva, Switzerland, 2 February 2009

Gisèle

Gisèle felt a rush of pride as she held open the door for the new girl. 'The best advice is to pay close attention to the patients' behaviour, especially those on the psych ward, because then you'll always have something useful to say – even if it's just that one of them has too many blankets!' She smiled to show that this was a joke, and added, 'Everyone is nervous at their first team meeting, so don't feel bad if you feel unable to contribute this week.'

Adelheid gazed at Gisèle. 'I'm not nervous,' she replied.

She was a little over-confident for someone who had been here just two weeks. Gisèle felt a twitch of irritation. Well, she would show her. She sat on the chair closest to Erich's desk. When he sauntered in, her heart leaped.

He smiled at her. 'Good morning, everyone. Ah, thank you, Juliana.'

Everyone had brought their own coffee in polystyrene from the canteen but Dr Erich had his served by his PA in a china cup. The meeting began with a long speech from the Director of Nursing but Gisèle barely heard the words as she was impatient to speak herself. At last, her moment came.

'Dr Erich, I noticed that one of the patients in the psych ward, Bessie Edwards, is on barbiturates *and* anti-psychotics, and, thinking of the side-effect risk, I thought that it might be wise to moderate her dosage. It seems curiously high.'

'Nurse,' said Dr Erich. He looked amused. 'You are referring to the patient who yesterday had to be restrained and sedated?'

'Yes, Dr Erich, but you see, there was a reason for that. I spoke to one of the healthcare technicians who took her to the restraint room and he said that she was lucid. She wasn't ranting, apparently, she—'

'Thank you, nurse. I'll look into it.'

He was brusque. She was nearly in tears. The meeting came to an end and she stood up.

'Wait here, nurse,' said Dr Erich.

She was mortified. The Director of Nursing was the last person to leave his office. Their eyes briefly met and Gisèle felt the silent sting of her rebuke.

Dr Erich walked swiftly across the room, passing so close that she inhaled the musky scent of his expensive aftershave. He sat in his chair and swung his feet on to the desk.

'Nurse,' he said. 'I admire your attention to detail. Bessie is a complex case, however.' He smiled. 'You are, what, three years qualified?'

She nodded.

He smiled. 'I and the Director of Nursing are looking after Bessie. Her prescription is under careful and constant review and her drugs have already been modified, but this ever-fluctuating assessment is a skill that has taken decades of experience to acquire. But I appreciate your concern, I really do.' He paused. 'There are two patients, also on the psych ward, whose pathology is a little less taxing, and I think it would be a beneficial exercise for you to monitor their prescriptions and report back to me with your thoughts and suggestions. Would that amuse you, Nurse?'

Gisèle could not stop the great smile from spreading across her face. 'Oh *yes*, doctor,' she cried. 'I'd be delighted.'

'Excellent,' he said. 'We'll go through their notes together after your shift.' He glanced at his watch. 'I'll see you back here at eight.'

She spent the rest of the day in a state of exultation. She noticed that both the new girl and the Director of Nursing gave her a suspicious look when she returned from his office, so she tried not to look too happy. But at a quarter to eight, she brushed and flossed her teeth, and applied lipstick.

At ten to eight, she stood outside his office door. His PA had left for the evening. She was too early, too keen. She was about to walk away when she heard his voice, harsh and loud. 'You asked to have her permanently removed – I provided that facility. One point five is *fair*. I could have asked for two. Thank you. OK. Thank you!'

Gisèle's face felt hot. She crept away, even though it was probably nothing and she had misconstrued the words, she knew he would hate her to have overheard his private conversation. She hovered at the far end of the corridor for five minutes, then she marched loudly up to his office and knocked.

Dr Erich opened the door. His tie was off, his shirt unbuttoned. He stared at her and her face fell. He had forgotten!

'I'm sorry, doctor,' she stammered. 'But you suggested that we talk over the patients' notes. I can always come back if—'

'Not at all,' he said. He ushered her in. As he shut the door, he rested his hand on her shoulder.

She jumped.

'I'm sorry, nurse, I didn't—'

'No, no,' she said, turning to face him. He didn't move back. 'It's . . . I . . .'

He bent towards her and kissed her. She pressed her body against his with a mew of desire. He pulled away immediately. 'Gisèle, please forgive me,' he muttered.

She stared at him, desperate. 'Doctor,' she whispered.

Tenderly, he straightened her collar. 'We should find our notes.'

Coquettishness masking desperation, she guided his hand to her chest. He groaned. As they kissed, she put his phone conversation from her mind. Her hands wandered down, but he murmured, 'I'm not ready.'

I'm not ready.

He was surely in love with her.

Mont Blanc Sanatorium, 3 February 2009

Bessie

Bessie lay on the bed like a slug. *Fool*, she thought, before her mind floated off in a haze of grey. She couldn't speak without slurring and even though she knew that bad people had imprisoned her here against her will, she couldn't tell anyone. If she attempted to speak to a nurse, her tongue seemed to expand to fit her mouth and she burst out laughing. It was impossible to avoid the drugs. That bastard, the handsome one, forced them down her throat if she hesitated.

Fat tears rolled on to the mattress as she thought of him. It was hard to think. She was so, so tired. Somewhere, a door opened with a click. She saw a smiling face loom. 'Hello,' said a disembodied voice. 'Oh dear, Bessie, don't be sad. We'll have you well and out of here in no time.'

You don't know the truth, Bessie wanted to say, but her thick tongue couldn't form the words. She barely knew the truth herself. What was the truth? She fumbled for the girl's arm. Then she felt the girl's warm hand grasp hers.

'I'm Gisèle,' said the girl, looking right into her eyes. Bessie's vision swam and she blinked. It was hard not to give in to the warm fuzziness, but she fought, trying to grip the girl's hand even though her muscles refused to function.

The girl's voice reminded her of people from her childhood; gentle women with smiling faces and kind hearts. This girl would be a friend. She would help her get out, get back. But where was it she needed to go? Her head was as thick as porridge. 'Help me,' Bessie whispered.

The girl patted her hand. 'Of course I'll help you, Bessie, don't you worry.' The girl moved towards the end of the bed. Bessie heard the clatter of a clipboard slipped off its hook, and then the girl said, 'Oh my. No wonder.'

The words merged and danced until they made no sense but Bessie's heart leaped. This girl was good. There was another click and a waft of air. Bessie shuddered. His aftershave hit her like chloroform even before he entered the room.

'Hello, nurse,' said the man. 'Are we behaving ourselves today?'

The girl giggled, and the hair on the back of Bessie's neck stood on end. She closed her eyes and feigned sleep. Through heavy lids, she watched. The man walked up behind the girl, as if he too wished to check on her notes. She saw him press his body against hers, saw his hand brush across her chest as he took the clipboard from her. She heard the girl sigh.

Bessie sighed too. Her friend was caught by the enemy, and therefore useless. She had no fight left. And it was difficult, now, to recall exactly what she was fighting for – or against. She closed her eyes and, with a sweep of sadness, let the drugs transport her.

Presidential Suite, The Cat, two weeks after the Grand Opening, 5 February 2009

Sofia

As the journalist drank his gently carbonated water, Sofia felt a tweak of annoyance that he wasn't paying for it.

The man had desperately thinning hair and was the shade of a corpse. He belonged in a drab office with strip lighting, rain falling outside. His rather fat bottom was wedged into a red sandalwood chair engraved with flowers and trees from the Ming Dynasty and he was surrounded by three-hundred-year-old landscape paintings by Wang Hui. He looked sadly out of place.

But one had to charm the press or they knifed you, and Sofia had put aside an hour of her day to dazzle the creature into submission. 'Oh,' she said playfully, 'you are *so* lucky to live in London. America just doesn't do chocolate or tea like Britain does! We're looking into importing Green & Blacks and PG Tips, allegedly for our English guests – but actually for *me*!'

The man scribbled obediently, and Sofia wandered to the vast window and gazed down on the velvet-roped Tiger Beach pool, the exclusive 'adults only' bathing area.

It was a neat symmetrical shape, three perfect conjoined bubbles of blue, surrounded by a lush barrier of pink flowering shrubs and flowers, and from her bird's-eye view, the clientele were little brown ants. It was hard to believe that peoples' lives mattered when you saw them from this far away.

Tiger Beach was fabulous. The beat of the hip hop juddered through you, so your insides danced whether you liked it or not. The sleek lagoon pools with their sandy bottoms and elegant waterfalls were gorgeously adorned by the young and beautiful. They craved pleasure; she provided it. All day long, they danced and flirted, lazed on the daybeds, drank frozen strawberry margaritas and Belvedere cosmopolitans and showed off their bronzed bodies.

Sofia felt like a puppet master.

She loved Las Vegas but now she had to leave it.

It was *wrong*.

Frank was a success at last and so much of it was her hard work. The thrill of reigning at the heart of such a powerful, important operation was unbeatable. When you made it in Vegas, you had the most amount of fun: you were *celebrated*.

And now, all of this was at stake.

The world falling to shit she could deal with. That was temporary. She and Frank were lucky. They hadn't got greedy. Personally, they were down to their last billion – it wasn't so bad. When Sofia was little and left food on her plate, her mother had told her, 'Your eyes are bigger than your stomach.' Now, she could thank her mother for checking her greed. Sofia and Frank owned four properties, not ten. Their share prices were down 70 per cent, but in this climate that was good. Las Vegas Shores was down *ninety*. Wall Street was confident in the Arlingtons. The interest payment on their debt was manageable: a neat $150 million a year. Frank had renegotiated his banking covenants shortly before the crash. He was smart like that.

No. The terror chewing up her brain had little to do with money. It was about the potential destruction of her entire *life*.

She had taken every precaution and yet every second she spent in Las Vegas was a risk.

Facing Bessie after twenty-five years was the most

frightening situation Sofia had ever been in. She kept reliving the hideous moment, and the panic swept over her in cold waves of sweat. It humanized her; it made her feel disgusting.

Even as she despised herself for her weakness, she went over the past in her head, trying to spot her mistakes.

There had been indirect contact twelve years earlier. Bessie had committed an indiscretion which had compromised the secrecy of the pact. Panicking, the stupid woman had contracted the Solicitor. Sterling and his boys had dealt with the problem, but it was a ruthless, ugly solution, and the woman should have learned her lesson then.

Sofia had no clue how Bessie had discovered her identity. They had met only once, in Dubai, briefly, just over twenty-five years earlier, and the woman had been blind drunk. It was on the basis of that single, chance meeting that Sofia had chosen her. Bessie's situation made her a suitable candidate for the proposal.

And yet, the first contact regarding their deal had been made more than two months after the Dubai meeting, when it was likely that Bessie's alcohol-fuddled brain had long forgotten a brief conversation with some woman at a bar. There was no way for Bessie to discover that Sofia was the author of the pact, for the subsequent approach and all arrangements had been made by a go-between. Could someone have tipped her off . . . ?

Well. This would be the end of it.

Sofia hated to make crucial decisions under pressure. But she had discussed it with Sterling and was almost certain she'd done the right thing.

The woman was now in a secure psychiatric hospital in Switzerland. Sofia had flown her there on her new five-million-dollar Hawker Jet two days after the Grand Opening of the Cat. Sofia was pleased with the new jet. She had matched its interior to the fur of her favourite golden retriever, Snoop. She had told Bessie they must be civilized; that they would discuss her grievances at a private spa. Sofia's lip curled; as if a *man* would be swayed by the idea of a *spa*! Sofia had a personal link with the Chief Medical Officer at the facility – or rather, with his bank account.

After a month of intensive electroconvulsive therapy, the woman would no longer be a threat. ECT had the benefit of creating short term memory loss. What had she said in the holding cell? *I feel as if I have missed my life.*

Oh, please!

ECT did not try to unscramble the egg, instead it erased all the shit you were moaning about, rebooting your brain as if it was a faulty computer.

In addition, the Chief Medical Officer would stick Bessie on a brew of medication that would do away with the *attitude*. A daily dose of 60 mg of citalopram and 25 mg of diazepam would mop up any dregs of memory that the ECT didn't catch.

Sofia would finally be free. Sofia didn't believe any of the woman's sorry talk. Her wails and threats were not caused by true emotion, they were the result of boredom and drink.

Sofia hadn't yet decided the woman's final fate. Perhaps she could remain in the psychiatric hospital until she died, happy as a lamb in a fuzz of meds. It was an upscale facility, all fresh-painted white walls and pretty nurses in white uniforms. She was lucky; Sofia was giving her the opportunity to return to a childhood state, where she had no responsibility, no worries, no fears.

There was another option but Sofia was reluctant to pursue it. Having her killed would just be lazy. Sofia had only ever had one person killed and she had not felt good about it.

Sofia's bleeper sounded and she jumped. 'Yes?'

'Darling, I'm coming up. If you have any young men up there hide them at once in the closet.'

Sofia laughed. 'Sweetie, I'm just finishing up with an interview. *The Times*: it's a British newspaper. One second,' she said to the journalist, and set off towards the entrance hall of the suite to greet her husband.

She kept an office adjacent to the massage room. Sterling was sitting at a desk, speaking on the phone behind the soundproof glass. Outside, in the reception area, was a small crowd waiting for an audience, among them her hairdresser, the chef, a designer, an astronaut (the skin on his face hung like a basset hound's from subjection to all that G-force), a Chief Rabbi, and the President of the World Wide Fund for Nature.

She had kept the journalist waiting long enough to name check them all.

'Krystal,' she said to Sterling's junior assistant, twenty-one and dolly, with a sunny personality and enchanting décolletage that made up for any mental deficiency. 'These people will need to be kept happy for at least another hour. Speak to Gloria-Beth.'

Krystal smiled and said, 'Yes, ma'am,' and skipped off to find Gloria-Beth, Sterling's senior secretary, whose hair was big enough to hide the vast wisdom accumulated over the last fifty years. Gloria-Beth would no doubt organize for Alexander, Frank's butler, to arrange food and drink.

Sofia still loved Frank. He knew how to make money, and that appealed. She was traditional; she felt that a man should provide. But she maximized his potential, and he was smart enough to value that. It was galling, of course, that the money-spinning wheel had slowed. The 'soft' – or trial – opening of the Cat, at the start of December, had been a success, but partly because they had been forced to offer rates that a motel would sniff at. One hundred and sixty bucks a night: *robbery*. But Sofia was confident that their new hotel was special enough that people would swarm there.

The consolidation of their success was important to her. She was well into her fifties now, and if you were old, you had better be rich, or people despised you. It had all been worth it. She had power; freedom; family.

She did not feel that she had missed her life. No indeed. She had grabbed it just in time.

Her bodyguard stood aside as Frank burst in. The door was always held open for him or else he'd bang it against the wall and leave a dent. Frank didn't care – he liked to make his mark. Like a Labrador, Sofia thought.

'Darling,' he shouted, lowering his voice as she flapped her hand. 'Have you heard from Ariel?'

'Yes, sweetheart,' said Sofia, the lie smooth and immediate. She did not want Frank agitated.

As she had told the journalist, 'A new hotel needs to be nurtured like a baby. And Frank and I are great parents. The tiniest details have the greatest impact. If a guest orders an English breakfast on room service, the bacon must arrive crispy and hot. Not that simple when you consider the distance it has to travel but it *will* arrive crispy and hot because that is the standard I insist upon. That applies to every single thing that occurs in this hotel. The scrambled egg will have a garnish of watercress and if some idiot in the kitchen sticks a sprig of parsley on top instead, and I hear about it – and I will – he is *gone*. But of course, he won't do that, because we employ the very best.'

The journalist had nodded and written it all down.

Of course, the hack was keen to focus on gloom. He had remarked that Frank had been 'surprisingly bullish' at his latest quarterly earnings call to Wall Street, and Sofia realized the journalist had listened in. Sometimes, the power of the internet surprised her and made her feel old. She was jittery about the Bessie thing and this made it worse. Her Head of PR had grilled the journalist, briefed Sofia and was sitting in on the interview, and yet she had the sense of jumping to avoid bullets.

It was impudent, considering this reporter had been put up for free in one of their finest suites. Now he was dragging up the Nevada Gaming Control Board's report that Strip gaming revenue had fallen approximately 14.9 per cent last month, with slot win down 9 per cent . . . Oh yes, and was the plot next to the Cat secure? Or could Castillo seize it and build a spoiler?

Sofia subdued her first impulse, which was to hit the journalist in the face. Instead she smiled and asked if the hack had seen the Forbes online Market Update: After Hours video report last night. It had announced that, along with Citigroup, Arlington Corp. was the only company whose stocks had 'rallied' – 26 per cent in fact. Perhaps he would like to see the video?

'I did see the report,' replied the hack. 'I hear it was in response to an announcement that one of your executives no longer worked for the company.'

'Indeed. It always hurts to let someone go, but the market response proved it was the right decision.'

'May I ask why—'

'I'm afraid not.'

'Are you making staff cutbacks?'

'These people are like family. If we have to let someone go, it is with the greatest regret.' Sofia glanced at her watch.

'We need to wrap up, now, thank you,' said the PR, perhaps aware that her job now lay on a knife-edge.

'One last question,' said the journalist. 'How do you feel about your son's plans to quit the company and launch a casino hotel in Macau with Charlie Ping?'

The Cat, three minutes later

Sofia

By the time Frank emerged from the lounge room, crunching popcorn, the journalist had been dismissed and Sofia had composed herself. To her husband, who mostly saw only what he hoped to see, she would seem normal. But she was in shock.

Frank fussed about Ariel, who predictably had gone missing after being passed over for promotion, and she had to force herself to respond. 'Ariel may have flown to Milan to look for chairs.'

Frank was emotionally retarded. He loved his children equally and yet had rewarded Ben – publicly, vastly, humiliatingly – above Ariel on the grounds that Ben was fit for leadership and Ariel wasn't.

'One second, darling,' she told him. 'I need to brief Sterling.'

She burst into Sterling's office and told him what the journalist had said. 'How *could* Ben do this to me – me and Frank? It's unspeakable! I need him! I need him for myself and for the business! He's dumping us for Charlie Ping!'

Her mouth shrank in a moue of distaste. Charlie Ping was another young business brain who should have approached *her*. She had marked Macau as her next territory to conquer; they had even hosted a dinner party for Arnold Ping. A former President of the USA had attended and bored the pants off everyone. It was outrageous that Arnold Ping, who reputedly kept the triads in order, was incapable of controlling his own son. Sofia had made her intentions clear; she had followed protocol – and yet Arnold Ping had snubbed her!

'I have to presume that Arnold Ping approves of Ben and Charlie's plans.' She supposed he didn't need his son by his side, as she needed Ben. 'Sterling, this is a disaster. *Another* disaster!'

Sterling's mouth was a thin line. 'We dealt with the first; we shall deal with the second.'

'But what about Frank? He will crumble when he hears about this! I need him to be strong; the company is as vulnerable as a kitten! If this gets out now, it will murder the stock price!'

Oh God, to lose Ben; to lose *Macau*. It was not going to happen; she would not allow it. They would work together, or nothing.

Sterling rose smoothly from his seat. 'This is a legal matter; it relates to privacy, as well as company law. The hack can have a word with our Head of Litigation.' He paused. 'I suggest you say nothing to Frank; say nothing to Ben. At this point, it could damage you.'

Sofia nodded. But her body still throbbed with fury. If a working relationship with Ben – let alone a personal one – was to be sustained, she would have to find a way to forgive him for his ingratitude, and the only way Sofia could forgive anyone was to punish them first.

She returned to Frank and scooped her arm into his. 'Darling, when Ariel is ready she'll call.'

'She's supposed to have her bodyguard with her.'

Sofia gritted her teeth to stop herself screaming 'I don't *care*!' Even before the kidnap of the Wynns' daughter aged twenty-six, Frank had been paranoid about Ariel's safety. He was probably right to be; she was an airhead. His own safety, he disregarded. But he was forever anxious that his daughter would be a target, because you were always pissing off *someone*.

They took the private lift down to Tiger Beach and Sofia let her thoughts tune out Frank's chatter. Out here, the spanking hot sun, the smell of tanning oil, the near-naked bodies and the endless supply of alcohol had the desired effect. The scene reminded Sofia of the last days of Rome. The poolside waitresses delivered drinks in the tiniest of bikinis. The place reeked of lust.

'I think a little prayer is in order,' said Frank, giving his wife a sly grin. He nodded towards the presidential cabana – aka the Temple of Heaven – at the end of the pool complex. It was available only to guests with suites on the penthouse floor.

Sofia smiled. It wasn't a bad idea. She was rigid with tension and yoga wasn't going to cut it. They sauntered towards the grandiose double-room cabana in the style of an eight-sided Chinese pavilion and named a Temple of Heaven (its namesake was an imperial sacrificial altar in Beijing). Frank pulled her inside the first room, lush with silk pillows, and billowing walls of red silk, and a ceiling of a hundred orange Chinese lanterns, and she yanked him towards her by his tie. Their lips met and . . .

A noise made Sofia pull away. 'Frank,' she said. 'The igloo is occupied!'

Stifling her annoyance, she marched towards the second room, 'the igloo'. The igloo contained a sleek white bar and a vast waterbed. The walls were made of hexagonal panes of frosted glass. If you pressed a switch, the igloo became a blizzard of cold white 'snow soufflé'. As the soufflé hit body temperature, it melted into sweet almond oil. The best way to get the oil to sink in to the skin was to employ friction.

There was a couple on the bed, doing that now.

Sofia's first thought was that they were beautiful. The woman was a gorgeous peroxide blonde – well, mostly. She was long, tanned, all curves and smoothness like an expensive car. The guy was tall and toned, his back rippled with muscles, with dark scruffy hair – oh *Jesus*! 'Stop it!' she shouted. 'That's disgusting! Stop it at once!'

Frank grabbed her wrist. 'Enjoy!' he called as he slammed shut the door. A few puffs of white soufflé escaped, and Sofia watched the foam settle on her six-inch patent heels. It was plain that Frank hadn't noticed whom they had disturbed. Had this been a pair of Ferraris shagging, Sofia had no doubt her husband's observational powers would have been keener.

'Sofia, are you crazy?' said Frank. 'These people are our guests! Lust and greed are our living! You're messing with the natural order of things!'

'Don't talk to me like that! How dare you! "Messing with the . . ." Ridiculous!'

Frank raised an eyebrow, and she felt annoyed with herself. It was amateurish to overreact. You might as well open a window to your soul.

'*I* know where we can go,' he said, and she laughed, a dirty laugh this time. He really found her irresistible. He thought she was beautiful, even though *she* couldn't

66

stand the idea that she was past forty. Past forty and you started to rot. But Frank acted as if she was twenty years old. It made her love him more than she would.

Ten minutes later, she screamed with the thrill of it as they clung to each other, 700 feet above the ground, on the silver-edged roof of the Cat. Her fingernails gripped the side of the building, and she looked down, hysterical and dizzy with laughter and the exhilaration of fear. 'Oh my God,' she shrieked, 'oh my *God*.'

Las Vegas in all its naked glory was spread below them, sharp, sunlit and beautiful, and as she forced her eyes open, gravity met her with a terrible force of suction, and she screamed even harder. There was nothing between her and the ground – the impulse to tip herself over the edge was strangely compulsive – and then Frank pulled her back, and they rolled away to safety, high with the adrenaline of lust and terror. She lay flat, panting, on the dusty concrete, the fierce heat of the sun boring into her skin, the warm, brisk wind lashing over her gently thrumming body. She smiled at Frank and groped for his hand.

'Sex and death,' he murmured. 'What else is there?'

The question hit her throat like a punch and the joy of the moment was squeezed out of her. *Death* . . . She had to decide if Bessie would live or die.

And now, snapping at the heels of the Macau problem: a further annoyance. Sofia had been delighted when Ben had stolen Sunshine from Castillo. But now it seemed that Sunshine would steal Ben from *her*. The sight of the two of them in the igloo would not have bothered her. We are all animals. We just disguise it with manners, laws and clothes. No: what had made her freak out was the fact that her son and this girl *weren't* having sex; they were making love.

Sofia did not intend to lose her son as a business ally. As for losing him to another woman: never. Ben and Sunshine's relationship was doomed, because Sofia was going to kill it.

Las Vegas, the following week, 10 February 2009

Lulu

Ben was driving Lulu home from her parents' house. Four days a week, they looked after Baby Joe while she earned a living. Ben glanced at her and grinned. 'You and your mom and dad all get on so well. You actually like each other! I wish my family was like that.'

'There's more at stake with your family,' she said. 'My lot have nothing to fight over except maybe a crystal ashtray and my granddad's old camera.'

Immediately, she felt awkward for bringing up the ugly subject of money, but he laughed. 'It's better that way,' he said. 'It's depressing when business gets in the way of your relationships. There's nothing' – he nodded towards Joe, asleep in his car seat – 'more important. But it can all get forgotten.'

He meant Ariel, she supposed. He was talking to Lulu

as an equal and it made her glow inside, which was pathetic. What was she saying: that having money made you a better person? All the same, she hadn't wanted him to see where her parents lived: their neat little house with its red-tile roof and off-white stucco walls could have fitted into the Arlingtons' broom cupboard. But Ben had insisted on giving her a ride. She had been about to collect Joe from her parents after work, as she did every evening, and her car had stalled. Ben had driven past her waiting at the bus stop and gallantly swerved across the road.

Her parents were their usual warm, welcoming selves when she introduced them. 'Oh, hello, honey!' her mother had cried. It was a long time, Lulu imagined, since anyone had 'honeyed' Ben Arlington.

Ben had shaken her father's hand with a wide grin, and kissed her mother and listened to them chat about Joe's day: 'He had Bolognese for lunch, he ate very well.' Lulu thought it must be all too parochial and suburban, and then she saw with surprise that Ben was touched.

And now he was about to see where she and Joe lived: a sweet, but tiny apartment. She didn't want to invite him in, because if he betrayed the slightest hint of distaste or condescension, she would feel ashamed and she couldn't bear it. She didn't want to be diminished in his eyes, but of course she would be. He would realize exactly how ordinary she was; what a normal life she lived in comparison to his gilded one. But equally, if he looked down on her, he would be diminished in her eyes, and she didn't think she could stand the disappointment.

'You can drop us off here,' she said.

'Is this it?'

'Yes, well, no, it's a bit further along, but it's fine.'

'You can't carry this great heavy chap in his massive car throne, or whatever it's called. Let me help.'

There was nothing she could do. She tried not to cringe as she led him up the stairs to her plain red door and unlocked it. Of course, the great Sunshine Beam resided in a vast mansion, impeccably decorated. *Her* palace had graced the pages of interiors magazines with its owner fetchingly sprawled over her enormous four-poster bed with its ferocious leopard-print pillows, bolsters, drapes and canopy.

Lulu had seen Sunshine parading around the Cat showing off the diamond bracelet Ben must have given her as a token of his esteem, and suddenly she had felt drab and dull and small and sad and foolish. So much for the wish. It was all very well to wish, but what if your wish clashed with someone else's? It was plain that in the wish hierarchy, as in most other areas of life, Sunshine was a lot higher up in the granting order than Lulu.

Ben turned around, smiling. 'It's lovely,' he said. 'It's very you.'

'You mean small and plain?'

'Well, no, actually, without coming off as a creep, I meant "warm and . . ." '

'Homely?'

He started laughing and she did too.

'Warm and . . . *pretty*.'

Pretty! Obviously a boss couldn't go around dubbing the payroll 'gorgeous' but she doubted that Romeo had ever called Juliet 'pretty'.

She pretended to be busy undoing Joe's seat belt. Ben knelt down beside her and watched as she lifted Joe out of his seat.

She put Joe to bed and walked back into the sitting room, half expecting that Ben would be gone. But he was sitting on her sofa, looking at the back of one of her Agatha Christie novels. It all went to prove how terribly unexciting she was. Now he stood up and wandered into the kitchen. 'Can I make you a coffee?' he said. He poked his head out of the doorway and grinned. 'Because I can see that the Strip will freeze over before you offer to make *me* one.'

'I bring you enough coffee in the day,' she replied, trying to look severe.

'True, that,' he said. He was opening cupboards, whistling. It annoyed her. It annoyed her that he was *dating* Sunshine Beam – and it was diamond-bracelet serious – yet he was *toying* with her!

'Ben,' she said, and he turned around. 'You know, I'm really tired, and I have some calls I should probably make . . . for Joe,' she finished vaguely.

Immediately he backed away from the cupboards, arms raised in mock surrender. If he was disappointed, he didn't show it. He kissed her on the cheek and said, 'You don't look like you need your beauty sleep,' and then he was gone.

She sighed and locked the door behind him. Then she sighed a little more, for the rest of the evening in fact, that fate had made Ben Arlington a kind and good-hearted man instead of a jerk.

Animal Bar, The Medici, a few weeks later, 1 March 2009

Frank

Frank seemed a great deal sillier than he was. Of course, 'silly' was an interpretation made by people who thought that to build a fortune one had to be sensible. It confused them to see a 'tycoon' joke around. Frank couldn't say that word with a straight face. The truth was Frank was a happy person! The happiest!

And yet he wanted to cry. The tension in his jaw was making his ears ache. His neck was so stiff it hurt. When he hunched his shoulders to relieve it, his joints creaked like old floorboards. His gut felt slack with a sudden sweep of sadness. He hadn't felt so wretched since his parents had died.

Money protected you from the harsher elements of this life – to a point. But there were times, and this was one, where everything you owned and had achieved was ripped away and you were left mentally exposed, trembling and defenceless, with the abrupt realization that you had stupidly, laughably confused what you had with what you were.

Frank had not touched a drop of the Jack and Coke that his host had ordered on his behalf. There were also monkey nuts in a bowl. He had successfully quit smoking five times, but now he tore a cigarette from the box on the table and allowed a girl to light it for him. He sucked the smoke into his lungs with the relief of a devil returning to hell.

The rage roared up inside him, and he wanted to wrench tables and chairs from the floor and hurl them through the tinted glass windows. It was almost impossible to contain his emotions by sitting still. But Frank wasn't as silly as people liked to suppose.

He would not have this incident reported, because as much as the media loved a poster boy, one day you would fall out of vogue and be torn down. That day, Frank decided, was a long way off. He would not make a scene: he did not wish to be reduced to a segment of light entertainment on *E!*

It was nothing to do with a juicy story being bad for business. It would be great for business. Hoi polloi had an insatiable appetite for proof that rich people were, despite their money, miserable. And the situation proved only one thing: that Frank would always do his best for the Arlington Corporation despite any personal consequences.

None of this was any comfort. He felt terrible. He had been naive. That was a stern accusation to bear when you were fifty-seven years of age. When Frank had received the call, his optimism had kicked in. His optimism was always kicking in. His optimism was faulty wiring, forever causing a short in his good judgement.

Frank hated Luke Castillo, yet hate was not a natural emotion to Frank. He had wanted to believe that even though Luke Castillo famously loathed and detested every bone, fibre, hair, toenail and piece of DNA that related to Arlington, when the man called him on his personal line, bright and breezy, asking after the wife, complimenting the new hotel, Frank wanted to believe (and, remarkably, *had* believed for as long as it had taken his driver to ferry him in the Bentley to the Medici's adult-only Animal Bar) that the scumbag genuinely wanted to be friends.

He'd shaken hands, settled himself in a comfortable chair, ready to be entertained, and then a sudden movement had made him glance again at the dancer slithering around the pole in a gold lace thong, fishnet tights, teetering stilettos and a barely there bra, shaking her luscious behind, spreading her endless legs, contorting her lithe body into the most provocative poses. Her golden hair was teased into a Brigitte Bardot style, her huge eyes were heavily made up and her pouting lips painted a deep, suggestive pink; she radiated sleazy, delicious abandon. The men in the place were red-faced with lust, their eyes popping like tomato frogs.

Then, swinging wildly around the pole, the girl lost her grip and fell on her back like an upended beetle. As she staggered to her feet, the men whooped, as if this gaucheness merely added to her allure.

It was Ariel.

Luke Castillo – that psychopath fat on Mob money – was enjoying the show, sat back in his chair as if he was at the seaside in a deckchair, chewing on an outsize cigar. He was still a fat fuck, despite the lipo; fucking ate too many sweets. Now he leaned over to Frank, all buddy buddy, wheezing, 'She's my new sensation, ain't she *wild*?'

Luke's new sensation had regained her composure and was now peeling off her pink sequinned bra and writhing more frenetically to the panting soundtrack, and the men were pushing, jostling to stick money down her thong. Smiling dirtily, Ariel slid off the stage and *winking at Frank* as, to catcalls and whistles, she pertly sat astride a fat, sweating creep. Frank could see the bulge in his nylon trousers and was at once glad and sorry he didn't carry a gun.

The compulsion to punch Luke Castillo in the face hard enough to ram his fucking cigar up his nose and singe his brain was so strong that Frank could taste the bitter desire in his mouth. He was, of course, expected to take a swing at Luke. Then Luke's men would get involved. Luke would have loved for Frank to be mortally injured in plain sight of a crowd of drunken idiots who could attest that the bullet to the head was self-defence. He'd probably rename the bar Crime Scene and it would do great business.

But Luke was a Neanderthal. Frank was more evolved. He looked Luke in the eye and smiled, showing teeth. 'Who knew there was such talent in the family?' he said, and the words hissed air.

Luke stared back, dead-eyed. Then he puffed on his cigar and grinned. 'You wait, Frankie, this next bit is real hot!'

Frank was momentarily suffocated by the phlegm in his throat and had to resort to deep breathing. He would not perform. He would defy both Luke and his daughter. Of course, he should have expected nothing less of Luke.

But *Ariel*. Stupid girl! How dare she debase herself? It was petulance taken to the extreme. It showed a basic flaw in her personality that she had so little self-regard that she could do this to herself – and to her *father*! If anything, it showed in a thousand ways that in passing her over for promotion, Frank had made the right decision.

He could barely believe, still, that she would hurt him this way. She must have approached Luke Castillo and suggested it. The thought made him want to vomit. She was messing with a dangerous man. The whole family was bad. They were so proud of what they were, yet their empire was built on criminality. The three sons, the mother: trash. Wasn't one kid a cop? A *cop*! What a fucking *joke*.

Ariel was a fool because she hadn't only punished her father, she'd humiliated herself by not having the wit to realize that Luke Castillo was using her rather than the other way round. So Frank sat back in his chair, finished his cigarette, sipped his Jack and Coke and watched his daughter cavort on stage with another woman. The smile was fixed on his face, and that was *her* punishment.

She had expected – wanted? Hoped? – that her father would storm the stage with a great bellow of anger and remorse, and drag her off it and home, and beg her to forgive him, offering her any position in the company that she desired, if only she would stay away from Castillo.

Frank felt that twenty-five years of doting on his daughter had been wasted. He was furious that she was prepared to throw their relationship away like this. Some kids didn't have that choice; their parents were torn from them. With that thought, Frank allowed himself to hate his daughter, and hate himself. It was *her* fault. *She* had driven him to the despicable position of sitting here, watching her act like a whore, and doing nothing.

A house in a quiet suburb in Las Vegas, thirty minutes earlier

Harry

Detective Harry Castillo and Sherlock Bones stared at the photographs of the dead man on his computer screen. Hank Edwards was a native of the city, but he'd died in Mexico. Gunshot wound to the base of the skull. Twelve years on and even though they knew who he was, they didn't know who'd done it.

'So, young Sherlock,' said Harry. 'Riddle me this. Chances are the identity of the victim points to the identity of the killer. If you know the victim, you're a step closer to understanding the suspect. The scene always gives you *something* – pity this one is gone to hell. But the way this guy's been dispatched . . . what do you think, Bones? A professional hit?'

Sherlock rested his head on his paws. His nose emitted a long whistle and he yawned widely.

Harry sighed. 'It's the easiest conclusion because there's no other lead. The Mexican authorities wrote it off as the work of a drug cartel, but I don't know. This guy owed a bunch of Las Vegas casinos a lot of money. That's right, Sherlock, he owed my daddy one *mil*.'

But there were no witnesses; no forensic evidence, not a hair or a fingerprint. Not exactly *CSI: Las Vegas*. Jen got a shoeprint one time and Harry had said, 'Hey, stick it in the Trainer Database!' and they'd cracked up.

His cell buzzed. He snatched it up like a teenager waiting on a date.

'Hey, Oskar, man, how you doing? The Arlington girl is *at* the Medici? You're kidding me. Jesus Christ. Sure, I'll look in. Unofficial. No trouble. Bye.'

His eyes flicked back to the screen. The man's brains and blood had soaked into the dirt. His foot was twisted round at an unnatural angle and the blood had pooled on the underside of his arms. His skin was an ugly yellow and, with the purple threads, the body reminded Harry of blue cheese. Harry was looking at violent death as other people looked at sandwich ingredients. Was that wrong?

He lowered the lid of his laptop. It was an old case; people had lost interest; it wasn't strictly Las Vegas Metro Police Department jurisdiction.

But *who* was responsible? Harry knew whom his father worked for, and there was nothing he could do about that beyond disown the guy. But if his father had had a man killed, Harry needed to know.

And now, his colleague Oskar had called, announcing that his father was up to new mischief. Luke was trying to start trouble with Frank Arlington via his spoilt little girl. Harry might want to swing by, you know, calm people down. Harry knew that Oskar felt sorry for him.

'He's throwing me a bone, Sherlock. Yeah, I know. I'm so ungrateful.'

But Harry was all or nothing. And right now, having been IOD – Injured on Duty – he was nothing. The doctor had printed out his exercises on a sheet. But Harry couldn't rouse himself to start. Injured on Duty; those three little words had taken him out of the field, away from the adrenalin rush of the streets. Jen, his partner, had moved on.

He couldn't stand the idea of returning to work half-assed, being stuck on 'Light Duty'. You couldn't even handle a weapon. He'd seen injured colleagues work Light Duty. You stood in the kit room handing out equipment to those that could.

Why did it astonish him that life could be ruined in a moment?

The team had just ordered lunch when the call had come on the radio. It was to a car lot; someone had heard what sounded like a gunshot. The whole team, Harry, Oskar, Jen, Jack, had burst out laughing. This was why Harry had joined Metro. Who wouldn't want to be a hero? People called when they needed you and you didn't ask why, you just went into the hail of bullets or into the homes of normal people having the worst day of their lives.

Harry hadn't imagined that this would be the worst day of *his*. He closed his eyes and saw the scene he always saw. His lieutenant getting out of the car, the screech of tyres, and *snap*, the resounding crack of a high-velocity round, and Jack, falling over.

As he'd leaped out of the car, he'd caught a bullet in the shoulder. But he was lucky. His lieutenant had not survived. Unless you considered paralysis and brain damage any kind of life. To his shame, he hadn't yet visited Jack. What was the point? Jack no longer knew who Harry was.

Jen had shot and killed the suspect as Harry lay on the ground. Harry couldn't think about the suspect or the pointlessness of the crime; the harm was done.

Of course, as a police officer, you took home every

case, thought about the victims, wondered if you might have done it differently, but you couldn't wallow because you had the next emergency to respond to. There was always another crime; 'job security', they called it. Vegas was slowly creeping up the chart for No.1 Murder Capital. Heck, Vegas was creeping up to be No.1 for every crime.

A long time ago, he had developed an ability to put a wall between himself and the victims. Empathy might keep him awake for a night or two, but then it went. It allowed him to protect them and to protect himself. The victims didn't need his pity, they needed his help.

The day Jack was injured, Harry had lost that ability. Now his head swelled with every tragedy he'd ever witnessed: the baby in the trash can with his toes curled around the wire mesh from freezing to death; the five-year-old who'd found his mother beaten to death in the bedroom, who'd whispered, 'Daddy did it'; the drunk driver and a little girl lying in the road bleeding, asking him, 'Are you my angel?' Harry had said, 'Yes,' and the little girl had smiled and closed her eyes.

Jen had it figured out. She got home, she took off the badge, she became a soccer mom. She didn't so much as smoke a cigarette; her biggest vice was a glass of wine on a Tuesday evening. It was hard to keep your humanity, but Jen was smart. She believed she made a difference.

'Jesus, Sherlock, I need a girlfriend. No offence, buddy.'

Trouble was that twenty-four hours a day, he was a police officer. At least, that was how he saw himself. And now he couldn't do his job. If he *was* his job, then that meant he was . . . nothing. He'd been offered counselling but he didn't want to sit there whining in front of some kid fresh out of college.

'So you can't run around,' Jen had said. 'But you can still *think*, can't ya?'

He needed to take charge of himself again because his mind was skidding out of control, like Vegas traffic in a rare snowfall. The prescription meds sat in a high cupboard; they were too alluring. You couldn't pretend that they limited only the physical pain.

'Ah, fuck it,' he said. 'Sherlock, let's go clear up someone else's shit.'

Everyone knew the Arlington girl had fallen out with her parents after being snubbed for promotion. Now she was using *his* father, Frank's mortal enemy, to make Daddy pay. What a brat. If he didn't get over there fast, her father might end up beaten or dead and she'd feel it was her fault. Harry knew what it was to feel responsible for that kind of tragedy, and he couldn't wish it on anyone, not even a person as obviously moronic as the Arlington girl. He had seen her on TV once, unveiling some new 'sleek, stylish and sexy' breed of car: she had pulled off the cover, lost balance and fallen flat on her face.

Harry stood up, wincing. His chin was rough with stubble. Slowly, he pulled on some jeans. Then he took everything off and had a shower.

Five minutes later, Detective Harry Castillo was driving towards his father's casino before Frank started something he wouldn't finish. Sherlock stuck his head out of the window, ears flapping in the breeze. Oskar had suggested that he break it up quietly before it began. This was hardly police work, more like babysitting. For the record, Ariel was exactly the kind of rich kid he instinctively despised. Their similar backgrounds made him loathe her all the more. And yet, as he swerved into the Medici's parking lot, Harry found he was whistling.

Animal Bar, The Medici, thirty minutes later

Ariel

'Gentlemen,' said the guy standing in the middle of the smoky room with, if her eyes weren't deceiving her, a real live basset hound, 'I think that's enough excitement for one night.' He looked at Ariel without smiling. 'Get some clothes on. I'm taking you home.'

'But my contract . . .' she began fearfully. She glanced at Luke but he merely shrugged, rose to his feet and left the room. Frank stood still for a second, as if frozen, and then banged out of the fire exit.

'Your *what*?' said the guy, and his dog gave an impatient sounding 'Woof!'

Now that Luke was no longer in the room, a few people started to laugh with nervous relief. Ariel ran out, her face scarlet. She felt like a lump of flesh. When she crept back in, wearing jeans and a baggy top and her hair pulled back, no one gave her a glance. She walked up to the man and said sulkily, 'Who are you anyway? I'm not about to get in a car with a stranger. I know the dog trick.'

The man looked down at her. He was tall, with tired green eyes and blond curly hair, and he'd cut himself shaving. Despite his stern look, he had laughter lines. Annoyingly, she felt her heart flip.

'I'm an off-duty cop and a concerned citizen. I'm concerned that you're getting yourself and your family into shit that you won't get out of.'

'I can look after myself,' she replied.

'Plainly,' he said and clamped a firm hand on her shoulder and propelled her towards the door.

She shook it off, even though she was secretly grateful. 'I'd like to see some ID,' she said.

He murmured, 'Yeah, well, I think I've seen yours,' and fished a card out of his pocket.

She blushed; it was so mortifying. She would never forgive Daddy. She snatched the card and her eyes widened. 'Harry *Castillo*, oh ho ho *ho*,' she said. 'Well, that accounts for a lot.'

'Quit talking and get in the car,' he said. She heard him mutter under his breath, 'The *dog trick*!'

'Great,' she said. 'So I sit in the back and the dog sits up front? That's nice. Oh my God, look at all these cans! And these empty packets! It stinks of rotting food back here. This is really gross. Don't you have a valet? And this car is like an *antique*!'

The cop snorted and screeched out of the parking lot. 'Bones is a working dog. He deserves to sit up front. And no, I don't have a *valet*. Nor do I have a butler, house-keeper, personal secretary or an employee to wipe my ass.'

He was so rude she could barely speak. 'Then do you', she enquired icily, 'have a garbage can?'

Harry turned around. 'Where can I drop you?'

'Look at the *road*!' she yelled.

'I'd like your address, if you know it, or do you keep a servant to hold that information?'

She told him where she lived as coldly as she could.

'Thanks for *nothing*,' she spat, slamming the door. She stormed up the path towards her apartment building and . . . oh shit. Knowing it was hopeless, she searched, just in case the keys to her front door had miraculously jumped by themselves from her locker at the Animal Bar into her jeans pocket. Out of the corner of her eye, she could see Harry Castillo, elbow out of the car window, waiting. The dog was also looking.

'Oh, just GO!' she shouted.

What could she do? The doorman did not keep a spare set; Sofia had vetoed this for security reasons. She had been furious enough that Ariel had chosen to live in a block.

Harry hooted. Reluctantly Ariel turned around and slowly plodded back to the car.

' "I can look after myself," ' he murmured, but otherwise made no comment. They drove in silence, apart from Harry saying to the dog, 'Bones, will you stop chewing the seat, how many times do I have to tell you?'

She was surprised when he drew up in front of a neat yellow house in a smart suburban neighbourhood. 'I guess you got money from your father,' she said, almost without thinking.

His face darkened with fury. 'Not everyone is like *you*.'

She felt bad, but he was so unpleasant, it was hard to apologize. She walked meekly in behind him and accidentally trod on the dog's paw. The dog yelped. 'Oh, Bones, I'm so sorry,' she cried. 'Are you OK? Oh no, I've hurt him, he looks so sad!'

The dog sat down and she crouched and stroked his long velvety ears. 'That's his normal expression,' said Harry. He chucked his keys on to the side and walked into the kitchen. She looked around. The house was messy and dirty, but it was beautiful inside. There were a lot of books on dusty white shelves and big squashy sofas.

Moments later, Harry walked back in carrying two mugs of hot chocolate.

'This is a nice place,' she said.

He rolled his eyes. 'But?'

'Well, it obviously could do with a tidy up but you haven't . . . and you don't . . . It's actually gorgeous. I mean, it's smaller than what I'm used to, but everything is smaller than what I'm used to. Oh dear, I . . .'

The expression on his face made her giggle. To her surprise, he laughed too. She was stunned at the transformation.

'I'm sorry about what I said about your father,' she blurted. 'That was so stupid. You obviously work really hard. It's just . . . you make me nervous. Disapproval makes me nervous, and then I say stupid things.'

'What makes you think I disapprove of you, Ariel?' He gestured that she should sit down on a sofa. He sat on another sofa. Then he raised a hand and disappeared off again. A few minutes later he returned with buttered toast.

'You gotta eat,' he said.

She took a slice and sighed. 'I think it might have something to do with how we first met.' She smiled. '*I* disapprove of me. I deserve to be disapproved of right now. I was a fool. Luke said I'd be expressing my . . . but it was just demeaning. It wasn't empowering, it was the opposite. Push-up bra! Panties made from scraps! Ridiculous platform heels! Wow, how did I not guess that this might not be a soul-enriching experience? I . . . well . . . Bones *does* deserve to sit in the front seat.'

Hearing his name, Bones leaped up on to the sofa. His head knocked her mug and she spilled hot chocolate down her front.

'Oh, *Bones*,' said Harry. 'Did it burn you?'

She smiled at him. 'It's OK. It was lukewarm. You should have probably . . .'

'Made it hotter?'

They laughed. 'Come on,' he said. 'Take a shower. I've got a nightshirt you can borrow. And then I'll show you to the spare bedroom.' He paused. 'It's not *so* dirty.'

She noted that Harry Castillo didn't exactly own any fancy products; she winced at the ingredient list of his shower gel. There were about ninety different chemicals in there. Maybe she could buy him an organic designer one as a thank you.

She dried herself on a thankfully fresh-smelling towel and changed into the nightshirt. It swamped her, which she was grateful for. She didn't want another man seeing her body for a long while.

'Harry?' she called in a small voice.

Immediately he appeared, tall and reassuring, and suddenly, she felt curiously tearful.

'Hey, kid, what's up?' he said in a softer tone than normal.

'Is it possible for me to go to bed now?' she said, struggling to keep the emotion out of her voice. 'I'm a bit tired.'

'This way,' he said. The room was white and airy and . . . 'No good?' said Harry.

'It's perfect,' she said and started to cry. 'Sorry,' she said through gritted teeth. 'It's just been . . . upsetting.'

'Ariel,' he said. 'Oh, Ariel.'

The sound of her name spoken by him made her shiver. She couldn't look at him because she so wanted to feel his arms around her, his strong hands stroking her hair. If she looked at him, she was lost. It would be a dreadful mistake. Apart from anything he was *Luke Castillo's son*.

As it was, Harry didn't move towards her, not one step. But his voice was like a caress.

'Don't look at yourself through the eyes of those douche bags – and I include my father in that definition. You're a good person, Ariel. And you're smart.'

She laughed then, and wiped her face. 'No one has ever said that to me in my life.'

'Well,' said Harry, his green eyes boring into her, 'you've been hanging out with the wrong people.'

Everything he said was like music. She wanted to kiss him so badly she might faint. 'Harry,' she said. 'You don't seem it, but you are kind in the *extreme*.'

He looked as though he might be trying not to laugh. 'Thank you,' he said, 'I think.'

'Could I', she said, 'ask you one more thing?'

'Your wish is my command.'

'It's just that, well, when I was little, I had a dog but only for a week, because Daddy is allergic. And he slept on my bed. The dog, I mean. And it was the best feeling. And I wondered if . . . if maybe Bones wouldn't mind. Does he . . . ?'

For a second, Ariel thought she saw a flicker of disappointment in his eyes. Then Harry grinned and said, 'I got to warn you, he's quite the sleaze hound. Don't let him hump your leg!' He turned away and whistled. 'Bones! Hey, buddy, your luck's in!'

'He snores like hell,' added Harry as she helped Bones scramble on to the bed. 'Chuck him out any time.'

Then he kind of saluted her and walked out of the bedroom, gently but firmly shutting the door behind him.

Mont Blanc Sanatorium, 30 March 2009

Gisèle

Gisèle chose the chair furthest from Erich's desk. The Director of Nursing was noticeably cool towards her these days and Gisèle could guess why. But beauty could not compete with youth. She couldn't stop a squirm of pleasure as she relived Erich's hands moving over her body. He kept a hotel room: a gorgeous, luxurious suite with a private elevator. His divorce would shortly be granted. Oh, he was ready *now*.

She ignored Adelheid, a girl plainly more interested in mascara than mental illness. Amusingly, Adelheid had chosen the chair nearest to Erich. Dream on, sister! The girl was chattering on, tossing her shiny hair, absurdly pleased with her own judgement. She had no insight and no humility. 'I did note that one patient was highly disturbed, doctor. It was Bessie Edwards. I believe I mentioned her at the end of last month and I know an adjustment was made as a result, but in my opinion she remains agitated. I'd recommend a change of medication to something stronger.'

Gisèle, speechless at the girl's nerve – 'I'd recommend'! – waited for Erich to crush her. She was too busy monitoring the two patients on psych to pay too much attention to Bessie. But the woman was practically a zombie. If anything, Erich and the Director of Nursing were being over-cautious with her treatment.

Dr Erich nodded sagely. 'This is interesting, nurse,' he said. 'Natalie' – he nodded to the Director of Nursing – 'you reported a disturbance last week also, as I recall.'

'But, doctor . . .' said Gisèle. She couldn't help herself.

'What is it, nurse?' he said sharply. She recoiled as if he'd struck her.

'Nothing, doctor,' she said. He nodded briskly and turned to the Director of Nursing. 'What's your opinion?'

'I agree,' the woman replied. 'It might be beneficial to try a new therapy.'

Gisèle stared fiercely at her lap. Was she going *mad*?

Here were three colleagues, two of them esteemed, insisting the earth was flat. Why would a medical professional lie about a patient's health? Nausea rose in her throat as she considered the two possible reasons: it was a genuine mistake or the doctor was corrupt.

Sadly, slowly, she dragged her mind back to that telephone conversation where – possibly – it appeared that her lover had been discussing payment of 'one point five' to provide the 'facility' to have 'her' – whoever *she* was – 'permanently removed'.

It couldn't be. She must have heard those words out of context. Furthermore, she was three years out of training, while Dr Erich and the Director of Nursing had half a century of expertise between them! As the meeting was concluded, she gazed, uncertain, at Dr Erich.

He grinned at her and winked.

She smiled back. Even so, when no one was looking, Gisèle was going to have another little check on Bessie. Just to be sure.

Mont Blanc Sanatorium, 1 April 2009

Gisèle

Adelheid's pale blue skirt had ridden up, exposing her white lace-topped stockings. Her long legs were splayed like an old-fashioned china doll and her white patent shoes – non-regulation, thought Gisèle with a burst of shock – stuck out in the air. She was gripping Erich's taut tanned muscled *derrière* with her neat French-manicured nails and she was squeaking like a hamster. It was disgusting.

Gisèle had only walked into the restraint room by chance. The day before, she had been called on to help strap down a violent, paranoid patient. Yes, it was Bessie, again. Well, they claimed she was paranoid. She had struggled against the wide leather bands on her arms and legs, until, at last, the sedatives had taken hold. Gisèle noticed that the hard leather had chafed Bessie's skin; it was red raw. She had a can of leather shoe-softener at home and today she'd brought it in to spray on the straps.

She stood frozen, holding the can of leather softener, watching the man she'd hoped to marry. Erich was licking and snuffling at Adelheid's body like a pig eating. Gisèle liked to close her eyes when making love to Erich. Their liaisons were romantic and tender. But with Adelheid he was like an animal. They had giggled about Adelheid wiggling around the corridors, her enormous chest busting out of her uniform; now Gisèle felt as if she and her silly girlish emotions had been run over by a truck.

Silently, Gisèle backed out of the room. She returned to the nurses' station and sat down, her legs shaking. Then she jumped up and started to run. She didn't stop until she was outside the sanatorium, swiping her key card on each heavy door with trembling fingers.

She collapsed on to a bench and stared at the glass lake, the jagged white-tipped mountains and the icy sky, seeking reassurance and calm, but saw instead a cool rebuke to her hysteria. She breathed in the chill air, like swallowing snow. A great rage billowed up inside her. How dare Erich treat her like this? How dare he do this – how *dare* he . . . Oh, and the things she'd done because he'd had the nerve to ask!

But Adelheid – why would he choose Adelheid? Did she, Gisèle, not know how to please a man? Was it the stockings? Was it the bosom? Gisèle's mouth closed in an angry line. Was Erich that much of a sex maniac that he had to seduce every nurse? He was an ambitious man and when he had murmured about 'risking' his career for her, she had been flattered. Now it seemed that he was also risking it for Adelheid. At a guess, he was risking it for the Director of Nursing as well.

Gisèle understood that many men were lazy. It wasn't always the most beautiful women they turned to, it was the ones who were there. But she knew Erich well enough by now to realize what drove him. It wasn't his you-know-what, nor was it power. It was money.

Perhaps Bessie was the key to everything.

Arlington Residence, Las Vegas, that same day

Sofia

Frank was singing in the bathroom.

Sofia sprawled on the vast bed, staring at the ornate

ceiling with a luxurious smile. She imagined all the poor married couples who fell asleep every night on the far side of a cold mattress: losers. Mostly it was because the wife was as fat as a house. Or the husband was a failure.

She fumbled in her bedside drawer for a cigarette. Where was the lighter? Stupid maid. Resenting the waste of energy she crawled over to Frank's bedside drawer. She fumbled towards the back of it and felt a small screw-cap bottle. Ooh, Valium! She pulled it out, and stared. Oh my God. You are *kidding* me.

The bastard was on Viagra.

Red Rock Canyon, five miles from Las Vegas, 1 May 2009, sunset

Harry

'So, sweetheart,' he murmured, 'was that smaller than what you're used to?'

Ariel giggled. 'To be honest, Harry, I don't have much to compare it to!'

She squealed with laughter as he pinned her to the ground. Bones, who had expected a walk, turned away in disgust. God only knew, thought Harry, as he sank into the kiss, that this was a bad idea. But she had melted his heart. She ran her hands through his hair and wrapped her long legs around him. 'Ariel,' he murmured, feeling the heat pulse through him, 'what are you doing to me?'

'Harry,' she sighed. 'You're so damn gorgeous. Please hush up and kiss me.'

She was irresistible. He hadn't felt like this ... ever. There was a beguiling innocence about Ariel that drew him to her. Despite all she had, she was a simple girl, and he didn't mean simple, dumb. She had honest values. And he had never seen such natural beauty. She took his breath away. When she smiled, he felt happy, even though he knew it was dangerous. He did not wish to think about his dad's reaction on hearing that he was in a relationship with the daughter of Frank Arlington.

'You know', he said, 'that I went to the trouble of packing a picnic.'

'I know; we just had a sausage roll.'

'You're *bad*,' he said.

She sat up, immediately embarrassed. Her cheeks were pink, and the setting sun framed her long blond hair with a halo of light. 'I'm not like this with anyone else,' she said.

'Concurrently?'

She grinned. 'Ever.'

She had dust in her hair and on her skirt. Everything about her made him love her.

The fact it *was* a relationship astonished no one more than Harry. It wasn't as if they had even discussed it. They belonged together and it was obvious. The morning after he'd hauled her out of the Animal Bar, she'd run into him as he'd exited the shower, a towel wrapped around his waist. She was flushed from sleep, and her hair was a mess, and he had felt his entire body tingle and zing with desire.

He'd quickly looked away. 'How did you sleep?' he asked, gazing at the floor.

'Good,' she'd replied. 'How did *you* sleep?'

'I slept OK,' he said. 'My shoulder ain't great.'

She had stepped close and very gently traced her fingertip along the scar. 'Ouch,' she'd whispered, 'I guess it still hurts.'

He didn't trust himself to move. He'd nodded, unable to speak. 'It wasn't', he whispered finally, 'a good day.'

And then she stood on tiptoe and kissed the scar and his skin burned at the touch of her lips – and suddenly they were kissing. And he remembered what she'd said, afterwards, stroking his hair and gazing into his eyes: 'I'll make it better, Harry.'

He was helpless. He was in love. He couldn't fight it.

'Come on,' he said. 'Let's climb higher.'

Harry whistled to Bones, who staggered to his feet. So did Ariel. She slipped her hand into his, and he kissed it.

They stopped talking as they ascended the rocky path. Bones was panting. 'Oh my God, look at that,' breathed Ariel.

The sandstone cliffs and ravines were red and grey and white, rising out of the huge empty plains of the Mojave Desert. Below, the land was dotted with scrub and red poppies, and in the distance the mountains were pink with flowers.

'It's another universe,' said Harry.

The sky was navy blue, merging with purple to yellow and orange, and the sun itself was a flaming red ball of fire. Harry and Ariel stood at one of the peaks and Ariel threw her hands wide and breathed in the cooling air. Las Vegas was a glory of twinkling light in the distance: it seemed a million miles away.

'From here,' said Ariel, 'you wouldn't believe there was any problem.'

'Yeah,' agreed Harry. 'The world is yours, once you escape the city.'

'Once you escape your *family*,' she said.

'That's not true,' he said. 'My family might be rotten to the core, but yours is all right.'

Ariel was silent.

'I stopped caring,' he added. 'You still care.'

'I suppose you're right,' she said. 'And it hurts to be judged by them. Not so much by my brother – I kind of know Ben adores me – but by Daddy. It's like he doesn't care.'

'Your dad cares,' said Harry. 'He's just . . . mad.'

'I guess he is,' said Ariel.

'Unlike *my* dad, who is just plain bad.'

Harry sighed, and he heard her sigh with him. He held her close and marvelled that they had found each other. Funny really, he wasn't a romantic kind of guy. When you fell in love, why the hell couldn't it be a cause for celebration? Why couldn't people be pleased for you instead of thinking about what it meant for *them*? Harry couldn't see that it should be a problem for either Luke or Frank. It was none of their business, especially as no one was even on speaking terms. All the same, Harry had an unpleasant feeling that Luke, at least, would make it his business.

Turtle Egg Island, the Bahamas, that same day

Sofia

As the speedboat bounced over the turquoise ocean towards the island, Sofia spread her arms wide and let the spray of the seawater anoint her like a queen. She always felt godlike approaching their retreat on Turtle Egg. Here was silence and stillness; here you could breathe. The only noise was the quiet *hush, hush* of the waves, and the gentle breeze, rustling the leaves of the palm trees. She had always insisted that the place was run 'like a magic trick', with no evidence of effort.

Today, however, was different. Turtle Egg Island was a business venue: a conference centre. She loathed the idea, but she had no choice. She loved her lifestyle; and she was not going to lose it. Therefore she was hosting a meeting to discuss the Macau question, followed by a small banquet in 'honour' of Arnold Ping. It was impossible, otherwise, to get the man to travel. If you issued a general invitation, it suggested you thought he could be summoned like a dog. Nor did Ping operate on short notice. It was fortunate that Sofia had been making overtures for some time. Most recently, she had invited Ping to the Pre-Grand Opening Party. He had sent a senior representative, and preliminaries had been discussed. Now Ping had agreed to hear further details of their proposal himself.

The location was a lure. The main house was magnificent: she had designed it herself. It was shaped like a huge curling seashell, and it was the pearly colours of the sand and sea. No one beyond immediate family and staff had ever been invited there. It was a sacrifice to share her sanctuary, but at this point, she would do anything.

Frank would attend, although Sofia had taken Sterling's advice and not told him of Ben's plans. She knew that, devastated as he would be, Frank would not override them. As far as Frank knew, this meeting was a routine step in the long journey towards winning over Ping. The Cat was a triumph, and if they wished to recreate the magic in Macau, they needed the approval of its king, an old Chinese guy without whose sanction, nothing ever progressed in Macau.

The boat approached the jetty, where staff stood in line. Sofia nodded hello and then swept towards the house to inspect preparations. Sterling marched at her heels. Every detail, down to the last blade of grass, was perfect, immaculate. Sofia rubbed her neck. 'My neck is *killing* me,' she said.

Sterling glanced towards the pool. Its glassy surface rippled in the breeze. 'A swim, perhaps,' he said. 'Followed by a massage?'

Sofia smiled. It was a pity that Sterling was gay, as he was her perfect partner in every other respect. He came from an old American family whose vast wealth and conspicuous philanthropy allowed them to lord it over the East Coast. Sterling understood her.

She slipped into the warm water. Sterling paced beside her along the edge.

'Sterling, is there any way that Frank could miss the meeting?'

'There is, but Ping would regard it as an insult, Sofia.'

Right now, Sofia despised Frank with the fierce, searing hatred that boils up suddenly in marriage and then pops like a bubble or ferments like yeast. Sofia loved the cachet that came with being Mrs Arlington; it had slowly dawned that the only drawback was *Mr* Arlington. Once she had given Frank a male heir, Sofia had never been bothered about mistresses, even though it was rumoured that Frank did not indulge. Well, now she knew why. He couldn't get it up without chemical assistance! It was insulting.

She had been a mistress herself and was aware of their lack of power. Sofia had always wanted to be the main event, and she was. And yet he'd found a way to cheat on her. She thought of him slipping a little blue pill into his mouth and she wanted to throttle him.

'He doesn't deserve me!' she gasped as she powered swiftly through the water, Sterling trotting at her side. 'I have *respected* this marriage. I have respected it as the foundation of my happiness, and I have maintained that pig as if he were an expensive car. I've lavished time and attention on him; I've given him exactly what he needs to function beautifully. And in return—'

She took an accidental breath as she dipped into the water and choked.

Spluttering and flailing, she grabbed at the side. Sterling, with no regard for his custom-made suit, pulled her out of the water.

'In return,' she croaked, 'he has made me feel fat, old, gnarly and disgusting.'

'Impossible,' murmured Sterling. 'You are exquisite.' He led her to a sun chair. 'You have endured a stressful few months. But this summit with Arnold Ping is a bright new beginning. Your worries are over. We have dealt with the woman and her pitiful threats of exposure. Dr Erich at the hospital assures me all is going to plan. The *Times* journalist has been silenced by our legal department.'

Sofia sighed. 'What about Ariel and . . . the boyfriend?'

Sterling came as close to a snort as was polite. 'Sofia, as with so many over-nurtured richlets, she is rebelling against every family value that springs to mind. This desire to annoy will swiftly pass upon receipt of the first stern letter from her bank manager. Even Luke Castillo can understand that.'

'Yes,' groaned Sofia. 'But Ariel seems to have managed to dream up a business idea for herself. Hotel *consultancy*, for crying out loud! And the boyfriend is a *cop*.'

Sofia didn't trust cops. You never knew which one had influence with the Gaming Board. And any of *those* bastards could walk into your casino on New Year's Eve and shut down every table for any political bullshit reason he felt like giving. Perhaps Frank had forgotten to stick his Gaming Card in his jacket pocket that morning. Or, hey, there wasn't enough money in the cage. You raised your limits but you didn't raise your reserve. Boom! Turn off the slot machines for eight hours!

'I could forgive Ariel going out with a cop,' she added. 'But I can't forgive her choosing the cop who is Luke Castillo's son.'

Sofia shuddered as Sterling began to massage her shoulders and closed her eyes. While Luke and Harry loathed each other, they were still blood, and Luke would not tolerate his son sleeping with the enemy – especially as the enemy had already stolen his Sunshine. He would take revenge, but how?

She sat bolt upright in the chair, almost knocking the bottle of Moroccan rose oil from Sterling's hands. 'What if Luke knows my secret? Do you think he could have traced Bessie and put her up to this? He could have paid her to ruin my life!'

Gently but firmly Sterling pressed her rigid form back down into the chair. 'Sofia,' he said. 'That would be impossible because how could he *know*?'

From nowhere, he summoned a servant bearing a glass of icy Diet Coke. Sofia sucked it down through a pink straw, and watched as a dragonfly the size of her hand buzzed its gauzy wings over the water like a small bi-plane.

'Hold your nerve,' murmured Sterling. 'The fact that Ariel has chosen Harry could bridge the gulf between your families. You don't have to like each other; you just have to observe protocol.'

'I suppose so,' said Sofia as the bubbles fizzed comfortingly in her throat.

Sterling coughed delicately. 'The situation in Macau is an interesting example.'

It was true. Ping was a billionaire businessman, the most influential individual on the island. As long as Ping reigned, brokering peace between the rival triads, ensuring that every faction got something (and that he got a little more than something), everyone made money; everyone tolerated everyone else.

Ping was the perfect person to advise her on diplomacy.

'You're right, of course. I could ask the old man's opinion. It wouldn't be too obsequious because Ping is incapable of finding any flattery disproportionate. After the private dinner I hosted, he thanked me, but so *mutedly* – with this shit-eating grin on his face as if he was enjoying some private joke – it was clear he felt this big show of worship at great expense was his due and that gratitude was a formality not a requisite.'

'The guy is hard work. But what he can give you is worth the floor-licking.'

Sterling was right; she would persevere. Mr Ping was due to fly in by chopper in eight hours' time. Frank was flying in direct from Las Vegas. He would arrive shortly before Ping, with a loyal and trusted secretary, probably Gloria-Beth. All Sofia had to do was relax, check her notes and look beautiful. The dress code was glamorous yet trustworthy: Donna Karan, perhaps. What could go wrong?

Turtle Egg Island, eight hours and fifteen minutes later

Lulu

Turtle Egg Island: the very name made her smile. Imagine bringing Joe to a place as magical as this; building castles together in the crystal sand and splashing about in the gaudy blue sea. It was hard to leave him;

thank God for her parents. Meanwhile, she felt as though she had climbed through the looking glass into another reality. She hadn't told Frank this was her first time in a Gulfstream V. Cool, if a little ridiculous.

She'd stepped on to the field, grinning at the exotic surrounds. Her grin had disappeared on seeing Mrs Arlington. Mrs Arlington had grabbed Frank's sleeve and hissed, 'You're *late*; how could you be *late*?'

Mr Arlington opened his mouth to answer, but was shushed by his wife. 'Ping's already here, he arrived ten minutes ago and he's terrible at small talk. And where's Gloria-Beth? She can't – this is – why did you bring *her*?'

Lulu pretended to be engaged with her employer's luggage. But it was impossible not to hear Mr Arlington explain that Gloria-Beth was off work with a periodontal abscess and he had walked into 'the secretary area' and grabbed 'the prettiest one'. Ah, thank you, Mr Arlington, good to know my years at college weren't wasted. If she was inclined towards litigation, she could have made a packet.

Mrs Arlington's face was scrunched up in a sneer. 'Go on ahead,' she snapped to her husband. 'I told him you were unavoidably delayed on a family matter, so don't make any other excuse. We're sitting on the veranda: it is civilized and sedate, and I'd like it to remain that way, so please, Frank, remember the rules. His rules – etiquette – don't be *noisy*.'

Mr Arlington smoothed his hair and rushed off.

Lulu felt Mrs Arlington's hand grip her upper arm, 'Frank has made an error bringing you here. But we need a typist. Now: this meeting is classified. Billions of dollars rest on its outcome, and if one word of what is discussed gets out to Ben, then I will sue you for breach of confidentiality in the federal court. Am I clear?'

Her heart raced; Mr Arlington had explained that the meeting was with Arnold Ping in relation to investing in a development in Macau. Ben, her boss, was a senior executive; he was on the board of directors. Why couldn't he know? Still, Ben could look after himself. She was not his keeper; no, that was his girlfriend, Sunshine Beam. And anyway, if she lost her job she and Joe were in trouble.

'Yes, Mrs Arlington.'

Mr Ping was travelling with a modest entourage: two colleagues, his current wife, one long-legged Russian girl and a middle-aged PA, all of whom now sat on squashy lounge chairs overlooking the pool. As they approached, Mrs Arlington made a squeak in her throat, and Lulu jumped.

Mr Arlington was shaking hands with Mr Ping; a great, hearty, vigorous handshake. Mr Ping, short and slight, looked as though he might blow away on the end of that handshake like a crumpled paper bag in the wind.

Mrs Arlington hurried over and bowed; Lulu did the same. Mr Ping bowed in return, although he didn't shake Lulu's hand. Mrs Arlington didn't bother to introduce her, but that was fine. She knew who *he* was, and that was what mattered. She took her place, a little back from the circle, and powered up her laptop. It was hard to sit straight in the squashy chair, rather than slump, and she wondered if Mr Ping felt as uncomfortable as she did. Mr Ping did not look like a slumper.

Mrs Arlington's butler had already served drinks and snacks. The garden was thick with blooms; a lot of trouble had plainly been taken to make the guests feel welcome. A huge bouquet had been presented to Mrs Ping; it now lay, discarded, on the floor beside her, fast wilting in the heat. Lulu vaguely remembered something about flowers. Did you give flowers to your Chinese guests, or did flowers symbolize death? These particular flowers were starting to symbolize death; she itched to put them in water.

Mrs Arlington talked a lot. Mr Ping listened. 'It's such a pity that you were unable to attend the Grand Opening of the Cat, Mr Ping, but your associate, Mr Leong, was terribly impressed with Xiqing, our superb Michelin-starred restaurant. We hope that when and if we open the Cat, Macau, our flagship restaurant will be named simply Ping, if, of course, you are amenable to this. You would have to try the food there first, of course, to ensure we weren't poisoning people in your name!'

Lulu glanced at the translator. She wondered if the girl had also been chosen because she was 'the prettiest'. Mr Ping's eyebrows twitched upwards, slightly, at her rendition of this speech. He was silent, almost to the point of awkwardness. Then he spoke, slowly and carefully, in Cantonese.

'Don't be this kind,' said the translator.

'You are too kind,' typed Lulu, trying not to giggle and succeeding. She couldn't be sure, but she suspected that Mr Ping, the old goat, was staring at her legs.

Mrs Arlington paused. 'Ideally, we would like to

situate our casino in old Macau. We feel the Cotai Strip is a little bit . . . off Broadway!'

Lulu wondered what the translator would make of this turn of phrase. The young girl chattered at speed; no hesitation or deliberation. Either she was very good or very bad.

Mr Ping's eyes narrowed. But Mrs Arlington was being politic: of course she would settle for a plot on the Cotai Strip. It was courteous to give Mr Ping the opportunity for tough negotiation. This was different to conflict, which was plain rude. Negotiation was about graciously permitting your opponent to feel he had talked you into granting a concession. Lulu was impressed. This could turn out well for the Arlingtons.

'We would welcome collaboration between our families, if this is not too impertinent a suggestion. For instance, we greatly admire your youngest son, Harold, and his work in, ah, contemporary theatre. We would be delighted if he could honour us in accepting a senior executive position in our entertainment division.'

Lulu privately thought this was a generous offer, considering Harold Ping was known for his impressive coke habit and being a bit of a prostidude.

Mrs Ping was clearly pleased – well, not clearly, but Lulu thought she noticed a gentle inclination of the head. Mr Ping sipped his green tea. 'The Cotai Strip is highly sought after,' stammered the translator. 'I will pass on your generous offer to my third son.'

Lulu wondered if this was a little curt, but perhaps Mr Ping was not a man who wasted words.

'We are hoping to receive permission for a gaming

licence early next year. But I understand that bureaucracy in Macau can be slow,' said Mrs Arlington. 'I have set millions of dollars aside for administrative fees.'

Lulu saw the translator glance at Mrs Arlington, and dip her head. The girl spoke softly, so softly that Mr Ping barked at her in Cantonese, and the girl jumped. He rattled off something in response.

'Tell me,' said the translator, recovering her poise. 'Who are you thinking of to run your casino in my humble kingdom? Perhaps you haven't decided as it is *very* early in the day and, as you say, you have no permission for a gaming licence. But your son, Ben, has proven himself to be talented in business, and he has experience, at least, of living in mainland China.'

Lulu stiffened. Oh *God*. Shut up, Ping. Ben was perfectly happy in Vegas, thank you. Although what was it to *her* where Ben was happy? He was unavailable, wherever he might be.

Lulu didn't look at Mrs Arlington, even though she wanted to jump up and shriek at her, 'Speak!'

Mrs Arlington's voice was smooth, emotion carefully contained. 'I am sure', she said slowly, 'that if his involvement was required, Ben could acquit himself in a fairly senior management role.' She paused. 'It may be a convenient time for my son to leave Las Vegas. He recently poached Luke Castillo's prize executive host, a Miss Sunshine Beam – oh, I'm sure you know what sons are like, Mrs Ping, they see a beautiful girl! The situation has caused bad feeling and one does not wish to court trouble in one's own back yard. Mr Castillo is not a man one crosses without consequence. Indeed, perhaps we could spin it as a *banishment* . . . Ah God, I can't believe I'm being pressured into this.' Mrs Arlington glared at the translator. 'Don't tell him that last bit.'

Sunshine Beam wasn't *that* amazing. She had the big boobs, the dyed blond hair, the throaty laugh, the vivacious allure – but she was smug. She was smart, but she wasn't *nice*. When Lulu saw her striding along, a little bit Barbarella, a little bit Scarlett Johansson, she wanted to stick out a foot and trip her up. Lulu was surprised that Ben had fallen for a woman as superficial as Sunshine.

'I have heard of Miss Beam; she is a valuable asset.'

'Indeed, Mr Ping. Sunshine is a diamond. Since Sunshine joined the Corporation – and she is only operating in one casino – our gaming revenue has shot up by six per cent. She produces six-figure players like a magician pulls bunnies from a hat. We would certainly consider sending her to consult at the Cat, Macau, perhaps for a few days every month. She would bring a lot of highly profitable traffic to the island.'

Inwardly, Lulu rolled her eyes. The genius of Sunshine. She'd wade through the mire of personal assistants ('I have those front-row tickets to the fight he wanted, but if he's interested, he should call in the next hour') until she got her fish on the line. She researched each player: his preferred game, his usual strategy, his average bet and his average loss, his biggest loss and his biggest win. She knew who was profitable and by how much. 'I want losers!' she'd say. But she'd make them feel like kings. Yes, that was her job. She was a sales rep, pushy as hell, with questionable morals. You couldn't trust Sunshine. She was out for herself.

The translator cleared her throat. 'We would consider it a sign of goodwill if Miss Beam's permanent place of work was Macau.'

Mrs Arlington was about to respond when Mr Arlington interrupted. 'That may well be possible. As you know, Mr Ping, I was late today – and I apologize unreservedly. The reason was that my son broke some news to me, good news, but news that it was very hard for me as a father to accept.' Frank smiled, sadly, Lulu thought, and added, 'If you are anything like me, Mr Ping' – Mr Ping bowed his head – 'we like to keep our apples close to the tree.'

'What?' blurted Mrs Arlington, silencing Mr Ping with a gentle touch on the lower arm. 'Ben told you he was leaving the company?'

'*What?*' said Mr Arlington. 'No! Who said anything about quitting the company? Did he tell you he was quitting the company? I just promoted him!'

Ben was *leaving*?

Mr Arlington babbled on while Mr Ping sat in silence. 'Why didn't you tell me, woman? How long have you known?'

'I was dealing with it myself, Frank, because it got in the way of *our* plans – and now . . .'

Mrs Arlington faltered into silence as Mr Ping rose to his feet. 'Mr Arlington,' he said in hesitant but perfect English. 'My eldest son Charlie Ping has invited your son to develop a casino in Macau as a shared venture, and I understand he is seriously considering the offer. You take offence that he does not tell you, but he may wish that you pursue your ambitions without reference to his own.

Your son is a capitalist; no doubt he believes in the health of competition.' Mr Ping bowed. 'You have been most hospitable, Mr and Mrs Arlington, and I thank you most gratefully for your kindness. However, there is a Chinese saying – in that I conceived it myself: Secure your foundations before you build the roof.'

Lulu let her jaw drop as Mr Ping, Mrs Ping, the Russian girl, the associates and the PA stood up as one.

As they bustled away towards the airfield, Mrs Arlington cried, 'Mr Ping! Please! I'm sure we can sort this out! This is a misunderstanding . . .' She stopped talking and gazed after Mr Ping's entourage as it toddled into the distance.

She whirled on Mr Arlington in a rage. 'So, Frank,' she said, voice acid. 'Please do share the news that managed to fuck up the deal I've been working towards for the past twenty-four months of my life.'

Mr Arlington glared at her, his face darkening. 'Don't blame this one on me, *baby*. Your Machiavellian scheming is what blew this sky high. Ping doesn't think he can trust you. As for the news that delayed my arrival: Ben told me this morning that he and Sunshine are engaged.'

As Sofia cried, '*What!*' it took all of Lulu's strength not to cry '*what!*' also. But no one noticed her horrified reaction; at that moment the Arlingtons were deaf and blind to everyone but each other.

Lulu stood up, muttered 'restroom' without anyone hearing, and stumbled off. She could barely walk; her legs felt like rubber. She found an outdoor bathroom, its mirrors festooned with yellow lilies and peered miserably inside. The cream shift dress she had so excitedly picked for the occasion looked crumpled and grubby. Her hair was tied back yet it had still managed to frizz around her ears. Her cheeks were uncomfortably scarlet and there were ugly beads of sweat around her upper lip. The expression on her face was broken.

A small apartment, Las Vegas, one month later, 1 June 2009

Lulu

'Oh God, *baby*! Give me a kiss – I love you so much!' It was 6.25 a.m., and Lulu was in bed with the most important man in her life.

It was no use; Baby Joe had slid off the bed and was waddling towards the door, bellowing '*Milk! Want my milk!*'

She changed his nappy, made his milk and stroked his hair as he drank it. In exactly one hour, her mother would arrive, leaving her fifteen minutes to make herself socially presentable, and twenty minutes to get to work. There was very little time to indulge in heartbreak.

The phone rang. As she heard her mother's voice – a hoarse croak – her heart sank. 'It feels like laryngitis. Dad has work today, but I don't think I—'

'You sound terrible, Mom, and of course Dad must go

to work. Poor you. Don't worry, just rest. I'll sort something out.'

It was easier said than done. She'd once got a girl from an agency who had lasted a day. She'd told Lulu that she and Joe had gone to the park, but the way she had phrased it: 'That killed an hour!' had planted a seed of annoyance in Lulu's head that had swiftly grown enormous. No one would look after Joe who didn't think he was a miracle.

And she knew what that meant.

The girls in the office went bananas. Joe was sung to, danced with and made a fuss of. But it was still embarrassing, as if she wasn't in control of her life. And, frankly, she wasn't. She was twenty-three, with a child and no partner. She had no social life, except when her mother begged her to go out ('and meet someone' being the unspoken end of the sentence). Her girlfriends occasionally set her up with men *they* wouldn't go out with. Sometimes Lulu realized that she had forgotten what she liked and had to remind herself. She liked happy endings that were truly deserved; she liked dancing until she was out of puff; she liked her bed; she liked singing to Scott Walker's most miserable songs. She liked high-quality chocolate and skinny fries and the first coffee of the day; she liked the shower almost *too* hot; she liked making her son laugh and kissing his silky fat cheek until he said, 'Get off me!' She liked *Seinfeld* and *Arrested Development*; she liked people who smiled at you just to be friendly. The craziness of a Las Vegas casino amused and delighted her, and she hated it as much as she loved it. It was a diversion from real life. As for men—

'Joe! Hey, buddy, give me five!'

Her son wriggled out of a colleague's arms and ran to Ben Arlington. Ben swung him in the air and he shrieked with pleasure. 'You're so big,' said Ben. He grinned at Lulu. 'Not long now and we can go surfing together.'

Lulu saw that all the women in the office had a misty-eyed look. She was unmoved. For all his chat and charm, Ben was intending to marry Sunshine Beam, and by choosing *her* – so callow and vapid despite her intelligence – he betrayed every woman in the room. Sunshine was loud and raucous (men would call it vivacious), but to qualify as life-affirming did you have to be unbearably full of yourself?

Lulu was employed by Ben but in the last few months, she had become his friend, and when he visited her apartment he *always* made the coffee. His friendship was precious to her; she would take what she could get. She flattered herself that he relaxed when he was with her, because she treated him as a regular guy.

She talked to Ben, a lot, about Joe. Joe's father had been an ill-advised fling who had disappeared into the ether; Ben tried to be a role model in Joe's life, and not out of some lofty do-gooding charitable inclination, but because he thought Joe was a fantastic kid. She tried *not* to talk about Joe, and, sure, they talked about other things – was it possible to go through school and not know what the word 'candelabra' meant; if you disliked your dentist because he wasn't as complimentary about your teeth as your old dentist, was he a *bad* dentist – but the conversation always seemed to revert to her son eventually.

'I hope you don't feel sorry for me,' she'd said one evening when Joe had caught a bug and projectile vomited on her twice (and once on her bed).

'Why would I?' Ben had said, and there was a touch of coldness to his voice. 'What a crappy thing to say. You're living the dream. *You* might not think so. You have a beautiful, healthy child, and you're still young. You have parents who adore you, and tons of friends, a job, a home. You're gorgeous, funny, clever, and, essentially, you're free. And I think you know it. You're a happy person. I should think if anything, it would be the other way round, *you* feeling sorry for me.'

'Don't be ridiculous,' she'd snapped.

'Why?' he'd said. 'Why is it ridiculous?'

'Oh come on, Ben!'

'Is it the money?' he'd said, and his voice was ice.

She'd laughed, even though her heart thumped at her audacity. 'Ben, people with money always say it's not important and it doesn't make you happy. And that's insulting to anyone who's ever experienced the soul-clawing dread that comes when you realize you can't pay your bills, you don't know what will become of you, or what the hell you can do about it.'

'I'd never say that money doesn't matter. I'm not a complete jerk. It's obvious what money does give you but if you don't have it, you don't realize what it can't give you. Happiness isn't found in a Maserati showroom. It's found in personal connections – and what tends to fuck that up more than anything? You can't make a first impression on anyone – it's already been made. It's lonely. It's an amazing, privileged life, but it's often quite a . . . *chilly* one.'

114

She'd reached out for his hand, and squeezed it, all animosity gone. It was true: Ben lived an odd life, highly superficial, showbiz and cut-throat, and yet all that was a very small part of who he was.

'Well,' she'd said. 'Then it's very good for you to be grounded,' and she'd handed over Joe, who'd obliged with a fourth *Exorcist*-style vomit.

Ben did the little things that she wouldn't think of doing with Joe, such as chucking him up so high in the air that he nearly hit the ceiling. She'd flap around, shouting, 'Careful!' while Joe screamed with laughter. But he also liked to read to him. Their favourite was a book Ben had found on his last trip to England, *Tatty Ratty*. Ben would call it *Ratty Tatty*, or *Fatty Ratty*, which Joe found hilarious. They'd sit there giggling, and Lulu would pretend to herself, in her rare indulgent moments, that this was her real family. It was strange to remember who he was outside her apartment. Out there Ben belonged to everybody except her, but in here, he was hers.

There'd be no more of that nonsense with Sunshine in charge. Lulu had thought of asking Ben to be Joe's godfather, to make the love in their relationship official, but while she knew that Ben would be honoured, she also knew how others would see it.

Ben confided in her also. As recently as last week he'd confessed to feeling bad about Ariel. Ariel refused to get in touch with any of them, and he'd driven round to her apartment three times but she was never home. Lulu had said that Ariel probably just needed space to grow up and gain some perspective. Ariel had actually, to everyone's surprise, managed to get herself a job of sorts. She'd set herself up as a 'hospitality consultant', which meant hotels paid her to test their facilities and criticize; nice work if you could get it. 'I'm not sure you need to worry *too* much about Ariel,' she'd said, and he'd laughed.

So! Had he been discussing the same tender subjects with Sunshine all the while? Lulu doubted that Sunshine's pillow talk would extend to other women, and certainly not Ben's sister. Sunshine wasn't thoughtful like that. Her focus rarely alighted on the bigger picture.

Lulu had once travelled in a chauffeured car with Sunshine, and Sunshine had stuck a piece of gum in her mouth and *dropped the wrapper out of the window*. To Lulu, it was a few short steps from litterbug to serial killer. Now she had Joe, she thought in global terms, of the world's future, and when she saw Sunshine dropping litter, she saw Joe, as an adult, scrambling over a great ugly sea of discarded trash.

'Have you set a wedding date, Mr Arlington,' simpered one of the bolder secretaries. 'Where will you go on honeymoon?'

'Bella, you seem worryingly keen to be rid of me . . .'

As everyone crowded round giggling, Lulu felt sure that not one girl there gave a toss about Sunshine Beam, but revelled in the opportunity to joke around with Ben Arlington and imagine for a few moments that he was hers. Oh Lulu, you sad sex-starved old girl, it's just sour grapes because you haven't got anyone.

'Are you having an engagement party, Mr Arlington?' said one of the secretaries, giggling.

'God, no, I can't think of anything worse. I—'

'Ben, my darling – oh goodness, is that a *child*? Whatever is it doing in a place of *work*?' At the sound of that voice, the warm atmosphere turned polar and people started shuffling back to their desks. Sofia Arlington's gaze rested briefly on Lulu, and Lulu's heart flipped in fear.

'*Lulu?*' she said. 'Is this yours?'

'Yes, Mrs Arlington. I'm sorry, I have childcare but it fell through, unfortunately, and I had to bring him into work. Delilah at the spa crèche says she will have him for the afternoon so . . . It's never happened before but—'

'Lulu primarily works for me, and I say it's fine,' said Ben.

Sofia smiled at Ben, a quick, professional smile. 'Well, dear, then we shall leave you to hold the baby. I have a special task for Lulu!'

'Oh yes?'

Sofia smiled again. 'Yes, darling; of *course* you are going to have an engagement party. Your father and I would be so upset if—'

'Mother, I—'

'Ben, please, as a favour to me. It would make me happy.'

Lulu watched Ben's face. Sofia was playing on his guilt about leaving, she knew it.

'Of course, then, thank you.'

Sofia clapped her hands. 'Excellent! There are a few possible dates at the end of August – let me know what works for you. I have decided, seeing as it is, one hopes, a once-in-a-lifetime occasion, to hold it on Turtle Egg Island. You can imagine the media furore that will provoke. Still, no publicity is bad publicity, and anyway, love conquers all – even hovering helicopters drowning out your father's interminable speeches. Of course, certain business associates will have to attend.'

'Of course,' said Ben drily.

'And it will be a suitable occasion on which to meet Sunshine's mother.'

Ben drew his mother to one side. Lulu heard him murmur, 'Sunshine and her mother don't speak, and haven't for some time. I'm not sure they need to be reunited. I don't think Sunshine even knows where her mother *is* – she tends to disappear. Her father's dead. Mom, I don't want a huge fuss. And what is it you need Lulu for?'

Sofia snapped her fingers even as Ben glared at her and said, 'Sorry, Lulu.'

Lulu smiled and walked over.

'Admin, Ben, I need her for admin. Lulu will advise me on the guest list; your most favourite people in the world. Come with me,' said Mrs Arlington. 'My dear,' she said, once they were out of hearing. 'I know I can trust you. And I know you are loyal to Ben. First, I *do* want you to help Gloria-Beth with the guest list – certain of Ben's friends will have to attend. But it's not entirely straightforward: I need you to trace certain people – Sunshine's family, for example. I am going to invite two hundred of *our* close friends, many of whom are public figures, so I require someone with sense, resilience and absolute discretion.'

Lulu nodded.

Mrs Arlington cleared her throat. 'Now, Lulu, there is another matter. I regret to say, I also know of someone who *isn't* loyal to Ben.'

Yes, thought Lulu, *you*. She still felt bad about the meeting on Turtle Egg Island with Mr Ping, but thankfully, no harm had been done. This at least was some comfort. Ben might not know how devious his mother had been, and how hard she had tried to ruin his plans, but Mrs Arlington had failed, which absolved Lulu, she hoped, of the moral responsibility to tell tales.

'And, because he is my son, I cannot bear to see him hurt. I certainly do not want him to marry the *wrong woman*.'

Oh God! Nor did she! Lulu hoped she wasn't blushing. But she understood the sentiment. She couldn't think of anything worse than Baby Joe growing up to marry the *wrong* woman . . . a harsh, selfish girl who wouldn't be tender with him. It was awful to think of your son in a bad relationship.

'So while this engagement party will be the most extravagant, glorious, impressive, public and luxurious celebration of love, it will also be a test . . . of the bride-to-be. And for that, dear Lulu' – Mrs Arlington smiled at her. Her red lipstick was uncharacteristically smudged and, for a second, Lulu was reminded of Heath Ledger as the Joker – 'I am going to need your help. Do you accept?'

As if she had a choice. 'Yes, I accept, Mrs Arlington,' said Lulu. The fact was, of course she didn't want Ben Arlington to marry Sunshine – and she knew in her heart that this was not entirely because of Baby Joe. Sunshine wasn't good enough for Ben; she wouldn't make him happy – well, not for longer than a *week*, and from what Mrs Arlington was saying it sounded as if she was possibly cheating on him already.

And even though Lulu didn't trust Mrs Arlington one scrap; even though she knew that Mrs Arlington was secretly furious with Ben over the Macau debacle, the fact was that Lulu was uselessly, hopelessly in love with Ben and didn't want to lose him, certainly not to a vain, shallow person who didn't deserve him, and she would grab at the smallest, thinnest straw if it meant that she still had a chance, however unlikely and ridiculous, of getting Ben Arlington to love her.

Despite every chance in the world being stacked against her, Lulu still held fast to the hope that her outrageous, outlandish wish could still come true.

Secure Unit, Mont Blanc Sanatorium, two months later, 28 July 2009

Gisèle

'Here you go, Bessie.' Gisèle took the little pot and counted the pills into Bessie's hand. 'How are you feeling?'

Gisèle watched as Bessie considered. 'I don't know,' she said eventually. 'I don't know how I feel.' There was a long pause. 'These taste like toothpaste. I am a small person in a small world.'

It *was* Bessie who had been put here with Dr Erich receiving a bribe of 'one point five'. Gisèle was sure. Yet she was intrigued as to how this woman could pose a threat to anyone. Her records said she was schizophrenic but Gisèle couldn't see it. It was normal for in-patients on the psych ward to claim there was a plot against them by evil people saying they were mad, but Bessie was the only person who Gisèle sensed might be telling the truth.

As an 'unstable' patient, Bessie was required to be accompanied in public by a nurse at all times. She was also heavily sedated, to the point of being unable to contribute to any discussion or activity. Gisèle had decided to fix this.

Dr Erich had thoughtfully chosen a drug for Bessie that no one else was getting. All Gisèle had to do was to swap Bessie's pot of pills for a placebo. As all drugs were locked away, she'd had to wait for two weeks before an opportunity arose to make the switch. It came one lunchtime; it was as simple as the key left in the door. Each pot had a month's supply. Gisèle swapped only a few pills in the batch that first month, April. Then she had to do nothing for a month: the pharmacy department would fill Bessie's prescription and the nursing staff would deposit the pills into her mouth each day.

In May, she had swapped half the pills for the placebo – mints. In June, it had been three-quarters, and finally, this month, July, the *lot*. Four weeks earlier, Gisèle had noticed, with both delight and fear, that Bessie was almost entirely cognitively intact. But it was imperative that no one else noticed. So she had brazenly suggested at the case review that Bessie might benefit from a mild benzodiazepine. She could see Dr Erich quench the impulse to cry 'the more the merrier!'

And so Bessie was taking Zopiclone – short acting, but rendering her sleepy-looking enough to seem to be on the major drugs needed to keep a dangerous psychotic well controlled – and a daily dose of extra-strong mints.

But, thought Gisèle with a shudder, the sleepiness could not hide the desperation in her eyes. She ached to know what Bessie had done. Perhaps, one day, Bessie would tell her the whole story over a cup of cocoa, while Dr Erich languished in *jail*!

Gisèle sat down in a chair. 'Bessie, I think we all feel very small on occasion in our lives.'

Bessie was twirling at her hair, except her hair had been cut short, and her fingers were twirling at nothing. She looked from the window to the bed, to the floor, but not at Gisèle. 'I wonder why I am here.'

'Oh Bessie,' said Gisèle. 'Life can be hard but I think we are here for a reason.'

Bessie burst out laughing. 'I don't mean here in the *creation* sense,' she said, fixing Gisèle with a hard stare. 'I mean here in this loony bin.'

Gisèle nodded, but it was hard to stop a grin creeping over her face. She was both ecstatic and terrified. 'I suppose', she said carefully, 'that someone put you here.'

Bessie looked startled. The hand fiddling with the air around her head became more frenzied. It looked as if she was making little devil horns with a finger, over and over again. Gisèle felt sudden nausea. What if Bessie *was* mad and there was an innocent explanation for Erich's 'one point five'?

'Look what I got you,' she whispered to snap Bessie out of her trance. She had bought Bessie a celebrity gossip magazine. It might aid her memory, provide her with context. But as she reached out to hand over the contraband, there was a click. Gisèle shoved the magazine under the bed. She was breathless with fright.

The door opened and in strode Dr Erich.

Gisèle offered Bessie a glass of water – anything to mask the guilt.

Since Gisèle had caught him with Adelheid, she had slept with him seven more times, even though his touch now made her skin crawl. *He* assumed she was shivering with desire. His ego was her only protection. He would have difficulty believing that a little nobody like her would stop adoring him.

Of course, he didn't know she'd seen them together. Yet her heart beat with a sudden fear.

'Good morning, Bessie. Nurse, you surprise me.'

Gisèle smiled weakly as Erich studied Bessie's notes.

'I was interested to see how the patient was progressing,' she stammered. 'I admire your work, doctor, and I am keen to learn.'

Dr Erich smiled. 'Wait for me in my office, nurse.'

'Yes, doctor.'

Gisèle scurried to the first floor. She nodded at Erich's PA, whose demeanour and teeth reminded her of Cerberus. Mont Blanc was stark, white, sanitized severity, but Erich's office was a refined level of shade-free chic. It had an entire atrium to itself, with white shiny flooring and vast picture windows, and Cerberus was sat at a white desk, angled in the corner. The inner sanctum was more of an apartment than an office: it contained sofas, house plants, mood lighting, a shower and a bed. Gisèle sat on the edge of the hard designer sofa, praying that Bessie would not say anything to Erich.

She jumped up as the door opened.

He looked at her, and she didn't know how to look back at him.

He beckoned her to walk towards him, and she did. She felt his fingers gently entwine in the hair at the back of her neck; he bent his head and nuzzled his lips at her ear.

Adelheid was slut of the moment, but Erich was such a politician that he couldn't merely let go. The week she had suggested putting Bessie on a benzodiazepine he had presented her with a bracelet! It was exquisite: diamonds, rubies, gold. Gisèle remembered the Christmas her father had given her mother a pretty apron. Dr Erich would never make such an elementary mistake.

Squashing her distaste, she pressed against his chest. A white-hot bolt of pain shot through her ear and she screamed, staggering back, gasping, clutching the side of her head as blood dripped through her fingers. Erich had ripped out her earring with his teeth!

She stared at him in terror as he spat blood on to the varnished antique-oak floor. He took a starched handkerchief from his breast pocket and patted his mouth.

'Nurse,' he said. 'You are conscientious, but do not exceed your medical duties. Your friend Bessie is a highly

124

unstable fucking nutter in the advanced stages of delusional psychosis. I am the only staff member adequately qualified to treat her. It is essential, for your personal safety, that you do not approach her. She may turn violent' – he nodded at her torn ear – 'and regrettably, if you have contravened regulations, the clinic cannot be held liable.'

He smiled and offered her his handkerchief. 'You understand me, yes?'

She took the handkerchief, pressed it to her bleeding ear and fled.

Mont Blanc Sanatorium, later that day

Bessie

After sending the nurse to wait in his office, the man had stared in silence at Bessie. She feared he could read her mind. He took a step towards her, then he muttered something under his breath and left.

She had to get out but the foreboding descended on her like a dark night. Somehow, the young nurse had found out and wanted to help but she was frightened – and with good reason. Bessie would have to spur her on to action because she had a horrible feeling that, if she didn't escape in the next few days, she would die here.

She rolled off the bed and picked up the gossip magazine. It was in German but full of photographs. She pored over it with a sense of wonder. Oh my *God*, oh my God. All life was here, so bright and full and happy! There were so many faces she recognized; perhaps she knew these people or had she seen them in films?

And then she turned the page to see a beautiful, elegantly dressed family standing on the rooftop of a tall, glittering building, against a crazy backdrop: a pyramid, the Eiffel Tower and desert. Her head swam with the sudden glut of information. It was too much to process. Her brain hurt. Slowly, tenderly, she traced a finger over the faces of Frank Arlington, Ben Arlington, a stunning creature who the caption claimed was 'Miss Sunshine Beam', and, finally, Sofia Arlington. Bessie's nails dug into the page and ripped it. Then she covered her eyes with her hands and shook with laughter that swiftly became sobs.

The door clicked open. She stuffed the magazine under her blankets. It was one of the orderlies. 'Therapy class,' said the woman, not bothering to say 'hello'.

Bessie rubbed her eyes. Her heart pounded with excitement, but she shuffled wordlessly beside the woman to the therapy room. It exhausted her even to walk 5 yards. She sat slumped and inert next to the orderly, who passed the time biting her nails. The man was there, his gimlet eyes passing over her like a curse. And oh, thank heaven, the nurse.

It took all her will not to make eye contact, but she wouldn't do it while the man was there. The nurse moved differently now. She seemed agitated, afraid, and, with a sinking heart, Bessie knew that he had got to her. It couldn't be. This girl was her only hope. She would have to fight.

The man stayed for most of the meeting and, more than once, Bessie felt his cold stare. She didn't respond, just sat there, muttering to herself. You want mad, she thought, I'll give you mad.

As the class ended, Gisèle helped the healthcare technician hand out plastic cups of weak orange squash to patients.

'There you go,' she said to Bessie. 'You like orange squash, don't you?'

Bessie stared at the drink, talking fast and low, rocking back and forth, her hand over her mouth, the picture of a disturbed psychotic babbling nonsense. But her words, audible only to Gisèle, were clear. 'I have three children,' said Bessie, 'two boys and a girl. And I know why Sofia Arlington put me here. I can prove everything. I beg you, get me out. I don't care how.'

Gisèle smiled and walked away without looking at Bessie. Bessie jumped, spilling the sticky squash over her tunic, as a hand gripped her shoulder.

'Chatty today, aren't we, Bessie?' said the man, his face like granite.

'I don't like orange squash, I told her I hate it, I want a G & T but she didn't listen.'

His eyes bored into her, disbelieving. He smiled and said, 'You're grounded, Bessie, pretty much for ever.'

He twisted her in the direction of the psych ward and marched her back to her room. She staggered and lurched, dead-eyed. She wasn't sure if he bought it.

'This is it for you,' he said, pushing her roughly towards the bed. 'You're lucky your sponsor wants you kept alive.'

She looked at him with glazed eyes and whispered, 'Yes, doctor, thank you, doctor.'

'Stupid cow,' he muttered, and stamped out.

Slowly, the fog was clearing, and Bessie knew it was because of the girl. The problem was, so did the man.

Staff car park, Mont Blanc Sanatorium, that evening

Dr Erich

Dr Erich sat in his Mercedes Benz and watched Gisèle leave the sanatorium from his left wing mirror. She hurried along, head down, her neat bob covering her torn ear. Dr Erich flicked his grey hair out of his eyes. He was a fool for having lost control. It was her fault for snooping. Did she know anything? His guilt made him suspicious. But suspicion was usually justified.

Gisèle was a pain. Her presumptions regarding their 'relationship' were insulting. He hadn't cared when she'd seen him screwing Adelheid. He had presumed it would teach Gisèle her place, and show her how a female was supposed to mate.

But instead of trying harder, Gisèle had turned sullen. Dr Erich clenched his fist. He had made another mistake. She felt scorned; she was angry; she was out for revenge. God in heaven! If Sofia Arlington even sensed that her watertight solution had sprung a leak, prison and being struck off would be the least of his worries. Unless he could stop this, *he*, not Bessie, would die. Sofia Arlington would discover the truth and . . . He would have to disappear well before then.

The bracelet he had given to Gisèle had come from a patient, now deceased. It was legitimate – she had left it to him in her will. They often did. There were rules, but you worked around them. Gisèle had barely raised a smile: ungrateful. No matter. It was a loan.

Dr Erich drew hard on his cigarette, expelled the smoke in a long, thin hiss through his teeth, and started the engine.

Mont Blanc Sanatorium, three days later, 31 July 2009

Gisèle

She tucked her hair behind her ear out of habit then quickly let it fall back. She had sprayed her ear with antiseptic, but the infection had taken hold. She refused to think of this as ominous.

Now that she had bonded with Bessie, the risk she was taking was about more than revenge – it was about a woman's life. That said, it gave her spiteful pleasure that in setting Bessie free she would ruin Dr Erich.

Bessie would see the sun again, because tonight, Gisèle

was going to help her to escape or, as they put it here, 'leave impulsively'.

She knew the name 'Sofia Arlington'. If you had heard of Las Vegas you had heard of the Arlingtons. This Sofia Arlington person certainly had the means to pay Dr Erich 'one point five' to confine an undesirable. And yet could it possibly be true?

Gisèle had a worrying suspicion that Sofia Arlington had featured in the gossip magazine she'd smuggled to Bessie. Bessie could have plucked a name from recent memory – she might equally have said, 'Homer Simpson put me here.'

But Gisèle trusted Bessie – if only because she distrusted Erich. And she had to act fast. She had been banned from the Secure Unit and Dr Erich might well attend another case review meeting and decide to change Bessie's medication. If Gisèle did not get Bessie out of here now, she might soon be lost again in a haze of pills.

Gisèle had finished her shift, and she knew Dr Erich was watching her from his car. She took care to cross the road only when another pedestrian stood beside her. Dr Erich was dangerous. But she was smarter. She would let him see her walk to the stop and step on to her usual tram.

She took a seat on the left, and watched his silver car zoom past.

As expected, her phone rang, and she smiled. It was her immediate superior. 'Gisèle, I'm so sorry, but you're going to have to come back to work. I'm coming down with some kind of bug. Peter and Colette have already gone home, ill. I wouldn't ask, but we're short staffed as it is.'

She descended at the next stop and returned to the sanatorium. She had considered all kind of ridiculous plans garnered from blockbuster movies, and then she had decided simply to take advantage of what was available to her.

She had chosen tonight because Dr Erich would be attending the University Summer Ball. Dr Erich was one of the scholars being celebrated: he was to receive an honorary degree. Education had gone downhill. There was no possibility his vanity would allow him to miss it.

Earlier she had made tea for her colleagues – they took turns – and poured a liquid laxative into two of the mugs: Peter's, because he smoked and tended to gulp his drink like a dog, and Colette's because she had a cold. It was unlikely that either would detect any hint of suspicious flavour. Also, both had access to the Secure Unit. She'd winced as she had dosed her superior's tea, but Dr Harris wasn't interested in food or flavours, her mind was on loftier matters. All the same Gisèle had crossed her fingers.

She signed in and hurried to the Nursing Station. Her superior gave a weak smile.

'Thank you. Oh Lord, I feel lousy. The whole staff seems to be coming down with a bug.'

'Dr Harris, you know I don't have access for the Secure Unit. What if . . . ?'

Dr Harris fumbled in her bag. 'Take my card. It's fine, just for tonight.' Gisèle watched as Dr Harris scribbled down today's code, and then staggered towards the door. She felt drenched in a cold sweat.

In fifteen minutes, she would 'check' on Bessie and

other patients, and do what was necessary. Half an hour later, she would make her rounds again, and the main phase of her plan would begin. Everything was in place. It was oddly fortunate that Mont Blanc fell short of its scientific, clinical and rehabilitative ideals. While the brochure boasted of their Michelin-starred chef, their medical equipment was less impressive.

Months earlier, Gisèle had mentioned to Dr Erich that the crash cart in the Secure Unit wasn't fully stocked. If there was a Code Blue, and a face mask was required, they'd be in serious trouble. Nor did the oxygen tank contain the regulation level of gas. And the drawer containing additional emergency equipment seemed to be stuck. She had been keen to prove she was a good girl. But he had only wanted her to prove she was a bad girl.

Now he would regret it.

She smiled at the guard, who smiled back, and swiped Dr Harris's card. Then she briefly checked the other patients before entering Bessie's room.

'Bessie,' she said. 'How are you? Time to pop that pill! I suggest you take it and lie down. I will come back soon.'

It was difficult to wait a full thirty minutes, pretend to write up notes, sip coffee and look unconcerned. But at last it was time. Slowly, Gisèle got up and walked to the Secure Unit. She opened Bessie's door, hardly daring to look. Bessie lay flat on her bed, gasping. 'Oh God, I feel so ill. Faint, sick, like I might pass out.'

Gisèle pressed two fingers to Bessie's neck. 'Your blood pressure is abnormally low.' She heard herself say the words robotically. If tests were done, it would be discovered that the patient had ingested acebutolol, a drug to reduce high blood pressure. But there would be no tests.

Gisèle closed her eyes for a fraction of a second, and pressed her bleeper. *Code Blue*. Minutes later, she watched as two healthcare technicians battled with the stuck drawer to free the oxygen mask. The crash cart was a rumpled mess: it was a disgrace.

'This is ridiculous. We need to load and go,' she said, her voice urgent. 'Make the call.'

The HCT stared at her, slack-jawed.

'Do you think that Dr Erich would like it reported that a patient died while he drank champagne and partied? Call an ambulance!'

On her side was the fact that it was a Friday night. Aside from the Head of Human Resources, all senior management had left the building. The Head of HR came scuttling down the corridor flapping her hands as the ambulance men from City Hospital rushed through the building, but Gisèle knew she would not object – medically she was not qualified, and she was also terrified of losing her job.

'I'll go with her, I know her case history,' said Gisèle to the Head of HR, climbing into the back of the ambulance. She added, 'Dr Erich is up to speed with the situation. His instructions are to keep this quiet, contain it.'

'Additional security is required for SU patients,' replied the Head of HR. 'Helmut will accompany you also.'

Gisèle nodded, as if unconcerned, as the silent, bulky guard, handcuffs on his belt, climbed in, but, oh joy, he was stopped by the paramedic. 'You'll have to follow separately, there's not enough room.'

Helmut looked at the Head of HR.

'We need to go before we lose her,' snapped Gisèle. 'She's unconscious, she's no risk.'

The Head of HR beckoned; a terse, angry movement. Helmut shrugged and stepped down, and the paramedic slammed the doors. Seconds later, the ambulance was speeding along the road, fast, furious and free. Gisèle kept her eyes lowered; she was afraid that anyone who caught her gaze would see the triumph in her eyes. Bessie was out of Mont Blanc, and the plan was a tweak or two from success.

City Hospital, Geneva, Switzerland, that evening

Gisèle

'Her blood pressure has been stabilized,' said the doctor. 'But I'd like her to stay overnight for observation. We'll put her in a private room. She is, of course, covered?'

'Yes,' said Gisèle. 'Mont Blanc HR will liaise with your accounts department. It's not a problem. Thank you, doctor.'

The room selected for Bessie was at the end of a corridor. The Nursing Station was down the hall. There was a lift and a staircase between the two: perfect.

Not so perfect was Helmut, the security guard; professionally immune to charm, he was standing like a robot outside the room.

Gisèle glanced at Bessie. She was still dozy from the anaesthetic. Gisèle tingled with impatience as a nurse connected the patient to the drip, took her blood pressure yet again; checked her temperature. Finally, *finally*, they were alone.

'Bessie,' she hissed into the woman's ear. 'Wake up. You're in City Hospital. This is your chance.'

Bessie's eyes popped wide open. 'What do I do?' she said, gripping Gisèle's wrist with surprising strength.

Gisèle told her and she laughed. 'That's ridiculous.'

'No, it isn't. You've lost weight; we're almost the same size. You just have to appear confident. And listen to what I say.'

Five minutes later, Gisèle lay back, exhausted, on the plump pillows of the hospital bed. She felt dizzy with elation. Helmut, so stand-offish, had barely looked at the nurse briskly walking down the corridor pushing a trolley. The keys and directions to her flat were hidden in the steel basin.

Gisèle had given Bessie enough money for the short tram ride to her flat. At Gisèle's flat, she would find a change of clothes and a little more money, enough to get her to where she needed to go. There was nothing she could do about Bessie's passport – no doubt confiscated by Erich – but Bessie would have use of her telephone and computer. The rest would be up to her.

And now for the hardest bit: Gisèle stood up, closed her eyes and, biting her hand to stop herself screaming, yanked hard on her torn ear. As she cried with pain, the blood dripped obligingly on to the floor. Carefully she arranged herself as if the patient had attacked her and she had passed out with pain. Of course there were holes in her story, but no one could prove anything.

This was uncomfortable; she willed someone to discover her. At last the door opened. Feigning unconsciousness, she didn't move. She stayed limp as she was lifted on to the bed. She had swapped clothes with Bessie and felt exposed in her hospital gown. In a moment, her rescuer would call for back-up; now was a good time to fake coming to.

She smelled whisky-infused breath on her face as warm hands closed around her neck and began to squeeze. Her eyes flew open. A tall, handsome, grey-haired man in a dinner jacket stared down at her. *Dr Erich.*

'No,' she choked, befuddled with shock. 'It's me, Gisèle!'

He pulled his hands away. 'I do apologize, Gisèle, I must have drunk too much champagne. I thought you were Bessie.'

Warped relief flooded through her. 'She must have attacked me, doctor, I—'

'She *did* attack you, Gisèle. She strangled you; all very sad. Now hush, little girl; time to shut up and die.'

Harry's house, Las Vegas, four days before Ben and Sunshine's engagement party, 27 August 2009

Harry

Harry sauntered into the kitchen whistling and kissed Ariel on the neck.

'Ariel, I got something I want to show you. A pre-birthday present. Hey, did you see this thing in the paper about your brother's party? There's a picture of that girl he's marrying, Sunshine Beam. I think she looks a little bit like you.'

'What! She looks nothing like me.'

'Well, you're prettier, obviously. Don't you wish you were going?'

'Not really.'

'There's still time to change your mind, even if you slum it and go via public airplane.'

'Harry, I'm not going.'

'It's a shame. He sent you an invitation. Isn't it a good occasion to make up?'

'No, I don't feel it *is* a good occasion to make up. The point of an engagement is to get engaged, not to have all the guests bring along their grievances to sort out.'

'Ah, come on, Ariel. Ben won't see it like that. He'll be happy you're there.'

'You don't know how he'll see it, or how my mom and dad will react.'

'You've got to make up some time, and I think you should go. Why are you being so stubborn?'

'Look, can you stop going on about it, Harry? It's annoying. I don't want to go!'

'Why? He's your brother! You miss him. I don't understand why you're not going to his engagement party when he sent you an invitation! He's called you and called you and I don't see why you're still sulking.'

'I don't feel like it, OK? Am I not allowed to have a *feeling* about this? I don't like her, that woman he's marrying. In fact I hate her!'

'You haven't met her!'

'Oh, she looks awful! I don't *want* to celebrate her joining my family.'

'It's not about her anyway; it's about being loyal to your brother.'

'What about my family being loyal to *me*? OK, maybe I didn't deserve the promotion that Ben was offered. I think we're all aware of how *limited* I am as a business person, even though right now I seem to be doing fine on my own. Wow, that must be a fluke! But my father humiliated me. And yes, I overreacted and did something I shouldn't, but my God! I have been a good girl for twenty-six years, I think it was time!'

'All right, so your dad was thoughtless and unfair, but none of this is Ben's fault!'

'I'm embarrassed, Harry! And I haven't got room in my head for all the emotional space that my family demand! I don't *want* to turn up at Turtle Egg like the wicked fairy, with everyone staring and gossiping.'

'I think you're making excuses.'

'Oh, like you've got it all worked out, Harry! I've seen you do your physiotherapy exercises, what, *five* times in six months? You're miserable about being off sick, and yet you can't face up to your responsibilities—'

'*Bullshit*, Ariel! What do you know about responsibilities? You've never taken responsibility for anything in your life!'

'How dare you! You know how hard I work. Let's talk about *you*, and how you are just frozen because you feel this crazy guilt about your lieutenant getting shot, when, gee, I think it was the fault of the guy who shot him! And how you are not *letting* yourself get better to go back to the job you love, because in your stupid warped head you think you don't deserve to!'

'Be quiet, will you! This is garbage!'

'No, Harry, you need to hear this.'

'I mean it, Ariel, shut up.'

'Don't tell me to shut up when I am part of this! I am in this with you. I am living it. When you feel it, *I* feel it.'

'You don't know what I feel. You can't imagine it. No one can.'

'Oh, spare me the self-pity, Harry.'

'Yeah, well, I guess self-pity is something *you* know all about. Just leave me alone.'

'Fine, then, I will. I'll go.'

'Go then.'

'I will. And don't think I'll come back.'

'Whatever.'

'This is it, Harry.'

'See ya!'

'You . . . *pig*!'

Ariel burst into tears and slammed out of the

apartment. Harry took the diamond ring out of his pocket and hurled it across the room.

Macau, three days before the engagement party, 28 August 2009

Ben

As he heard the tread of the man's shoes in the hall, a trickle of sweat ran down his back. The heavily wrought wooden doors opened. Ben stood and bowed as Ping entered. He gave Ping a slight nod and shook his hand light and quick. He handed Ping his gold-embossed business card, presenting it the Chinese-side up.

As long as he managed not to behave like a crass American, the meeting would be a success.

He then singed a finger on the cigarette that Ping was smoking down to the filter. He drew back his hand a little too fast, hoping Ping hadn't noticed. There was no air conditioning, and the smoke tasted bitter in his throat. He was gasping for a glass of water, but to ask would be to insult the host, as it would suggest that the host was lacking.

It would also show weakness. Everyone in the room – from Ping's men lounging on the sofas to the Russian hookers standing in a beauteous gaggle by the wall – knew that Ben was weak. Ben's only strength was his youth, which could be dispensed with in a single gunshot. Ben felt he would rather die of thirst than bleat for water.

On advice, he had brought protection, Tom Hawk, ex-SAS, with a Stanley knife in his belt. Ben introduced Tom as 'Head of Marketing'. Everyone understood; everyone pretended not to.

Ping sat stiff-backed and unsmiling in a dark navy suit. His antique chair was like a throne. Ben could see the intricately carved wood, inlaid with mother of pearl, depicting scenes of battle. The man's personal taste was different to his casinos, which were vast and brash with yellow fluorescent lotus flowers and glow-in-the-dark dragons.

One of the girls stalked over and mixed a can of orange Fanta into Arnold Ping's glass of 1945 Château Pétrus. Her long brown hair fell in a silk sheet. Her hand trembled slightly as she poured.

Ben shifted on the sofa. It was squashy and low, forcing him to look up to Ping. Ben's opinion of himself was not swayed by what other people thought or how they treated him. He liked the Chinese saying: 'You cannot push a cow's head down unless it is drinking water of its own freewill.' Concede to the ego of the other man, and then business would progress.

Ben said, in Cantonese, 'This is a beautiful room.'

He was politely reminding Ping that, were he to converse with an associate in Cantonese, Ben would understand what was said. And the room was breath-taking; it was on the ninth floor of one of Ping's properties and its view swept across the sea, which today was a surprisingly clean fierce blue. There was no wall, just window: a single sheet of curved glass, at least seventy feet in length.

Ping nodded coldly.

His men sprawled in the background, in dark *Top Gun* sunglasses and shiny *Miami Vice* suits, their guns spoiling the line of their jackets. Ben saw the odd flash of a knife in a belt and felt uneasy. For the first time it occurred to him that Ping might not see him as a potential investor in the island, but as a threat.

Ben's shirt was sticking to his back. He could not imagine that the air conditioning was broken; someone had turned it off. The sun heated the room like a greenhouse. Even the Russian hookers grew silent. A pink Nintendo DS sat untouched on a side table, and one girl held a lipstick, frozen as if she were a statue.

Ben prayed he wasn't making the last mistake of his life, and said, 'Mr Hawk, if you wouldn't mind, I'd like to speak with Mr Ping alone.'

Hawk glanced at Ben. His eyes said, *Bad idea*. 'Please, if you would, Mr Hawk. The botanical gardens here are spectacular.'

Hawk stood up and bowed. 'Excuse me, gentlemen,' he said with almost imperceptible sarcasm. 'Mr Arlington knows I cannot resist a pink azalea.'

Ping sipped his drink.

Ben waited.

'So, Mr Arlington,' said Ping in English. 'Las Vegas is in deep recession. Macau has a six-billion-dollar surplus. What is it, besides greed, that attracts you to the city of Macau?'

Ben smiled, although Ping's decision to speak in

English was a snub: a way of reminding him that he was still a foreigner.

'If I was driven by greed,' said Ben, 'I would have stayed in Vegas and grown fat. My mother and father kindly believe I am of use to their business and are forever generous in promoting me beyond other well-deserving candidates and showering me with money and privilege.'

He took a breath. 'I've been fortunate to work along-side my father. But perhaps you understand how it is in a family business. Colleagues treat the boss's son like a Ming vase. I have learned a lot in spite of my situation, not because of it. I work differently from my parents and I would like to work independently. I want to be known for who I am, not who I was born to.'

Ping's face was devoid of expression. 'Perhaps', he said, 'you wish to hop from one gilded lily pad to another. You perceive that my son has connections and you see an easy ride.'

Ben paused. 'Mr Ping, I want to work with your son because our business visions collide, and I like and respect him. He and I would make a strong team. As a businessman he has proven himself without anyone's help. He is extraordinarily successful.'

Charlie was certainly a lot more than his 'connections'. Charlie had attended Eton, possessed an MBA from the London School of Economics and spoke with a cut-glass English accent. He wore a baseball cap pulled down over his dark shiny hair, and had a remarkable intellect and a disgusting sense of humour. He'd done his time at the family firm and had made money selling derivatives in Hong Kong.

'So you admit that he is the stronger candidate, Mr Arlington.'

'Without doubt,' replied Ben with a smile, 'as he has already struck out alone and succeeded admirably.' Ben refused to remind Ping that Charlie had the advantage of age; he was thirty-two. Lulu would laugh at that; the idea of Ben squeaking, 'But he's seven years older than me!' He only hoped he'd get the chance to tell her.

But sod it, if Ping could show spirit, so could he. Ben added, 'Wall Street estimates my potential annual worth to a gaming company as twenty million dollars. And Macau could do with some of that. It may be the world's hottest casino market. And it may have a six-billion-dollar surplus, but many of the Cotai Strip developments are in jeopardy. Developers are struggling to find new sources of funding. I am not arrogant, but Charlie and I have an astute business plan and I don't think that we would have trouble raising capital.'

Even though I see now, talking to you, that I am an idiot, added Ben gloomily, in his head. Charlie was not an independent operator. He came from a close-knit community; he intended to earn a living within his father's kingdom and so Arnold Ping would have to approve the match. What if he had already disapproved it? Now Ben saw that Charlie's word meant nothing to his father; Arnold Ping made up his own mind. Charlie's relationship with his father was all about humility: impressing Ping; being of use to Ping; earning Ping's trust. Ping expected his son to figure out success alone.

Perhaps Ping considered that in choosing to work with Ben, Charlie had made a grave error of judgement.

Ben tilted his chin. He met Ping's eye, then politely he looked away. So often, the American ideals of strength – a firm handshake, a steady gaze – coincided precisely with the Chinese idea of vulgarity.

'Do you not think you insult me with a bare face – coming to my island to try and take away my business and enlisting my first son to help you?'

Ben sensed fidgeting gangsters removing weapons from their belts.

'Sir,' said Ben, 'if I wanted to insult you, believe me, I would do it from far away. Charlie and I are certain that there is room for us all to thrive. My parents could still fulfil their dream in Macau, even if I built my hotel directly across the street. China has one point three billion people and just thirty-one casinos here. Meantime, over seven hundred casinos in Vegas serve three hundred million Americans. Further investment on the Cotai Strip will only increase the island's appeal and its revenue.'

Ping made no indication that he had listened or even heard. Another hooker, with hair in pigtails, lit another cigarette for him. Ping nodded at her. To Ben's surprise, she returned with a glass and a bottle of mineral water, already open, which she placed in front of Ben and poured. Ben felt Ping's gaze. It was another test, but of what? If he drank the water, to show that he trusted Ping, was he proven brave or foolish?

Ben was thirsty. He raised his glass and drank.

'I hear you are not too much of the politician,' said Ping. 'Here, you know, people are easily offended.'

Ben sighed. 'It's true. I am not a politician, I am a

businessman, and I find that it helps *me* to be direct with the people I work with. People know that I tell them the truth. To lie wastes time and causes trouble. When you flatter, people are briefly pleased. Then they discover the truth for themselves. And so you offend them twice instead of once.'

Ping eyed him as if he were a piece of trash. 'I am talking of your competitors in business. I hear that you are quick to make them your enemies also. It speaks of someone who is rash and hot-headed.'

'Ah,' replied Ben, 'you are thinking of Luke Castillo.' He paused. 'Even if I tried to please him he would find a reason to despise me. It is futile to adjust your behaviour to pacify a person who is angry like a volcano. Luke Castillo will hate me whatever I do, so I do what is best for me and my family.'

'You do not think that there may be consequences? People who annoy Luke Castillo have a habit of disappearing.'

Ben did not want to disrespect Ping, but he failed to keep the scorn from his tone. 'If there are consequences, I will face them. But Luke, despite his reputation, is a careful man. He might like to make me disappear, but for the trouble it would bring, it is not worth his while.'

He could feel his heart race as he talked of Luke, even though he had resolved to remain calm. The fact was Ben hadn't considered that Luke would actually *punish* him for taking Sunshine. Luke had too much to lose. But Ping's question unnerved him. Maybe he wasn't up to this. He half wished one of the henchmen would shoot him and get it over with.

Ping, through a haze of cigarette smoke, announced: 'You aim to open a casino across the street from the City of Gold. I own the City of Gold. Why should *I* not make you disappear right now for your audacity?'

'Ours would be a very different venture,' Ben replied quietly. 'One does not always have to go head to head like two bulls fighting. Sometimes one can help the other like a butterfly and a flower.'

Ping seemed to contemplate the silver wallpaper. 'I think', said Ping, 'that you are a young man who thrives on danger. And perhaps, because you are not scared, you do not always see the threat when it is close at hand.'

Ben swallowed. Was there a threat close at hand? 'It's true that there are safer things to thrive on: exercise, meditation, and fresh air. Perhaps I should be content to follow in my father's footsteps. But it is stifling, Mr Ping. I crave freedom. Perhaps I am stupid to crave it *here*. I am not naive. I understand that I will have to make compromises. But I also believe that a man should set himself as the standard. That is the most I can do.'

Ping looked at Ben. The men around Ping were talking quietly among themselves, but Ben knew that they were attending to every word spoken. He resisted the temptation to pull at his collar. He felt choked by the heat. He had no bloody idea what Ping was going to do next.

Ping raised a hand and a man swaggered over, a sneer on his face. Ben kept his expression impassive as Ping murmured in the man's ear.

The gangster walked slowly away, opened a small cupboard set into the wall and reached for something.

Probably, thought Ben gloomily, he'd be dispatched by a small, neat gun, something that wouldn't blast a hole in the wallpaper or shatter that expensive window. There was a sharp *click*, and he glanced at Arnold Ping, forcing himself not to betray his anxiety.

'Nice and cool,' said Ping, and Ben felt the cold caress of the air conditioning whirr into action and tease the back of his neck.

He smiled at Arnold Ping in relief and, to his surprise, Ping started to laugh. 'Tatyana,' he said, 'pour Mr Arlington a drink.'

Ben watched as the tall blonde sashayed over with a bottle of '45 Pétrus. Ping was still chortling as the rich red liquid swirled into the glass like liquid rubies, and Ben breathed in the delicious scent. The girl then expertly cracked open a can of Fanta and tipped a great slug of the bright orange liquid into the alcohol. She mixed it with a swizzle stick shaped like a dollar sign and shoved it into his hand with a malicious grin.

Ping leaned forward and clinked glasses. 'Your health!'

Even though elation couldn't make Pétrus and Fanta taste good, it was the best drink Ben had ever had in his life.

Lulu's apartment, Las Vegas, two days before the engagement party, 29 August 2009

Lulu

'You can stay here,' said Lulu. 'I know it's not what you're used—'

'It's lovely,' said Ariel. 'You've made it beautiful. And it would be wonderful if I could stay here. I just can't face going back to my apartment. I've spent my birthday and last night in a hotel all by myself! I just—' She put her face in her hands. Her whole body shook. 'I'm so embarrassed. I'm such an idiot! What I did! Pole dancing was miserable. I didn't feel ironically post-feminist at all. The things I said! And now . . . Harry and I have broken up . . . I don't know what I'll do without him.'

Lulu gave Ariel a hug, at the same time admiring her designer top. It looked like a normal T-shirt but you just knew it cost four hundred dollars from Kitson in LA. Poor kid. Ariel was three years older than Lulu, but she was very *young*. Lulu had barely believed it when she'd received the call – Ariel Arlington, begging Lulu to let her come over!

Reluctantly, Lulu had given her the address. On arrival Ariel had rung from her cell to check she had the correct street. Lulu, looking out of the front window, could see Ariel peering from the taxi, phone clamped to her delicate ear, presumably unable to believe that not *all* Arlington Corp. employees lived in vast luxury penthouses.

Once the truth was established, Ariel adjusted fast. 'Oh

Lulu,' she sighed, tiptoeing into the hall as if it were pixie-sized. 'It's *so* wonderful to see your friendly face. I've just split up with Harry. I didn't want to, but I was kind of *forced* into it. You know when you try and trick a man into saying, "No, stay, I love you!" and it backfires? Then we got into this massive row, arguing over the family. You know, like he tells me I'm ridiculous for not calling Ben, but he won't take a single step towards dealing with any of his own old shit! Of course I want to make up with Ben, but I feel so ashamed. And I don't really like Sunshine. I know that's mean, seeing as I never actually met her, but just the look of her scares me to death. I don't really want her to be part of our family, and I know that's selfish but I can't help it.' She smiled sadly. 'Lulu, you're the only person I know close to Ben who won't judge me and come to a mean conclusion.'

'Ariel, you must call him, then. I know he'd love to hear from you. He doesn't care about all that's happened. I think he was horrified at your dad's decision. He'd want you to be at the engagement party, I know he would.'

Ariel stared at her. She was very beautiful, a fragile beauty, Lulu decided. 'I don't know. I can't face the thought of seeing my parents. I just want to hide for a bit. I am miserable without Harry, I am *nothing* without him. I don't feel up to a big social appearance. But would you tell Ben I send him all my love and kisses? When he gets back into town, I will call him. I'll make it up to him.'

Lulu nodded. The girl was in a state. Lulu found her a bit of a mystery. She had been given every advantage, and yet she was a mess. To say you were nothing without a man! Maybe, without the man you loved, you were *lessened*. She, Lulu, had also been stupid. She had persisted in imagining that because Ariel and Ben had been born into wealth, they were immune from the pressures and strains that *she* experienced. It was naive. Lulu cherished her family; his family just fought. It was horrible. Unseemly. She felt sad for Ariel and Ben that their parents were so wrapped up in selfish ambition that they were willing to destroy their children's happiness if Ariel and Ben's wishes clashed with their own. She was immensely fortunate and it took the Arlingtons to make her see that.

'Ariel,' said Lulu, 'stay here and make yourself at home. There's food in the freezer. It's mostly Bolognese. Just eat it. Joe will be staying with my parents for the next few days, so the apartment is going to be empty. Call me if there's anything you need. And listen . . .' She paused. 'Don't be sad about Harry. If you love each other – and it sounds as if you do – you'll get back together. If you're meant to be with him, you will be.' She added in a flourish: 'Because that's how the world works!'

Her reward for delivering this unlikely fairytale was a heartfelt squeeze on the hand from Ariel and a whispered 'thank you'. Lulu smiled as best she could, and murmured about going to pack. As she walked into the bathroom, she glared at her reflection. *If you're meant to be with him, you will be.* Oh, sure that was how the world worked; yes, and she knew all about that, seeing as she was about to get on a plane to celebrate the engagement of the love of *her* life to Sunshine Beam.

151

En route for Turtle Egg Island, the morning of the engagement party, 31 August 2009

Lily

The sleek private jet soared over a cluster of tiny islands, scattered white and green amid the topaz blue of the sea. Sunshine's mother, Lily Fairweather, adjusted her shades and smiled. A heavy rumble in the distance suggested thunder, but it must be a long way off. As far as she could see, the skies were clear.

She disliked flying, yet reminded herself it was a little pain for a lot of gain. An engagement party is to be suffered rather than enjoyed, but *this* engagement party would be sublime.

She shivered with anticipation (or was it trepidation?) and fiddled with her invitation (gold script on a thick cream heart-shaped card, embossed with a hologram to thwart crashers). She had read in gossip magazines that Sofia Arlington had wanted the envelopes to be delivered by carrier pigeon, a charming idea that had only been rejected because of paranoia over avian flu.

Lily recalled the moment she'd found out about the engagement. She had become quite overwrought. But after the initial shock, she felt calm, as if this was meant to happen; as if Ben and Sunshine's union was merely part of a wish that had been granted.

To receive an invitation had stunned her. Apart from anything else, she and Sunshine were barely on speaking terms. They hadn't seen each other since meeting in England for a supposed spa weekend at the end of last year. And yet a fine-quality envelope addressed to Mrs Lily Fairweather, from Mr and Mrs Frank Arlington, had been *hand delivered* to her current address.

Lily smiled to herself. The official engagement of Ben Arlington to Sunshine Beam – Sunshine *Beam*! That girl was so Vegas! – was going to be spectacular, and she planned to play a major part in the spectacle. When she and Sunshine had stayed at the hotel in England, trying in vain to find something in common as mother and daughter, Lily had been a mess; fat, wretched.

She couldn't wait to see Sunshine's face as she stepped out of the plane. Her daughter would be expecting a lardy, junk-eating, chain-smoking alcoholic: no doubt she had warned the prospective in-laws that her mother was . . . *different*.

Well. She had certainly changed.

Lily looked down at her slim, elegant legs, and tensed her stomach, just for the pleasure of feeling its toned muscles obediently ping taut like viola strings. Her reddish hair was fashionably cropped, unlike when Sunshine had last seen it, straggly and chewed. Her one accessory was a gold bracelet studded with diamonds and rubies. Her shift dress, showing off her toned arms and fake tan, was white. After all, this wasn't a *wedding*.

Lily beckoned over the gorgeous steward and requested the time. She didn't wear a watch because she didn't own one.

'I do have the time for you, madam,' said the steward with a look. Lily decided not to pursue it; this was not the place or the time. And after a pause, he added smoothly, 'It's ten past eleven in the morning.'

153

'Thank you.'

The young man nodded. 'Would you care for another drink, madam?'

She returned a gracious smile. 'Thank you. I *will*.'

Lily sank back into the soft luxury of her padded recliner chair, pushed the array of travel and fashion magazines to one side, and sighed. The plane did a little bunny hop and she gripped the armrest, with a little *huff* of annoyance: the ordeal of flight. Never mind. In two hours and ten minutes the plane would land on Turtle Egg Island and she would see her child – and her child would see *her*.

Turtle Egg Island, the afternoon of the engagement party

Sofia

Stormy weather had forced the plane carrying Sunshine's mother to make an unscheduled landing in Hong Kong. Sofia could barely believe that there was a higher power with the ability to override *her* plans.

She was anxious to meet Sunshine's mother and establish that while they were soon to be in-laws, *she*, Sofia, would be top dog. It annoyed Sofia that Sunshine didn't even have a family photo of her mother, but Sofia had no doubt the woman would be plain and unremarkable, and suitably awed to be joining Vegas royalty.

So she was outraged that the woman had missed the engagement ceremony. Never mind that it was being blamed on 'the weather'. Arriving late suggested that this Lily person considered herself more important than all of them. When she was nobody – a poor relation!

Sofia took a deep breath. Well, the woman was now on her way, and would join them for the cutting of the nine-tiered chocolate and butter-cream cake. Sofia did not intend to honour her in-law-to-be with an introduction.

She would just have to fit in.

The event was, as expected, spectacular. Sofia's instruction to the planners was: 'I want a party that would make Marie Antoinette blush.'

The dregs of the media had flown to the nearest mainland and attempted to hire helicopters, but there was only one local charter company and Frank had already rented its entire fleet. Plus, there was a 2-mile exclusion zone around the island. So, Ben and Sunshine had celebrated their engagement on the pink sandy beach, prettily fringed by palm trees, the waves gently frilling the shore, without the paparazzi buzzing overhead. Never mind; Sofia had received a payment of two million dollars from *Vanity Fair* for the exclusive rights. They would spread the news of Ben and Sunshine's embarrassing split around the world.

The native flora of the island was a little understated for the occasion: thousands of violets had been flown in from Europe.

'You look beautiful,' said Frank. For a second, Sofia thought Frank was talking to *her*, then realized with irritation that he was addressing Sunshine.

'And so she should, in her custom-made pink Dior gown by Galliano,' said Sofia lightly, smiling at Sunshine.

Sunshine gave her a hard smile back. Ben had given her a 15-carat diamond engagement ring from Graff; Sofia estimated its price at one and a half million dollars. Yes, dear, you can regard it as a keepsake.

The fiancée was certainly gorgeous; it was a pity this day was to end in public humiliation for both. But Ben had really been inexcusably ungrateful to Sofia. He had no idea what she had done for him, as a mother, and it was only right that he learn a lesson. He would discover, by the close of the weekend, that you really cannot have everything your own way. He would go to Macau to open a casino without the family if that was his wish, but he would go as a single, more humble man.

Ben was dressed in a white Armani suit and diamond cufflinks. His collar was open; his tie had remained on for about one second. She had always said he would be a heartbreaker; he had certainly broken *her* heart. It was only right that he feel her pain.

The higher you flew, the harder you fell, so they said. With this moral in mind, Sofia had arranged for the guests to dine on blue crab salad and lavender-grilled prime beef tenderloin, prepared by their personal chef. Later, Cher would sing for them, because as much as people rolled their eyes, the woman was beyond fabulous, and she sold papers. Sofia wanted every lavish detail reported. Ben had made a sweet speech, after which Sunshine had been serenaded by the Christ's College Boys Choir from England. It was a nod to her mother's British roots, not that the woman had been here to appreciate it!

'So what do we actually *know* about Mrs Sunshine senior?' murmured Frank. 'Is she a Vegas stalwart or an import like the rest of us? Is she one of us, or is she ... one of *them*?'

Sofia sipped her mint julep. 'I doubt she's one of us, Frank. Sunshine managed to crawl out of obscurity and left this woman behind, along with her whole family. I should think her mother is a drab little suburban bore and the most exciting event of her week is if the supermarket reorganizes its shelves. An event like this is probably terrifying to her, as are we. Lulu found her – I think she lives in a *mobile home* on the outskirts. I told Lulu to send a jet, which must have freaked her out, but it was that or she probably wouldn't show. And goodness knows, we want to meet her if only to see what's *there*. If she's too bizarre we can distance ourselves, but I don't see it as a problem. Most celebrities have an embarrassing relative. It's merely a burden of fame.'

Frank nodded. 'Well, if she is not quite the thing, after this week we'll follow her daughter's lead and have nothing to do with her.' He grinned. 'But who knows? She could be cute!'

Sofia pursed her lips and turned away. Sterling approached, immaculate in his trademark black suit, immune to whatever climate he was thrust into. 'Miss Fairweather's plane will land in three minutes; she will be here in ten.'

Sofia nodded. It had not occurred to her that she might *like* Lily Fairweather, although it had occurred that she might be 'cute'. Sofia regarded all women as competition. Until she had seen Lily Fairweather, Sofia would not be able to relax. She needed to establish that Sunshine's mother was uglier/poorer/fatter/older/stupider than her, and that if anyone dared to compare the 'mothers-in-law' then Lily would always lose.

'Good,' she said, with all the grace she could muster. 'I look forward to meeting her.'

Turtle Egg Island, the evening of the engagement party

Lily

Lily couldn't suppress a grin as she stepped into the heavenly light of a desert island evening. The pilot had radioed ahead and a small welcoming party stood on the tarmac. Sunshine looked as pretty as an angel in her frock, but where was the fiancé? Lily supposed it would be ill mannered to leave the guests unattended.

Her face carefully shielded from the sun's glare with a vast gold and white Philip Treacy hat and her eyes protected with gold and white Chanel shades, she stepped down the stairway, and bestowed an air kiss on the fiancée. 'You look amazing, dear,' she said.

Sunshine's eyes widened. 'Oh my god, Mom, so do you!'

Lily smiled graciously.

Sunshine added, 'Mom, this is Frank, Ben's daddy.'

'So wonderful to finally meet you, Mr Arlington,' she murmured.

'Frank, Frank,' boomed the man. 'It's my pleasure entirely. Welcome to the family!'

He was stunningly attractive for a man wearing winkle-picker shoes.

'And this is my mother-in-law-to-be, Mrs Arlington.'

The woman, as cold and thin as an ice pick, held out her hand. 'Call me Sofia, please.'

Lily laughed. She removed her shades, and then her hat, and grasped Sofia's hand. 'Sofia,' she said. 'It's so lovely to meet you' – a delicate pause – *'again.* I am Lily Fairweather but my friends call me Bessie.'

BOOK 2

Portsmouth, England, February 1963

Sofia

Sofia was not the sort of child to beg, or pray, but it was irrelevant: there was no way in a million years that her mother would permit a Birds Eye Fish Finger to infiltrate the Kirsch family residence.

Sofia had heard tell of the Fish Finger – its delicious orange crust, the hint of goo beneath, and the soft white inside; 'They taste *nothing* like fish,' her friend Daisy had marvelled, wide-eyed. Daisy's mother was equally above the Fish Finger, but Daisy had had the great fortune to have visited her Auntie Doreen and Uncle Paul in Golders Green. Uncle Paul was doing well in the *schmutter* trade and they were well off but – Daisy had wrinkled her delicate nose – lacked class.

'*Alef, Bet, Gimmel, Duled, Chey,*' mouthed Sofia and Daisy as the rest of the class chanted the Hebrew alphabet. Miss Feinstein, who taught them, was the worst teacher. She was 104 with ferocious breath and she never explained, she just shouted. Sofia's twin brother, Jonathan, was so quick to learn, he had been put with the

163

older children. But every Sunday morning, Sofia attended Cheder at the synagogue and learned nothing. She had been learning nothing at Cheder for the last five years.

It was as if her brain was officially closed to the Hebrew language. They read, week after week, from the Festival Prayer books. Sofia understood none of it. The one advantage to being the stupidest girl in the class was that she got to do 'extra reading' with the student volunteers.

There was a knock at the door, and – joy! – Zach poked his head around it.

Miss Feinstein nodded curtly at Sofia. Sofia tried to keep the smile off her face.

Zach was her favourite volunteer. He had brown floppy hair and was dreamy – a *total* LG. An 'LG' was her and Daisy's secret code for Good Looking, but Zach was more than an LG, he was a *triple* LG.

They'd sit outside, in the corridor, which smelled of bleach and oil, faintly musty and sweet, side by side on hard wooden chairs, and Zach would gently correct her mistakes. He wore jeans and a red jumper obviously knitted by his grandma, but he still looked dreamy. Once, without saying a word, he had passed her a pink flying saucer. She had let it melt and fizz on her tongue, grinning with happiness.

She wanted to tell him that she lived only two streets away. She had seen him walking out of his house one day, as she and her parents had driven past in their 3-litre Rover coupé. It was an automatic and had cost a whopping £1,662! Her father loved that car. He washed and polished it every Sunday morning, and covered it every night in a black tarpaulin. But Sofia was cool. She would die rather than have Zach think she had a *crush*. She was, after all, ten years old. Double figures; hardly young.

It galled her that her mother was so strict. Every Friday afternoon after school, Sofia would have to lay the table for Friday Night, with their best Mappin & Webb cutlery, and polish every silver knife and fork until it gleamed. For her birthday, Sofia had asked for the *Valentine Pop Special* – it was only 5s. 6d. – but instead her mother had given her the *Look and Learn Book For Girls* – so boring she hadn't bothered to open it.

Their house was beautiful, but who cared? The chandelier-style candlestick wall lights, the cream-striped wallpaper, the gilt-framed paintings, the antique wood armoires, the vase of deep yellow roses, the little china statuettes and busts, the chairs and sofas upholstered in red and gold silk with their elegant clawed feet, the gaudily patterned carpet – all that stuff and her mother *still* refused to buy a television! Daisy's parents had one. They had worn evening dress for the first broadcast!

They were fun. One time, Daisy's parents had sat in the back of their little Ford and pretended to bicker, like Daisy and her brother. This kind of behaviour was almost beyond Sofia's realm of imagination. Sofia's father was a big deal in the community, second only to the Rabbi. Her mother enjoyed the prestige and felt it appropriate to remain humourless at all times.

The only nice thing her parents had ever done for Sofia was to buy her Noodle. Noodle was her poodle; he was white and fluffy and she adored him. It didn't matter that Noodle was only there because Sofia's father loved dogs. Noodle would be waiting for her when she got home, licking her face, even though her mother always snapped, 'How many times do I have to tell you, don't let the dog lick your face!'

She wished that Noodle could sleep at the end of her bed, but he had a cardboard box in the kitchen and wasn't allowed upstairs. The first week he had howled and whined the entire night every night. It had broken her heart to hear him so wretched; he was only a baby, six weeks old. But her mother had said, 'He has to learn.'

Her mother extracted fun from every situation like juice from a lemon.

'For those who sanctify thee, thou hast sanctified with thy holiness,' said Sofia, her voice flat with lack of interest. Zach nodded, stifled a yawn, and pointed to the next line. Oh my God, she was boring him. She stared at his hand, and imagined him stroking her hair. Sofia was glad that Zach's sweater was home-knitted. It made her feel better about her own clothes. She was wearing a cream tunic and a white polo-neck jumper that itched, and red tights. She must look about six years old.

Her mother had also bought her a tartan coat with large white buttons. It had come with a cape, but this was an indignity too far and Sofia had lost it.

Her mother knew exactly what Sofia had done but, aside from calling her 'careless' and 'spoilt' and to add that money didn't grow 'on trees', could do nothing about it. Sofia didn't care about being told off. It was worth it. A cape on a ten-year-old was *idiotic*. It was strange, as if she and her mother were engaged in an unspoken battle to undo each other. Sofia had no idea where this hostility came from, but she was up to the fight.

Sofia sighed heavily. At least Zach was letting her read in English, though they both knew it was a waste of time, as the whole point of the exercise was to improve her Hebrew. He felt sorry for her. It was embarrassing. She did not want pity. And how dare he yawn!

She wriggled a tiny bit closer to him, and pressed her lips hard together to make them swell. Daisy had smuggled in some lipstick; she had scraped a tiny amount off the top of her mother's least-used brand and smoothed it back again. Sofia's lips were a deep alluring pink, although they had only dared use a touch, because if Miss Feinstein detected cosmetics there would be hell to pay. She breathed in: Zach smelled gorgeous, all clean and fresh, but *masculine*.

Sofia knew she was beautiful. But did Zach notice, even a little bit? She really thought she would like to marry him. Obviously not *yet*, but in ten years. Now, all she required was that he noticed her. She had time. Zach wasn't going anywhere. This was a small community, and there was zero competition. Daisy was pretty, but plump. Beverley Michaels was always staring at Zach, but Beverley Michaels had black hair on her arms like a man.

Well, Sofia would make sure that Zach noticed her. She shook her blond glossy hair from its tight ponytail, murmuring, 'It was giving me a headache.' Then, in a Marilyn-Monroe-type breathy rasp, she continued, 'And praise is comely . . . to the Holy One . . . from those who are . . . *aaah* . . . sanctified.' She paused and glanced at Zach. He was trying not to laugh. She stifled a giggle of triumph. 'And thus . . . may thy Name, O *Lord*—'

She stopped abruptly as the door to the classroom swung open. Miss Feinstein's gargoyle head peered out into the corridor. There was a weird expression on her face Sofia had not seen before. She was . . . *smiling*.

'Sofia, Zach, come back to class now! There is news!'

Great: just as she was getting somewhere with Zach. Oh, but she couldn't *wait* to tell Daisy – she would just die!

Pink with triumph, Sofia marched back into the classroom and dropped into her chair with a bump. Five minutes to one; freedom was nigh. She smirked at Daisy, and rolled her eyes towards Miss Feinstein, who was clapping her hands for attention.

'Congratulations are in order,' she boomed in her thick Polish accent, undiluted after twenty years. 'Sofia is making *aliyah*!'

The words warped in her ears, as in a dream, and Sofia felt her head turn in amazement and horror as Daisy, a mirror image of distress and disbelief, turned towards her. Was this senility? Was it a joke? Was there another Sofia in Cheder class whom Sofia didn't know about?

But, frozen, she stared at the teacher, who was nodding her addled old head, and displaying yellow teeth, and looking right *at* her.

Sofia stood up, knocking over her chair. 'Miss Feinstein,' she said, her voice raspy with shock. 'I think you must . . . I'm not . . . I mean . . . you can't mean . . .'

'You and your family are going to live in Israel! Your father mentioned it yesterday in *shul* to the Rabbi. *Mazel tov*, Sofia! At last, after so long resisting, you will finally learn Hebrew!'

Portsmouth, two weeks later, March 1963

Sofia

Sofia watched as her mother dumped a small brown overnight bag in front of her. 'This is your suitcase. Whatever you can fit in here you can take.'

Sofia looked at her mother but Mrs Kirsch avoided her gaze and left the room. Sofia flung herself on her bed and covered her eyes. She was dizzy. Her mouth hung open like a trap. Her entire body seemed to buzz and fizz. *It was true.*

'We are going to live in Israel,' her father had said as they ate lunch.

Sofia had remained silent, looking at her twin brother. Jonathan had crinkled his eyes at her as if to soften the blow, then he put down his knife and fork and said, 'When?'

It was the only permissible response, as it implied acceptance. *Why?* would have been sacrilege.

'In three weeks.'

They had been told nothing more. Sofia felt dead with the misery of being ripped away from all that was precious. Now she realized how much she loved her best friend Daisy; she loved her private girls' school and the kind teachers; she loved the little family outings to stately homes that they went on at the weekends; she loved – oh my God – Noodle; and she loved Zach.

Noodle, her mother had informed her, was to be given away to some other family. How could they do that? Noodle loved them; *they* were his family! Sofia felt ill at the thought of parting with him. In her heart, she felt his pain which, because he lacked understanding, would be all the greater. It was like abandoning a child. The agony was so acute that she blocked it out.

And she would never see Zach again. It was unbearable.

Israel! She knew nothing about Israel except from the Bible stories. Israel was desert, camels, tents, wells and black-veiled people. Israel was thousands of miles away, as distant as the past, and when her father said, 'It's going to be wonderful,' she looked at him as if he were an alien talking.

'Sofia!' called her mother. 'Hurry up! We're going to the coffee shop!'

Jonathan wasn't invited. Listlessly, she put on her tartan coat and walked beside her mother. They didn't talk. Her mother only spoke when she greeted her friends Bernice and Maureen at the Lyons parlour.

Sofia sat at the table, staring at her chocolate éclair and trying to look pleased. Her mother would not tolerate a sullen face. She picked up the éclair and took a small bite. Normally, she would relish it, but today the cream tasted sour and the chocolate refused to melt on her tongue.

Sofia became aware that Bernice was smiling at her.

'Pardon?' she said.

'You're going to live in Israel,' she said. She was pretty, but her red lipstick melted into the creases around her mouth. Sofia wondered if she didn't realize or didn't care.

'Yes,' said Sofia.

'How do you feel?'

'I don't want to go,' said Sofia. She was so surprised to be asked that the truth came out. So what if she sounded rude? Her life was ruined. Everything that was precious to her had been snatched away.

As the ladies sighed with impotent sympathy, Sofia noticed a change in her mother's expression. No one else did – why should they?

Sofia counted down in her head as goodbyes were said, hands shaken, kisses received, until it was Zero Hour and she and her mother were alone.

'I *never* want to hear you say something like that again,' said Mrs Kirsch. She slapped Sofia on the arm and said: 'You are going to be *very* happy.'

Jerusalem, Israel, April 1963

Sofia

As Sofia gazed at the fields of orange trees, the scent of the white blossom filled the truck with a delicious perfume. And then the smell faded, to be replaced by the stink of manure. Everything here *stank*. She felt like a leaf blown off her tree. A thousand images filled her head, jostling for attention: the aunts and uncles crying at the airport; the enormous plane; the terrifying noise of the engine; and landing with a bump on the tarmac while men in black hats clapped and sang, '*Avenu shalom alechem!*'

'I don't feel well,' she gasped to the teacher. She always got travel sick, even in the squashy back seat of the Rover with her father driving at 10 miles an hour. Here, bumping along in the back of a dusty old army truck, like one of a herd of cattle, she felt weak with the urge to vomit. None of the children in her class spoke English – Hebrew, French, Arabic, yes; English, no – and the teachers refused to understand her. But a green expression did not require translation. Miss Sachs thrust a lemon half under her nose and said, 'Lick, lick!'

She stuck out her tongue and licked the fruit. To her astonishment, she felt the nausea fade. She smiled weakly. Miss Sachs nodded and said, '*Tov.*'

Good.

Nothing was good. Sofia couldn't believe the roughness of her new life. Before, it had been so controlled, so comfortable; pretty dresses and lovely shoes. Now, she was sitting on the floor of an open truck with a mass of foreigners. They weren't Israelis; they were from everywhere *else*: Morocco, Romania, Germany, Iraq. At first, she thought the boys had their heads shaved because of the heat, until Jonathan had explained that it was lice.

At her English school, the twenty pigtailed girls with

ironed shirts and shiny shoes had sat rapt, listening to the teacher teach. Here, it was chaos: forty children in one dirty little room and no discipline. She had asked her mother if there was a uniform, and her mother had laughed.

A lot of the children wore rags. They were living in Jerusalem, near the Absorption Centre. Their home was a couple of rooms in a tatty old building. There were no carpets; the floors were stone; and there were spiders. Sofia was not scared of insects but she hated what the spiders *meant*.

The first time she had been invited to play by a child at school, she had been shocked to see one dirty mattress on the floor, for so many people. It seemed that everyone lived with their mother, father, and at least one grandmother.

These people had nothing but they always fed her: bread, jam, cheese, or some strange but surprisingly delicious bowl of stew that reminded her of fairytales, *Ali Baba and the Forty Thieves*. The food was the first thing she liked about Israel, even though the only time they ate meat now was when people visited from abroad. Once a week their father would take them to a stall on the street that sold chips and doughnuts. Here, people ate on the street and it wasn't considered rude. The smell of fried food got in your clothes; her mother told her off for sniffing her sleeve. On Fridays, the smell of fresh bread wafted through the city like magic.

While Sofia could not be pleased about bumping down a smelly dirt road, she was determined not to be miserable any longer. Her mother sulked, because her mother was powerless. She, Sofia, was a fighter. Even having no money could be romanticized because *no one* had money. She grabbed her brother's arm and as they bounced along in the army truck, shouted in his ear, 'Are we poor, Jonathan?' She half hoped for a yes, so she could imagine herself the heroine of her favourite book, *A Little Princess*.

He beckoned her to lean close, even though none of the others spoke English. 'When you are poor,' he replied, 'there is no hope. We are broke, but it's just for now, because we, Sofia, are clever enough to *change* our situation. *You*, sis, will always be clever enough to change your situation if it doesn't suit you.'

She stared at him with a kind of wonder. He was ten years old, and the smartest person she knew.

It was hard, having to learn a whole new way of life, but having Jonathan there made it an adventure. The week before, she and Jono had gone to the Post Office with her mother, and she could not understand why the people in the queues were so clumsy: again and again, they dropped *agorot* – pennies – on the ground. Sofia would have kept them, but Jonathan ran and gave them back to people – and they smiled and dropped them again.

When Sofia told her father, he explained that it was a tradition: people dropped this money on purpose, and the beggars, who lived in caves on the outskirts of the city – *caves!* – would pick them up.

She was learning to survive, and her resilience impressed her. She was an *olah*, an immigrant. It meant 'one who goes up.' It was curious to think that when you came to Israel, stuck in the Middle Ages, they considered that you had gone up in the world. She wasn't yet convinced. In this morning's maths lesson, she had given a correct answer. 'Speak the numbers in *Ivrit*,' Miss Sachs had replied, 'then you take part.' Apparently, Sofia had a right to citizenship here. And yet, she saw no one rushing to include her.

The truck jolted to a halt outside the Holocaust Centre. Sofia knew about the Nazis. They had been taught about the gas chambers in school. Six million Jews had died. It was terrible; unimaginable. The first time she had seen numbers tattooed on an old man's arm she had had to force herself not to stare. The twenty-third time; you stopped looking.

Sofia jumped down from the truck and followed everyone into the building. It was nice to have a day out. They were going to watch a film – a *film*! The last film she had seen was *The Hundred and One Dalmatians*. She would sit next to Shai. He was nothing compared to Zach, but he had beautiful eyes and his head was a good shape. His hair was growing; it looked bristly, but she knew that if she stroked it, it would be soft to the touch.

An unsmiling woman ordered them to sit down by flapping her hands, then she began to talk in impassioned Hebrew. Sofia looked around for a clue to indicate that there would be snacks. She could see Jonathan sitting in the front row. He felt her gaze and nodded at her, reassuring.

The lights snapped off, and the words *Nuit et Brouillard* – Night and Fog – appeared against a black background. An image of fields of grass, shivering in the breeze, filled the screen. The music was jaunty. The camera swept along like the wind, to high walls, topped with barbed wire.

The soundtrack was in French but there were English subtitles. Next to the screen, the words appeared in Hebrew also. Some children were chattering and whispering. They stopped as the film showed how the concentration camps had been built – all so well prepared, so efficient – and told how Elizabeth here and Samuel there went about their daily lives 'not knowing that a place was being prepared for them'.

The hairs stood up on the back of Sofia's neck; to see the image of all these people – *so many people* – queuing, clutching bags as if they were going on holiday.

A small child gazed into the camera, holding the hand of his big brother and sister, and Sofia stared, disbelieving. Daisy had a little brother, Tommy, he had red cheeks, white-blond hair and was as fat as butter. How could these Germans – they looked normal – take a baby and kill it? Sofia couldn't comprehend the killing of one person. Here, in Israel, they didn't say 'six million' – they said *'six million and one'*.

Hypnotized she stared at the screen. Each image was more terrible than the last.

She saw naked, skeletal men, and women, and *grandfathers*, herded like cattle, the papery flesh barely covering their bones.

She saw the inside of the gas chambers, with nail marks clawed into the grey concrete ceiling.

She saw the piles of dead, like rag dolls, tipped into a hole in the ground.

She saw the stone 'operating' table, for torture and

experiments. The grooves were, she supposed, for the blood to flow down.

She saw a neat row of headless bodies, and then a pile of heads, in a wide plastic bucket.

She saw a man whose foot had been burnt with phosphorus. His skin was eaten away, almost to the bone; he was curling up his foot in agony.

She saw a mountain of spectacles, and then a great field of women's hair – acres and acres of it, piles and piles.

The Nazi officers claimed, one after the other, 'It was not my fault.' The film had showed how one of them kept a splendid home, adjacent to the camp, with his plump, primly dressed wife sitting on a cosy sofa, with lampshades, and a table laid with candles and a tablecloth.

'We pretend it only happened once,' intoned the voice, in sombre, mellifluous French. Minutes later, the film ended. Sofia could hear her classmates softly drawing breath. Some were sniffing, a few were sobbing. Her eyes were dry.

Sofia stared at the black screen, slowly absorbing the evil of mankind.

Haifa, Israel, July 1966

Sofia

The first time she had raised her hand and given the answer in *Ivrit*, the whole class had clapped. She had managed to find a few friends. And then her father had announced over breakfast that they were moving to Haifa. Sofia stared at her mother, incredulous; her mother busied herself with lifting the plates off the table, *always taking away*. Sofia looked at Jonathan and he shrugged.

In Haifa, they had moved to a large, airy apartment at the top of a mountain, facing the sea. They lived on the third floor of the block, which housed just three families. Hannah, who lived on the ground floor, was Sofia's age and friendly, even if it was only because she thought Jonathan was hot. The grass in the communal garden was rough and tall, but shaded by pine trees.

Sofia sat alone on the ground, bashing open the black and brown pine-nut shells with a stone. The heat of the morning sun was fierce on the back of her head. She would have a headache later, but she didn't care. She bashed and bashed, picking the shell fragments off the creamy nuts. After an hour of this, she had a large pile of white little pine nuts. Then, crossly, she started to eat them.

An argument immediately began in her head, and she sighed. She divided her pile into two, tipped the one half into a plastic bowl, and trotted up the milky-white stone stairs. She kicked on Jonathan's door.

''Sme!'

'C'm' in!'

'I hate sharing with you,' she said. 'It's just pro-grammed in.' She dumped the bowl of pine nuts in front of him.

'I should probably eat these at the dining-room table,'

he said, and they giggled together. Then she lay on his bed and stared at the light dappling the white ceiling, while he read a book. He was only five minutes older than she was, but he was most definitely her 'big brother'.

Their parents thought so too. In England, when they had their friends round to play poker, Jonathan was allowed to play a hand before he went to bed, while Sofia served 'nibbles'. In Israel, their parents didn't know anyone to play poker with, but now that Jonathan was thirteen, he was occasionally allowed to invite *his* friends for a game. The boys played for shekels around the dining-room table and drank root beer while Mrs Kirsch fluttered around them, and Sofia was mesmerized by the camaraderie and glamour of it. *She* would certainly not be allowed to join in. Jono wouldn't mind but her mother would object.

'One day,' said Sofia, 'after the army, I want to go to a real casino and play.'

Jono looked up and grinned. 'Las Vegas it is! We'll go together.' They shook hands on it. She could have stayed there, saying very little, for the rest of the morning, but then her mother called, 'Sofia! Lay the table for lunch!'

She got up with a groan and was about to go, when Jonathan said, 'Hey.'

She looked at him and he chucked her a package.

'Oh God,' she said. 'I love presents!'

She ripped it open. It was from Daisy. Inside there was a letter and a black and white photograph. 'Oh my *baby*! Oh, look how happy he is!' The picture was of Noodle, leaping mid-air to catch a stick, on the beach. Sofia pressed the photo to her chest and brushed away sudden tears. 'I can't believe she wrote, she's so lazy!'

Sofia scanned the letter for gossip – she would read it carefully later.

I miss you sooooo much, Sof! That brother of yours is such a pain. He nagged me like an old woman to write – he even sent money to pay for the photo. I only did it because he's so dreamy – ha ha – sorry to make you feel sick! Do you know he even wrote to my parents to ask them to track down Noodle's new owners? They did it though, because if they didn't they knew he'd tell your parents and then my parents would look bad, ha ha!

Sofia could hardly speak. 'Thanks, Jono,' she said. 'Thanks.'

Jonathan grinned. 'I only asked.'

But she knew it was more than that. It took effort to force people to go to unnecessary trouble from another country.

'Sofia! Now!' shouted her mother.

Sofia hugged Jono awkwardly; the Kirsch family were not big on hugging. The knowledge that Noodle was happy was the most precious gift that anyone had given her. It touched her that Jonathan *knew* this, even though most of the time he acted like a normal boy, kicking a ball against a wall ninety thousand times a day.

Sofia set the table for lunch while gazing out of the window at the glittering Med. This winter, she had stood at the window for hours, staring at the grey sky, which seemed to merge into the sea. Sometimes she would see a small tornado, merrily whipping up the water, and the wind would rattle at the shutters. She loved the howl of the wind. The winters in Israel were surprisingly cold. In Jerusalem, in December, there was often snow on the ground, and half of her class would stay at home because they didn't have shoes.

Here, in affluent Haifa, it was different. She attended a private school; the children were European, or Israeli-born, and clever. Sofia, who had barely learned the language, felt dull and stupid again. She was glad it was Sunday.

She pulled the photo of Noodle out of her pocket and stared at it, tears welling. Wiping her eyes, she saw that her mother had marched out of the kitchen with the salad bowl and was staring. 'What's the matter with you?'

'Nothing,' replied Sofia. Then, with a surge of defiance, 'I don't fit in at school.'

For a second, Sofia thought her mother was going to cry too. Then, almost begging, Mrs Kirsch replied quietly, 'Don't be ungrateful, we've sacrificed everything.'

Sofia tried not to wince. 'I'm sorry, Mother,' she said. 'It will be fine.'

There was a knock on the door. Sofia's mother smoothed her hair and went to open it. '*Chhhhannah!*' said Mrs Kirsch, overdoing the Hebrew pronunciation. 'Sofia, it's *Chhhhannah* from downstairs!'

Hannah had probably come to see Jonathan, but Sofia came to the door. 'Hi,' said Hannah. 'You want to go to the beach later? You and your brother?'

Sofia glanced at her mother, who nodded stiffly.

Three hours later, lying on the beach, slathered in olive oil, Sofia and Hannah found they could communicate very well. 'In England, you have great clothes – here, *nothing*. But your food is shit!'

'Not true; we invented fish fingers, Hannah. My friend Daisy will visit soon and I am sending her money to bring me a skirt so I can look like Twiggy. If you pay, I will get you a skirt too!'

'Sure! You, and him, you are cool, but those English girls – they think they are so great with their lipstick and their stockings. They are soft! They know nothing about hard work and fighting for their country! You think Daisy can bring the lipstick and stockings also?'

'Mm,' said Sofia. She checked her arm to see if it was tanning. Her skin was used to the sun now. She was no longer a soft, English girl. She couldn't *wait* to be sixteen so she could join the army. She was born to fight.

Golan Heights, the Syrian border, 12 October 1973, Yom Kippur War

Sofia

Sofia swallowed her nausea as they listened to men screaming for their mothers. No one looked at each other as the screams bounced around the tiny tin-roofed shack. The radio crackled, or maybe it was the sound of the soldiers burning alive.

That morning she had laughed as the tanks were called earlier than the girls had expected. The night before, tired of feeling filthy, they had washed their underwear in a couple of tin helmets and strung them out to dry between two tanks. When the tanks had left the base, they trailed a string of flapping knickers.

She thought of Raphael, the way he tilted his head just before they kissed. She shivered, recalling the desire she felt as she smoothed her hands over the muscular curves of his shoulders and biceps. She knew what his body would look like: small, black, charred, curled up.

The first time Sofia had seen a burnt body, she had gagged. It was an image that she was sure would stay with her for ever. Then she saw bodies number two, three, seventeen, and they became a blur.

Sofia sat, dry-eyed, in the shack, until it was over. She would not be thought a coward, which would be the shaming verdict had she asked to be excused.

She was required, anyhow, to type up orders (field phones could be tapped, and men didn't type). Her job title was Secretary to the Head of Tanks of the North-East Command, but it was far more than a secretarial position. She was only twenty but she was in a fighting unit, out in the field, and from necessity you were given the responsibilities of which you proved worthy. Sofia had a high level of security clearance.

Raphael's screams lingered in her head. 'You are at *war*,' she told herself. 'What did you expect?'

When her superior finally indicated that she could go, Sofia left the room slowly. She couldn't think what to do next, so she cleaned her gun. Your gun was more important than your boyfriend, she thought blankly. No matter where you went, your gun went too. If you went to the toilet, or to bed, your gun went too.

If there was so much as one grain of sand caught in your gun, your superior would roll it in the sand for you. And if there were two grains, the guns of your entire unit would be rolled in the sand. When that happened, your popularity took a dive. Sofia's gun had never been rolled in the sand.

Now, she sat on the ground, her face loose with the absence of emotion, and cleaned her gun till it glinted in the sunlight.

A shadow fell and she glanced up. Her boss stood before her. She jumped to her feet.

'It's been a rough couple of days,' he said.

'Yes.' Sofia nodded. She could barely believe that it had only been one week of actual war. There had been a lot of body bags. But she was not going to ask for special treatment because Raphael was dead. Everyone lost someone. It was shocking, but you had to go on living. The training and the conditions were tough – the six-day marches up mountains with full kit – but what did people expect? They were living outside in the middle of a desert; in the day, the heat was ferocious, at night, it was so freezing that half the unit wore boots three sizes too big so they could stuff them with newspaper to try to keep out the cold.

'My driver is going to my house to pick up some clothes.'

Sofia allowed herself a small smile. The attack had been launched on Yom Kippur, the Day of Atonement, the most sacred date in the Jewish calendar when every-one might be supposed to be fasting and praying at synagogue. Truth was, the Israelis were a secular bunch – it was hard to believe, given the circumstances. Everyone had been pulled out of their houses with no warning; there had been no time to pack so much as a toothbrush.

Reservists arriving at the base had stepped off the bus, been assigned to tanks and packed off to the front. There was not one spare minute to wait for the crews they had trained with, there was not even time to install machine guns on the tanks. The Israeli Defence Force was a step away from fighting this war in its pyjamas.

'You don't live so far from me, so if you want to go home for one night and get some stuff, fine.'

She hesitated. In the IDF there wasn't that curious, divisive formality as in the British military; no one called anyone 'sir', and if her boss was making himself a coffee, he'd make her a coffee. Yet she felt unwilling to accept the favour.

'Go,' he said. 'Come back tomorrow.'

'If you're sure,' she said. 'Thank you.'

It felt bizarre to knock on her front door and see her mother, in an apron, her hands covered in flour. She was wearing foundation and lipstick. Fuck Zionism, no way was Sofia's mother going barefaced.

'Sam*yooool!*' shouted her mother, before saying so much as a hello.

Her father appeared at the door, a picture of delight, alarm and confusion.

'Raphael's dead,' said Sofia. 'I'm going to have a bath.'

Her mother's hands flew to her mouth. 'I'm so sorry,' she said, and turned away. After a moment, she turned back: 'Dinner will be on the table in half an hour. We're having fish.'

Sofia tried to get comfortable in the narrow bath but it was impossible. The water was lukewarm. You couldn't *wallow*. Israel was not a country that understood or condoned the concept of luxury. Even if people were kind, which they frequently were, their kindness was brusque, as if it were an embarrassment and not to be dwelt on.

On the fifth day of war, a lorry had arrived full of food from a restaurant in Tiberias. And, if you got through the shelling, the kibbutzim doors were always open to the soldiers. But any 'thank you' was received with a dismissive nod.

Sofia sighed and got out, drying herself with a small, rough towel. It felt good to be clean, and fresh. She smelled of the orange carbolic soap her parents used. At least she would sleep in a soft warm bed tonight. The smell of frying fish wafted into the room, and she could hear her mother banging pans about. It was strange that home felt more confining than an army base.

After dinner, Sofia's mother washed up and Sofia sat with her father.

'So what's going on?'

She told him, and, in the telling, tried to remove the emotion. When she looked up, her father was staring at her in alarm.

'What?' she said.

He shook his head. He looked pale. 'I know what this is,' he exclaimed. 'This is shell shock. We had this in the

Second World War. Tell the driver to take you back tonight.' He gripped her arms and said, almost kindly, 'You must go back tonight or you'll never go back!'

'But we'd have to drive past the front line! I . . .'

Her mother had come out of the kitchen and was standing at the door. In a daze, Sofia dialled the driver's number. He registered faint sarcastic surprise, but didn't argue.

Ten minutes later, there was a knock. Wearily, Sofia picked up her small bag and opened the door. 'Thanks, Avi,' she said, but it wasn't the driver. A man and a woman stood there, both in army uniform, both of senior rank. As the man opened his mouth to speak, her mother bustled up to see who it was, emitted a strange rasp and tried to force the door closed.

'Mum, what are you *doing*?' said Sofia. Her mother prided herself on being civilized, especially here. She wouldn't even shut the door on a Jehovah's Witness.

'No, no,' her mother was gasping, 'go away.' Only then did Sofia understand, and the shock and disbelief paralysed her.

She watched, as if she were watching a film, the officers gently edging into the apartment, and her mother screaming for her father, who came running.

'Mr and Mrs Kirsch?' said the man. 'I'm afraid I have terrible news. I am so sorry to tell you that your son Jonathan has been killed in action in the Sinai.'

Her mother collapsed into her father's arms. Sofia stood there, unable to move or speak. She had never heard her father weep and it was a horrible sound.

'Do you want to sit down? Can I make you a drink?' said the female officer. Sofia shook her head.

Then Avi, the driver, arrived. He assessed the situation and started to back away. Sofia gripped his arm. 'Let's go,' she said.

She did not try to comfort her parents, and they did not try to comfort her. As she sat in the silent car, gripping her bag, all she knew was that her precious twin brother, the one person she had truly loved, was dead. The words her mother had sobbed as she fell into her husband's arms rang in Sofia's ears: 'Why *him*? Why did it have to be my *son*?'

Heathrow Airport, London, England, 1975

Bessie

'I'll manage,' said Bessie.

Her father smiled anxiously. He was so frail now that it was painful to look at him.

'You go through security,' he told her, and his voice wavered. 'And then you go to the check-out desk and show the hostess your ticket.'

'The check-out desk?'

He patted her on the arm. 'If you're not sure what to do, ask someone.'

'I'm sure I'll be fine,' she said, although secretly she was terrified. 'I better go through now. Love to Mum.'

Her father nodded, and waved as he tottered away. Mum had wanted to come to the airport, but bad health had prevented her. Not that she had a broken leg, or the measles. She was depressed. Apparently, mental illness ran in the family – oh, hooray!

Bessie managed to get through security and to the check-in desk – not the check-*out*! She didn't look like an idiot in her smart pink shirt and her flared jeans, but she felt like one. She sat in the orange plastic chair and gazed at the planes taking off. They were enormous.

'Ma'am, is this seat taken?' said a soft drawl.

Bessie looked up and saw a tanned man in a crumpled linen suit, with long hair tied in a ponytail. He smiled, showing gap teeth.

'No, it isn't,' she said, and smiled back.

'You OK, ma'am? You look a little peaky.'

'I haven't flown before.'

'Oh!' said the man. 'You got nothing to worry about, all you got to do is put your feet up and sip on cocktails and nod hello to the clouds!'

Bessie laughed.

'Hank Edwards,' said the man, 'at your service. Let me get you a drink.'

She expected water, and was charmed when he brought back a little plastic cup of vodka and Coke.

As they boarded the flight, Hank pointed out the emergency exits and the little toilets.

'Can't we sit together?' she said to the air hostess, but the woman checked her ticket and shook her head.

Bessie shuffled along to her window seat and stared out of the window. What if the plane crashed?

'Hello again!' said a cheerful voice.

'Hank!' she cried.

His eyes twinkled. 'Your neighbour agreed to move to business class,' he said.

Bessie beamed. 'Hank! That was really so kind of you!'

She gripped his hand as the plane took off. Afterwards, she looked and his fingers were white. 'Hank, I'm sorry,' she gasped. 'I just about crushed all the life out of you!'

He grinned. 'Sounds like the kind of girl I'm accustomed to!'

He was thin but sweet, and he was so interested in her. He asked her why she was travelling to LA.

'Well,' she told him, 'my father used to run a law firm – he's retired now – and I've been working there, as a legal secretary, but I wanted to do something different. I'm twenty-four, and I still live at home. My dad spoke to an old colleague, who knows someone who has a law firm in Las Vegas. Not in the *gambly* bit, of course. I'm sharing an apartment with other girls, it's all been arranged.'

Hank smiled, and the skin at the corners of his eyes crinkled. 'Well, I guess we'll be on the next flight together, because Vegas is where I'm headed.'

Bessie was delighted. It was silly of her to be so nervous, but twenty-four years of her parents fussing around, believing her incapable of so much as walking to the shops to buy milk on her own, had damaged her confidence.

Hank nodded as he poured the rest of the vodka and Coke into her glass. 'You'll have to come over to my place and I'll make you ribs. I got a new barbeque and it is the business!' He grinned. 'You are going to *love* Las Vegas. I'll show you around if you like, take you to see the sights. Maybe we'll visit a casino, take in a show, go for a walk in the mountains, or just splash around in my pool.'

Bessie's eyes widened. 'It sounds very different from where I grew up.'

'Where did you grow up, Bessie?' enquired Hank. She looked at his nails. They were very neat. He was obviously wealthy. If a man had money, it meant he could keep you safe.

'Have you heard of Hampstead Garden Suburb?' she said. 'It's an exclusive, leafy, uptight area in north-west London, where people are programmed to keep their hedges trimmed to an exact height and never give way to oncoming traffic. It is very smart and it doesn't have any casinos.'

Hank smiled. 'And how did you fit in?'

Bessie shrugged. She felt a little tipsy. 'It was very comfortable, although I suppose I've been sheltered from anything bad and am probably rather spoilt.' She leaned across to Hank, trying not to slur her words. 'I'd like to see *more* of the world than I have.' She giggled. 'I'm craving vice and variation!'

Hank roared with laughter, and patted her hand. 'You stick with me, sugar; I'll show you both!'

She giggled. 'What do you do, Hank? Ooh, I feel dizzy.'

'I run my own little business, selling liquor to casinos and hotels. Not so fine and fancy as a law firm, but I do OK.'

Her head was spinning by the time they reached LA.

Bessie blindly followed Hank, who managed to retrieve her luggage and help her make their connection to Las Vegas. He had also been kind enough to give her black coffee and mints. People had started to look at her.

'Hank,' said Bessie a little drunkenly, 'I don't know what I would have done without you!'

She stood on the tarmac outside the airport, holding her suitcase, and felt quite swept away with the romance of it all. It was evening, but so warm, and the lights and the buildings were awe-inspiring. It even smelled nicer, and the sky was vast.

'I feel like I'm in a film,' she said. 'I've never seen anything so pretty in my life!'

Hank smiled at her. 'I was thinking the same thing,' he said.

Slowly, she moved towards him, and his lips met hers, warm and soft.

'Don't leave me, Bessie,' he said, 'stay with me a while.'

She giggled. Everything he said sounded so funny. 'Hank,' she said. 'You know I'm not that sort of girl.' She tried to look severe. 'We've only just met.'

'You're so right,' whispered Hank, lighting a cigarette. She took it from his hand, and drew on it, after him. As she did so, she felt a heady surge of desire. She *was* that sort of girl; she just didn't like it to be obvious.

'How about we make an honest woman of you, Bessie?' he murmured. His breath tickled her ear and gave her goose pimples.

'Get married?' she squealed. 'You aren't suggesting that we get *married*?' She started laughing so hard she could barely breathe. She finally managed to stop howling with laughter and stand up straight.

Hank was looking a little peeved. He muttered, 'It's not *that* funny. I'm really attracted to you.'

'Hank,' she whooped. 'It's a great idea! I don't want to share an apartment with girls anyway! Let's do it!'

The Medici, Las Vegas, 1981

Luke

Luke was laughing, but he was annoyed. He liked to cast his eye over the Las Vegas pretty girls who applied for work at his hotel. They were always compliant; this one was not.

'Handsome' Stan had brought her down to the vault. It was a little arrangement they had. Stan knew what Luke liked, and if he had a candidate, he'd give Luke a call. Then he'd tell the girl that he was taking her to meet the Boss.

It scared them just enough to make it exciting. Handsome wouldn't speak, or answer questions; he would pad silently past noisy conveyor belts, under great silver worms of vent pipes, into the vault, where Luke would be waiting.

Luke liked to screw surrounded by stacks of money; hard silver pillows of it, stacked in plastic bags, millions of dollars, wall-to-wall cash. Money reassured him. There was nothing prettier than lots of money.

The girls knew the score. They knew it when they sent in their photograph. They *loved* it.

So Luke could see that Handsome was quite mortified when this girl bluntly informed them both that she was 'over-qualified to be a dealer'. She had a 'different job' in mind! Yeah, thought Luke, us too. But at the same time, he couldn't believe the girl's nerve.

Then the girl turned to Handsome and said, 'I'd like a position in security. I could do *your* job with my eyes shut. *You* do your job with your eyes shut.'

And so he was laughing with disbelief. He lit a thin cigar. It would be amusing to see how this turned out.

The smile dropped off Stan's face. 'What the hell are you talking about?'

Luke stared coldly at the girl. She was more than beautiful: she was luscious. He couldn't stand emaciated women. This one was all curves. Even her blonde hair fell in waves. Her eyes were hard and blue, and her tits were high and full. She had a big mouth. He had to have her.

'Your security is behind the times,' said the girl in a bored voice, 'and it's losing you money. Just spending a little time in the Medici, I see that quite a few cards – twenty-three or twenty-four – on the Mini-Baccarat table are marked: a tiny scratch on the back of the card, and I'm guessing those cards will be mostly eights or nines. That was today. Last week I came in here, and Mini-Baccarat was being played with an incomplete deck! And right now, on the floor, there's a guy working with two other men and a woman. He's placing late bets – one colour chip and two cash chips, actually – while pretending to place a new bet for the next game. His friends are claiming the winnings, and his girl is distracting the games supervisor – she's very pretty. And did you notice that every time the slot machines are close to the maximum jackpot win, they are hogged by the same bunch of guys – a professional gang, surely? And I *suspect*, because I only took a quick look, that someone has been tampering with your slot machines. I think a triangular piece of plastic has been wedged into a coin chute. I'd check that out if I was you, could be the same thing in quite a few of them.' The girl shrugged. 'People *cheat*.'

Luke nearly choked on his cigar. She had to be talking shit. This town was full of mad people.

The veins on Handsome's neck swelled purple. 'What the *fuck*?' He glanced helplessly at Luke. It was the wrong thing to do, and Handsome instantly knew it. He addressed the girl: 'You have a wild imagination. And the Medici did not advertise a vacancy in Security. So, baby, I suggest you show Mr Castillo how sorry you are before I throw you out on your ass.'

It stank that Handsome cared more about looking bad than the possibility that people were stealing.

Luke stepped forward and looked at the girl from an inch away. 'Are people trying to *scam* me?'

'They aren't trying to scam you, Mr Castillo,' said the girl. 'They are scamming you.'

Luke jabbed out the cigar and lit a cigarette. He clicked his fingers. Handsome scurried to the fridge and poured him a Diet Pepsi. Luke dug in his trouser pockets for a toffee and jammed it in his mouth, tossing the wrapper on the floor. 'Handsome,' said Luke. 'You need to make it all right. All of it.'

Now and then, Luke reached a place beyond anger. And that was when people knew to be frightened. 'People are stealing from me,' said Luke quietly. 'Deal with them. And then come back here so I can deal with you.'

Handsome ran from the room. Luke took a few deep drags on his cigarette and chewed the toffee. 'Sit down,' he barked at the girl, indicating a cardboard box. He turned away. What the fuck else had the girl noticed? It pissed him off that people like Handsome were careless, because if he fucked up, it was Luke who paid for it. How did it get so bad so quick? How did it change so horribly, in only three years?

Three years ago, thought Luke, he was living in Munchkinland and he didn't even appreciate it. Every day, the quarters from the slots poured into the hoppers and the total sum of their weight lit up on the screens, and a guy from the Nevada Gaming Commission sat by those screens every night, faithfully copying down every total in his little black notebook, unaware that the machines weighing the quarters from the slots had been recalibrated to weigh a thousand dollars in quarters as nine hundred dollars.

The extra hundred in quarters was placed in locked coin cabinets around the casino walls, and every time a change girl was given some bills, instead of going to the cashier's cage, she'd go to the cabinet. At the end of an average day, there might be eight grand in bills in each of those coin boxes.

Everyone on a senior level knew what was going on. But no one ever let on. Ah God, it was sweet! Now, Luke looked back on those days as golden. He couldn't believe he'd taken them for granted!

Then the Feds had got all busy with electronic and visual surveillance, and fucked it all up. Yeah, he should thank his stars that the Argent casinos and the Trop were taking all the heat; it looked as if a bunch of guys were going to be indicted over that one. But he wasn't grateful – he was pissed off. It made his job so *difficult*.

He'd had the coin boxes removed, and thought up a new plan. A year ago, a friend of theirs had been employed as a cashier. Bluntly, this guy stole from the cashier's cage and falsified fill slips to account for the missing money. It was less profitable and not as slick, but Luke didn't need the attention. He didn't want a problem, but he had a nasty feeling that this young girl was going to give him one.

Luke turned to the girl. 'You want to be successful, right?'

'Of course I do,' said the girl.

Luke nodded and tapped his ash on the floor. The girl looked as if she might smoke, but she could buy her own. 'Yeah,' he said, 'then you got to learn to please people. Lose the attitude. I've never regretted how I got my success. If other people hadn't put up some of the cash I needed to buy this place, I'd be running the gift shop.'

Luke sat down beside the girl. 'You got to impress people, not just by being smart but by being ready to see things *their* way. Then you get to do things *your* way. A little bit their way, a little bit your way.' He grinned. 'I mostly employed my own men, all of them good clean citizens. And then one or two appointments were made over which I had no say.'

The girl looked at him, and he shrugged. 'I get along with those guys. I don't make a fuss – I let them do what they need to do. I ain't no Glick. You know who Glick was, right? I wasn't stubborn, I made a few compromises, and I tell you, it was a small price to pay. Every month, the Medici does us proud. I'd rather die old and rich than young and greedy.'

The girl nodded. 'I understand, Mr Castillo. While your so-called security chief was in the room, I only mentioned the ways in which the public were cheating *you*.' She cleared her throat. 'How many change booths do you have up there?'

Luke felt the sweat clammy on the back of his neck. He was glad for the roar and clatter of the machinery. It would be pointless to bug this vault, you wouldn't get a thing. All the same, he glared at her, 'Do you ever shut up?'

She gazed at him. 'Only when I'm being kissed.'

He smiled as she carried on talking. 'You're clever, Mr Castillo. The extra, unregistered change booth is genius, because who the hell knows how many change booths there are *meant* to be? But if anyone *did* notice – anyone who *cared* – that would be awful. I worry about things like that.'

He didn't want to get rid of the bloody thing: all the profits went directly to Chicago.

He pressed a finger to his lips. 'You know a lot about my business. And I think I could find a place for you here. I think you'd make yourself useful in all sorts of ways.'

'Oh, I would, Mr Castillo. It angers me when people are lazy. I'd look after you and your interests. I'd keep you safe.'

He laughed, partly because he couldn't recall the last time someone had spoken to him like that. Maybe his mother, when he was six.

'Tell me,' he said. 'How is it you know so much about all this shit and yet you don't know how to dress? You look like a cheap hooker, honey; tight jeans, that bodice thing, and those crazy high heels.'

'Oh,' said the girl. She looked hurt. 'Well, I *like* how I dress. I have my own individual style and—'

Luke held out his hand to the girl. 'Sofia, right?'

She nodded.

'Sofia.' Now he was murmuring in her ear. 'You are beautiful, smart and you are driving me *insane*. Will you shut up?'

He pulled her to him, and kissed her. She grabbed his hair and kissed him back hard. His hands were all over her, and she writhed against him. Finally, he broke away. They were both breathing hard and flushed with desire. He grinned because that boyish smile always got them, and because, in the end, no matter how cute they thought they were, he was the boss. His gaze flickered downward.

'Got something that'll keep you quiet, baby,' he said, and watched her sink to her knees.

An upscale suburb in Las Vegas, June 1982

Bessie

'Why am I standing outside my own front door unable to fit my key in the fucking lock, Hank?'

Little Sam and Marylou jostled each other, giggling and fighting on the white steps, as their mother's scream bit through the quiet air of one of Clark County's premier neighbourhoods. Bessie's heart pumped rage. She knew she was out of control and that she shouldn't behave like this in front of the children and that the neighbours were agog, their ears pricked for scandal behind their white shutters, but the sudden terror she felt roared out of her in a rush.

She knew what this was. She didn't need to hear Hank's bleating voice on the end of the line to know what this meant.

'Honey, I love you . . .' he began, and her entire body clenched like a fist. Hank said those words as other people invoked the Lord's name to protect them from the devil. When Hank told Bessie he loved her she knew that something terrible would follow.

'Where are you, Hank? What have you done? What have you done?'

The children had stopped fighting. Sam, nearly three, was clinging to her leg like a fat little koala on a branch, lisping with anxiety in his baby voice, 'All right, Mommy? All right?'

Marylou, a cool and self-assured five-year-old, was sitting on the step chewing her hair.

Hank's voice was a whisper. 'I lost some money at Casino Joe's. I had to sign over the house.'

Bessie sat down on her beautiful white stone step, each paving stone so creamy, neat and perfect, and tried to catch her breath, but it was gone. She sat there, hyperventilating, unable to speak, dry-eyed with shock.

'Honey, I—'

'Shut up,' said Bessie, and her voice was no longer hers, but the hiss of a cat. 'Get here.'

Sandra from across the street was already hurrying towards her, her eyes sharp and bright like an eagle's. She and Larry had once invited Bessie and Hank to lunch at a restaurant and afterwards Sandra had split the bill with the aid of a calculator. There had been a bowl of wrapped chocolate mints in the lobby, and Sandra had stuck in her whole hand, taken as many as she could grasp and dropped them into her handbag.

Sandra opened her red lipsticked mouth to impart the juiciest news she'd ever had the pleasure to report and Bessie let her get as far as 'drilling the locks' before pushing her children towards the woman and saying, 'Please, just for an hour.'

She found herself unable to kiss her children goodbye.

She didn't want to cry in the street so she cried in the car.

She was shaking, and howling, and now and then she banged the steering wheel and screamed, 'Why?' Her nose and eyes streamed and she felt crazy, like an animal. There was no sign of Hank. 'Probably getting drunk somewhere,' she hiccoughed, and then she screamed, 'Probably getting *drunk*!'

A sharp tap on the window made her jump. She jammed on her sunglasses and let down the window. Sandra stood there. 'Bessie,' she said. 'You need to control yourself, for the children's sake. You can all sleep at our house tonight, as I'm presuming you have nowhere else to go and can't afford a hotel.'

'Thank you, Sandra,' said Bessie through gritted teeth.

Sandra nodded. 'I'll be doing a cold dinner tonight. The children aren't fussy, are they?'

Her tone indicated that they damn well shouldn't be. 'Goodness no,' said Bessie. 'What small child is fussy about food?'

'I think you should come inside, Bessie,' said Sandra. 'You can leave a note on the windscreen for Hank.'

Bessie did as she was told and followed Sandra into her immaculate, ornament-filled home. Sandra was a person who required exacting gratitude for every tiny thing that she did for you. Bessie watched as Sandra switched on the television – 'We don't want them running around out of control' – and her children sank hypnotized on to the sofa, staring ahead at the screen like robots. It was *The Simpsons*, a cartoon that would teach her two-year-old to say 'jerk-off', but who cared?

There was a loud knock at the door. Sandra opened it, and Bessie could hear an accusatory tone. 'You've been . . . your children see you like . . . Your wife . . . very upset . . .'

Hank slunk into the kitchen. Sandra suddenly screeched, 'FOOD, LARRY!' right behind Hank, causing him to jump and drop his briefcase. He stumbled to a chair. Bessie couldn't look at him.

'Can I help, Sandra?' she said. Sandra was roughly removing clingfilm-covered plates from the fridge and dumping them on the table.

'The cutlery is in the fifth drawer along,' replied Sandra. Bessie opened three possible drawers before Sandra, huffing, opened the one that was 'fifth along' from hell knew where.

Two-year-old Sam dunked his smoked salmon in his cup of apple juice and then decided it would be easier to simply pour the apple juice all over his plate like gravy. Finally he pushed away the plate, waving the soggy bread and wailing, 'Is broken!' Meanwhile, five-year-old Marylou poked her salmon around the plate, saying, 'I hate fish, it makes me feel sick.'

Hank sat there in silence, trying to swallow his burps. Sandra radiated disapproval, her body tense with irritability. '*Don't* let Sam get down from the table,' she snapped, 'his fingers are all greasy!'

It was plain that Sandra thought Bessie was a terrible mother; a self-fulfilling prophecy. 'Sit properly!' Bessie shouted at Sam. 'Eat with your mouth shut!' she snarled at Marylou, 'we're not savages!' Sam's lower lip trembled and he started to cry.

'So, Hank,' said Sandra, having dismissed the children to watch more corrupting TV, 'what has been going on? As you can imagine, Bessie has been distraught. Where did all the money go? How did it go? When did it go? Are you *sure* these people have the right to take your house?'

Bessie felt sapped. She let Sandra ask question after question as if *she* were the wife. Bessie felt that her decline in status was immediate and absolute. She sat silent and meek at the dinner table like a disgraced child.

Through Sandra's interrogation, Bessie learned that three months earlier, when Hank had claimed he was away on a business convention, he had gone to Casino Joe's and, over the course of two nights, smoked Cohiba cigars, enjoyed gallons of vintage cognac and lost three hundred thousand dollars. He had begged his host for more credit. When credit was refused, he had emptied every cash machine in the house.

'Oh my God,' said Bessie. 'Oh my God.' She fiddled with her hair, twisting it around and around her finger. She couldn't stop twisting her hair – if she stopped she didn't know what she might do. She could see Sandra's eyes upon her, but she couldn't look at the woman.

Hank slurped his bitter black coffee. His voice quaked, which made Bessie want to hit him. 'I just wanted to win that money back for you,' he said plaintively.

'Oh, *shut up*,' she said.

The ninety days he had to pay off the $300,000 in out-standing markers passed, so the casino had run the amount through his bank account. Well, there was $4,035 in his bank account. And he had racked up $50,000 on his credit cards, which he'd also blown.

'Shit, Hank!' screamed Bessie. 'Fifty grand!'

'Oh dear,' said a strange voice, and everybody turned in its direction as Larry so rarely spoke. In happier days, Bessie had bitched to Hank that when Sandra fell in love with Larry it must have been like falling in love with a bath sponge.

'But', croaked Bessie, turning away from Larry, 'can't we get a mortgage?'

Bessie then discovered that they already had *two* mortgages. He'd been taking out loans against the house: her pride and joy, *all bought and paid for*. Over the past three years he had lost nearly two million dollars in various casinos.

'Sandra,' she said as her neighbour showed her to the tiny guest bedroom, 'I had no idea.'

Sandra pursed her lips as if it were Bessie's fault for not being a snooping wife and then stalked out.

Bessie smiled bitterly at the closing door. She would have sent her husband to jail in a shot rather than lose the house but this casino had romantically assumed otherwise and taken their home.

There was a quiet knock; Bessie assumed it was Sandra. Hank walked in. 'Honey,' he said. 'I know you're mad. But don't be blue. Tomorrow we'll cruise around the county and look at some mobile-home sites. Some of them ain't so bad.'

She just looked at him. 'Can we not afford a small, shitty apartment, Hank?'

Hank's gaze slid all over the bedroom; anything but look her in the eye.

Mobile homes were basically a step above homelessness.

'People think stuff like this is bad,' began Hank, and already she hated him. 'Life could get so much worse. We don't appreciate that.' His voice increased in volume as he warmed to his subject. 'We think we're hard done by, we're so busy hankering for a bigger house, more money, and yet we don't consider ourselves fortunate for what we do have: two healthy, happy children. Hell, there are people out there with crippled kids, eaten up with cancer. We think we're so damn entitled to the perfect life, we don't consider that it could all go the other way.'

There was no way she could strangle him in Sandra's house, even though Bessie was a substantially sized woman and Hank was a weedy little man. So Bessie nodded and smiled as if the inside of her wasn't a seething black mire of fury and loathing. Her husband was talking as if this had just happened and it could have happened to anyone, it wasn't anyone's fault so there was no point feeling sorry for yourself; just pull yourself together and get on with pretending you aren't miserable. How dare he bring cancer and dying children into the equation? How dare he force her to eat her pain!

'Go and sleep on the landing, Hank, or in the bath, I don't care.'

He hesitated, and she added, 'And, honey?'

'Yes?' said Hank, an element of hope in his tone.

Bessie smiled sweetly. 'I'm going to get you back for this.'

An upscale suburb in Las Vegas, a month later, July 1982

Bessie

As Bessie rang Sandra's doorbell, she couldn't stop herself from turning to look at her old house across the road.

It was already sold and the new owners had repainted the front door and replaced the shutters.

She had left a small box of clothes in Sandra's garage, and Sandra had asked her to come and collect it. From the way Sandra spoke it was as if Bessie had dumped the entire contents of her house in the woman's front hall.

There was the rattle of a chain being fastened and the door opened a crack. 'Hello,' said Bessie to the maid. 'Is Sandra there?'

'Who are you, please?' said the maid, peering through the crack in the door.

'It's Bessie,' said Sanda. 'You know Bessie. Dear, how was the drive? Would you like to sit and have a cold drink?'

Bessie wanted to say no, but the lure of sitting in a real, luxury kitchen and pretending, for just a few moments, that *she* still lived like this, was too great. 'Yes,' she said. 'That would be lovely.' She paused. 'I just need to use the . . . ladies' room.'

Sandra hesitated, long enough for Bessie to realize that she was no longer worthy of a piss in Sandra's house.

Bessie washed her hands, avoiding looking at herself in the mirror. Losing all her money had changed her: she was like a beady-eyed rat, digging through rubbish desperate for a crumb. Even as she drove the car into town, she'd worried about the cost of petrol.

She allowed Sandra to bustle and fuss around her. The woman even cracked open a biscuit tin. The air con was blissful. 'So how are you managing, dear?' said Sandra, beady eyes wide with faux concern.

It was plain that she was feeding off Bessie's woe, but Bessie hardly cared. After a month of exile, she was desperate to speak to someone.

'Well,' she began, 'we found a place that isn't so bad. It's a little mobile-home site' – she refused to say the words 'trailer park' – 'run by Hank's cousin. Some people use it as a vacation home. It's small, and each plot is actually very nicely maintained. There's even a swimming pool in the middle, built around a huge cactus. It's in bloom right now and all the butterflies flutter around it. It's ever so pretty.'

Sandra made a snorting noise but managed to disguise it by sniffing. 'It sounds positively luxurious!'

Bessie sipped her drink and muttered, 'Yes, it's very comfortable.'

The mobile homes were old-fashioned and tiny; the size of her old hallway. The cousin had proudly told Hank that some of them had 'vinyl underpinning'. They were not 'double-wide'. Bessie hated that she was *au fait* with trailer-park terminology, that she knew how to describe one of the hulking new modern trailers: two trailers welded together so that they aped the look of an actual house. Yes. Well, let's not pretend.

At one point, the cousin had looked at Bessie and said, in a low, tactful tone, 'Some people, they like to hide the wheels on their trailers with attractive skirting.' Bessie had stared at her trying to work out if she were joking, and said, 'I see.'

'How do you cope with it being so cramped?' murmured Sandra.

'Oh,' said Bessie. 'It's actually quite . . . spacious.'

Their rented trailer, 14 feet by 70, would cost them five hundred dollars a month, 'including taxes, water and sewage'. The other trailers were so close that if they ran out of salt, she could stick her hand out the window and borrow from Next Door without getting up from the table. When she and Hank screamed at each other, their neighbours would hear every word; they might as well be in the room. On the third day, a mouse had run up the heating vent.

'I expect the people take a little getting used to,' said Sandra.

Bessie smiled. 'What is so nice is that everyone is so accepting and friendly.'

The sense of community was horrific. Everyone in each other's faces, the entire time. Bessie thought they must be mad: these nutcases couldn't get enough of each other. Bingo nights, pot-luck suppers, barbecues, craft club, beautiful back-yard competitions, raffles, quiz nights: didn't anyone want any privacy *ever*?

'It must be terribly hard. You must miss your gorgeous house and your pretty garden.'

Her head was stuffed with dreams of her beautiful sandy brick house: four bedrooms, four bathrooms, a mature garden and a swimming pool tiled around the perimeter with a mosaic of blue curling waves. She'd interviewed a nanny to look after the children, and the woman had said, with longing in her voice, 'I'd like a home like this one day.'

'Oh, not at all, we have the sweetest yard.'

The cousin had given them some red petunias as a 'house-warming' gift, and helped Sam and Marylou plant them in the patch of earth beside their caravan. I am not one of you, Bessie had thought, staring blankly at the wall. Her neighbours' wind chimes were like water torture; you could go crazy, waiting for the next *ting!* Bessie thought of her lovingly landscaped garden and wiped her nose on her sleeve.

'What on earth does one do about schools, in your situation?'

'It's the funniest thing, but the local elementary schools are of a high standard, so the children are very happy, as am I.'

The other children called them *white trash* and the mothers looked at her with pity and the teachers were surprised that Marylou loved to read. Neither child would ever have a friend back to play. When she took Marylou to school, she might have dressed smartly for the sake of the other mothers, but what was the point? They knew where she lived.

'And how are you getting on with Hank?' purred Sandra.

Hank acted as if Bessie should be grateful that their new home wasn't a stinking wasteland of crime and poverty, littered with burnt-out jalopies, and populated by hookers and drug addicts and wild dogs.

Hank was in a dream world, curiously shut off from reality. Once, in the car, which was all they had left, Simon and Garfunkel had come on the radio, and Hank had whistled along to 'Feelin' Groovy' while she fought to control the violence from spilling out. She realized after several seconds that her breath was all pent-up and stale inside her and she'd exhaled in slow, short,

210

shuddering bursts, to avoid throttling him at the wheel and killing them all.

She smiled again. 'Hank is being very supportive.'

'LARRY!' shrieked Sandra, making Bessie jump. 'DON'T USE OUR BATHROOM – THE MAID JUST CLEANED! Ah, well, it's not about your home, in the end, is it? Family is what matters.'

Bessie couldn't stand the cousin observing them in their poverty and shame. She felt so exposed, she might as well be wandering around town naked from the waist down. Bessie shuddered at the idea that strangers and acquaintances alike were party to her failure. She had presumed it wouldn't be so bad with people who didn't know her history. But it was. She was appalled that *these* people must presume she had *always* been this. It was as bad as the people who had known her before and despised her for failing.

'Of course,' she replied, 'and it's so sweet that we're getting to know Hank's cousin.'

Short of combusting in a fireball, there was nothing a trailer park could do to please her.

'Hello. *Hello!*'

Bessie stood up, smiling with pleasure. Sadie, another neighbour, was standing at the kitchen door. Unlike Sandra, Sadie had been a genuine friend. Bessie was ashamed to realize that her gaze flickered straight to the heavy gold jewellery on Sadie's ears, throat and wrist. *I could sell that.*

'Darling, we miss you! It's not the same!'

Sadie and her husband were fun. They had been round for dinner, she had squeezed them fresh orange juice; their children had played together; they had gossiped over the fence; Bessie had attended her father's funeral. When Sam was born, Sadie's little girl had drawn a picture for her of a rainbow. Underneath she had scrawled: 'When you get a baby boy you get a rainbow.'

'So,' said Sadie with a frown, her voice a hushed whisper, 'how are you managing? It's hideous, isn't it? As you know, Peter works in construction, and because of the recession, contracts are being cancelled all over the place. If it weren't for our savings, and the fact that Peter's reputation means he's still in demand, we'd be' – Sadie mouthed the word – 'fucked.'

Bessie felt her face heat up with crawling embarrassment. Sadie was dripping with gold! She had no worries; she and her children were safe, and yet, out of misplaced social courtesy, she was lying to Bessie. Bessie felt sick. She realized that Sandra and Sadie were observing her with curiosity as if she were a zoo animal.

Bessie picked up her bag. Her situation in life made her alien to these women.

'We must get together some time,' called Sadie as Bessie picked up her box of clothes and hurried to her car.

Bessie didn't bother to reply. She had never been a social person, and this was why. People always disappointed you.

She drove back to the trailer park, sobbing. Occasionally, she stopped crying to cringe. She couldn't even have a conversation because she was so ashamed of her situation that she hated to reveal a single fact about herself. She couldn't even think freely. To think of the future in more sweeping terms than what was for supper was petrifying, and to think of the past was to be crippled by regret.

Short of suicide, there was nothing she could do to get out of this hell. No – there had to be some way of escape.

Luke's estate, Crystal Bay, Lake Tahoe, Nevada, September 1982

Sofia

Sofia gazed at the clear waters of the lake and the Ponderosa pines beyond as the girl rubbed Moroccan rose oil into her shoulders. The massage room was a little beach-style hut at the end of the pier. She might have closed her eyes but the girl was nineteen, hadn't travelled further than California and was full of questions. Sofia didn't mind. Luke was not a talker; it was nice to *converse*.

'I suppose Israel must sound like a frightening place to you, but it was my home and I was used to it. Do I miss it? Oh no. I cut all ties the second I decided to move on. They make it easy: "*Lama yaradat?*" they ask. "Why did you leave?" But the literal, insulting translation is: "Why did you go down?"'

'Why did you go down?' said the girl. 'That is literally mega insulting!'

It was strange, Sofia thought, how the passion seeped

away the second you left the country. Seeing Israel from afar gave you emotional distance as well as physical. In that beautiful country, lush and desolate by turn, in the thick of it, under threat, you were united by blood. But it was no longer so simple.

'In their hearts,' she said, 'my Israeli friends might understand why I'd want to go, but it would be treason to admit it. The nation no longer knows what it wants. People, between themselves, are asking, "What is the price?"'

'Oh, right,' said the girl. 'Is it expensive over there?'

'It's hard when your grandfather, your father, your . . . brother has died . . . for this piece of land . . . for that piece of land . . . It's taken, it's given; it goes back and forth. At the end of the day, you want a life. You see the TVs, the cars, that the American teenagers have, and you want them.'

'Oh my God, do they not have *cars* over there?'

Sofia smiled. 'Not like here. Although, when I first moved to LA, I didn't have a car.'

The smile froze as she recalled her 'freedom' years. She had rented a small apartment in Brentwood, CA. It was all she could afford. She had taken a course on property ownership and financing and got herself a low-paid job with a broker. She was a natural saleswoman and knew she would make a lot of money down the line. But she was bored. Every month she could afford it, she flew to Vegas to play poker. It was the only time she felt happy; in Vegas, she dreamed of Jonathan.

'Do you act?' breathed the girl.

'Everyone acts,' said Sofia. 'But I realized I didn't

belong in LA. I quit my job, and came to Vegas. I had a military background and I knew my way around a casino.'

'Well, that is a good skill to have because some of them are mega huge!'

A quiet cough interrupted them. Sofia looked up and smiled. It was Sterling, her new aide. He was a poor little rich boy who was bored of privilege and had dropped out of law school. Sofia had found him cheating the slots. He reminded her of Jonathan, to the extent that she couldn't throw him out. When she asked him what he wanted to do in life, he'd replied, quite seriously, 'I want to be a spy.'

Sofia's patronage had saved Sterling from prison. The authorities did not take kindly to those who ran illegal gambling enterprises, and the court would have ruled a custodial sentence. She simply destroyed the evidence and claimed a misunderstanding. 'My dear,' she'd said to him. 'I need someone brilliant to snoop around for me. You'll never be bored and you can delegate the paperwork.'

Sterling ignored the girl and said to Sofia, 'Your presence is required by the pool.'

Sofia pouted her scarlet lips around the pink straw of her amaretto sour. She shook back her hair and sucked the liquid from the maraschino cherry like a spider extracting the juice from a fly.

'Thank you, darling,' Sofia said to the girl, and stood up. Her white bikini showed off her toned, tanned body to great effect. She slipped into her high white heels, and wiggled down the pier with Sterling walking faithfully beside.

The bright blue sky of Nevada smiled down on her as it did every morning; she had exchanged one desert for another. Luke's estate was lush and gorgeous and private, and commanded a vast stretch of the lakefront. When she wallowed in the huge oval limestone bath, the blue waters of the lake sprawled beyond, and she felt like a mermaid. Behind the estate were the slopes of Mount Rose Wilderness – in the winter, they skiied. Across the lake was Nevada State Park and National Forest.

The house itself was as tall as it was wide, and finished in granite, marble, black walnut and copper. All the furniture was white leather, and the carpets were cream. Sofia loved it and, providing she did as she was required, he spoilt her.

Thanks to her tax-deductible salary, this year she had been able to buy a large, luxurious property in an exclusive area of Las Vegas that reflected her success – as a Medici casino executive for IRS purposes but actually as a girlfriend. While she lived in Crystal Bay and Luke's opulent penthouse apartment in town, she cherished the cosy privacy of her condo and was happy to run to it when they argued. Luke would storm after her and bang on the door. The make-up sex was wild.

She breathed in the air, sweet with blossom. 'I don't think I could live in a country where oranges don't grow,' she murmured.

'One would have to be a savage,' agreed Sterling.

Her only complaint with her new life: Luke made it plain that as far as business of any kind was concerned, she was not to be involved.

They were approaching the pool area. 'How do I look?' she said.

Sterling gazed. 'The bosom needs adjusting,' he said, and tactfully turned away while Sofia lifted and shifted.

Sex with Luke Castillo was no hardship – in fact it was glorious: he was a good-looking man and he knew how to work it. She was required to stay beautiful, always oblige, and be charming to important players and guests. To be fair, the men, who she presumed were connected, she found charming. They treated her with respect. She only wished she could have more assurance from Luke that he considered her to be permanent. He saw other women, but from what she could tell, their status was come and go.

'Has he been with anyone lately?' she breathed as they approached.

'You are the fairest of them all,' murmured Sterling, and she bit back a sigh.

When she saw Luke look at this or that showgirl she felt a flash of rage, but they were all so tawdry. Close up, past the pink feathers, sequins and thick make-up, most of them had bad skin, halitosis and could barely speak English. Even long, fabulous legs and a pretty laugh couldn't compensate for total idiocy. She tried not to feel threatened. If Luke had to let off steam, as it were, with a tart or two, she could live with that. She had no choice.

Sofia consoled herself that she was number one and Luke liked that fact to be visible, which was all the reassurance she required. She possessed rooms of stunning designer dresses and shoes and handbags; such a surfeit of stuff that she was almost bored by it. The Hawker 800 was at her disposal, although she had to ask permission. Luke did not like her out of his sight unless he knew exactly where she was going and who she was with.

She went to Rodeo Drive. Sterling came too, as did Luke's 'bodyguard', no doubt to ensure that she behaved herself.

'He likes burger as well as steak; maybe that's why he's so paranoid,' she muttered. It astonished Sofia that he thought she might cheat: why would she? Luke was darkly appealing, deliciously powerful. Did he think she'd be tempted to play away with some fat movie director? These days Sofia thought with her head, always, and she had added up the advantages of being Mrs Castillo, as opposed to the advantages of being anyone else.

'He requires total commitment, total obedience,' said Sterling. 'That's the way you keep a man like him.'

'Mm,' said Sofia, no longer listening. If she married Luke – a natural progression – she would be a slave to his needs, but she would have status, wealth, power and a life of privilege. Luke was sharp: he knew to whom he owed his lifestyle and he understood how to stay out of trouble. Within the perimeters of his world, he was honest. When she married Luke, she would never have to worry again.

Sterling nodded goodbye and swept into the house.

Luke was reading the paper on a sun lounger. The remains of a Diet Coke and a bowl of toffee popcorn were being cleared by a maid. Sofia scowled at her, then knelt at Luke's feet and licked and sucked his big toe. Thankfully, he was a man who appreciated a pedicure, and was forever in and out of Jacuzzis.

Luke flipped down the paper, 'All right already. Get over here.'

Sofia pushed a sun lounger close to his with her foot and then rolled on to it and lit a cigarette. Luke reached over and slapped her hard on the behind. He wore a plain gold watch. She had once suggested that he might try something more ornate, with diamonds, and he'd said, 'Do I look like I have lady parts?'

She did have lady parts, therefore her watch had diamonds. She was sure that Luke had bought her at least five million dollars' worth of jewellery. One evening as he had placed a diamond necklace as heavy as an iron chain around her neck, she had remembered an old boyfriend. Two weeks before he was killed, Raphael had slipped the pull of a Coke can on her ring finger, and kissed her hand.

Her stomach lurched and she put a block on the memory. Raphael had been a boy. Luke was a man.

This indolent life was what she wanted now. It offered a different kind of excitement. Her boyfriend's dangerous, unpredictable edge provided a challenge. She would have loved to become involved in the casino management, but it angered Luke. Once, she had pursued the argument and he had slapped her. She had slapped him back, and then time had stood still for a moment where her heart quailed in genuine fear, but then he had laughed, and roughly pulled her to him, gripping her hair in his fist. He had ripped a bespoke Valentino blouse but the sex had been worth it.

Now she squirmed obligingly as his hand wandered beneath the material of her bikini.

The staff melted away as he rolled from his recliner on to hers. His bodyweight crushed the air out of her lungs. He yanked off her bikini bottoms. She pressed against him, always willing. Lucky for him she found romance a waste of time.

She was just getting into it, when he stopped.

'Oh my *God*, Luke!' she said, glancing up to see Miranda, Luke's secretary, standing at the side of the recliner holding a phone.

'I'm so *extremely* sorry, sir,' said Miranda. Her round shoulders shrank with embarrassment.

'This better be important,' snapped Luke. 'What do you think we're doing here, playing chess?'

'There's a phone call,' said Miranda, somewhat unnecessarily. 'It's urgent. I've said but he won't—'

'Here,' snarled Luke, snatching the phone. Sofia, butt-naked, squashed beneath him like a cushion, felt humiliation vie with irritation.

'Actually, sir . . .' Miranda's customary squeak turned into a wheeze. She fumbled for her inhaler. By the time she had recovered her breath, it was too late. Luke was already barking into the phone.

'*What!* You should not be ringing here. This is an unlisted number. Jesus fucking Christ!'

Luke reared up like a serpent, pulled his Versace silk robe around him, and flung a towel at Sofia. She declined to cover her modesty and sat up. Glaring, he thrust the receiver in her face. She indicated her surprise, and regret. Who could it be? Whoever it was, they were going to pay for getting her in the shit. It better not be a man, was all Sofia could think. How could it be? She didn't *know* a man!

'Who is this?' she said, in a voice of ice.

'Sofia Kirsch? *Shalom.*'

A chill ran up Sofia's spine, despite the ferocious desert heat. She knew, of course, of the assassination attempt on the Israeli ambassador to the UK, by the ANO, the Palestinian terrorist organization. She knew that the Israelis and the PLO had been lashing out since the previous year. The trouble with Israel being smaller than Wales was this: every time a larger, hostile country so much as stuck out its tongue, Israel felt obliged to cut off that tongue.

If Israel didn't massively overreact, launching a disproportionate counter-offence, it would be invaded and crushed. It was essential that Israel was feared by its enemies; that she demonstrate size was no indicator of strength. War had not yet been declared against Lebanon, but Sofia knew enough about the IDF to suspect it was imminent.

She also knew that she was still, technically, a reservist, but it had been so long – surely she could be of no use? But the honour of being asked was enormous, plus the fact that you couldn't legally refuse unless you were pregnant or terminally ill, and even then only a coward would ask for exemption. Sofia felt her blood rage with fresh purpose. She was tired of sitting on her ass. She wanted to be of *use*.

'Yes, Elan,' she replied in Hebrew.

Luke had become still and silent.

She knew what Luke was capable of, even if he wasn't aware himself. Sofia had never feared men who attempted to intimidate with threats, who boasted of their terrible victories. The real tough guys didn't advertise. And yet Luke was in a position where he had to be careful.

Of course she feared Luke, but she wanted him to know what *she* was capable of. She wanted to remind him that she was different, better than all these ten-cent showgirls. It would do Luke good to miss her, to want her and not be able to have her because she had more important things to do.

Sofia glanced at him only once as she received brief instructions. Her boyfriend was watching her, his face as cold as death. She could sense his tension but she was too excited, too full of herself to acknowledge what it meant. She needed one last fling. She would serve the Land of Milk and Honey; she would return to America triumphant. Luke would realize that he had a capable, useful, belligerent partner. He would reconsider; allow her a little more autonomy, a whisper of influence. That was all she could realistically hope for, but it would be a foundation on which she could build.

En route to Las Vegas, 26 October 1982

Sofia

Sofia chucked *Princess Daisy* to one side and irritably waved away the saucer of Krug. She did not need alcohol clouding her thought, or her appeal, as she reunited with Luke. The plane was bumping through cloud and she pulled down the shutter. She hated the whiteness; it made her feel blind.

In Israel she had embraced the physical hardship. She had pulled on her uniform, the colour of the desert, grasped her Uzi and felt her body and soul warp into that of a warrior. But the second she quit the Middle East, she discarded this part of herself like a snake shedding its skin. Sofia had scratched the itch. Now she could devote herself to Luke.

Sterling, sitting across the aisle, leaned over. 'Would you like to choose an outfit, Sofia?'

She had flown to New York from Tel Aviv. Sterling had met her in the business lounge, along with Molly Sykes, former fashion director of US *Vogue* and one of Sofia's favourite personal shoppers. They were making the last leg of the journey to Las Vegas together, where Sofia was going to surprise Luke.

As Sterling jumped up to fetch Molly, Sofia noticed his fingernails. 'Sterling,' she cried. 'Since when do you bite? You weren't worried about me, were you?'

Sterling curled his hands into fists. 'Of course, but the fighting wasn't my main concern.' Sofia had asked Sterling to visit Atlantic City while she was away. While the place had always played second fiddle to Las Vegas, the popularity of Atlantic City was on the rise, probably because of the crime in Las Vegas, rather than because Atlantic City possessed any alluring properties of its own. But it was worth having Sterling take a look and report back.

'You are sweet, Sterling. But don't fret. I know what men are like.'

'I know more,' murmured Sterling. The fact that the smooth, unflappable Sterling had bitten his nails to the quick unnerved her, but only momentarily. Sterling was agitated because he had been unable to watch Luke while Sofia was away. Sofia had no doubt that her boyfriend had gorged himself on floozies, but she could understand that he might feel entitled to a final fling or five.

'Sterling,' she said. 'We both know that my darling is rotten to the core. That's his appeal. I don't care for nice guys: they're as dull as boiled potatoes.'

'Yes,' said Sterling, 'whereas one does have to be a bit of a bastard to reach the top.'

Sofia grinned. Bad guys were picky, and it was flattering to be chosen to join Luke in his ascent. Her status in the IDF gave her unique satisfaction; in the real world she could only match that by aligning herself with Castillo. She was a perfect fit for him, in personality, will and intelligence.

'Now it is going to be all about *him*,' said Sofia. 'I've indulged myself, and now I'm going to indulge him. Tell Molly to bring out the slutty stuff first!'

Molly was able to source the most desirable pieces of haute couture as they left the catwalk. A few of the edgier designers knew whom Sofia went home to and declined to take her money. It was better that Molly shopped on her behalf.

Molly marched to the front of the plane with armfuls of booty. She was stick thin, with dyed black hair, and she wore the most dreadful hats. But she understood what other people liked – mostly.

Molly said nothing to Sofia, just held up a crystal-studded black leather jacket like Neville Chamberlain brandishing Hitler's autograph.

When Sofia said nothing, Molly exclaimed, 'This is the jacket worn by Isabella Rossellini on the latest cover of *Vogue*, and when I say people would kill, I do not exaggerate.'

'Molly, I'd look like a Hell's Angel. I'm trying to look soft and kittenish.'

'Sofia! I swear, if I see you in another off-the-shoulder leopard print, black split-leather skirt, and a gold leather belt, black fishnets and spike heels, I will rip that belt off you and strangle myself with it. Mr Castillo likes what he knows – which is a problem because he knows nothing. And no, I haven't brought a fur. How many furs do you need in the desert?

'No fur, but here is something soft and deferential. Limited-edition red Chanel mini-skirted suit embroidered with gold and silver thread. These shoulder pads will make your waist look *minuscule* – you'll have the hip-waist ratio of an ant!'

Sofia slipped on the jacket. Sterling had somehow appropriated a full-length mirror. She stared into it and shuddered. 'I look like an old witch out of *Dynasty*.'

'Her personality is powerful enough, Molly,' said Sterling reprovingly. 'We want to minimize it.'

'Hey,' said Sofia. 'What's *that*?'

Molly was trying to hide an item under the leather jacket. It was bright pink, cute and fabulous.

'It looks like something you'd put on a Barbie doll!' said Sofia.

'It's a ra-ra skirt,' said Molly. 'You could wear it with legwarmers and a headband and put your hair in bunches. And I have glitter mousse. You could team it with a leotard. It's very California.'

'I'm *thirty*,' whispered Sofia, 'although I shall always claim twenty-six.'

'There's no shame in a twenty-three-year-old dressing up like a sixteen-year-old cheerleader,' said Sterling firmly. 'This, Sofia, is the sartorial equivalent of crawling back to Luke on your knees.'

Her heart beat fast as she stepped into the private limousine. The car had taken her from McCarran airport to the Tropicana; Sterling had booked a suite in the Paradise Tower so she could prepare herself for the grand reunion. Molly had styled her hair and done her make-up. Now they kissed goodbye, and Sofia called, 'Wish me luck!'

She had picked up a Rubik's cube at JFK. Now she twisted it, sharply, this way and that, hoping that it would calm her nerves. It had the opposite effect.

'The best way is to pick off the stickers and rearrange them,' said Sterling.

She jammed the stupid toy in her bag, sucked on a cigarette and tried to relax on the blue crushed-velvet cushions of the Cadillac Fleetwood. It was impossible. The wire support of the black camisole bra dug into her skin – she couldn't wait for Luke to peel off the damn thing.

Sofia stubbed out her cigarette and lit another. She gazed out of the window as they rolled slowly down Las Vegas Boulevard. Apart from the mighty Kirk Kerkorian, these days there was pretty much no one with the fight to take on Luke and build a major new casino on the Strip.

So when she saw a great dusty hole in the ground where the Burlesque had stood only months before, her eyes widened in disbelief. She tapped on the window.

'Sterling! Who blew up the Burlesque?'

'Frank Arlington. You know the one. He looks like a young Elvis and milks it. He plays tennis with Kirk. He owns a property downtown and thinks he can handle the big time. He told the *Sun* that he's going to bring show-biz back to Vegas – pardon me if I didn't notice that it went away! Mr Castillo tried to put a spoke in his financing, but it didn't work.'

Sofia sat back, dazed. Her heart beat fast; she felt the insolence on Luke's behalf. 'Oh, I know Frank Arlington,' she said snappishly. 'He has two successful properties on the East Coast, and thinks he can handle Sin City. He's cute but so bright-eyed and bouncy he makes you want to puke.'

Luke kept a gimlet eye on anyone whose licence application had been approved by the Nevada Gaming Commission. Frank had been steadily buying up shares in the Burlesque for a couple of years. But to have taken over! She wondered whom he knew.

'I don't think Frank plans to go anywhere, Sofia,' said Sterling. 'His new golf course and country club is apparently breathtaking. It's already been rated one of the top in the country. It's a smart move, considering that for some truly unfathomable reason so many inveterate gamblers – sorry, I mean *whales* – love playing golf.'

'Oh!' said Sofia with disdain. 'He only built it because Wynn refused him membership! Frank Arlington is a nobody! And now, because of him, my man is going to be in a crappy mood.' She couldn't wait to soothe his pain. She couldn't believe what she'd missed. But an hour in this city was the equivalent to a week elsewhere.

She sighed as the white crenellated walls of the Medici and its great gold domes blocked out the afternoon sun.

'Home, sweet home!' murmured Sterling.

She was a little anxious about her reception. Bursting in on Luke, luscious and contrite, was her best option. Of course, she couldn't guarantee total surprise; her image would be captured on film fifty times en route to his private quarters.

'Sterling,' she said. 'Why don't you go back to my place? Take the car; I won't be needing it.'

Sterling looked doubtful, but obeyed.

She swept through reception, past the poker lounge and the steakhouse. As she scurried along a thin 'staff only' corridor, the noise and hubbub from the casino floor faded. At last, she stood before a thick bullet-proof door of reinforced steel. It was time. She pulled out her mobile phone and dialled his desk number.

'Guess *who*?' she cooed as someone picked up.

'Who is this? I don't know who you are.'

Sofia glared at the phone. 'Bullshit, Miranda. Put me through to Luke.'

'Mr Castillo is unavailable right now. Can I take a message?'

Sofia was speechless. No doubt Luke wanted a little more humility. She snapped shut the phone and kicked the door. No response. She buzzed the intercom.

'I'm sorry,' said Miranda again, 'but Mr Castillo is—'

'Miranda,' she shouted into the intercom, 'could we talk face to face . . . please?'

Eventually the great door clicked open and Miranda appeared, looking ruffled. 'I'm not supposed to—'

Sofia grabbed her by the arm and squeezed, digging her nails into the woman's spongy flesh. 'Miranda, I know that Luke is trying to teach me a lesson, but it's learned. He is *always* in his office at three p.m. on a Tuesday. If he isn't there, where is he?'

'He's in the chapel – but it's a private ceremony, Miss Kay, you can't—'

Sofia barged past Miranda, and sped towards the Medici's Wedding Chapel. She could almost feel the eyes on the ceiling bulge and ogle in her direction. The security team were sitting on their asses cracking up at the sight of her in that dumb ra-ra skirt. Suddenly she felt ridiculous. She ripped off the headband.

No doubt some lowlife billionaire was tying the knot, and out of deference to Luke had decided to do it here. The Medici Wedding Chapel was a gaudily tacky take on the Sistine Chapel, and no one was claiming otherwise.

Excessive security, noted Sofia as she approached. At least ten guys surrounding the area. Five of them – the senior echelon – were armed. She nodded to Steve, the boss, who usually saluted her. She had trained him, after all. She just *dared* him to laugh at this outfit. But his face was blank, even severe, and she was stunned to see him actually step forward and block her path.

'Stevie,' she said. It was beyond a joke. 'You have *got* to be kidding me.'

Steve stared through her. If she was that way inclined her feelings would have actually been hurt. This was blatant disrespect, and it could only be the result of a direct order from the boss.

'Out of my way, kid,' she hissed. She tripped him on his back, but was instantly surrounded and pressed face to the ground. A cold circle of steel jabbed into her neck: the hell they were going to shoot her!

She wasn't frightened; she was shocked. Her dumb girly miniskirt had flipped up and Medici Security had a great view of her red-and-black lace knickers. All she had been taught in the IDF was not applicable here: Sofia opened her mouth and started to yell.

Now, she thought, let Luke's precious corporate event continue through *that* noise.

Sure enough the doors of the chapel burst open. With difficulty – her hands were restrained behind her back, and Steve was forcing them closer to her neck until she felt as if her arms might pop out of their sockets – Sofia raised her face from the cold peach marble floor.

Out into the hallway swept a beautiful bride. She had long bouncy dark hair, *big* hair, and a thousand tiny diamonds had been woven into her shimmering locks. Her dress was long, white, and exquisite, thickly embroidered with cream lace. She was at least five months pregnant but – fecund beauty – the swelling belly added to her allure.

She laughed as confetti fluttered softly around her and her teeth were even and sparkling. Her eyes were dark with the passion of deep joy. She was stunning. Her husband must be very rich, thought Sofia.

Sofia's view was limited and, despite straining her neck, she found the groom was still obscured by the mass of guests and security; but as the bride triumphantly pulled her groom towards her and the cameras flashed, he burst into view. For a few long moments, Sofia stared right at him.

Lasciviously, the groom bent his head and drew his new young wife towards him in a greedy kiss. They were really getting into it there. Everyone cheered. Sofia couldn't take her eyes off him as she was yanked to her feet and dragged away.

The groom wiped his mouth on the back of his hand, smiled at Sofia and winked.

Luke.

The Arlington Golf Course & Country Club, one month later, 30 November 1982

Sofia

It was Frank's party, and Sofia was the only woman who hadn't made a move. Instead, she circled Frank, talking to every other guy. They surrounded her like lumps of rock orbiting a star. She was dazzling, glossy; untouchable. Her hair was swept up, delicate tendrils curling around her elegant neck, her skin was tanned and looked butter soft, her body was toned, but not skinny. When she smiled, dimples formed. The men were competing for those dimples like dogs for a biscuit.

Her dress was eye-popping. The pale gold bustier cupped her boobs like scoops of ice cream in a bowl. The material clung to her slender waist and flared out, prettily, girlishly, to the knee. She had long legs and high peep-toe shoes. The effect was mesmerizing and no man seemed able to resist.

Sofia was only bothered about one of them.

She saw Frank glance at her, and she smiled, quick, shy. The trap was laid. Sofia glanced inside her handbag where Sterling had written a five-point plan on a scrap of paper, the first three of which were:

- *Ignore him*
- *Smile shyly*
- *Walk away*

He had been forced to commit her seduction routine to paper, as she couldn't remember it.

'Oh God,' she'd said to Sterling as he'd seen her into a taxi an hour earlier. 'It would be so much easier if I could just hit him over the head with a mallet and drag him back to my cave.'

'You'll be fine,' Sterling had replied. 'Frank isn't like the other one. From what I hear, he can be persuaded.'

Now Sofia carefully took off her shoes and walked barefoot out of the door. The men were all panting, desperate to reunite this modern-day Cinderella with her designer heels, but none would be so rude as to pursue the main prize. It would be like killing the stag in the king's hunting party.

Frank followed her down to the water's edge, a child following a trail of sweets.

Sofia bent to pick up shells (carefully scattered by Arlington Corp. employees on the beautifully manufactured faux beach beside the lake each morning) and saw Frank retrieve one himself and hand it to her. As she took it from him, their hands touched, and they smiled at each other. He really was very attractive, though in a less *brutish* way than Luke. This was a pity, as she liked brutish.

'You really shouldn't be here,' he said, standing carefully away from her. She noticed he was drinking orange juice.

She shrugged. 'You held a charity golf tournament,' she said. 'And while I *hate* golf, I do like to help raise money for old soldiers. It is a cause close to my heart. Isn't *my* money any good to you?'

'Miss Kay,' said Frank, and she almost laughed at the formality, 'it's insane of you to have come.'

'And why is that exactly?'

'Oh come on, honey, you know why.'

His voice was a soft drawl and as he gazed at her from under a shock of jet-black hair, Sofia smiled tightly, surprised to feel a ripple of excitement. She was supposed to be charming *him*, remember?

'I'm a free woman, Mr Arlington. No one tells me what to do these days. And no one cares.'

Frank smiled, scraping a line in the sand with his shoe. 'Ah, I think we both know that isn't true. Say you had a special toy when you were a little girl. And say you got

233

to be too big for that toy. Your little brother comes along, and he wants that toy. Now, you're too big for that toy, you don't want to play with that toy any more, but you sure as hell don't want your little brat brother playing with it. Cos in your crazy little mind it's still *your* toy and it always will be.'

Sofia uncurled Frank's hand and took the shell he was holding. 'I dislike what you're implying, Mr Arlington. I'm going to translate the code just so we're both clear what this conversation is about. Am I simply Luke's discarded toy; a possession that must belong to him for ever? And' – she raised an eyebrow – 'who is it, exactly, who wants to play with me?'

Frank blushed.

Sofia gazed at the shell; it was warm to the touch, spiky, but smooth and pink inside. Then she looked at him. 'Oh honey,' she said, softly, stroking his hair. 'Vegas doesn't *get* you, Frank Arlington. You're weird. But you're not *Vegas* weird.'

He laughed. 'Whatever do you mean?'

'Vegas is traditional, in its own curious way. And you don't buy into that. You have your own ideas about what Las Vegas requires, and I'm not so sure that everyone agrees with you. Those African masks in your first hotel were spooky as hell.' She leaned close and whispered, 'They were too authentic. It felt like death was in the room.' She shrugged. 'Fear works. Anxiety means bigger bets, but you need to do it in the right way.'

His expression grew cold. 'I might not have the force of organized crime behind me, Miss Kay, but please don't treat me like a fool—'

'Sofia,' she said. 'Don't call me Miss Kay again. I hate it.' She tossed her hair. 'I'm not playing with you, Frank, or treating you like a fool. I think you need a friend. I want to help you.' She pouted. 'And I don't think you should care or ask why.'

He raised an eyebrow. 'I'm listening, Sofia.'

She took a step back.

Sofia was not the sort to sit and mope after being discarded by a man. Her incredulity and rage became energy and power. When Luke met her gaze after kissing his wife, he had given her invaluable information: he cared. He was hurt – not that he would ever allow such an emotion to filter into his consciousness. And Sofia intended to hurt him further. She didn't love him – how could one love such a monster? He'd got another woman pregnant while he was living with *her*! But they were linked, for ever, through bitter memories.

Luke had ordered his security to let her go. His exact words had been: 'Escort Miss Kay the fuck off the premises.' Sofia had decided that he was cursing to disguise the fact he was showing her mercy. She had fled home to the condo she had bought with his dirty money, but she considered that she'd earned every cent. She had the locks changed, but she knew that Luke would let her keep it. She was almost sad about that. Even to fight with him was better than no contact at all.

After a month of self-imposed exile, and barricading herself from the press, who never seemed to tire of printing gorgeous happy photos of the blissful newlyweds, Sofia had decided on a course of action.

'How do you like this one?' Sofia murmured to Frank,

delicately tracing the frilly line of the shell with her fingernail.

'It's perfect,' said Frank, and she heard the catch in his throat.

She would marry Frank Arlington because Luke hated him, and together they would crush Castillo underfoot. Sofia knew she should be careful but she couldn't help herself. Luke would regret the way he had treated her. She wasn't some dolly bird to be used and thrown aside. He was a fool, because she could have helped him; but Luke believed he didn't require help. He thought he didn't need her because he had *them*.

She would prove him wrong. Frank Arlington, with his clear smooth skin and slicked-black hair curling over his forehead like a rock star, was the way forward.

'Excuse me a second,' murmured Sofia, and dug in her bag, perhaps for a light, but actually to check point number four:

• *Listen*

'You know,' she stammered. 'I'm sorry but I don't actually know very much about you. How did you end up here?'

Frank sat down on the sand and smoothed a place for Sofia to sit beside him. She was in for a long listen.

'It was my father's fault. He was an engineer. He worked on one of Kerkorian's projects and impressed him.' Frank grinned. 'He was an impressive kind of guy. He was . . . patient. Nothing fit in the architect's design, and my father reassembled a lot of parts in the field to make the project work. Kirk told me so himself. He appreciated it, that my father went the extra mile.' Frank looked at her. 'I try to remember that.'

'How lucky you were to have a father like that.'

'Absolutely,' said Frank, 'in every way. I think of how he was, and that is the kind of father I would like to be to *my* son.'

'I didn't know you had a—'

'I don't.' He smiled. 'But I will. I *will* have a son. I just need to find his mother first.'

Sofia's heart lurched. So he wanted a son. Hey, she was prepared to do whatever it took. She paused, then asked delicately. 'Is your father . . . ?'

Frank sighed. 'He died in a car accident with my mother. He was only sixty-five and she was sixty-three. I just wish . . . ten more years, you know?'

Sofia nodded. 'I suppose after that you didn't have the heart to leave.'

Frank smiled. 'The city was part of him, he was part of the city. What could I do but apply for my gaming licence?'

Sofia knew the rest. He had aimed for a plot that no one else was much interested in; it wasn't a prime location. When the site came up, Arlington was able to get a bank loan, at a decent enough rate. His investors were clean. He was wise enough to make his friends before he made his application: he employed locals, donated to charities, avoided making enemies.

'I'm never going to be one of the boys, but Kirk's approval helped. And maybe the Commission didn't want any more of the boys. All the scandal over Mob rule' – Frank looked at her directly – 'has made it easier for me to progress.'

'Not to mention that you were already running successful casinos in Atlantic City and the Bahamas.'

Frank grinned. 'I love it. I have the most fun of anyone I know.'

'I hear you make your hosts work like they're selling on the stock market.'

'I do, because they *are*. If they're not on the phone hustling my product, they're wasting my time. The worst thing is a "greeter" host – those sixties throwbacks who sit on their fat backsides and wait for the clients to magically *rrrrrrrrrroll* in!'

Sofia burst out laughing. 'That's what happens at the Medici!'

Sofia would have given Luke some advice about 'greeter' hosts, but he had never wanted to take it. Not since their first meeting had she had any influence on his business management. The day Handsome Stan was fired changes had been made, but she was not allowed to be involved. *She* was a greeter host.

She smiled at him. 'You're a little more forward-looking than Luke.'

'Well, I'm from NYC. I'm a superior kind of redneck.'

'You are,' she murmured. Frank had his hosts seduce clients: bribe them with offers of free dinners, free accommodation, tickets to a show. People liked to think they were getting something for nothing. Even though no one got anything for nothing, perception was all. She smiled at him. Frank was getting to a point where he'd made enough money to be a little more of a jerk.

His next venture was also small. The Burlesque had been at the dog-end of Las Vegas Boulevard, but it was on the Strip. He was moving fast in the right direction.

This time, Sofia would make no mistakes. She had failed to punish Luke into marrying her; her tactics had misfired horribly. This time, she would bewitch her man into wedlock. She would get right down to the serious business of making Frank fall in love with her and then *trap* him.

Sofia knew that all women thought like this, even if they didn't see it. The fact was, once it occurred that they liked a guy, they did their damnedest to be irresistible with the application of make-up, the careful choice of outfit, the editing of the more disagreeable parts of their personalities. Perhaps the only thing she had got wrong was the use of the word 'trap'. It wasn't a word that people willingly applied to a romantic situation. Had she simpered about 'dreaming that their bodies and souls be entwined for ever' everyone would smile and agree.

'The stars are different here,' she said, abruptly. 'Like diamonds in the sky. It makes you think you can dream.'

Frank stared at her. 'You captured me,' he said, finally, as their lips met. The passion of his kiss seemed to melt her and she trembled with a sudden weakness.

She shivered a little in the cold, and he led her boldly through the parting crowds of guests as if they had nothing to hide. She could sense the click of a thousand long lenses: nothing in the twentieth century could be kept secret now for longer than it took to draw breath. Let the news get back to Luke Castillo immediately: his loss would be Frank and Sofia's gain. Each had something the other wanted, and both would benefit from the alliance.

• *Make him wait*.

Sofia crumpled Sterling's note into a tiny ball and allowed Frank to lead her upstairs to the honeymoon suite. If you had a *real* connection, you didn't have to make him wait. You only made a man wait if the relationship was, at heart, dishonest. They tore off each other's clothes and fell on each other. Oh *yes*, she groaned, as she pulled him into her. *Fuck you, Castillo*, she thought as they moved together, and maybe Frank thought it too.

Sunrise Valley Trailer Park, January 1983

Bessie

Bessie lay on the lumpy little bed, wincing every time her husband said, 'Uh!'

There was little worse in a marriage than having sex with your husband (as opposed to some other man) when you didn't feel like it.

'You're just doing your wifely duties,' puffed Hank.

She smiled, with effort, and said, 'No, I'm not, I'm really enjoying this.'

She forced a sigh. This was going on for ever.

'Oh *yeah*,' said Hank.

'Don't wake the children!' whispered Bessie as he finally rolled away. She flipped down her nightdress.

'Good for you?' sighed Hank as he started to snore.

'The earth moved,' replied Bessie, and then, under her breath: 'Must have been the San Andreas Fault.'

She lay like a log, staring at the tin ceiling. Tomorrow, the woman in the trailer next door would give her a look that said: *I know what you did last night*. Yes! The whole pack of losers might as well live in the same room! She had to get away or she would slit her wrists. She had found the place she wanted to move to. It was called Angel, and it sounded like heaven. Hank had already said 'no' three times. But she knew that if she was obliging enough, Hank would relent, if only to get her to shut up.

Bessie jabbed her husband in the leg with her toe. 'Sweetie? Shall we do it again?'

Private hospital, Las Vegas, nine months after the five-point plan, 28 August 1983

Sofia

It was astonishing, thought Sofia, that the baby started crying right away. As she lay stunned and empty on the bed, luxuriating in the sudden absence of pain, the baby screamed; a fast, angry sound, shockingly loud, shattering the peace. The abrasiveness of the noise and her instant irritation surprised her. She brushed it away and said to the nurse, who was wrapping the baby in a blanket, 'Hurry up, I want to see him.'

'*Her*, my dear, *her*. You and Mr Arlington have a beautiful little girl,' said the woman, her stupid face all smiles.

'A girl?' said Sofia. The nurse must have made a mistake.

'Here you go, Miss Kay, oh, she is just darling! Congratulations!'

Sofia stared at the baby, whose mouth was open in a great roar. She unwrapped the blanket – the nurse had bundled up the child like a parcel – and peered at its bright red little body. The parts required to qualify one as male were notably absent.

'A *dear* little girl,' said the nurse, a touch sternly. 'Of course you want to inspect your miracle, but we do need to keep Baby snugly and warm!'

Sofia covered up the baby, and said to it, 'Shhh!'

She couldn't believe it. And Frank wouldn't believe it either. He had presumed that she would give him a son. Sofia had been so sure that fate would oblige with a boy that she had had the nursery in her house decorated in blue; indeed every item of clothing, blanket and bootee was blue.

She had been nervous about telling Frank that she had fallen pregnant that first night, in case he thought, heaven forbid, that she was a gold-digger. But gold-diggers had nothing to offer but their bodies, and Sofia had so much more. Frank, who was strangely naive when it came to women, had been thrilled. 'The time is right, Sofia,' he'd whispered. 'Let's create a dynasty.'

You didn't create dynasties with *girls*.

'Shall I call in Mr Arlington?' said the nurse. 'He and his employees have been pacing the corridor.'

'Yes,' said Sofia, adding to herself, 'might as well get it over with.'

Seconds later, Frank burst in, banging the door against the wall and prompting the baby into a fresh jag of crying.

'She's gorgeous,' murmured Frank. 'She looks just like me!'

Sofia smiled, trying to feel joy. The nurse must have broken the news. A girl was all well and good for those with no direction, but useless if you wished to pin down an empire.

'Well done, girlie,' murmured Frank, kissing Sofia on the earlobe. 'I have a daughter!' His voice caught and he fished around in his jacket pocket. Suddenly he leaped up, ran from the room and could be heard shouting down the corridor to his PA, 'Clive! Clive! Did you get the thing?'

Thing . . . or *ring*? Sofia strained her ears but there was no further exchange. Her heart beat fast – maybe it wasn't the disappointment of the year. Frank had choked back tears as he looked at the child. Maybe he would propose regardless! Birth, like Christmas and Valentine's Day, was a catalyst for proposals. From what Sofia could tell, men proposed at births, Christmas and Valentine's Day without necessarily thinking the situation through. If the day passed and they *didn't* propose, either they genuinely loved you enough to consider it another time without a prompt, or they weren't going to propose at all.

Frank dashed back into the room, holding a velvet box. 'For the mother of my child,' he said, as the baby howled. 'Wow,' he added. 'That kid sure can yell.'

'Thank you, darling,' said Sofia, and opened the box with as much slow decorum as she could muster. Inside was the regulation diamond bracelet. 'It's really beautiful,' she said. Her voice was choked, but for all the wrong reasons.

'Three carat, every single one,' said Frank. 'Those things are the size of pebbles!' He grinned. 'I guess I better go tell Clive to get the nursery redone.'

Frank had also had the nursery at *his* place done up entirely in blue.

He stood up and gently stroked the baby's head. 'You did good,' he said to Sofia. 'For a boy I liked the name "Ariel". And now I like it for a girl too.'

Sofia's eyes filled with tears. 'Sure,' she said. 'It means "Lion of God" in Hebrew.' She added feebly, 'And hear her roar.'

There was a soft knock on the door and the nurse bustled in. 'Shall we try to get Baby on the boob?' she said in a loud voice, so as to be heard above the screaming.

Frank backed smiling out of the room with promises of another visit tomorrow.

As Sofia suffered the indignity of a strange woman grabbing her nipple and trying to wedge it into the infant's mouth, she replayed the image of her boyfriend backing out of the room.

'Nurse,' she said. 'In my bag I have *Christie Brinkley's Outdoor Beauty and Fitness Book*. Can you pass it to me?'

Sofia tried to balance the book on the bed while keeping the baby clamped to her breast, and failed. She stared at the white walls of her vast private suite, and felt as if she needed a bath. Certainly, Frank was delighted to be a father, but he had failed to propose and she understood why. With no heir, there was no incentive.

Sofia attempted to kiss the baby on its head, but she was too sore to move and gave up. This kid was a start. She was impatient, but practical. If at first you didn't succeed, you should try again. She had not succeeded with Luke, and so she had tried again with Frank. But this birth, while sweet, was another failure. And if you failed more than once, as Sofia believed she had, the next time you tried, you were entitled to cheat.

Angel Trailer Park, somewhere in the Mojave Desert, near Area 51, September 1983

Bessie

'Why did we come here, Mommy?' sobbed Marylou. 'I hate it! And I hate you! You're the worst mommy in the world! I want to go back to Sunrise Valley!'

Bessie wiped the sweat off her upper lip, and swigged her water. If only Marylou would just *shut up*. The child never stopped whining. 'We moved because it's peaceful here.'

Angel was little more than seven or eight trailers

scattered around a gas station in a blind valley in the middle of nowhere, not so far from Area 51. It had once been a mining town, but the mineral had run out and the place was truly forsaken; being more or less inaccessible with no amenities besides an inn, and the nearest town thirty minutes drive away. The inhabitants were curious, but they were loners themselves, and Bessie found that she had space to breathe.

'Marylou,' she said. 'Please don't whine. I can't deal with your whining. It's actually making me feel queasy.'

In Sunrise Valley Trailer Park, that gossipy little village, she had felt her grasp on sanity slipping. She had begged Hank to let them move. Nagging and sex; it was a potent combination. Eventually, he had agreed; only because to live in the middle of nowhere meant that he could stay in Vegas during the week. Bessie no longer cared what he was up to. They had no money left to lose.

'It's boring here!' wailed Marylou. 'And I don't like my new school! And it takes too long to get there!'

'I think it's very pretty, driving past all the alfalfa farms.'

'Alfalfa is the most disgusting food in the world!' retorted Marylou.

'Don't be so selfish, Marylou!' snapped Bessie. 'Your brother likes it fine!' It was true. Little Sam liked to lie on the dusty ground at night and try to grab the stars.

Now, she found a warped pleasure in scraping by, spending as little as possible. Hank still sold alcohol in the city, which meant she was able to take the edge off, and he had promised on his mother's life (his mother was dead) that he would never set foot in a casino again.

Bessie was no longer hanging by her fingernails on the edge of society. She had dropped off into the abyss. It was the difference between being despised by society or showing that you despised society *more*.

'Look!' cried Sam. 'That's Daddy's car!'

There was a rumble of dust as the old 4x4 sped along the road towards them. Marylou tossed her hair. 'Daddy is my favourite,' she said to Bessie. 'I don't *like* you, you're horrible.'

Bessie watched as the children greeted their father. She smiled tightly. God, he was ineffectual.

'Hey, chick!' he said to Marylou, ruffling her hair. 'Hello, little guy!' he said, swinging Sam into the air. He winked at Bessie. She had drunk a little too much recently and had slept with him a couple of times. What else was there to do?

'I managed to get myself a nice little gig,' he said to Bessie, lighting a cigarette and smoothing his hair. He turned to the children. 'In a few months' time, how do you fancy going on a plane holiday, to Europe?'

As the children screamed with excitement (even though Sam didn't know what he was screaming about) Bessie frowned at her husband. 'What on earth are you talking about?'

Hank linked an arm through hers. 'Honey,' he said. 'I've just signed the contract to provide the liquor at *the* party of the twentieth century! There's a top flight hotel opening in Dubai next February, and anyone who's anyone is going to be there. I'm talking Oprah Winfrey, Diana Ross, I'm talking Presidents, Heads of State, rock stars, movie stars – and Bessie, Hank, Marylou and Sam!

We got free bed and board, like, you know, in an ordinary kinda room; we got flights for a discount; we got champagne. Baby, get ready to live it up!'

Private hospital, LA, five months after Ariel's birth, 30 January 1984

Sofia

This time she was ready to abort the kid, right there. She'd have them wheel her straight from the scan to the fucking scrape room.

Why not a boy? she screamed in her head.

Sofia sat up. Why *not* a boy?

Sterling indicated to the lab technician that they were done.

'It's probably Frank's fault,' he murmured to Sofia as they were driven back to the airfield. 'If his boys are fast swimmers, you'll get a girl baby every time.'

Sofia stared straight ahead at the polished walnut interior of the car. She was rigid with doom. 'How do you know this stuff?'

'I had a classical education.' Sterling glanced at her. 'Don't do anything rash. You still have options.'

'Oh,' she said, sarcastically. '*What* options? I feel like Catherine of Aragon. If I can't give him a boy, Frank will get rid of me and find someone who can. And it won't matter if it's *his* fault and he only makes girl babies. By the time he works it out, I'll be his ex-girlfriend, waitressing in a café.'

'Sofia,' said Sterling. 'Don't panic. You just have to think creatively. Bonny Baby Number Two does not arrive for six months. And half a year is time enough to come up with a plan. Some happy solution will present itself, and that will be because fate wishes it.'

Sofia felt reluctantly dragged from her self-pity. 'That's very poetic of you, Sterling.'

Sterling smiled. 'I have my moments of glory, Sofia, and you will have yours.'

Dubai, 18 February 1984

Bessie

This child was barely old enough to be using scissors. She stood by a wooden table on which lay a sheet of paper, a tube of glue, and twenty-five thousand English pounds in fifties. The little girl was cutting out Queen's head after Queen's head from one of the piles of notes. She was making a collage.

The girl's father was standing in a corner of the room on his mobile. Minutes before, the little girl had been hanging off his leg. The man had jammed his cigarette in his mouth, nodded to his assistant, who had opened a leather holdall, and dumped an avalanche of money onto the table.

This was Bessie's first impression of the Paradise Special Members (Under 11s Only) Club. Bessie was staying on the Executive Floor, albeit in what appeared to be a broom cupboard, so her kids were eligible. The club nannies would look after her children until bedtime, and she could, supposedly, enjoy the party.

Sam, now four, had disappeared the minute he'd seen Luke Skywalker offering Jedi training, and Marylou, six, had run off to play in the architect-designed doll's house with the real live fairy godmother. Bessie was so mesmerized by the little Arab girl that she forgot her own children the second they were out of sight.

Bessie had opted out of society as far as she could, so she didn't have to think about what she couldn't give her children. But here, there was no escape from the enviable options of the wealthy.

She plodded back to her room, and imagined snatching up piles of tattered notes and running away with them. But it was too late: the house was gone.

Perhaps tonight she would pretend that none of it had happened. She would be Cinderella at the ball. She would imagine she didn't live in a trailer with *wheels*.

And yet, it could always get worse, said Hank. How true. Lately she and Hank had allowed themselves a little free entertainment and now she was paying for it.

She'd squeezed into a black decade-old Diane von Furstenberg wrap dress. She'd pulled it from the box she'd collected from Sandra's house. A few dresses, a couple of photo albums, plus some old toys, were the only items salvaged. The casino had auctioned their furniture, TV and wedding crockery.

She applied lipstick and she kept on her shades. She took the lift down to the ground floor and stood on the beach, gazing at the sky as the fireworks exploded. Bessie didn't see the stars; she just saw cut-up money.

As the fireworks lit the night, Bessie scrutinized the crowd on the beach: rich, beautiful, famous, privileged people basking in excess. The white frill of tide against the dark ocean, the luscious scent of the evening breeze: every exquisite detail would be a reminder to them that they had made it *for ever*. Their greatest dilemma: caviar or lobster. For them beauty was everywhere: in the millions of red tulips ruthlessly harvested for this one night; in the endless sky full of spark and fire.

Bessie, however, was a fraud. She took two champagne flutes from a passing waiter. She had managed to block out the shame but now it had returned with great force. What sort of adults couldn't pay for themselves? What people couldn't afford to raise their children? They were falling, and they would fall still further. She could not see an end to it. Oh, yes, Hank was working tonight, but they were still paying off debt.

She stood there, rigid, only moving robotically to exchange her empty champagne flutes for two glasses of vodka. Yes, the party was lavish but she could take no joy from it, just as the beauty of a lake was of no consequence if you were drowning in it. The Hotel Paradise was owned by an Australian tycoon, who wanted to make the world gasp at his genius. Paradise, built in the alluring curvy shape of a US dollar, had been constructed on a man-made island off the coast of Dubai.

It boasted an exquisite seafood restaurant 5 metres

beneath sea level. In the shape of a long tunnel, its curved ceiling and walls were made entirely of glass. Rays and octopi and lion fish billowed past as the guests sipped champagne.

The most expensive accommodation was a Line Suite, which bridged the curves of the hotel and commanded spectacular views of the bay. A Line Suite, named after the stroke in a dollar sign, cost twenty thousand dollars a night and contained gold-leaf furniture. Bessie and Hank's room was at the far end of the Line Suite level; she had experienced a ripple of excitement until she walked in: it was tiny and overlooked the staff car park.

At last, the fireworks came to their violent, crashing finale. Most of the guests chose to remain outside and eat, but Bessie needed to sit down. She sprawled on a lavishly upholstered armchair under a gargantuan chandelier in one of the ballrooms – she dared the thing to fall and squash her flat – and ate steadily, gulping more champagne between each bite.

She had just jammed a parcel of egg pasta filled with wild boar Bolognese into her mouth when she saw Kathleen Turner, the beautiful actress from *Body Heat*, staring in fascinated disgust. Bessie smiled widely, showing orange-stained teeth.

Tina Turner was singing after dinner. How could Bessie care about a concert? She staggered towards a bar, giggling. She needed another drink, just one more drink.

'Mind if I sit?' said a cool, assured voice.

Bessie shrugged. 'No,' she said, only because it was easier to say than: 'Oh God, do you have to? I'm out of my skull. I can hardly see, let alone talk! Can't you just go away?'

She glanced at the woman sliding on to the next stool; looked again. Bessie blinked, and grabbed the edge of the bar to stop herself falling off her stool. Either the woman had two heads or Bessie was so drunk she was starting to see double . . .

The woman seemed preoccupied. She went to light a cigarette, then she snapped shut the lighter and threw the unlit cigarette in her bag. She sighed and retrieved it, gave a little shrug, and put it to her lips. She drew on it heavily, saw Bessie watching, and offered her one.

Bessie nodded, and drained the dregs of her tequila. The woman's fidgeting was making her feel sick.

She needed to get very drunk, to escape the guilt that came with getting only slightly drunk. The glasses were getting smaller. She lifted hers to be refilled. The barman turned away without noticing. You are *nobody*. Bessie slumped on to the bar, before lifting her head and smiling.

She had brought another old dress to try on besides the von Furstenberg. She'd said to Hank: 'What do you think about what I'm wearing? This, or—'

'Yeah, what you're wearing's fine.'

Hey, death, why don't you come for me.

Bessie looked at the woman, who was smoking fast, as if she had somewhere to be. 'Not having fun?' she said, stumbling over the words.

'I've enjoyed it,' said the woman coolly, 'but I'm a little tired. Well. Good night.' The woman stubbed out her cigarette.

Bessie felt suddenly desperate not to be alone. 'I'm pregnant,' she slurred. She raised her glass. 'Last drink. Last smoke. Just found out.'

'Congratulations,' said the woman, gazing hard at Bessie.

Bessie felt a silly relief. 'No, comish—— commiserations,' she said. The words slid out of her mouth like jelly off a plate. 'No money, see. Poor as *dirt*. I'm only here cos Hank's working. Urrgh, it'll be a boy, because it *will*. That's my luck!'

She started to laugh, knowing that it was too late to salvage normality, and too drunk to care.

The woman said nothing. Bessie rested her chin on her hand; her elbow slipped off the counter. 'Whoops,' she giggled. 'And you? Why are you here?'

The woman smiled, and signalled to the barman to refill Bessie's glass. He did so immediately.

'It's a business trip for me too,' she said.

The Paradise, Grand Opening, Dubai, later the same evening

Frank

Frank had finally met a woman who understood him. And yet, despite the birth of their little girl, Ariel, last year, he hadn't proposed. He knew she wanted it. She hadn't said, but Frank was learning that women did most of their communication in silence.

Frank didn't have the energy for marriage. Not right now. He needed to focus on his career. And he wasn't yet convinced that Sofia could be part of it.

At school, Frank had excelled at long-distance running. He didn't have a natural aptitude for it, but he refused to quit. His need to win made him the best. Nothing else would do.

It was galling, then, to be losing. He craved victory and the fact that he was struggling in Las Vegas was hard to bear. Frank had hoped to take inspiration from his friend Richard's Grand Opening in Dubai. The party was sumptuous and the place was stuffed with celebrities; Sofia would happily entertain herself; she didn't need him.

'Arlington!' he boomed as the phone rang. It was Bill Asquith, his Chief of Design. Frank planned to spend the night sitting on his enormous bed under the pale gold eiderdown, by himself, making notes on his laptop. 'Bill, I've checked out this vanity project. I think we can improve on Paradise!'

His new casino hotel would open within the year: although it was small, it was his first venture on the Strip, and he intended it to redefine the concept of hospitality. Here, he had a chance. You couldn't compete with Caesar's Palace from Fremont!

'Bijou is going to be small but sparkly like a jewel. I want to fill it with precious things: paintings, sculptures ... Huh? Sure the punters will appreciate that stuff! They're tired of all these great gaudy palaces with bad impersonators, burger bars, plastic trees and theme-park rides!'

Bill voiced anxiety that the idea was too niche.

'Bill,' said Frank. 'The super rich will flock and my drop per table is going to exceed anything in the state of Nevada!'

Bill worried that size might be an issue for the super rich. They liked to spread out.

'Bill,' said Frank. 'It's all about *perception*. You don't call it small, you call it exclusive. I've put a lot of goddamned work into this. I've got psychologists on my books telling me how people gamble and why. I've got marketing experts showing me how to get them to spend.'

Frank was proud of his sophisticated approach. Luke Castillo's marketing strategy was to stick a titty bar next to the baccarat lounge and make people fear for their lives if they didn't give you all their money.

'Bill,' he bellowed. 'I have three wishes for *my* guests: I want them to step into the colour, light, noise and magic of my hotel and to be wowed out of their tiny minds. I want my guests to go home feeling elated, feeling as if they have been personally hosted by Mr Arlington. I want them to quit my property poor, but happy. And it's your job to make that vision sing!'

There was a quiet knock on the door, and Frank started in irritation. There was a 'do not disturb' notice on the door. Perhaps Bijou should be the first hotel that issued electric shocks to those who were incapable of reading and following a simple order on a sign.

'Who is it?' he barked.

'Me,' said a voice.

Frank sighed. 'Bill, I'll catch you later.' He put down the phone. 'Come in.'

Sofia was wearing a dress that shimmered pearlescent like a mermaid's tail. Large diamond pear-drop earrings flashed as she shook her long blond hair away from her face. Her skin was suntanned and creamy smooth, and there was a smattering of freckles on her delicate nose. Adorable. She had long lashes and a generous mouth, and her huge green eyes bored into his soul. She was wearing high silver heels and wobbled slightly as she stood away from the wall. She radiated vitality. He tried to resist.

'I don't know that Richard's gone the right way here,' she cried, throwing her hands wide as if she was about to sing a song. 'It's grand and imposing but it's too big, too impersonal. I feel like a little lost girl.' She paused. 'I don't want to spend money here, and I don't want to gamble. He's showing off; he's not giving me enough love. He's not making me feel *lucky*.'

Frank jumped up from the bed, jabbing his finger at her. 'That is *it*, Sofia, that is *it*. I couldn't agree more. Is it just me, just us, or is the Paradise the Emperor's New Clothes?'

She tilted her head. 'There is a fine line, isn't there, between nurturing your patrons and overwhelming them? I want to feel spoilt; I don't want to feel as if I'm not worthy.'

Frank stared at her. So she *did* understand. She understood the business as well as she understood him. She really was quite perfect.

He touched her hand and felt, suddenly and strongly, as if he must never let her go.

He led her to the sitting room. She stopped, briefly, as

she walked in, then whirled around, smiled, and sashayed to the huge floor-to-ceiling window. The view was of endless night. It was surprisingly black: the hotel was right off the coast, and the sea met the dark horizon without interruption.

Frank looked, instinctively, for a star, a sliver of moon – any glimmer of light. He was superstitious in a lazy way, choosing to find auspicious symbolism in co-incidence, discarding anything that could be perceived as a bad omen.

As it was, the universe rose to meet Frank's high expectations and provided him with an aeroplane crossing the night. It was not a star, but it would do. He leaned against the vast window and pulled her to him. His hands travelled slowly down her dress, and she tipped back her head, grasping his shoulders, and he kissed her neck, and behind her ear.

'I want you,' he whispered.

'I'm right here, Frank,' she murmured, and his insides melted at the sound of his name on her tongue.

Afterwards they lay on the bed and brainstormed ideas for the new hotel. She had a nice idea for the foyer, and he kissed her. She looked into his eyes before leaning in to kiss him back, and the unspoken words made his heart thump.

'What is it, darling?' he said.

'I'm pregnant again,' she whispered. 'And this time I'm sure it's a boy.'

Frank's heart swelled with love and pride. *Anything Luke can do, I can do better* . . . He held her hands in his and gazed into her eyes. 'Then,' he said, kissing her fingertips one by one, 'I might just have to make an honest woman of you.'

Sofia screamed and hugged him, and bounced on the bed like a child. Frank, laughing, jumped up to bounce with her. There was no harm in getting engaged. An engagement was merely a reservation. One could always cancel.

Angel, two months later, 2 April 1984

Bessie

She checked her watch. It was 9.59 a.m. The kids were at school. Hank was in Vegas. They'd said 10 a.m. Maybe it was a joke. Maybe nothing would happen. Or maybe the trailer would explode.

She was wearing the Diane von Furstenberg dress again. It was the only decent item of clothing she owned, although at the moment she had a little bit of cash hidden under her mattress. If today wasn't a trick, organized by Hank to make a hot, exhausted, pregnant woman even wearier than normal, then Bessie might well buy another dress.

The initial approach had been casual but, she was sure, serious. When you lived in a desert trailer, and found an envelope under your door, with your name on it and a thousand dollars inside, your interest was piqued. She'd called the number, and a male voice told her that she would be paid another thousand dollars if she fulfilled his request.

The request itself made no sense, but if there was money in it, wonderful money, Bessie would do it. She couldn't see the harm. She didn't *want* to see the harm.

The roar of an engine cut through the quiet. She stared into the distance. Oh my God! A silver car snaked towards her. As it drew near, she gasped. The locals would mistake it for a Ford, but *she* knew it was an Aston Martin. The man driving it was freshly shaven and his black suit looked expensive. He stepped out, held open the door and called her 'madam'.

'Thank you,' she whispered, stepping clumsily into the leather interior. The man looked normal, but perhaps he was a psychopath who liked to kidnap and murder pregnant women.

Someone had provided *English* chocolate – three Cadbury's Flakes! – in a porcelain bowl, and there was a silver cool box stuffed with cans of Coke. No alcohol though. She ate all the Flakes and drank two Cokes. She was driven to a private airstrip in the back of beyond and ushered on to a plane.

'Isn't there a place in Las Vegas that's suitable?' she said to the man in black. She was petrified, but didn't dare to refuse.

'Don't worry,' murmured the stewardess. 'We're all here to look after you, miss.'

The woman had called her 'miss', but she liked it. She didn't feel bonded to that scumbag Hank in any way. She'd divorce him, except that it would upset the kids and she wasn't up to the fight. She relaxed in the soft chair and tried not to grip the armrest on take-off; instead she crossed her legs and admired how long they looked in the pillar-box-red stilettos she'd bought with a little bit of her thousand dollars. She'd made a special trip to the city in their banger of a car.

She hadn't spent one cent on Hank. She had bought Sam and Marylou five outfits each, and toys: Cabbage Patch Dolls, Care Bears, My Little Pony, GI Joe, He-Man, Lego, a football, a tricycle, a bicycle. Their delight had shocked her, because it made her realize that not having money *did* matter. Marylou was in girl heaven because she had a pretty dress. When her children were happy, Bessie found it possible to be a good mother. But when they were miserable, she turned cold; she couldn't help it. If she allowed herself to love them then, she would have to feel their pain. And the agony was simply too much to bear.

Bessie allowed the stewardess to fuss around her for the duration of the flight. The woman offered her strawberries, and she had a flashback to eating strawberries smothered in vanilla cream on the deck of her old house. There was a raw ache for her old life. She tried to brush it away and enjoy the moment. The plane landed as softly as a feather, and Bessie was ushered into another plush car.

She gasped inwardly when she saw the private hospital. Oh my God. Back in England, she remembered going to Harley Street as a teenager with her mother to see a surgeon for 'women's problems'. She recalled the grand white pillars and Queen Anne windows, the musty smell of antique chairs and ancient rugs, the rows of lipsticked secretaries, and how the pollen of the lilies in the vase tickled her nose.

This American hospital, however, crushed this small stuffy English claim to élitism underneath its gargantuan, white, new-moneyed foot. Everything was pristine, gleaming, clinical; as if Bessie had been transported to the future instead of, as she suspected, LA. The man in the black suit checked her in, and she was immediately spirited away to a private room.

'Thank you,' said Bessie as the pretty woman in the white coat gave her a mug of creamy hot chocolate 'to get the baby moving' before the scan. She tasted the drink and it was so luxurious, her eyes prickled with tears. She blinked them away, mortified. She couldn't resist glancing at her reflection in the great gilt mirror. She had applied her new lipstick and she barely recognized herself.

'Well done, miss,' said the technician, smiling, as she completed the scan. 'All is exactly as it should be.'

She wanted to ask if it was a boy or a girl, but suddenly, she felt sad and curiously empty, as if it and nothing mattered, and the words died in her mouth. It was a strange thing to pay a stranger a thousand dollars to have a private pre-natal scan. She felt oddly detached from this baby and she knew why: she had nothing to give it. As Bessie left the room, she saw the technician pick up the phone and dial. The look on her face, as she glanced towards Bessie closing the door, was *furtive*.

Sofia's residence, Las Vegas, later that day

Sofia

'So far, so good,' she said to Sterling, when he rang. Her voice was calm but her legs wobbled and she collapsed on her bed.

After the phone call, she began to worry. What if she had misjudged the woman? What if she were, in fact, a smug earth mother, who sang to the baby in the womb, the sort who couldn't wait to flop out a boob for the kid to suck on, who dribbled with adoration over her progeny as it slept, who snatched at the opportunity to wear bin-bag dresses and stop plucking her eyebrows and get as fat as a house because she was engaged in loftier matters – yes, frivolous world! – the pious job of *motherhood*. If Bessie were that type, she hadn't a hope.

But somehow, Sofia didn't think so. Bessie was a decent enough parent, but she was weak, weary and resentful of what she had been reduced to. Sofia knew that poverty, as much as power, corrupted. And as Frank always said, perception was all. If Bessie was persuaded that this course of action was selfless, sacrificial, the best for her children, then Sofia was confident the woman would be as pliable as dough.

Angel, 27 April 1984

Bessie

When she understood the facts of the proposal, she sat down on the grubby little foldaway stool in the trailer and cried. But not for the reasons one might imagine. The deal, offered out of the apparent blue by a stranger, crystallized every wretched feeling she had about the ugly mess of her life, and she cried because she saw that she was in acute crisis.

It was a good minute before she thought of the baby.

Now she considered. Had she bonded with it? No. If it had been Charlie's child, it might have been different. Ah, Charlie. If she only had money, she could buy a house near town and return to her part-time job as a legal secretary, all glamorous and well kept, and get on with the serious business of seducing her boss. There was chemistry, but she had resisted Charlie's flirtations because at that point, she was married.

Now, she no longer considered herself married. She and Hank were emotionally divorced; they just needed their feelings to be ratified by law. Not that Hank would ever agree. She was too frightened even to approach the subject. She didn't want to make life even *more* wretched for her kids. But Hank had ruined everything for her. She'd had to quit her job when he'd lost the house; not only had they been forced to relocate to the back end of nowhere, but she couldn't afford childcare any more.

Charlie had murmured, 'There will always be a place for you here.' She dreamed of him at night. He was the only person she could recall who treated her with respect.

She could be herself with him, although she had lied to Charlie about one thing. When Hank had lost the house and she'd had to quit her job, she had told Charlie they were moving to England.

This proposal could change her life in so many wonderful ways. And this life inside her didn't really feel like *her* baby. It was the foetus of Hank. But – her stomach turned frightened somersaults – what a thing to *do*. And yet, other people in the situation she was in had their kids adopted; they abandoned them, or worse . . . She had to talk herself round. When you were raised in Hampstead Garden Suburb, that sense of primness never really left you, even if you had rebelled against it.

Bessie rubbed the sleep from her eyes. What would they think of her in Hampstead Garden Suburb, all those little princesses she'd been to school with, if they could see her now, see inside the grubby depths of her tainted mind; if they could see how she had lived, how far she'd sunk, and the hopelessness she felt when she looked at her prospects? She was a woman who no longer washed her face, who didn't bother to justify sipping gin throughout the long, boring, carbon copy of every day. If food fell on the unwashed floor, she'd pick it up and eat it, hating herself.

No doubt, she thought, feeling the ugliness of her sneer, those little princesses were all wisely married to their boring, balding hedge-fund managers, all reigning over their vast triple-fronted mansions overlooking parkland, barging around the same square inch of globe day after day in their huge, black 4x4s, having the same conversations (husband problems, my builder, her house, which school), tanning themselves wrinkly and black in the same three destinations (The Algarve, Florida, Eilat). She hated them because she envied them. No, not envy, it was worse than that; it was jealousy, poison and undilute.

Bessie snatched up the heavy cream envelope that lay on her pull-down table and ripped it open.

Sofia's residence, 28 April 1984

Sofia

On hearing that Bessie had agreed, Sofia ran to the bathroom to be sick. It was excitement, fear, and morning sickness. Bessie had agreed – oh, she had a greed all right. Sofia laughed as she dabbed her mouth with a fine cotton towel. The plan would go ahead. She splashed her face with chilled Evian and gazed at her perfect reflection with controlled calm.

Then she threw the towel in the air, screamed with joy and clapped her hands, watching her mirror image dance like an imp. She was triumphant, and resolute. No regrets. She understood exactly what she was doing and she was psychologically at one with it. Biological ties were overrated. It was easy to cut off; one merely had to be convinced of *why*. If you had doubts, then you were making a mistake. Sofia had no doubts.

This was not a whim.

She had tried with her mother and father, but the relationship never worked. Her parents had done their best for the family, but mainly for themselves. Their children had been forced to play along. She and they had nothing in common; it was as if they were from different planets. Her entire childhood had been spent in awkward civility, fury and bewilderment at their weirdness – until the death of her twin brother.

Grief had not brought them closer; just the opposite. Sofia blamed her parents for bringing them to Israel. Never mind that she had loved the army life, she blamed them for sacrificing her darling brother to politics and religion. Her mother, she knew, wished it was Sofia who had died; Jonathan was everyone's favourite. With family, life had convinced Sofia that it was better to choose.

Angel, 30 April 1984

Bessie

Bessie sat on the steps of her trailer under a makeshift canopy and laughed at the hot blue sky. She felt light as dandelion fluff, despite the cannonball weight of the baby. She pouted a little and tossed her hair, just like a movie star. She'd even found an old lace fan – some Spanish get-up she'd discovered while riffling through

Marylou's 'secret' box – and she fluttered it in front of her face, narrowed her eyes and dreamed of new possibilities.

She wasn't doing this for herself. This way, everyone was a winner – even Hank. She'd tell him her parents had died, leaving her everything. She hugged herself in delicious anticipation. 'This is a seven figure arrangement,' the note had said. She guessed they would pay her in instalments, maybe a hundred thousand dollars a year. Hank would want to know how much her 'parents' had given them, of course, so she'd make arrangements. She would put a small portion of her fee in an account, say, twenty thousand, and the rest she would squirrel away. Never again would he have access to *her* money.

The baby boy would go to a privileged home, she presumed. Perhaps it was royalty – secret agents acting on behalf of Diana! Bessie's bloodline would eventually ascend the British throne! Girls were less trouble than boys, at least, they ate less and they were tidier. But listen to her, thinking like a pauper! This arrangement meant she would no longer have to live in a filthy pig sty and scrabble for food, picking up the half-mouldy bargains, dented tins, and biscuits with torn packaging.

She heard a faint purr and peered into the bright horizon. As the noise became louder, she saw a motorbike speeding along in a regal cloud of yellow dust. Bessie squealed with delight. It was all so exciting! She felt special, she felt important – she mattered, for the first time in years. Now, she could have *diamonds*.

She had kind of let her imagination run away with her, based on the thousand dollars and the Aston Martin and the private jet. So she had said 'yes' and signed a piece of paper. Nothing enthralled her, except money. Today, she could sit in admiration of the wide blue sky, only because she was drunk on the thrill of imminent wealth, instead of just drunk.

If she had money, she could love her kids – any kid. Money would free her from that cloying, debilitating cloud of misery. Everyone would have a better life: to live in a real, proper *house* again; to have staff, to feel *good* again! With money, she would be a happy, even-tempered mother. Without it – if she had said 'no' – Hank's foetus, along with her other kids, would grow up in a tin can.

The motorcycle roared to a standstill. The driver dismounted and, with leather-gloved hands, unclipped a large cardboard box from its tie-casing on the back of the bike. Without removing his helmet, he nodded to Bessie, who scrambled to open the trailer door.

On the side of the bike was written 'Spirits of the Valley: Fine Wines'. She was impressed at the trouble someone was taking to deceive. Her neighbours would assume she had just taken receipt of a case of cheap booze.

'Thank you,' she said as he dumped it on the dirty floor. She could barely hold herself back from ripping open the box with her teeth, but she waited until the bike had roared off and then slowly locked the door. She knew what was in the box. It would be money. Trembling, she drew the thin curtains, and picked furiously at the tape binding the box.

Gibbering with joy and disbelief, Bessie tore open the box.

She looked inside and choked: a single dollar bill. Her eyes bulged in rage. What was this, a joke?

Then she noticed the paper, caught in the flap of the box. Bessie snatched it up, and read the words with boggling eyes.

> $999,999 has been transferred to an account in your name. A further $1,000,000 will be transferred on successful completion of business. Thereafter, you will receive $1,000,000 annually, in perpetuity, on condition of discretion eternal and absolute. Take your silence to the grave.

A chill ran from the back of her neck right down to her toes. There was no need to be sinister. Were they implying she was untrustworthy? She felt affronted. But, oh my GOD! She was as rich as Paul McCartney!

There was no order to 'destroy after reading' as in the spy movies, but like a good little collaborator, Bessie hung out of the window, lit a match, and watched the evidence burn. She understood what was required and would fulfil her obligations with precision. Sobbing with elation, and relief, she lay on her bed and stroked her stomach. 'I've made the best decision for both of us,' she told the baby. She had given both Sam and Marylou nicknames inside the womb. Sam was 'the Bean' and Marylou was 'the Wriggler'. She wasn't going to call this one anything. It was better that way.

Private hospital, LA, 20 August 1984

Sofia

The baby screamed shrilly and Sofia was glad that Frank wasn't a father who wished to be present at the birth. In fact, he was in Macau, attending the Grand Opening of Arnold Ping's Good Fortune. Good fortune indeed.

Until Sofia had that plain gold ring on her finger, she didn't trust him with the truth. Frank was, he said himself an 'easy-going' kind of guy. Did that mean he would easily go? There was no end to the beautiful women who threw themselves at him. Sofia had given birth to his daughter a year earlier. This time, she would give him what he craved: a boy.

Sofia watched through half-closed eyes as the midwife weighed the child. She could hear the midwife crooning softly to the baby, and her heart flipped over. Sofia squeezed her eyes shut tight.

Frank wanted to keep his fortune in the family. And Vegas was redneck at heart and sexist to the bone. Aside from herself, Sofia didn't see that it was possible for a woman to run a gaming empire. Maybe in twenty years it would be normal, but right now it was unheard of. And Frank wasn't good at thinking long-term.

Frank had made a fuss on the arrival of his first child: thrown a party, given a lump sum to every premature baby unit in Clark County, and set up a trust fund for the baby in Sofia's name. He'd placed five million dollars in there, and joked about the 'tax break'. He'd opened an account for Sofia too. The money, he told her, was so that she could sell her old house and buy a bigger one for herself and Ariel, 'not too near, but not too far'.

Sofia appreciated a man handing over ten million dollars for the delight of her 'not too near' company, but she didn't feel that Frank had got it right. She already had a perfectly lavish home. Sofia wanted a house that came with status, and power. This would only be attained when Frank married her.

They had been engaged since February, but Frank would not commit to a wedding date. This lack of action, Sofia believed, was far more telling of Frank's feelings about girl babies than all the party-arranging, money-throwing hoopla. Her position would not be secured until she had provided a son.

Sofia accepted a cocktail of painkillers from a nurse and swallowed, wincing. She wished the midwife would just get on with it; the woman was dithering. She couldn't risk a repeat of the Luke Castillo situation. This time she would give her man what he wanted. It was harsh, and of course it affected her. But it had to be.

With this in mind, Sofia had not bought a new house but rather saved the money to buy something she actually had need of.

She looked up in annoyance as she realized that the midwife was actually standing by her bed. The woman had her instructions and yet her stupid instincts were fighting against them; she was holding out the baby for Sofia to *cuddle*!

'You're making it worse,' said Sofia. 'I don't want to see her. Just take her away.'

Private hospital, LA, the following morning, 21 August 1984

Bessie

She pushed the baby to her breast; it fought and screamed, scratching at her with tiny, mole-like hands. She lay back against the soft goose-down pillows, closed her eyes, and pressed the bell for the midwife.

'She won't feed.'

'Ah,' said the midwife, a brisk Australian, 'you need to be patient. Baby is learning too, and she'll tell you when she's hungry. We call it feeding on demand—'

'I'd like to give her a bottle.'

'But, Bessie,' said the midwife, doubtfully, 'all that lovely breast milk is *perfect* for your little one. Formula is great for calves.'

When she'd popped out Marylou at the tail end of the seventies, formula was regarded as the Bollinger for babies. Now this midwife was turning up her nose!

'I need to sleep,' said Bessie. 'I'm so tired, and my stitches hurt. Could you take her to the nursery and give her a bottle, please?'

The midwife pressed her lips together, but did as she was asked.

It was curious. She hadn't expected the baby to look so ... *alien*. Sam and Marylou had looked just as she had expected babies were meant to look. This one, however, looked different. She had gazed intently at its face, trying to see if it resembled Diana or Charles in any way ... but it was just a run-of-the-mill nondescript baby.

She wondered, with a pang, if *her* boy was also fighting, screaming at some other woman's breast. She felt sick, then, and tried not to think about it. She'd done the right thing. She had made a noble sacrifice, so that her child would grow up with every opportunity – that *four* children would grow up with every opportunity that wealth could provide.

Some women might not mind hardship, their parenting wouldn't be affected by it, but hers was and her children had suffered because of it. She had a cool relationship with them, because it was too painful to care. If she let herself care too deeply about Sam and Marylou, she would just kill herself with the misery and regret of it all. But here was the chance to love them again. She could not feel bad, or sorrowful. And, most importantly, her baby boy would never know.

The exchange had been swift and discreet. She had been flown, again, by private jet, to a small private hospital at an undisclosed location, and wheeled into theatre, where she had been given a Caesarian section.

Peering from her drugged-up haze, she had seen a squalling red creature emerge from her innards with a shock of black hair. Then the baby had been whipped away 'to be weighed and dressed'.

Panicking that this was it, she'd rung for the midwife. 'Please,' she'd whispered. 'I'd like five minutes alone with him.'

The woman had hesitated, then she brought her baby back in and left them. With tears streaming from her eyes, Bessie had fumbled inside her handbag and, with shaking hands, taken a photo of him on her new Canon

T70. Then she'd hurriedly stuffed the camera back in her bag and rocked him, gently.

Seconds later, the midwife came in, held out her hands for him, and he was gone. When 'her' baby was returned, half an hour later, in a white all-in-one, it had a fine dusting of blonde hair.

It felt so dreamlike that Bessie couldn't be certain it had even happened. She felt floaty and unreal on wonderful morphine, which she topped up herself with a hand pump. Who was her mystery benefactor? How had she been chosen? *Take your silence to the grave*: really! Of course, she wouldn't try to discover the woman's identity; it would be dangerous and crazy. But, say, ten years down the line, if idle curiosity persisted, then she'd investigate. By then, no one would be watching.

Once the blonde baby had been taken to the nursery, Bessie felt a great sweep of misery engulf her. To make it go away, she asked a nurse to pass her handbag.

She fished out a number, and made a call to her (she couldn't really believe it) 'personal manager' at the bank.

'Yes, Ms Edwards' – she had the sense that he'd call her Your Majesty given the chance – 'your balance stands at a rather resplendent two million dollars.'

She put down the phone and burst out laughing. Then, gritting her teeth against the surprisingly insistent pain of abdominal surgery, she reached out for one of the glossy property magazines that adorned the polished walnut side table, alongside a large bowl of exotic fruit.

If she was to enjoy the chances she had been given, she had to believe that she had done the best thing for her baby – for *all* her children. There could be no doubt or regret. It was time to put sentimentality behind her, and embrace her shiny fabulous new life.

An upmarket suburb of Las Vegas, thirteen years later, 10 September 1997, 7 p.m.

Bessie

Beautifying in anticipation of sex with her lover was Bessie's favourite pastime. Her sweet fantasy was real, she thought as she stepped out of her gold and black onyx power shower, wiggling in time to the beat. She swathed herself in a soft fluffy peach towel, luxuriating in the caress of it against her skin.

Mariah's voice joyously belted out of the Bose speakers implanted in every corner of every room – one of the many bespoke specifications for this glorious house. This house made her old one opposite Sandra and Larry look like a shack.

Bessie ignored her reflection in the faux antique floor-to-ceiling mirror (it was wired so as not to steam up – although if Bessie got any fatter she'd have it rewired to steam up the second she took off her shirt). But although she was heavy, she was shapely. And now she could afford to have regular facials, manicures, massages, and haircuts, she looked ten years younger and quite delicious.

She was still singing as she shimmied across her vast

bedroom and into her walk-in closet. Every day she appreciated the luxury of her situation – *every single day*. She loved the grand French windows that sucked in the light, the elegant carving on the banisters, the pretty little lights set within the wall at ankle level alongside the staircase, so that if you crept downstairs at night for a drink of water (or whatever) the stairs were softly lit and there was no need to turn on a harsh glaring bulb that would make your head thump.

Bessie loved that she could lie in a well-padded hammock on the rose-filled balcony and gaze at Red Rock and the endless desert sky. Their back yard, as Hank insisted on calling it, was ostentatiously large, with a long viola-shaped heated pool, and a pagoda smothered in orchids and desert marigolds, and a mother of a barbeque. The grass was plastic. They had gardeners, of course, but it was still tradition to mow your lawn on a Sunday and as Hank said, 'I ain't mowing shit.'

She guessed she was stuck with Hank. The continuation of the marriage had been one condition of the deal, and she supposed she understood. God forbid he hired some nosey divorce lawyer to investigate her finances. Still, their relationship was bearable now: the house was so huge they rarely saw each other.

Their neighbours in the gated community were gracious but reserved; Bessie loved it. Actual millionaires tended to privacy, it was mostly the poor and the in-secure middle classes who felt compelled to bitch and spy. She couldn't stand it; she felt so above them now. Even though Casey was thirteen and attended the

Meadows, she avoided socializing with the other mothers. She resented their curiosity.

The nanny was a blessing. Bessie had no tolerance for all that crap about children being miserable when their mothers worked. It was *fabulous* for the children that their mother worked. It meant that the times they weren't at school were spent with a jolly young woman, with bundles of energy, who could relate to them about whatever it was they were interested in (Bessie assumed computer games).

She was tempted to pay the nanny to live in, but even though the house had an annexe, she resisted. Marylou was twenty now, taking a law degree at Berkeley. And Sam was a hulking eighteen-year-old, so the nanny was mainly there for Casey. Casey would have loved it, but Bessie wouldn't have been able to relax knowing the nanny was sleeping in her house. As it was, the girl always got a prim look on her face and shepherded Casey out of the room when Bessie and Hank were fighting. Bessie preferred not to be observed.

Bessie trailed a finger along the plastic-coated rainbow of outfits. Each had a little photo attached; she'd read about this idea in *Vogue* and thought it fabulous. Her maid had done it. The trouble was that everything seemed to have shrunk at the dry cleaner's. Bessie didn't step on the scales any more: they were obviously broken; that or the guardian angel who these days sat on her shoulder was bloody overweight. There was no way she weighed *that*. She didn't eat *so* much.

But when you had Cook who made orange and Grand Marnier pancakes for breakfast or a rum baba decorated with raspberries and grapes and double whipping cream, it was a crime to subsist on crackers with cottage cheese. The Nevada heat made it uncomfortable to be anything other than skinny, but then Hank was thin and it was like getting it on with a coat hanger. Charlie, however . . . *mmm*.

Bessie loved it when a plan came together – and she and Charlie had. As soon as she had become accustomed to her new, luxury life, she had simply rung him up and asked if he had a vacancy for a part-time legal secretary. He had reinstated her the same day. And they had become lovers the day after that. Gosh, it was *thirteen years* ago now. She had rescued Hank and her children; she felt she deserved her little reward. And Charlie *swore* that his marriage was over, even though his wife stayed fatly put.

Charlie liked her plump, and meanwhile, Cook made lobster Benedict, and the lobster just melted in your mouth, and eggs set you up for the day. Cook always said, enjoying the joke, 'You can't beat an egg!'

But the good thing about Cook was, you rarely saw her, and if you did she was half obscured by a towering stack of pancakes. She had no interest in Bessie beyond as a receptacle for her talents. Cook did not understand the word 'greedy'; to Cook, an 'appetite' was an asset; people who didn't eat fit to burst were disappointing.

Cook adored making chocolate puddings with oozy insides; she made sweet and sour pork that made your taste buds dance; she made Lancashire hotpot, pumpkin risotto, pineapple upside-down cake, savoury chicken pot pie, meat loaf with mushroom gravy, corned beef, potato and pepper hash, sausage spoon bread; she made banana coconut chiffon pie; she even made fish curry steamed in banana leaf, and deep fried spare ribs with chilli and lemon grass. The whole world was her recipe book, and Bessie had just about fallen in love with her.

But, damn, her Chanel skirt was a tight fit. She closed her eyes and yanked up the zip. It held; a tribute to quality tailoring. It was too hot for stockings, but Charlie Jay did so love her in stockings. She was wearing her littlest prettiest knickers, but it was hard to disguise that her bra was hardworking. The lace and the seed pearls didn't quite camouflage those heavy-duty straps. Hank said she had a flabby ass; it took a big man like Charlie to appreciate a woman who refused to starve herself to the girth of a twig.

She checked her watch (today it was a diamond-encrusted white-gold affair from Harry Winston). She should hurry; Hank was due home in half an hour. She found it easier to lie via the nanny: 'Nicola, I'm going to the office, there's a case file to work on before tomorrow, so I may have to pull an all-nighter.' She giggled as she sat at her white vanity desk in front of her mirror and applied her Christian Dior crimson lipstick, imagining herself pulling an all-nighter with Charlie.

Carefully, Bessie descended the sweeping staircase. It was carpeted in royal blue with a gold border. Sam and Casey were playing in the pool; the garish plastic lilos made the scene look messy.

Bessie paused and gazed at them from the safety of the living room. There was a deviousness about Casey. Marylou was direct in her ingratitude. Marylou had made it plain she couldn't wait to get the hell away. Bessie feared it was because her daughter had seen her parents at their worst during her formative years; the damage to their relationship was irreversible. Sam was her favourite – her only boy. Ah, it gave her a pang, every time she thought about it. But she didn't think about it much.

Casey, leaping off the diving board, caught her eye – the girl stuck out her tongue before bombing into the water.

'Brat,' muttered Bessie, and turned on her heel.

As she zoomed off in her black Range Rover – a conservational booboo, but better that than the un-American act of driving a *small* car – she glimpsed her husband's Mercedes in her rear-view mirror, turning into the road. She turned the corner in a hurry, not that she cared if he'd seen her. She was going to the office, what could he do? He'd landed on his feet; their sumptuous lifestyle was all thanks to her. The trailer-park episode was a dark blot in the past; in her head, she denied it had ever happened.

She had a little electronic device in her purse that activated Charlie's gates. She drove her car straight into the underground garage. She had one of those too, only hers had a remote-controlled turntable that rotated your vehicle so you didn't have to go to the trouble of reversing. She wasn't great at reversing.

Charlie walked into the garage and opened the door for her. She twisted around in her seat, her eyes bright. He didn't even wait for her to exit the car. They slid towards each other, urgent, and ready. It was fast and rough and she squealed with pleasure; she loved the heaviness of him; he was a big man, with carnal appetites.

Afterwards, they sat in his hot tub, giggling and coy. There were rules to their relationship: they met only once a month, when his wife flew to Miami to visit her sister; and there was no inappropriate behaviour at the office. Apart from the fact that a lot of work got done, this drove him crazy. She was partly punishing him for being married. He claimed they slept in separate bedrooms, but early on Bessie had seen the wife's slippers tucked under her side of the bed. But she said not a word to Charlie; by then, she was too far gone.

After the bath, they ate a sumptuous dinner courtesy of a chef from Caesar's: they gulped champagne, and pulled at pink lobster flesh, their fingers greasy with melted butter. Dessert was creamy and sweet, spurting with syrup and melted chocolate. She and Charlie ate with glee but their gluttony was pinched because their eyes were half on each other. They sat at the table, their knees touching, and as they sipped coffee and nibbled at chocolates, his hands wandered.

'Your hair is so shiny,' he sighed. 'And it smells of meadows. Do you know, on the way to work this morning, I saw a woman at the traffic lights and I swear she had tied up her hair in a pair of *panties!*'

Charlie was very appreciative of her, because she made an effort. Sometimes she wanted to tell him the truth. She wanted to show him an old photograph of her in cheap shorts and a torn T-shirt and flip-flops and hair like straw, looking a thousand years old, taken in Angel when she was as poor as a church mouse, and ask him, 'This is what I was. Do you still love me?'

But she was afraid she knew the answer, so she didn't ask. Charlie liked the finer things in life. He was a snob. He had never in his forty-nine years been less than comfortable and cared for and had a limited understanding of those whose lives weren't as smooth and well oiled as his own. Surely all women had for ever, each morning, to locate a suitably decent hair-ribbon and to make themselves pretty for the menfolk?

'You're so *handsome*,' she sighed like a teenager. They made love on the dining-room carpet and then tiptoed up to bed holding hands. She drifted into pleasant doze, relishing the feel of Charlie's arms around her and her own gently buzzing body. She was silly to torture herself with the sadness of the past. Her present was perfect and no one could take that away from her.

The Medici, that same evening, 9 p.m.

Casey

Even before her father became famous in the worst way possible, Casey Edwards had decided it was wiser to bet on the side of the house. It wasn't hard to tell who made all the money. The Medici was crazy beautiful; Dad looked like shit.

And Luke Castillo, who owned the Medici, was, like, *wow*. She stood in reception, clutching her school bag, trying not to stare. He was old, maybe forty or fifty. But he was ice *cool*.

She wished Luke was her dad. He wore a cream suit with a black shirt and he made things happen. His hair was shiny and brown, and he had big brown eyes like a puppy. He was a bit fat, but tanned, and he smelled of perfume, but not too much. He smiled a lot, showing white teeth; she guessed he had a lot to smile about. He wasn't a nice man, but Casey was not interested in nice. Luke was capable, and powerful; that was enough. He wore a big gold watch; it was hard to take her eyes off that watch: it was so bright, the sunshine gleamed off it.

And yet, despite her fascination with Luke, she really did not want to be here. It was nine o'clock at night, on a Wednesday.

She had an English assignment that needed to be handed in the following day. She had to write a story starting with the words: 'I should never have opened the box.'

Her mother was out, at the solicitor's office. There was an important case, Mom had told Nanny Nicola; she would be working all night. When Nicola had passed on the message to Dad, Casey knew immediately from his face – half angry half pleased – that she and he would be sneaking off to the Medici.

Dad had been sneaking off to the Medici, the only casino that would let him play because of his bad credit rating, a couple of times a month for the past year. He took Casey with him because Nicola finished work at eight, and Sam was too self-absorbed to be trusted to look after her. If Mom ever found out, she would go *nuts*. So Casey didn't tell.

Mom was a legal secretary, and it pissed her father off. He didn't think they needed the money. *Her* parents were always giving them money (Casey knew this because her mother said so). And Hank's earnings from his job as a wine merchant were more than enough to comfortably support a family of five (Casey knew this because her father said so). Also, Hank suspected that his wife and the solicitor were hot for each other (Casey knew this because no one said so).

Casey gazed at her spotless white sneakers as Luke gripped her father's hand and kind of shook his shoulder. She couldn't look at her father. She couldn't stand the way he acted around Luke: subservient, hopeful. Perhaps Luke didn't notice.

Luke was polite to her father; he knew that Hank came here to be treated well. It was a big compliment for Luke to come over to a guest: it made other guests think you were an important player. But Casey knew that Luke came over because Hank lost money in the casino. Hank's suits were crumpled and his watch was gold plate. Mom had bought him a nice one but he'd sold it to pay off a debt.

'Hey, sweetheart,' said Luke, turning to Casey with a wink. 'I hope you've brought your swimsuit!'

In what she hoped was a flat voice, Casey replied, 'I've brought my swimsuit, and my homework.'

Luke nodded, as if this wasn't unusual, and pinched her cheek. Her skin burned at his touch. 'What a choochy face! Now, sweetheart, if you need a thing, Nancy will take care of it. Hot dog, burger, French fries, ice cream – you name it, she'll get it. Now go spoil yourself!'

Casey nodded coldly and stalked off towards the pool area. She glanced back, and her heart went *pang* in fright. Luke and her father were talking, but in that quiet, hissing way that adults talked when they were angry. She dropped her bag and tried to listen as she scrabbled for pens and pencils on the marbled floor. She was still close, but the false merriment of the slot machines paying out next to nothing made it hard to hear. It was only because Casey dreaded the key words that she heard them: *loan against . . . house . . . outstanding markers . . . one five . . . jail . . . ruined . . . soon . . . good for you.*

Casey shoved rulers, pens and notebooks into her school bag and ran to the exit; she wanted to unhear every word.

Nancy was her favourite waitress. She was grey-haired and jolly but terrible at math. Casey knew this because the other week, Nancy had paused from handing out blue-and-white-striped towels to help Casey with her homework and Casey had got an F.

Casey walked out of the swing doors and breathed deeply as the heat smacked her in the face. She lay on a deckchair, ignoring the stares from the older clientele (everyone), pulled off her shirt, and closed her eyes. Nancy brought her a glass of chocolate milk. 'There you go, honey, and shall I put into the kitchen to make you a burger, extra pickle?'

'Thank you,' said Casey. 'Yes please.'

Nancy always made sure Casey had enough to eat and drink, because the one time she didn't, Casey had immediately ordered a Coke with two shots of scotch from a new waiter. The guy was cute but a sleaze; he made it plain he expected a favour in return. He murmured in her ear, suggesting they meet on the roof. Casey was horrified and stupidly giggly. Nancy had flounced over narrow-eyed and shucked out the truth. She'd sacked the waiter instantly. To Casey she'd said, 'Honey, if a person gets Mr Castillo in any kind of trouble, that ain't wise.'

It wasn't fair.

No one was allowed to get Luke in trouble, but he was allowed to get her father in trouble. Oh God, oh God, what had he done? What did he owe? She wished it was different, but she knew it never would be: Casey was not a gambler. Twenty dollars was a bunch of money. It bought you magazines, lipstick, Diet Pepsi and gum. She wasn't supposed to know how much her father threw away playing baccarat and craps and hunch 21, but she had a good idea.

She could see it in his face; every time it drooped a little further, in anger, greed, disbelief, fear. Casey could not even process the idea that her dad could blow fifty thousand dollars on a bad night. It was obscene to think it was that much. He might as well go to the bank, have them tip all his money in a sack and then drop the whole wedge of notes down a drain. And now, it seemed that he'd blundered beyond his limits to the point of no return.

As Casey sipped her chocolate milk through a pink straw, she realized that her hands were lightly trembling. She hated losing money, even a cent. To anyone outside the family, the Edwardses appeared wealthy. They were wealthy, like, *today*. Today, they lived in a beautiful white pillared house with six bedrooms and a pool, surrounded by palm trees and landscaped gardens.

But what about tomorrow? Unlike orphan Annie, Casey did not believe the sun would come out tomorrow. Tomorrow terrified her with its awful possibility.

When her big sister Marylou had told her they'd lived in a trailer park for two years, until just after Casey was born, she hadn't believed her.

But her brother, Sam, confirmed it. 'It was cool,' he said, dreamily. 'There was a bunch of trailers all clustered around a diner and a gas station. We just played in the dirt. Some nights, we got tacos and chicken cooked by a truck driver. The TV didn't work out there, but you couldn't have heard it anyway because most nights the Air Force would be testing experimental jets overhead. We'd look up at the sky – it was awesome. You could see every shooting star, and every galaxy.'

'We had nothing,' Marylou had snapped.

'But having nothing made every little thing you did have more special,' said Sam.

'It was shit,' said Marylou. 'Mom couldn't even afford to buy me a dress.'

Sam was a stoner. Casey was more like her sister, not that Casey ever saw her sister these days. Having nothing was her worst fear, and no number of stars or galaxies could make that special.

Casey had never dared ask her parents why they'd lived in a trailer park. Mom and Dad were emotionally brittle people. Casey didn't have to ask: it was obvious.

She knew that when her parents first married, they had lived in a pretty, sprawling house in a smart suburb of the city, with four bedrooms, four bathrooms, a double garage and a pool. Of course they had: her mother would never have married a poor man. But because Hank was a gambler, she had ended up with one.

Casey opened her workbook, shut it again and stood up. 'I'm going to the restroom,' she mouthed to Nancy who, despite being on the other side of the pool, had whipped around the second Casey had risen to her feet. Nancy seemed to sense movement like a battleship's radar.

Casey crept back into the casino. Her father had told her, on pain of death – or at least a beating that would leave her close to it – that she was not allowed in the casino. Fuck him. In her opinion, he wasn't mentally fit to issue orders, and fuck Luke Castillo too. *Good*, if she got Mr Castillo into trouble. He got *her* into trouble by making it impossible for her to finish her homework.

The Medici's high-limit room was merely a raised area, adjacent to the main floor, with more comfortable chairs and a few extra plants. Casey wedged herself between a large plant and the gold railings. She could see her father sitting at a table by himself, beckoning to the dealer. She couldn't see his face, but his feet were at her eye level. He was rubbing one shoe fast against the other; she could hear the faint *squeak, squeak*, and her heart sank.

Just walk away, she willed him, but the wish was futile. He didn't understand how it worked. *She* did, and she was thirteen years old! That money he'd lost was *lost*, as surely as if he'd hurled that sack into Lake

Mead. And yet, he wouldn't stop trying to get it back.

It was impossible to get it back; it was only possible to make new money – by working. But Hank was set on getting back the lost money by winning at baccarat – a house game. He panicked, lost all sense of reality, of probability. He persisted in believing in luck. If he lost tonight, as she knew he would, they could be out of a home.

At least, if you must gamble, she thought, try black-jack; give yourself more of a chance in hell. She watched, heavy with dread, as an ugly waitress dumped a glass of vodka on the table and her father downed it in one angry gulp.

How did she know the tricks instinctively, and he knew nothing? Her father was an ingénu in Vegas. Casey was a native; the grit of the city was in her blood. When Casey was four and Sam was eight, they were being driven down the Strip and he'd pointed at a passing truck; it had a billboard with a life-size photo of a near nude woman plastered over it, plus a number to call. 'She's *naked*,' said Sam. 'Ha ha! I can see her boobies!'

Casey had replied witheringly, 'Of course she's naked, Sam! She's a stripper, it's her *job*!'

Now, in her makeshift spy position, she shivered. It was cold in here. And there were no windows; it could have been twelve noon or midnight. She yawned. The strain of worry was exhausting.

When she opened her eyes, her first emotion was surprise that she had fallen asleep in this uncomfortable crouch. Oh my, what time was it? Two a.m. Crazy.

Her legs felt as if they had solidified and, trying to shift position, she winced. But her head was full of noise – no, it was *outside* – it was right in front of her: Dad, jumping up from the table. His five o'clock shadow could almost be classified as stubble, and it was an unnerving shade of grey. His tie was askew, and his hair stood on end, stiff with grease from his hand raking through it a thousand times.

But the sound coming out of his mouth was pure *joy*.

'Yes! Yes! Fucking yes!'

He was punching the air like a schoolboy, his face screwed up in brutish triumph.

Casey sat up, stunned.

He had *won*. It was incredible. It was unbelievable. He had WON!

The future rushed towards her, rosy-cheeked and full of celebration. She saw her family, her mother and father, their arms around each other, prosperous and blessed, with healthy children and a luxurious home, her father carving the Thanksgiving turkey, praising her mother for cooking such a delicious meal, and Casey, Sam and Marylou, joking and affectionate, instead of distant, drifting, with nothing in common. She would change her name from Casey to Sunshine: Sunshine was the prettiest thing in the world, as precious and sparkling as the gold on Luke Castillo's watch.

In a daze, she watched as Luke's general manager approached: Ted. Ted was her father's host, although he did little more than slap her father on the back every time he showed up. If her father was lucky, the guy would order him some ribs without him having to ask. For some dark reason, her dad seemed nervous of Ted, even though it appeared to be Ted's job to serve *him*.

Ted clapped his hairy hand on Hank's shoulder. It seemed vaguely threatening, or was it merely patriarchal, comforting? Either way, it indicated that the Medici was king, and Hank was the servant, if not the slave.

Here, at least, it was quieter than on the main floor; she could listen better. 'Sure, Hank,' Ted was saying, in his gravelly voice that never varied in tone. 'We'll cut you a cheque for half a mill. You go home, wave it around; show the little woman you won big. But after you show her, you better come right back here and pay it back: *two million*, Hank, *two million*. That's a chunk of change to owe, and Mr Castillo, he gets impatient.'

Casey felt the jubilation leave her body in a rush. She slumped to the ground. She didn't cry. She had never seen the point. She felt that crying was a weird alien mechanism within the human body which you chose to access. *One and a half million*. Her knees felt liquid at the thought.

But at least her father would keep his fists to himself tonight.

She stood up and walked towards him. Hank nodded, dazed, as if she were an acquaintance he'd met maybe twice. The valet called a cab and they rode home at speed.

Her father was still drunk. He flapped the cheque in her face, slurring, 'Five hundred big ones, that ain't luck, that's skill!'

Casey returned the faintest of nods, and stared out of the window at the night sky. She guessed she'd better start looking for galaxies and shooting stars.

Charlie's house; 11 September 1997, early morning

Bessie

Bessie awoke, confused. There was a sharp, discordant *crack*; a rock hitting glass. And there was shouting, harsh and abrasive. Even before her woozy brain deciphered the identity of the voice, her instinct had nailed it. She clung to Charlie, who shrugged angrily from her grasp and ran to the window, cursing.

She pulled on the peach silk robe, this month's gift, and scurried, tripping over her discarded shoes in the dark, to the window. She cowered behind the curtains as her husband's loud, brutal roar tore into the night.

'I know you're in there, slut,' screamed Hank as he hurled another stone at the window.

'Oh my *God*,' she whispered. 'Oh my *God*, how does he know, how did he find out?' Her heart hammered with terror, but rage soon overcame everything. How *dare* he, after all she'd done for him?

Charlie opened the window and calmly told Hank to go away. 'You have disturbed me, my neighbours and my wife,' he said in his smooth, authoritative tone. 'You have also cracked my window. Not only are your allegations wild and false, you are drunk and should not be driving. Do you have a child in the car? If I were to take this further, and call the police, as far as criminal charges go, they would be spoilt for choice.'

Bessie let his words wash over her. She lifted the tiniest corner of the curtain and peeked out. Hank had

Casey in the passenger seat; the kid was wearing head-phones and was, no doubt, listening to Madonna at ear-damaging volume on her Sony Walkman. Shit, what the hell time was it? Bessie glanced at the bedside clock: 3.40 a.m.!

She closed her eyes. What a nightmare. She had been careless, she knew it; too smug. Of course Hank knew she was sleeping with Charlie. She squeezed his name into conversation. Lately, she'd stopped showering after their liaisons because she liked the scent of him on her skin. It was a way of showing Hank she loathed him without wasting words. But surely now, with Charlie so imperious and unruffled, Hank would slink away. The following day, they would all act as if it was a dream.

'Come out, slut!' screeched Hank as she cringed behind the curtains. 'I know you're in there, and there's something else I know. This kid ain't mine!'

Bessie felt her entire body clinch in a spasm of horror and the realization hit her: how could she have been so rash and so stupid? Only now did she understand the possible consequences of her carelessness. She was a fool, she had goaded Hank into his terrible suspicion.

'Be quiet and go home,' called Charlie in a low, tense growl, but Hank was out of control.

'I'm going to get me a fucking paternity test, I'm going to get her spit and my spit tested in a lab, and when it comes up as "no match" I'm going to sue your fucking ass for mental cruelty and the fucking house!'

Bessie's head swam; she felt dizzy and ill. She grasped at the curtain and the room turned black.

She woke minutes later with a gasp. Someone had thrown a glass of icy water in her face!

She stared, confused, at Charlie. His face was like thunder. He had thrown water at her, as if she were a fighting dog!

'I'm sorry,' she stammered. 'I have low blood pressure. If I'm in a stressful situation, I black out sometimes.' She stumbled to her feet, staggering towards the window.

'I persuaded your husband to return home,' said Charlie.

She couldn't meet his eyes. He sat on the bed, his head in his hands. He was rigid with anger.

Paradise was lost.

She couldn't believe what her husband had destroyed. Silently, in quiet mortification, she dressed. Then she sat at the kitchen table and stared out of the window at the emerging dawn. Charlie stayed upstairs. At 7 a.m., she quietly let herself out and drove to her health and fitness spa. She sat in the juice bar until 10 a.m., pretending to read the newspapers, half choking on her cappuccino. Then she called the nanny, to check that Hank had left for work.

She called in sick – hey, Charlie would understand – returned to her beautiful home, her only consolation in life, and ran upstairs to bed. She rattled through her closet and pulled out a vodka bottle. She ripped off the stopper and drank from the neck. She was in a state of shock. She burst out in a fit of crying, and then abruptly the tears dried and she spat and cursed. What would she *do*?

She glanced at the cupboard above the plasma screen.

It appeared to contain only shoes, therefore there was no reason that Hank would ever dig through it. But behind the shoes was a locked safe with a combination. Inside that safe was a phone number. She was to call it only in an emergency. Bessie was certain that that emergency was *now*. She was about to reach for the phone when there was a timid knock on the bedroom door. Bessie sniffed and wiped her eyes. 'Yes, what is it?'

'A call for you, Mrs Edwards. It's the school.'

Bessie rolled her eyes. The school overestimated her interest in the minutiae of her children's education. It was *their* job! But the headmistress was a force like a tornado.

Bessie took the call and tried not to slur her words. 'Good morning . . . Yes . . . Oh dear, that's terrible! I'm sorry. Casey is usually very diligent about her assignments. I've probably been unable to commit to the time. Casey's nanny should have . . . An important case, so her father . . . Asleep in class! I suppose men don't quite understand the importance of a reasonable bedtime. It won't happen again. I'll have a . . . *Pardon?* She said *what?* . . . I'm astonished. I mean, without getting into personal details, my husband sought assistance from Problem Gambling. He hasn't set foot in a casino for . . . I don't mean to malign Casey, but she is thirteen. It's not always an age that can be relied on . . . She was specific? . . . The *Medici*! Well, I intend to check. If you don't mind, today isn't that convenient, perhaps some time next week? Meanwhile, I will certainly have words with my husband, but please rest assured, I cannot imagine that he would . . . It would contravene the terms of . . .

Well, thank you for the call, I appreciate it, goodbye.'

Bessie found she was shaking. She had to get a grip. She needed to think clearly. The call to the emergency number would wait for a few minutes. First, she needed to secure her home. She took a deep breath, and called the operator. 'VIP hosting at the Medici, please.'

'I'd like to speak to whichever of you thieving bastards looks after Hank Edwards, please. This is his wife. Yes, I believe he owes you money which I am in a position to pay.'

It wasn't strictly true, and the owing money part was a guess, but if she knew Hank, he was in the shit up to his scrawny neck. Also, if anything would make those lying schmucks rat out her husband, it was the promise that his debts could be paid. Hank was a loser, and he always would be. If he was gambling, he was losing, and she only needed to know how much. She had lost Charlie, she had lost the love of her children; she would lose her house again over Hank's dead body.

An upscale suburb in Las Vegas, nine days later, 20 September 1997

Sandra

'Oh my *God*, Larry, it's Bessie and Hank in the *Review*, the front page, take a look at this! Oh my God!

'"MEXICO CITY, AP. In a gruesome sign of the

mounting drug-related violence, a Las Vegas resident has been found murdered in an upmarket suburb in the south of the capital.

' "Police found Hank Edwards's mutilated body dumped in the road by a bus stop in the usually peaceful neighbourhood of San Ángel on Sunday at 3.17 a.m."

'Good Lord! Hank! Mutilated!

' "Mr Edwards, 45, a wine merchant who sold alcohol to casinos, was shot in the back of the head. He was attacked with an axe post mortem."

'They've not really included the details.

' "He was married with three children. A local official told AP on condition of anonymity that Mr Edwards was suspected of distributing narcotics for a notorious drug cartel."

'I said there was something fishy about him.

' "Mexican drug cartels are responsible for" – boring boring boring – "These cartels are reported to employ" – boring. OK, here we go – "According to a police officer who did not wish to be named, Mr Edwards may have been used because his day job provided convenient cover."

'Well of *course*, it all makes sense. Larry, we were harbouring a *serious criminal*. He could have killed us in our beds!

' "Officer Alfredo García of the Agencia Federal de Investigación told AP, 'We believe Mr Edwards owed a lot of money to several Las Vegas casinos and was in danger of losing his home. It may be that Mr Edwards attempted to short change the drug cartel to raise money to pay off his losses. His brutal death may have been a tragic consequence.' "

'He was a criminal and an idiot!

' "Mr Edwards, who lived in a 2.5-million-dollar, six-bedroom house in a gated community in the north of the City . . ."

'What! How? Well that proves he must have been a crook. There is no *way* they could afford a house like that. Fourteen, fifteen years ago they were penniless!

' ". . . leaves a widow, Bessie."

'I never liked her.

' "She told AP, 'I cannot believe that people are accusing Hank of these horrible things. It disgusts me. He may have gambled a little, yes . . .' "

'Enough to lose his whole house! They should have interviewed *me*!

' " . . . but I have an independent income.' "

'Excuse me, *what*? Is she talking about being a secretary? You know, maybe her parents died, they had money.

' "Hank does not owe anyone a cent, and I challenge a single casino representative to come forward and claim otherwise.' "

'Well, we'll see won't we?

' "Meanwhile, I will consider suing any person or organization making false and defamatory claims against my late husband.' "

'Oh my God, Larry! Should we send flowers? I'd love to see the house. I can't believe Bessie Edwards is living in a two-point-five-million-dollar house! She has no sense of style – any wealth is wasted on her. Oh my God, so who do you think actually killed Hank? Do you think it was drugs or do you think Castillo was behind it? He keeps his nose clean, but we all know his money is *their* money – although aren't the Mob supposed to stay out of drugs? Larry, what do—? Larry, are you listening? Oh for God's sake, *LARRY*! Wake up!'

BOOK 3

Turtle Egg Island, the day of the engagement party, 31 August 2009

Sofia

Sofia felt panic rise within her as if her lungs were filling with blood.

How could this be?

Bessie was Sunshine's *mother*.

The implications were horrible. Her head felt thick with stupidity. The reality was such a shock that she was slow to process the facts. She wasted precious seconds, stumbling, wondering how Bessie had escaped from the nuthouse, how it could be that she, Sofia, hadn't realized who Sunshine was, hadn't seen the obvious links. Well, it wasn't all her fault. The girl had lied. She had given herself a breezy Vegas name; she had constructed herself a new glamorous identity, and she had said her father had dropped dead of a heart attack. Whereas everyone knew how Hank Edwards had died. If Sunshine had been truthful, instead of coy, this disaster could have been prevented.

Sofia's determination not to lose this fight remained.

But for the life of her, she couldn't see what she could possibly do to stop Bessie now.

How careful she had been – Ariel and Ben had been educated outside the City and Ben had rarely appeared in a newspaper – but she had not been careful enough. She had watched Bessie for the first ten years, but then grown complacent. Her mistake had been to take care of every problem as it arose, instead of before. Dr Erich had failed her. It was hardly a surprise that the immoral were untrustworthy.

Ben kissed Sunshine's mother on the cheek and Sofia felt the blood drain to her feet.

It took all Sofia's will not to wrench the woman away from her son and hurl her to the ground. Bessie had wormed her way into the heart of Sofia's family, to the core of all she held precious. Any moment, the woman could open her mouth, and Sofia would lose all she had.

'Welcome to the family,' cried Ben. He'd changed and was wearing blue surf shorts and a white T-shirt. His feet were dusted in sand.

Earlier that morning, Ben had approached her and Frank and told them about his plans to quit and set up alone. In a flash of honesty, she'd said to him: 'I hate it, but I can't stop you.' Her hurt at his betrayal remained, but her disappointment had been blunted by Frank's chief accountant pulling up some figures. The CEO of the Las Vegas Shores Corp., had lost sixteen *billion*. Now was not the time to expand. Perhaps Ben had even done her a favour.

It felt irrelevant in the light of Bessie's appearance. And it was Sunshine's fault. Sofia felt weak with rage.

Even as it sank in that Sunshine was her own flesh and blood, Sofia couldn't look at Sunshine for hating her.

Sofia watched, dumbly, as Lily Fairweather – ah yes, the sly reversion to the maiden name, the different abbreviation of Elizabeth – returned Ben's kiss.

Oh Ben, she loved him so much. She felt sick with love, looking at him. She couldn't lose him to Sunshine, and she sure as hell couldn't lose him to Bessie. She had a plan for crushing Ben's relationship with Sunshine, but she didn't have a clue what to do about Bessie.

Ben drew away, still smiling.

Sofia's blood roared loud in her ears.

The woman breathed in sharply. She placed one hand on his arm; her grip tightened. Oh God, if she said it now? Sofia had no choice. It would be terrible, inexplicable, to attack this woman. She had no idea where it would end, but if she did nothing she knew exactly where it would end – and that was worse.

As Frank, Sunshine and Ben stood politely, Sofia stepped grimly forward. She was about to raise her arm.

'I feel odd,' gasped Lily.

Sofia froze.

Lily's eyes rolled and she staggered.

'Mom,' said Sunshine a trifle sharply. 'Is it your blood pressure? Do you need to lie down?'

Lily opened her mouth to speak, and promptly collapsed. Her body crumpled like paper and her head hit the concrete. Her Chanel shades flew off her face and snapped.

Sofia could barely stop the smile spreading across her

face. In this most hideous swill of circumstance, here was a shred of good fortune at last.

Sunshine dropped to her knees. 'She's blacked out. It's her blood pressure – but I think she's hit her head. Call someone!'

Ben dialled emergency services. Sofia watched, wiping cold sweat from her forehead. The woman was trying to present as tough, but she was weak. At the most crucial moment, when Bessie planned to break her silence, she had become so overwrought she had *fainted*.

Bessie groaned. She made a choking sound. Sofia turned away as the woman vomited.

'Keep calm, Sunshine,' said Sofia. 'The chances are she'll be fine. She'll be confused and talking nonsense – a crack on the head will do that to you. I'm sure it's OK to move her.' She gestured to Sterling, who she could see was as pale and shocked as she was. 'She needs to be in the shade. The air ambulance will be here in minutes. I can't imagine she'll be hospitalized for more than a few days. It's so unfortunate. It would have been wonderful to spend some time together.'

Sofia felt like a robot trying to impersonate a human being. It was only a shame that convention forced them to call a doctor. If only she could have sent the woman to bed and found her happily dead the following morning from a brain haemorrhage.

Ben turned Bessie carefully on her side, and then pulled Sunshine close. 'Are you all right, babe?'

She nodded.

Sofia smiled. I'm going to ruin your life, my dear, she thought, and I am going to do it today.

Her composure was nearly regained, but she couldn't stop herself from babbling in spite and relief. 'Dear Lily probably hadn't recovered from making the emergency landing in the storm – and on a private jet, one does experience every little bump. And I'm sure it's intimidating to meet a family like ours. It's startling, if one is not used to the life. Wealth, power, success does frighten, if one is living a . . . small, ordinary sort of existence.'

This speech earned her a glare from Ben and a roll of the eye from Frank, who patted Sunshine's shoulder and said, 'They're taking her to St Christopher's. It's a private hospital and the staff are excellent. They know us. She'll be in good hands.'

'Thank you,' said Sunshine. She gestured around the little airfield, to the gauzy blue sky and the coconut trees that framed it. 'Look, please attend to your guests. There's no point us all waiting.'

'It's true,' said Ben. 'Dad, you should go.'

'I suppose you're right,' said Frank. He kissed Sunshine on the cheek. 'I'm sorry, sugar.'

The whirr of a helicopter tickled their ears, and Ben sighed.

'I'll go with her,' said Sofia suddenly. In a hospital, anything could happen.

Lily moaned again, her eyes hazy and unfocused, and Sunshine glanced at her in alarm. 'I'll go,' she said.

Sofia felt her pulse race. But then, Bessie had had all the time in the world to tell Sunshine the truth, and she never had.

'I'll go with you,' said Ben.

'Of *course* you won't!' cried Sunshine as Sofia bit her tongue. 'One of us has to stay!'

Ben raked a hand through his hair. 'Fine, but call me,' he said, and kissed her. The medics placed an oxygen mask over Lily's face, and lifted her on to a stretcher. Sofia sighed.

But it was a temporary relief. Nothing was certain. Sofia had to *make* it certain.

Turtle Egg Island, later that day

Ben

His parents had reacted with astonishing calm to the news of his Macau plans, which led him to believe that they had already known. It made Ben wonder what tricks his mother had up her glitzy designer sleeve, God help him. Sofia did not abandon her dreams that easily.

He must try to enjoy the party. His parents had gone to so much effort to organize a spectacular celebration, they deserved for it to be a success, despite the missing bride-to-be. Actually, Ben suspected that his mother wasn't *that* distraught by the bride-to-be being missing; in an ideal world, this would be her perfect situation: no bride, and Ben in a basket at the end of Sofia's bed.

He wandered on to the beach. It was beautiful, but he couldn't wait to leave. Sunshine had been irritable and fussy for weeks, bothering him about the style of his tie, and the other day he'd actually caught her checking his phone. She'd claimed it had rung; an obvious, checkable lie. Afterwards, he had brooded about it, thinking, *Do I even know you?* But it was normal for men to have cold feet before a wedding, just as it was normal for women to briefly mutate into psychopaths.

All the same, it wasn't a great start: the mother-in-law cracking her head on arrival. He sighed. The woman was odd. She hadn't looked *at* him; she'd looked right inside him. He didn't like her at all. It was creepy. She made him feel like prey.

He shook hands, accepted congratulations. Beautiful girls in butterfly-coloured baby-doll dresses kicked off their designer shoes into the crystal sand and skipped into the turquoise lagoon, until the warm shallow water surrounding the island was bright with glistening tanned bodies and the sparkle of diamond accessories gleaming in the sun.

He had the abrupt thought that he would like to be at Lulu's apartment, splayed on her soft old sofa, drinking kick-ass red wine and French onion soup (her recipe), watching *30 Rock* and talking shit. Only they didn't talk shit. She told him little things about Baby Joe, such as when she stubbed her toe on the door and cried, and he put his little chubby arms around her and said, 'You all right, Mommy? Are you OK?'

Ben had felt quite choked. 'You're *so* important,' he'd said in wonder, and she'd laughed.

Sometimes Ben amused himself by counting how many friends he'd keep if he suddenly lost all his money. Lulu topped that rather short list. When they were together, laughing and talking, he felt an overwhelming sense of wellbeing; they had a deep, real, honest connection. She was about the only person in his life who didn't want anything from him beyond companionship. It made him feel good about himself in a way that all the razzmatazz never did.

Where was she today? He wondered if she'd heard about the accident. Ben tipped his shades over his eyes and watched a tiny spider crab scuttle over the smooth crystal sand. Pale pink flowers lined the edge of the beach; the DJ's music was disco fabulous; sounds of the eighties – his mother's favourite decade – blared out with poppy optimism.

He shook his head as a statuesque waitress in a white-tasselled bustier and hot pants bent low to offer him a trio of Kumamoto oysters. He refused caviar with smoked salmon and yellowtail sashimi; he turned down the salt-crusted snapper and the black truffle creamed spinach. The French cheeses with fresh figs and candied walnuts were wafted under his nose and he stifled a shudder. Another willowy blonde approached with a tray of flourless chocolate cake and vanilla marshmallow; that stuff was usually irresistible but it made him heave. Perhaps he was allergic to being affianced.

He felt bad, quitting the glorious heat, the exquisite blue skies, the delicious scent of the light salty breeze, his friends – the few he trusted. He placed his untouched glass of champagne on a tray and walked to the villa, trying to smile as the laughter, joyful and carefree, celebrating the rest of his life, wishing him happiness, rang in his ears. He felt as if he were being boxed up, like a gift; the sense of it made him gasp for air. As he walked, he turned, and saw his mother staring at him; it was as if he was still ten years old.

Ben knew she couldn't understand why he wanted to be independent from the family firm. To her, he was living the dream – he was living *her* dream. Sofia would have loved to have been born into wealth. Throughout his childhood, if ever he had been less than happy, she had screamed, 'You don't know how *lucky* you are. At your age, I had NOTHING!'

To Sofia, Ben had nothing to run from, no reason to go.

He willed her not to follow him. He took the private lift to the subterranean pool level and spa, pressing the entrance code – known only to Sofia, Frank, Ariel, and himself – and pulled off his T-shirt, grabbed a pair of swimming shorts from the wardrobe, and dived into the cool water.

He swam lengths, fast and furious, without stopping. When he heaved himself on to the side, panting hard, he found himself gazing at an elegant pair of feet, encased in gold stack-heeled mules. He looked up to see a tall, slender goddess of a woman regarding him loftily; she had long dark auburn tumbling curls and dark eyes, and wore a flouncy dark scarlet halter-neck evening dress, the edges of which were thickly encrusted with rubies, rose quartz, pink sapphires. It clung to her remarkable figure.

She was very . . . *Lulu*?

She sighed, and said, 'I *was* waiting for an invitation,' and peeled off her dress.

Underneath she wore the tiniest white bikini. Wow.

He frowned. He actually couldn't believe it. He stared. She blushed.

'I got my hair done. Sofia gave me a wardrobe allowance.'

He shook his head. 'You look . . . cool,' he said.

She laughed. 'I was hot, actually. Your mother suggested I come down.'

'Right,' he said. He tried not to look at her. Lulu was sweet. He thought of her as a sister . . . he'd presumed he thought of her as a sister. And you did not think about your sister like *this*. This was not a case of changing into a pretty dress. This was a major overhaul. She was still Lulu; he just hadn't realized that Lulu was . . . *this*. And he didn't know why. Maybe she had always presented herself as off limits, assuming he felt the same. She had never given him a hint of liking him, not in that way. He knew she liked him as a friend, not a . . . *lover*. Not to mention that she was employed by him. He didn't think she wanted a big leery man slavering all over her; she wanted a knight, a prince, a chivalrous gentleman, who respected her and Baby Joe. And anyway, sex got in the way of friendship; it never enhanced it, no matter what people said. Their connection was far too precious to him to mess up with sex. Oh yeah, and he was engaged, that little thing. It was one of the only times he'd argued with Sunshine; she'd been snippy about him going round to Lulu's place to fix a cupboard. 'Can't she get a man to do it?' Yes, he'd replied, she can, *this* man. 'You know she's got a thing about you,' Sunshine had sneered, 'you're her route to easy street.' It was the only time that Ben had ever considered his fiancée unattractive.

'Come in then,' he said. He flicked a little water at her. She giggled.

Ben watched as Lulu slid into the water. He was transfixed; he felt like a mouse staring at a cat slinking towards him. She tilted her head back against the pale stone and nodded towards the open shower that rained prettily down from the arced ceiling into the Jacuzzi bath.

'Do you want to shower?' she murmured.

He couldn't believe it. Lulu had never looked at him in that way. And now she was looking at him in that way, giving him permission to . . .

'No,' he said tersely. Then, kinder: 'No thanks, Lu.'

'Are you sure?' she replied. Suddenly she had hooked her arm round his neck. She pressed herself up against him. 'Because, you know' – she blushed again – 'you look kind of dirty.'

Ben laughed, more from shock than amusement. He lifted her off him, and out of the water, and sat her on the side like a small child.

'Lu,' he said. 'It's me. And today is my engagement party. What are you *doing*?'

All the gloss and bluster left her and she hung her head. 'Well,' she said. 'Oh God. I'm sorry. Sof— It was stupid.' She pressed her lips together and then blurted: 'I'm mad about you, Ben. I just am, and I can't help it. I've tried to, you know, hunt for other men. But I just don't like any other men. I'm sorry.' A tear ran down her cheek. She grabbed a towel and wrapped it around herself.

'Hey, Lulu, don't cry.' He stroked her hair out of her

face and lifted her chin. He gazed into her dark eyes. 'Now I have a disturbing picture in my head, of you hunting for men.'

She stared at him, half laughing, even as her eyes spilled over with tears. Slowly, time wound down as he pulled her towards him. Her towel fell away, and he closed his eyes for a second as she tilted her face to be kissed. His lips touched hers, so soft, then firm, and he felt a bolt of desire rip through his body so strong that it stunned him, and he grasped her to him, hard, and—

Your mother suggested I come down.

He pulled back just as Lulu leaned forward into the kiss. She lost her balance and fell with a shout into the water. She gasped, thrashing about. 'My hair!' she wailed. 'It's ruined!'

Ben grabbed her and hauled her out. He felt guilty and irritated. Did she love him? *No!* Sofia had sent her. His own mother was trying to get him to cheat on his fiancée at his own engagement party! He knew that Sunshine was too much for Sofia: two alpha females, battling like stags over . . . *him*. But he felt sick with disappointment that Lulu could be persuaded to *this*.

'Your routine needs finesse, Lulu,' he said coldly. 'Right now, it's a little coarse.'

He jumped out of the water, flung a towel at her and walked into the changing rooms. He yanked off his swimming shorts and hopped back into his surf shorts, nearly ripping them.

How dare Lulu allow herself to be used by Sofia? He was angry with himself: that he had been tempted, that he couldn't resist. Sofia was clever. She hadn't sent one of

314

the Beautiful Women of America. She had sent Lulu. He was angry, he realized, because his head was a mess. He was about to marry Sunshine; Sunshine was everything he should want and need. Sunshine was the woman that all the men were in awe of. It was astounding that he was . . . shaking. It wasn't entirely rage; it was shock, from the intensity, the compressed passion of that brief kiss.

Sunshine did not make him feel like that. She was an enthusiastic but selfish lover. You half felt that after sex she might devour you like a female spider.

He crushed the treacherous thought, but it was too late. He had given it headroom. He felt sick.

He marched back to his wing of the villa.

The aggravation had burnt him out. He fell on to his bed and was asleep in minutes. When he woke, it was 3 a.m. and strangely quiet. The guests were housed elsewhere on the island in the pretty beach villas, but most of them would still be partying, yet he could hear nothing. The walls were soundproofed; he was in a luxurious open-plan cell. Ben stood up and rubbed his eyes, the unpleasant events of earlier coming back to him like a bad taste in his mouth.

The main villa was designed in the shape of a seashell; his suite was on the outermost curl, light and airy, with the ceiling open to the stars and a sweeping view of the dark ocean, edged with a frill of white lace.

It was a paradise, and a prison. Ben opened a window. It might help to hear the sound of the ocean. He listened for a moment. The hiss and rush of the sea was interchangeable with the roar of the freeway. Then he heard a rustle outside in the foliage. Ben froze. 'Who's there?' he said.

Of course, there was no answer. He closed the window and stood, silent, peering through the shutters. Noiselessly, a figure slipped from the shadows and vanished into the night. The adrenalin pumped. It wasn't a guard, it wasn't a guest – it must be a spy. A photographer. Sofia had organized today's media coverage, just as she had organized everything else. Presumably, the paparazzo had been sent to catch Ben being unfaithful with his secretary.

He needed to get away from Turtle Egg Island, from the temptation of Lulu and the menace of Sofia. As for Frank . . . Ben just felt guilt, as if he were leaving a puppy on the side of the road. Frank was rarely in control of his own feelings, let alone anyone else's, and that made him emotionally weak.

Ben and his father would always have a special bond. On his sixteenth birthday, his father's media chief had put together a movie of his life so far. There Ben was, on grainy video footage, aged two. Frank was lying on a sofa, and Ben was snuggled like a fat little koala on his stomach. His father was gleefully plastering Ben with kisses: 'We're having romance!' he cried, as Ben squealed and giggled and shouted, 'Stop lat!'

His mother was different. Her love for him was both passionate and cold. She was not affectionate, but he felt her intense preoccupation with him. She had always watched him closely – understandable, considering his family's enemies in Vegas – and yet her obsession with his safety and every detail of

316

his every day was as much about her as about him.

Frank, ultimately, would put his personal sadness aside and take delight in his son's fulfilment of a dream. Sofia regarded Ben as *hers*. This was revealed in the depth of her outrage at his resignation; of course she had already known, and that was why she had tried to destroy his relationship with Sunshine.

Ah, Sunshine. He felt lousy with guilt. He needed to see her and be absolved. He pulled his phone out of his shorts pocket. As he did so, a small square of paper fell out. He picked it up. It was a photograph, old and the colours were faded. He peered at it. Who was it . . . ? It was hard to tell. To him, babies all looked the same. He had no idea how it had got there. Was it of Ariel?

His heart ached at the thought of his sister. Her self-imposed estrangement felt wrong and distressing. He had tried to call her but she always turned off her phone. She had spoken only once to the press, declared that 'the family had made a mistake' and that 'they would be sorry', lumping all of them together as the enemy.

Ben didn't believe that she was plotting a great revenge; it was just talk. Ariel was gentle; she was hurt, and lashing out. He missed her.

He held the photo in his fingertips, and stared at it. Someone must have put it there. Sofia? Lily? She had grabbed at him as she fell. Was it a photo of Sunshine? He couldn't tell if it was a boy or a girl. Well. Something was odd. He remembered Sofia – he was sure that she had lurched forward a second *before* Lily had crumpled to the ground.

Sighing, he shoved the photo back in his pocket and

pulled on his shoes. His behaviour had been wrong, and he needed to see his girl and make it right.

St Christopher's Hospital, late night 31 August – early morning 1 September 2009

Sunshine

It was impossible to get comfortable in a hospital chair. Sunshine glanced at her mother, sleeping peacefully in her soft bed.

Bessie had certainly done a number on herself. Presumably some rich boyfriend had paid for her to spend a few months in an exclusive spa. Her cheekbones were pronounced and her forehead was wrinkle-free. Bessie had a way of taking over any social situation, and while a fainting fit caused by low blood pressure was involuntary, Sunshine blamed Bessie.

This was *her* special day and her mother had spoilt it. Sunshine should have been the centre of attention. Occasionally, Sunshine felt guilty that she only saw her mother every few years. But every time they met, she was reminded of *why* their reunions were so rare. The woman was a pain.

Instead of cavorting on the beach amid tiny pink shells scattered like jewels in the white sand, the warm water lapping at her toes, sipping a Bacardi, accepting congratulations and flirting with the rich handsome man she was going to marry, she was stuck in a small cold room that smelled of air freshener and bleach, with her tiresome mother hogging all the oxygen.

The fact was, Bessie – Sunshine refused to call her Lily – was deeply asleep, pumped full of medication. Sunshine's presence was a formality, if not an inconvenience. When Bessie awoke the following morning, her prime concern would be getting back to the island fast, to take advantage of her new connections and to impose the full extent of her personality upon the other guests. A slight concussion would not slow her down.

Ben was about to jet to Macau for further meetings. She'd known that Arnold Ping would be charmed by him. What was not to like? Ben was humble, smart, wise and *good*. And he was brilliant in this business, yet never complacent. He worked hard; he never stopped trying.

Sunshine had been propositioned by high rollers more times than she could count (thirty-two, actually), but she'd shunned them all because she liked to consort with the biggest boys. Luke had been her first crush; she'd always had an eye for the guy who owned the joint. Never Frank; he was too soft, as soft as butter. But Ben was destined to rule. She shuddered at the idea that he would reject his inheritance, but further down the line, she'd get him to change his mind. Their first kid would be good leverage.

She stood up. 'Mother,' she said. 'We never liked each other, did we? Why the hell did you come?'

She sashayed out of the room and took the lift to the penthouse. She would stay the night and check in with Bessie the next day. If her condition had improved,

Sunshine would return to Turtle Egg and whip Ben away from his nutcase mother and the bitch secretary.

Sunshine was successful, special, stunning, and yet this poor little mouse was a threat. Lulu, with her silly dog's name, was a typist who took home a nominal salary, who lived in a tiny little apartment at a nowhere address, who had been stupid enough to have a kid without hanging on to a man, and yet she was *irrepressible*.

Weeks earlier, Ben had told her about playing soccer with the secretary's kid. The girl's nickname for the kid was 'Fat Sue'.

'I thought it was a boy,' said Sunshine sharply.

'Yes,' Ben had replied, and she'd detected impatience in his tone. 'Joe. His name is Joe, but he's so plump and beautiful, he *is* Fat Sue.'

Sunshine had immediately seen that Lulu had a thing for Ben and that Ben had a thing for Lulu and didn't yet know it. Sunshine knew it and hated her. Call it a woman's instinct for danger. The second that Sunshine became Mrs Arlington, that bitch secretary was going to be out on her ear.

Sunshine tapped her staggeringly high stiletto heel on the polished antique oak floor of the penthouse. Tall kick-ass shoes were her trademark; they gave her no trouble because she was toned. Only fat, lazy women who didn't exercise and had a weak core got back pain from heels. To her, a six-inch heel was like walking in slippers!

She flared her nostrils and surveyed the room. The floors, whitewashed walls, vases of fresh white flowers and sandstone bathroom gave it the feel of a gorgeous apartment. The hospital was on the seafront, and Sunshine had a panoramic view of the other, smaller islands dotted about them. It was as if she were on the upper deck of a yacht.

But Sunshine was unimpressed; she had expected to be staying the night with Ben. Sulkily, she unzipped her sundress. Underneath she was wearing a bikini; it was hot pink. And now it was *wasted*!

There was a knock. It was four in the morning. These doctors didn't leave you alone. This better be serious. She yanked open the door.

'Oh—'

Ben swept her up, silencing her shriek of delight with a kiss.

She wrapped her legs around him and pushed at the waistband of his shorts with the heel of her shoe. She was frantic to re-establish ownership, but she could sense, immediately, that something wasn't right.

'What's wrong, Ben?'

'Nothing . . . I wanted to see you.'

He smelled of sand, of the sea breeze, sweat and salt. 'Why?' she said. 'Did something happen?' She felt the anger of suspicion drag the muscles in her face downward.

Ben raked his hands through his hair. 'Jesus. Don't look at me like that. Nothing happened. You're stuck here in this hospital. I wanted to check you were OK.'

'That's great,' she said. She couldn't help the whiny tone of her voice. 'But why not just call? Or wait till morning? And seeing as you are here now, why don't you want to fuck me?' She saw his face. The expression was almost a wince. What? He was prudish all of a sudden? 'What's going on, Ben? You're acting totally weird.'

'What? Because I've just walked in after a stressful day and I don't feel like ripping off your clothes?'

'Newsflash, darling. *All* men feel like ripping off my clothes.'

'Well,' he said, more coldly than she'd ever heard him sound before, 'I'm here, and you're here and yet . . . I couldn't feel *less* like ripping off your clothes. So work that one out.'

The unfriendliness of his words made her feel ugly inside, as if he were looking into her heart and despising what he saw. As if the spell of attraction was broken. It was horrible; she was instantly wretched. She could never bear being judged for what lay within. It was one of the perks of being beautiful. It deflected from your personality flaws.

'I can't believe you said that,' she blurted. 'I'm irresistible and you know it.'

Twelve years earlier, Sunshine Beam – or Casey Edwards as she was then – had found the scrutiny that came with sudden notoriety disturbing and invasive. She had always intended to change her name – she couldn't wait to formally detach herself from her parents – but the additional horror of her father's murder had given her more reason to bury Casey Edwards and regenerate as Sunshine Beam.

She guessed her mother had turned into a near recluse, squirrelled away God only knew where, for identical reasons. She no longer saw her brother or sister. Marylou was a tight-assed lawyer in New York, and Sam lived on a commune in the Midwest. She had nothing in common with either except bad memories.

'And yet,' said Ben coolly, 'here we are.'

Sunshine had wanted a new start with Ben, and now it was all going wrong. Her stupid mother had ruined it. He was off to Macau for a week, and in Vegas, Fight Night was coming up. She had two high rollers being picked up in the Gulfstream, and one flying in on a Lear Jet. One of them was Trey Millington. He hadn't got her into bed yet, though not for want of trying. Well, this time, he just might succeed.

She disguised her restlessness as energy, but the truth was she was constantly searching for something unknown. Despite all she had achieved, she was not content, and her hope was that out there was someone who could fulfil her. She'd thought Ben was that someone. Money and power were a prerequisite of course, and Ben had both, but he was also gorgeous and very desirable. All the same, she could take her pick – didn't he know that?

'How's your mother?' he said, clipped and formal.

She shrugged. 'The doctors will tell me if she gets worse.'

'What?' he said. 'You haven't checked?'

'Yes, I checked earlier. Jesus. Why don't *you* check?'

He gave her a look. 'I just might.' He paused. 'You're not big on family, are you, Sunshine? Are you sure you even want this . . . *us*?'

Her heart was bursting with rage and fear. How dare he pull that one on her? Something had changed, but why . . . and how? Oh my God, it was a woman. 'Who was it?' she hissed. 'Who was it? You've done something, haven't you? Don't pin this on me!'

'What are you talking about?'

She knew. She could see it in his eyes. She wagged a finger at him. 'Three words, Ben: shame on you!'

There had to be evidence: a little text on his phone, or a love note in his pocket. Men, they were all the same, they had to have a trophy. She flew at him and started rifling through his pockets.

'Sunshine, get off me!'

He pushed her away, but not before she had extracted a scrap of paper from his pocket. She narrowed her eyes. It was a photograph – of him, as a newborn. He was crinkly and covered in that white waxy stuff, but it was unmistakably his face.

'Who gave you this?' she shouted, feeling foolish that it was not incriminating. 'Where did you get this? I thought you said you didn't have any photos of yourself as a baby.'

'It's mine. Give it to me,' he said in a flat voice. She was about to rip it in half but she didn't quite dare.

She handed it back. Sofia must have slipped it into his pocket. At a ceremony to celebrate her son's alliance with another woman, she had given him a photo of himself as a newborn – the time when he was purely *hers*. It was warped.

'It was that secretary, wasn't it?' screamed Sunshine.

He *blushed*.

She ran to be sick.

He stood over her, awkward. 'Sunshine, please, it was a kiss.'

She spat the vomit into the pan, and choked, 'I'm waiting for you say "it meant nothing", but you can't say it because it did *mean* something, or you wouldn't feel this shit!' She grabbed the mouthwash and swilled out her mouth. 'I'll kill that little slut,' she hissed, her eyes blazing. 'I will—'

Ben gripped her upper arms with surprising force. 'If you so much as touch Lulu or threaten to harm her or anyone close to her in any conceivable way, if you even speak about her, then *I* will kill you and go to prison for it, and you know I'm not joking.'

She stared at him in shock and burst into tears.

He turned away, breathing heavily.

'Well,' she said finally. 'There's not much I can say to that. I'm leaving now. Frankly, I don't care what happens to my mother. We've never liked each other and, to be honest, Ben, I'm a host, not a carer. If Sofia wants to play nurse, that's up to her. As for our cancelled engagement, you can break the news to your parents.'

She wanted to throw his diamond ring in his face, but she just couldn't. Despite her tattered pride, she still wanted to marry him. Yes, even though he was in love with another woman. He was more than a man, he was a lifestyle. Even though she wanted to scratch out his eyes, she couldn't quite bring herself to throw millions and billions of dollars off the side of a cliff and watch them flutter away.

As Sunshine stormed out of the suite and stamped down the stairs, she hoped that he'd come after her, pull her to him and kiss her passionately as they always did at the end of old movies. But he didn't. It seemed that Ben Arlington was quite happy to let her go. Well, screw him and screw the whole rotten Arlington dynasty. She was Sunshine Beam, and she had better options.

Turtle Egg Island, the morning after the party, 1 September 2009

Sofia

Sofia awoke and tried not to scowl. The scowl was her mother's natural expression. Her mother had looked sour in every photograph and in the imprint of her memory. It enraged Sofia that she had fallen asleep, even if only for a few hours. Somehow the act of falling asleep minimized the extent of her fury.

Frank was asleep, blissfully unaware of all the shit he had to worry about. Looking down at his open mouth, she felt a sudden urge to smash the heavy glass ashtray on his head.

She showered quickly in the open-air shower outside their room, staring clench-jawed out to sea as the hot water ran over her hourglass body. She must remain calm. Everything was under control – or it soon would be.

She hoped that Lulu hadn't fucked up. The silly fool had always been in love with Ben, only Ben, because he wasn't interested, hadn't noticed. Sofia had gone to some trouble to *make* him notice. She had ordered her personal stylist to transform the girl. She was lovely, but hid it beneath dull practical clothes. She also wore glasses, lazy cow! She worked in a Vegas casino: half the *men* had whitened teeth and tinted eyelashes.

Sofia had told Lulu that if she didn't try to seduce Ben, she'd be fired. So Lulu had trotted down to the pool, and Sterling had reported seeing them kiss. In many ways, humans were like dear little robots: utterly predictable. Now all she needed to do was to catch them horizontal, and the paparazzo that Sterling had sent to stake out Ben's room was sly and persistent. He'd sell the shots around the world and the engagement would fall apart.

Then Ben would go to Macau, chastened and single. Sunshine would remain at the Cat. This might even be the deal-breaker for Ping, forcing Ben back into the Arlington Corporation fold. As for Bessie: by the end of today, she would be dead. And then Sofia, at last, could relax for five minutes. Jesus Christ, was a fag break and a quick flick through *People* magazine too much to ask?

Sofia checked her watch. It was seven in the morning: time to check on the lovebirds. She dressed fast, slipping on her Aurora cuff in diamonds, pink opals and pink sapphires and her Ambrosia necklace in diamonds. The more anxious Sofia was, the more jewellery she wore.

She jammed on her sunglasses and hurried to Ben's wing of the villa. It was quiet. She pressed the entrance code, scurried to his bedroom and knocked. There was no reply and the door was locked.

Was there a chance she had misunderstood about Lulu? Sofia turned and ran to the staff quarters. Maids flattened themselves against the stone walls as she passed. She reached the large airy room assigned to Lulu and threw open the door.

There was a lump in the bed. She ripped off the cover. There was Lulu huddled in a ball. She was tearstained, and wearing a shabby cotton nightdress.

Sofia shook her awake. 'Where is he? Where is he? What happened?'

Lulu looked confused and terrified. 'Mrs Arlington! *Nothing* happened. I feel so ashamed. I made such a fool of myself!'

Sofia hissed: 'Where *is* he?'

'I don't know. He just . . . left.'

'You were supposed to *tell* me. If it wasn't fine, you were supposed to—'

Reprimanding a person who had made a mistake was a waste of breath; the damage was done. 'You fool,' Sophia said hoarsely. 'You love him and you *blew* it. You'll never get him now.' She stalked out. As she ran down the corridor, she rang security. 'Who left the island last night?'

The man stammered as he listed the names. 'Louis Prince—'

'*Who?*'

'Louis P—'

'There is no Louis Prince. There is a Louise Prince, also known as Lulu, who, alas, is still very much with us. Are you telling me that an unidentified male left the island last night? When?'

'It was three fifteen a.m. He said he was – and I did say—'

Sofia should have brought in Manhattan Karl, her Chief of Security at the Cat. This idiot was overwhelmed

328

by the calibre of guest. Because the guy had been leaving rather than trying to get in, he couldn't see the harm.

It could be that Ben merely wanted to see Sunshine. But what if he suspected that something was up with Bessie? As soon as that woman regained consciousness, she would spill every secret and ruin them. Sofia had been too kind. Bessie would have to go. Weak people made surprisingly nimble opponents.

As she whipped down the curling corridor towards Sterling's quarters, a woman scurrying the other way ran smack into her.

'*Sunshine!*' The bitch was carrying a Louis in each hand. 'What are you doing here? How is your ... mother? Have you seen Ben?'

Sunshine put her designer luggage on the floor. 'Mrs Arlington,' she said. 'Ben and I broke up. I'm sorry for the wasted party. He'll explain. Right now, I don't feel like talking. I'm going home. Goodbye.'

Sofia managed not to smile at completion of Plan A. *Where* was Ben?

'Ben's at the hospital,' added Sunshine. 'Is there a boy available to carry this to the chopper?'

'You'll have to wait,' replied Sofia. She left the girl standing there, mouth open. Looking at Sunshine, Sofia felt no remorse, and no love for her biological daughter. Let her resign. Her contract stated that she was not allowed to be employed by a competitor for twelve months – so fuck you.

When Sofia knocked, Sterling slid out of his room like a viper out of a tree. Sofia pulled him back inside and shut the door.

'I am a wreck, Sterling,' she hissed, 'a wreck! Ben is at

the hospital. Bessie might be talking to him right now. I can't stand it! I just need her . . .' Sofia drew her hand across her throat.

'Happily,' said Sterling. 'Bessie is in the right place. Her notes could be confused, the wrong medicine administered – a decimal point moved so a concentration of drugs becomes lethal. We'll have dear Bessie on her way by lunchtime.'

'Do what you think is best,' she said. 'I don't want the details. I want it over.'

They took the chopper. It was a bright, beautiful morning but there was a strong breeze: a reminder that it was nearly the rainy season, when the world turned grey and the rain fell hard and heavy, in sheets. The pilot landed on the hospital roof.

'If you find Ben,' said Sterling, 'I'll deal with the other thing.'

Sofia rapped on the door of the penthouse. The second she found Ben, she would spirit him out of here. She would send him to Macau herself to get him away from Bessie. Her CFO would rustle up some nice figures. She would persuade Ben to accept Arlington Corp. as a major shareholder in his venture with Charlie Ping; he would be crazy to turn down an investment offer on such friendly terms. Especially as he no longer had Sunshine Beam as a sweetener for Arnold Ping.

'Ben!' she called. 'Ben, darling; it's me.'

She waited; tried again. Then she had hospital security open up the suite. It was deserted. She rattled through the bedroom, hunting for his passport, his phone, clothing: nothing.

'Perhaps he has gone for a walk?' said the guard.

'Why?' said Sofia.

She called his phone. No answer.

She took a breath. Was he in Bessie's room? Oh God. Sofia flew down the stairs and rapped hard on the reception desk. 'Where's HDU? I need to see Lily Fairweather! Now!'

Even as she approached HDU, she knew. Senior doctors and security guards swarmed round the entrance, and there was an uneasy buzz. Sterling was nowhere to be seen.

Sofia's hope was that Bessie had died, but her gut knew otherwise. 'Ben!' she shouted, not bothering to disguise her panic. 'Ben, are you in there? Where are you?'

Sofia burst into the room, praying to see the tall, slender frame of her son: safe and alive and *here*.

The room was empty. The bed . . . empty.

'Where is she?' said Sofia as her throat closed up. 'Where is Lily Fairweather?'

A female doctor shook her head. 'They don't know. She's vanished! One minute, she's lying here; the next, she's gone! They're checking surveillance but security says there's a technical fault.'

As the nightmare took hold of her, Sofia all but lost her power of speech. She had to puff to force the words out. 'She's gone . . .' she gasped. 'And she's taken my son.'

Her head swam. It was too much. She had lost control, and even Sterling was no use to her. There was only one person who could help her now.

So be it.

Presidential Suite, the Medici, a day later,
2 September 2009

Sofia

Luke Castillo liked to have sex holding a cigar in one hand and a woman in the other. Despite this affectation, he managed very well. Sofia, bent over the edge of the bed, felt as if she would go faint with lust. He gave the impression of being fat but he wasn't; it was his personality and other parts that were big.

She had contacted him directly while en route to Vegas. They hadn't spoken for over two decades, and yet, hearing his gravelly voice at the end of the phone, she felt dizzy; its familiarity was hypnotic and immediate. She hadn't introduced herself; there was no need. She had merely said, 'I need to see you.' Without pause, he had replied, 'Come over.'

She'd worn a slinky dress with a plunging neckline, high shoes, black stockings and meek hair; she looked sadly beautiful. Luke didn't respond well to ugly, confident women. Assistants ushered her up to the presidential suite. She barely knew what she would say. She would admit defeat. He had won. He held all the cards. She was desperate, at his mercy. That would be enough.

It was essential to surrender completely. Only then would Luke grant her wish.

When she knocked quietly on the grand doors, they opened slowly by remote control. Luke was sprawled on a massive sofa at the far end of the suite. She had to approach him, like a slave approaching a king, as he watched.

'Crawl,' he said.

'*What?*'

'Do it!'

So she had sunk to her knees and crawled, although she had managed to give the crawl a little pizzazz, so it was more of a prowl. Her cleavage was shown to its best advantage, and he hadn't taken his eyes off her. She watched him, too, moistening her lips with her tongue; she watched his cold handsome face, and his dark eyes, his unforgiving expression. When she finally reached him, she was panting with desire and so was he. He'd hauled her up by her hair, up and on to him, and they kissed ferociously. She breathed in the hot, ashy taste of his cigar smoke as if it were nectar.

There were no words of love, or even like. She was submissive, remembering exactly how he liked it and what he liked to do, what pleased him, what made him crazy. He taunted her, about Frank, and she let him. No, he didn't make her want him like this. No, it wasn't this wild with him.

Sofia felt as if she were having an out-of-body experience. She had come to Luke for a purpose; it was insane that she was revelling in the task, that it was an incredible, fantastic release, a joy, a pleasure, suddenly separate from the goal at hand. It was horrible to realize that she was still obsessed with him, that in a warped way, Luke Castillo, a stone-cold, immoral man, was and always would be the love of her life.

Afterwards, he lay on the bed, and she stroked his hair,

and kissed his face. He stared at the ceiling, impassive. She was in an aroused state of fear and excitement, and she knew he felt her hand tremble.

'I'll run you a bath,' she whispered, and he nodded. The huge sunken Jacuzzi bath was the place to beg her favour. She brought him a towel, wrapped it around him, and he walked to the Jacuzzi. Sofia walked behind him like a geisha. With any other man, she would have found this despicable and ridiculous. With Luke, it was erotic, and *right*.

There was no sign, in the presidential suite, that Luke was a married man, no framed photographs of the wife: *she* was now fat, desperately over-made-up, like a clown, a pastiche of beauty, her clothes trashier, her jewellery louder; and yet Sofia hated the idea of her existence. No doubt the wife was snacking on her third Krispy Kreme of the day while frantically scouring Robertson for the magic dress that took 50 pounds off your ass.

Sofia stepped slowly and gracefully into the Jacuzzi, glad that she had worked like an athlete to keep her figure lithe, tanned and irreproachable. Luke groaned as she swam towards him. She sighed as he pulled her to him; reverently, she traced the powerful lines of his shoulders and biceps with her fingernails.

'What is it you want, baby?' he growled as she dug her nails into his back. 'Because, right now, you know I'd give you anything.'

'Only you,' she whispered, and she watched the wolfish grin spread across his face. She tenderly soaped him down, massaging his body, marvelling at how the mere touch of him sent electric sparks of desire through her. Then she led him back into the bedroom and dried him, softly patting him with the fluffy towel. She was on her knees when she finally got up the courage to speak.

'Luke,' she said huskily. 'Back then, when we were together, I was arrogant, and I apologize.' She looked into his eyes. 'I wish I hadn't left you. The only person in my life whom I have any genuine love for is my son, Ben, and I am begging you not to take him away from me. When you married ... your wife ... I wanted to hurt you. Frank wanted me, and he wanted a family, a son, and – well, I was half mad with grief, I would have done anything to make you feel the pain I felt.

'But when I met Bessie Edwards – Lily Fairweather as she calls herself – at the hotel launch in Dubai, it seemed like fate. We were both pregnant, both miserable: the solution was right there. We both got what we wanted. She got money, and I got my boy. Ben was my consolation prize. I might not have you, but I had Ben. And I loved him, I love him and I cannot lose him. And so I am begging you, please, call Bessie off, just make her disappear, or do whatever it is you do, because if Frank finds out that Ben is not his real son, it is the end for me, for Ben, for all of us. Please, Luke, I am begging you, *please*!'

All the while, she had been slowly rubbing rose oil into his back, whispering into his ear, gently massaging her body against his, and now he stood up and threw her on to the bed. She cringed, expecting to be hit.

Luke stubbed out his cigar. Then he scooped her on to his lap like a kitten. Very softly and tenderly, he stroked the line of her mouth with his finger. She was almost crying. 'Baby,' he murmured, his voice husky and low with thrilling emotion, 'you'll always be my number-one girl. And I will always hate you just a little bit for marrying that imbecile. And I will never forgive him for taking you from me – because, sweetheart, you could have hung around. There are benefits to being a mistress these days, they have rights.'

Her eyelashes were wet with tears. 'I know,' she whispered. 'I made a mistake.'

'But' – and she felt the rasp of his calloused fingers caress her neck – 'you chose to align yourself with the enemy who, very publicly, humiliated me again and again by taking what was mine. He took *you*; Ben took Sunshine; Ariel took Harry! Frank and his kids are all up in my shit!'

Sofia shivered, suddenly, in fear. He kissed her gently, just below her earlobe. 'And so,' he continued, 'I considered it only fair that when I got the chance, I took what was his.'

Oh *God*, maybe Luke had already *killed* Ben.

Luke stood up, forcing her to slither off him. He pulled a robe around him and kicked her clothes towards her. He smiled at her, but this time, there was no softness, it was a hard, cruel smile. She scrambled into her dress and jammed on her shoes, not bothering with her stockings. This was no longer about seduction, but survival.

'But, Sofia,' said Luke, 'I didn't take Ben. I took *you*. I know that I have your heart, and he knows it – he always has. And that is enough for me. It's also enough that I rule Vegas because I *am* Sin City. We understand each other, me and this hot desert town. Frank is an outsider, and his success, if that's what he chooses to call it, will always be forced.'

Luke laughed as he lit another cigar. 'Baby, until you came to me, I hadn't a fucking clue what dirty little schemes you'd gotten up to, how you've been lying to your husband, letting him raise another man's child all these twenty-five years.'

Sofia stared at him dumbly. 'You mean you didn't put Bessie Edwards up to this?'

Luke shook his head.

Sofia felt hysteria rise. 'You know who she is, right? She's Sunshine's *mother*.'

'Bessie Edwards,' said Luke. 'Sure I know Bessie Edwards. I never met her but she was married to Hank. He owed us a shitload of money, and she paid off half a mill, right before Hank was killed.' Luke paused and raised an eyebrow. 'That wouldn't have anything to do with *you*, would it?'

Sofia closed her eyes and sighed. There was no point in lying. 'It was about thirteen years after we . . . made the deal. Bessie was cheating on Hank and Hank found out. He told her he suspected their youngest kid wasn't his and that he was going to check. Bessie panicked, and got in contact – indirectly, of course; Sterling had set up an emergency number – to a lawyer we could rely on. Hank probably wasn't a threat but Sterling didn't want to risk it. And Bessie needed to be taught a lesson. Sterling knew people and they took care of it. They made it look drug-related.'

A muscle twitched in Luke's cheek. 'It was handy for you', he said, 'that Hank's murder almost got pinned on me. I took a lot of heat when Hank died; despite his wife's kind contribution, he was still in the hole to the tune of a million bucks. When you had him disappeared, you wrote off *my* debt. You owe me, baby, you owe me big.'

Sofia put her head in her hands. 'If you didn't find out that she had given her baby to me and tell her, how did she find out?'

'Christ, Sofia, she must have found out on her own. She's a mother! Mothers are psychotic. But' – and, for the briefest of seconds, Luke Castillo looked almost wistful – 'I always felt an affinity to Sunshine Beam, little Casey Edwards – and now I see why. I loved the mother; I loved the daughter.'

She gave him a sharp look, and his face darkened. 'Not like that, Sofia. Me and you, we had something. And you fucked it up. And it's only because I am soft on you, soft as a rotting pear, that I am not going to throttle you with my bare hands. So get out, Sofia. Get out before I have a chance to think about what you have done to me and how angry I am.'

So Bessie had acted alone – and now Luke knew everything. Instead of helping herself, she had made the situation worse. Sofia fled, and her heart was a small, mangled black knot of fear and regret.

St Christopher's Hospital, one day earlier,
1 September 2009

Ben

'My darling son,' said the stranger. 'Come and give your mummy a kiss.'

Ben was in shock. His brain was running around in circles. He didn't know what the hell he was supposed to do. He was operating from a place of helplessness and raw fear.

'Lily.' She lunged at him like a bad date and there was a feverish brightness to her eyes. 'Stop.'

It was too much to grasp; he was reeling. He'd leaned over her hospital bed to see if she was OK and she'd grabbed him by the wrist, digging her nails into his flesh so hard she had drawn blood.

'Did you see the photograph? Did you?'

He sensed her irritation at his confusion. 'The one of you as a newborn,' she said, her voice still hoarse from the tubes.

'Yes,' he said, fumbling in his pocket. 'My mother gave it to me, but how do *you*—?'

'I gave it to you. Ben, my darling, I'm your mother . . . I said, I'm your mother, your real mother. I gave birth to you . . . Yes, that's right. Look at me, look at my face, it's *me*, I gave birth to you, but *Sofia* took you away. I was desperate and she took advantage . . . I was at the end of my— She offered silly crazy money . . . No, please don't go – *wait* – wait,' she said fiercely, 'because I have. I've waited for twenty-five years.'

He'd stared at the photograph. 'Look,' she said greedily, 'see, that's *my* hand holding you, see that wedding ring?' It was an ugly yet distinctive ring: a bulbous frog-green stone surrounded by rubies, set in wrought gold. He flinched as she shoved her hand in his face: she wore the ring; it was undeniably the ring from the photo. 'Hank, your father, gave it to me when we got engaged.' She snorted. 'I should have dumped him then.'

As everything that held him up fell away, Ben struggled to prove her wrong. 'That baby could be *any* baby. How do I know it's me? It could be Sunshine!'

Even as he said the words, he remembered that Sunshine had seen the photo and recognized it as him.

She laughed. 'Ah, my darling, you can see it's you, I see it in your eyes. And the date is on the other side.'

He flipped over the photo. It was his birth date. 'But Sunshine was born just the day before me,' he said. He felt if he kept arguing, she might stop.

'My dearest, has *Sofia* ever shown you a photograph of yourself as a newborn, still covered in wax?'

Ben was forced to admit she had not.

'No,' said Lily, her mouth a snarl. 'She *can't*.'

His throat seized up with dread. 'I don't understand what you're saying. Sunshine and I . . . are we *twins* . . . ?'

'No!' said the woman, her voice shrill. 'Sunshine is *their* daughter – Sofia and Frank's. She's an Arlington, through and through. Sofia needed to give him a boy and she found *me* – and so we made an exchange. I thought it was for the best; you would have been raised in poverty otherwise. This way, I could give you the best chance to have a good life – you have to understand that. It was a selfless, kind thing I did! This way, I could give *all* my children the best chance. And I thought I could bring up Casey – Sunshine – as my own. But . . . we just didn't gel, although I tried.'

She paused. 'And then, when Casey was thirteen, my husband . . . began to suspect that she wasn't his child. I knew if he took a paternity test . . . well, I was terrified, and so I contacted *her*. At the time, I didn't know who she was, all contact was made through a go-between. Within ten days, my husband was *dead*. Killed! She had him murdered! Could you even believe that? I loathed the guy but he didn't deserve *that*. After Hank died, everything changed. I just . . . missed you more and more. And I wished . . . I wished I could have gone back in time, and kept my baby. And then I realized I didn't care what she did to me. I was determined to find out who she was and get you back.' Her voice oozed syrup. 'Oh my precious, my darling baby, I've *yearned* for you.'

Ben drew back; he felt sick. All his life he'd stood, in a proud and elevated position, at the top of a mountain; today it had crumbled to nothing and he was scrabbling on his knees in mud.

'Right,' he said. 'So how *did* you find out who she was?' He watched her closely. If she couldn't give him an answer, he'd know she was lying.

'It was simple,' she said. 'I paid a private detective. He found your original birth certificate, and the amended one. It took him a week. I paid him twenty thousand dollars. I have all the documents, for proof. I thought you might . . . resist the truth.'

'I'm not resisting anything,' he said sharply. He

needed her to shut up. 'Stop talking for a moment.' He sounded like a child. But he didn't want to be hers. She was a stranger, and her intensity was terrifying.

'I'm sorry,' he said eventually. 'I believe you – every word.' He had to work to keep his voice steady. 'But it's not going to change a thing. It *can't*. It's . . . too late. Frank is my father because . . . he is my father. As for Sofia . . . What she did . . . it is . . . not out of character. It's extreme . . . evil. She had a difficult life. She saw things that change a person. I don't know what to feel about her. But she is my mother and she is what I am used to. The thing is though, the thing is, that Frank can't know.' Ben paused. 'You won't tell him. He doesn't deserve all this shit. If you tell him, you'll never see me again.'

He jumped up. He guessed he'd take a plane home and pack. He'd go to Macau tomorrow – he'd ask Lulu to come with him. And Joe. And if that meant Lulu's parents too – well, the whole family; he just needed to get away from all of this.

'Wait!'

The desperation in her voice made him turn at the door. She was scrambling out of bed. She looked half crazy.

'Sofia knows I've told you.'

Ben shrugged. 'Then she'll have to live with that.' He paused. 'Goodbye, Lily. I'm sorry it didn't work out.'

He suspected that he was fooling himself. But he still hoped that if he acted as if her words meant nothing, they would mean nothing and his life could go on.

'I need your help, Ben. Please. I am begging you. You have to take me away – take me with you. *You* don't want

Frank to know because you . . . love him. *She* doesn't want Frank to know because she loves power and she'd hate a divorce. Please, Ben. If you don't help me, she'll kill me. I know it. She'll kill me today.'

For a second, he considered abandoning her, and letting Sterling deal with the 'problem'.

But he couldn't let it happen. He was not a killer.

He didn't know if, by walking back into that hospital room, he was weak or strong.

'We need', he said, without smiling, 'to disappear. Get dressed.'

Then, forcing himself not to shudder, he slipped his arm into hers and they strolled out of the building. As soon as they were in the street, he jumped apart from her, and hailed a cab to the airport.

'You know . . .' she began coyly, but he shook his head. There was no beginning.

'I need to think,' he said, and she fell silent, but he could feel her eyes on him.

He began to text Frank, but he couldn't finish the message. He didn't know how to explain. He didn't contact Lulu for the same reason. He would have to keep silent and let the people who cared about him worry, and he hated Lily for forcing him to make such a decision.

'Where are you taking me?' she husked.

Ben ignored her.

Sofia kept a private jet in a hangar, but the tail number was traceable. Still, if he avoided flight following, he'd be just about invisible to radar. He'd head for one of the smaller airports around LA, and then . . . work out their next move.

343

'It's like we're running away together.' She giggled.

He didn't reply, but stood aside as she jiggled up the steps to the Cirrus.

She said, 'I hate these little tiny planes, and yet I don't feel afraid of flying with *you*.' Her eyes slid over him. 'You're such a talented boy.'

He slid into the cockpit. It was an hour since they'd left the hospital. Soon, people would realize that he and Lily had disappeared. He couldn't stand to think of Lulu's bewilderment. And yet they'd parted on the worst terms; why was he even concerned about her? He was worried for Frank too. Why wasn't he worried even a little about Sunshine? Because he sensed that whatever truth emerged from this sorry episode wouldn't touch her. Nothing really did. But Lulu and he had a bond. It felt like a betrayal, to leave without so much as a word. He hoped that he would have the chance to explain.

Ben stared at the controls and his vision blurred. His eyes felt hot and tired.

'Where are you taking me?' she said again.

Finally, he turned and looked at her. The triumph died on her face as she saw his expression.

'I don't know,' he said. 'I can't think of anywhere I want to run to.'

He saw her eyes narrow, assessing him.

'OK,' she said briskly. 'Let me be in charge. So' – Lily twisted her hair into a knot – 'I keep a little place north of Vegas. We'll be safe there.'

'Right,' said Ben. 'Right. Fine. If you're sure?'

'Oh yes.' She smiled.

He stared at her for a second and then started the

engine. He had no intention of spending a moment longer with his new-found mother than necessary. She'd made decisions that in his mind identified her as crazy. Flying to Vegas was fine by him, but he suspected he knew *her* motive for the choice. In this woman's warped mind, Sofia was the one block between her and happiness. Lily must be plotting to kill before she got killed.

She would fail as Sofia was better qualified, better connected and better armed. Ben would talk Lily out of attempting anything stupid. It was the weirdest thing: even though he now knew Sofia was amoral and psychopathic, he couldn't entirely detach himself from her. She was a poor excuse for a mother, but she was still his mother. He didn't exactly love her, but there was a bizarre bond, borne of habit and familiarity, that he couldn't shake.

And yet, Lily, poor put-upon Lily, weak as a wilting flower . . . she was emerging as his own flesh and blood and yet he couldn't feel a link. As soon as she was hidden from Sofia, and safe, Ben would get away from her.

'Are you sure this is the safest place for you? Because my mother' – he felt Lily's hostility at his choice of word – 'doesn't quit.'

'She won't find us. I've owned this place for nearly thirty years, and no one would ever dream of it.'

An image of Frank discovering the truth flashed into Ben's mind. His father would be crushed. For a moment, Ben despised Sofia. But he despised Lily more. Sofia was selfish and cold, but she was not a hypocrite. Somehow, Lily worming away from all responsibility felt more repulsive than Sofia's ruthlessness. Lily blamed everything on Sofia, as if she had not agreed to sell her child for money, and that was vile.

Now Ben understood Sofia's bizarre behaviour the previous day. Christ. No wonder he had been strangely attracted to Sunshine. Beyond her obvious charms, he had been raised by her blood parents. He was lured by her curious familiarity.

'You're quite tall, aren't you?' sighed Lily, gazing at him.

He smiled tightly. There was no question of persuading Lily to stay away from him; so he would give her no choice. Macau was looking like the smartest decision he'd ever made. That said, he was about to go missing for a short while when he had a business meeting scheduled for Thursday. Well, Charlie would forgive him for not showing up when he heard the news on CNN. Ben suspected that if Sofia had her way, his vanishing would be spun as a kidnapping.

'I did this out of love,' said Lily. 'I hope you realize that.'

Ben nodded, but he didn't agree. Sofia and Lily had both been driven by greed. They could have ruined his life, and the lives of those who might have reasonably expected to be loved by them, and they hadn't cared. But they hadn't ruined his life. He would recover from this.

'Who I am', he said, 'has nothing to do with where I came from.'

There was a subdued gasp. He could sense that she was crying, but he didn't look at her.

Las Vegas had an unhealthy disregard for the past. He

346

had always respected history, believing it told you who you were. Now he saw it merely showed you who you might be.

'Can you keep it down?' he said when her sobs grew louder. 'I need to concentrate.'

He'd avoid the airports that the police would check. Bravo airspace was heavily controlled; to fly into B Class without clearance was the fastest way of drawing attention. The weather and landscape made it tricky, but the prospect of wind, updraft turbulence or thin air didn't bother him. Nature he could work with. His likeliest source of trouble was man-made – and the skies above the Las Vegas Bowl were teeming with busy-bodies: there were Military Operation Areas, Alert Areas, ultralights, model rockets and skydivers.

Lily dried her eyes. She tapped on the control panel with a varnished fingernail. 'Head for between Tonopah and Alamo.'

'There's nothing there.'

'*Almost* nothing there.'

It was still dark when they approached. It *was* the middle of nowhere: he saw a dirt landing strip next to a scatter of trailer homes. One had a blinking red light on its roof.

'What is this? It's bloody close to Area 51. Any tighter and they'd scramble jets.'

'It's called Angel,' said Lily. She paused. 'It's where you would have lived, had I kept you. That trailer is where we lived when I was pregnant with you. Would you wanted to have grown up in a tiny trailer home just . . . *nowhere*? Nowhere on earth, with your parents miserable and fighting? Don't you see? I did the best I could for all of us.'

Ben felt nauseous. Would he have wanted to grow up there? The fact was, he hadn't been given the chance to find out.

'Why did you keep it?' he said. 'You don't strike me as the sentimental type.'

She sniffed. 'I started a little business. And it's been useful. As the whole world knows now, good fortune is not a constant. Lately, I've used it as a . . . base. And for now, that's where we'll be staying: the Bunny Fluff Hotel.'

'We're hiding out in a *brothel*?'

'The girls are discreet.'

'How do you know?'

She smiled at him, not happily. 'I told you. It's my business. Beggars can't be choosers.'

Ben brought the little plane in to land on the bumpy strip. He felt as if he had hopped into someone else's life – and he didn't like it at all. He couldn't stop thinking now that, even though their actions had been immoral and disgusting, Sofia and Lily had done him a favour.

Arlington Residence, Las Vegas, 3 September 2009

Sofia

Sofia pursed her lips as she slipped on the white silk gloves and opened her private safe. She had never wanted it to come to this.

Carefully, Sofia placed the items – each one had been labelled – into a padded case. Then she changed into the maid's uniform. She looked at herself in the mirror: Luke would have *died*. It was a pity she was married to Frank. Still, all good things must end.

She walked into the private parking area and pressed the keys that Sterling had left on her bed. She wrinkled her nose as a battered grey Ford flashed its lights. She hadn't driven a car this primitive in a long while. She placed the bag gently on the passenger seat and drove to Ariel's apartment.

Carrying a mop and her bag, she let herself into the building. It was upscale but not prohibitively so. You could still be a relative nobody and live there. That annoyed Sofia. Ariel's naive desire to be a 'woman of the people' really got up her nose. The people were scumbags!

As she was over forty and dressed as a servant, the young, handsome doorman barely acknowledged her. Perfect – but fuck him.

She let herself in. Sterling had copied the keys for her six years earlier, when Ariel had first rented the apartment; Sofia had told herself then that it was about security. Now she knew she was right. It *was* about security: her own.

She was sad and sorry that the situation had become so dirty and tangled. But she had no choice. It was all about saving herself, and Ben.

Sofia unzipped the bag. Then she did a little scene-setting.

The bottle of Grey Goose vodka, she placed on the lounge table. Next to it, three black and gold goblets, all released from their plastic packaging. Wearing her silk gloves, she poured a spot of vodka into each.

She took hairs from another plastic bag with tweezers. Two belonged to Ben: she had taken them from his pillow. Then she placed Lily's sunglasses on a chair. They were cracked from their bounce on the tarmac.

You had to spell it out for the police or they didn't solve shit. If that idiot Frank paid the ransom, Sofia would ensure its transfer to an account that would be traceable to Ariel. Of course, no charge would stick, but Ariel's publicly aired resentment of Ben and her dealings with the Castillo family made her involvement possible, if unlikely. Luke was notoriously vengeful, and Ariel was weak enough for it to be plausible Castillo was using her as a pawn. Sofia knew her plan was imperfect, but it was a delaying tactic only. By the time the police figured out that the Castillo family and Ariel had been set up, and that Bessie was to blame, Sofia would have found Bessie and dealt with her.

On her way out, Sofia accidentally brushed against a framed photograph and knocked it off the wall.

The glass broke. She looked down. A shard had

gouged the picture; a white scratch now eviscerated the image of a young laughing Frank holding five-year-old Ariel aloft to blow out her birthday candles.

Frank had always had been superstitious and Sofia had always barely hidden her scorn. Perhaps his gipsy beliefs were justified after all. Ah well, the mess would add to the veracity of the scene. Sofia stepped daintily over the smashed glass. She really wasn't cut out to be a maid.

Las Vegas Metro Police Homicide Department, later that day

Jen

'I can't drink this,' said the woman, pushing away the Styrofoam cup.

Detective Jenifer Madison said nothing. After a moment, Sofia Arlington sipped the coffee and wiped her eyes. In different circumstances, Madison might have enquired as to where she had bought her bag. It was large, aquamarine, with white trim and silver buckles and it would have been perfect for carrying her gun.

Mrs Arlington looked too put together for a parent whose son had vanished in suspicious circumstances. Jen didn't care *who* she was, billionaire casino-owner or janitor, you were a human being and a mother before your job. Mrs Arlington was dressed beautifully, but there was roaring emotion beneath the sleek façade. She appeared devastated, but that didn't mean she wasn't involved. Guilt looked remarkably similar to grief.

Madison tapped her pen on the table. Privately, she wondered if the son wouldn't just turn up in a few days' time sunning himself on a beach with the future mother-in-law, claiming: 'We just fell in love.'

Her colleague, Ed, had flown to Florida and spoken to the Commissioner – tough job etc. – and processed the hospital room, but it was an empty scene. A single drop of blood, belonging to Ben Arlington, had been found close to the woman's bed. The blood drop didn't have a tail, meaning that he was stationary; possibly leaning towards the patient when a minor injury was sustained. But the guy could have scratched himself, or knocked a scab. The woman, one Lily Fairweather, was slight. She was recovering from a head injury. There was no other disturbance to indicate a struggle.

Ed had canvassed the area but no one had seen the subjects leave the hospital. The guard had led Ed with great pride to the security camera and demonstrated how you could remotely swivel the lens to cover every angle of the exit. Ed had asked to see footage from earlier. 'It's live,' the guard had admitted. 'The VRC isn't hooked up.' He'd added, 'If it was, it would have recorded everything!'

ATC reported a private jet leaving the main airport and landing at Ontario International in California; the tail number was registered to Arlington Corp. – but then it had disappeared.

Arlington or Fairweather must have had a car

waiting, or another plane, but where had it taken them?

'So, Mrs Arlington, why is it that you think they're somewhere in Las Vegas? If you're not straight with me, I can't help you.'

Mrs Arlington shifted uncomfortably on the plastic chair. 'I'm being straight,' she said. 'I *feel* that they are close. It's what you people call a hunch.'

Jen's phone rang. 'Hello, ma'am. It's Cory McCloud, LAPD.'

Jen stood. 'Excuse me for a minute,' she said.

It never hurt to leave a witness or a person of interest alone in the box with their conscience. Her ex-partner, Harry Castillo, had a theory: if a witness fell asleep in the box while waiting to be interviewed, chances were they were guilty. Harry reckoned it was evolutionary: the bad guys knew a shit storm was coming their way, so they rested to gather strength. Yeah. It was a shame about Harry Castillo flaking out. In this job, it was important to surround yourself with things that made you happy.

'Hello, Cory. What you got for me?'

LAPD had sent patrol to canvass the area around Ontario, but it was like they had disappeared into thin air. Like, you understand, it was a physical impossibility. They'd checked out Ben's apartment: it was deserted. The last known address for Lily Fairweather was a ten-million-dollar property in an upscale suburb; the current owner had bought it via auction five years earlier.

Jen thanked the officer and walked back into the box.

'What do you know about Lily Fairweather, Mrs Arlington?'

The woman met Jen's eyes. 'Not a great deal. But I

know her history isn't trouble-free. She had money and lost it. I believe her husband gambled.'

Physical evidence was what closed a case, but a person's history might reveal motive. The more you knew about a person the better idea you had of who might want to hurt them. Jen just didn't yet know how.

Jen nodded. She suspected that Ben Arlington would soon be found alive. She also had a feeling that Mrs Arlington knew this.

'Excuse me for saying this, but you don't strike me as behaving like a mother who thinks her child is dead.'

Mrs Arlington's face turned pink with rage.

Good.

'How *dare* you!' Mrs Arlington seemed to gather herself. 'I feel like I've been ripped in half. I am trying to keep myself from falling apart.' She managed to dab at her eye with the back of her hand.

This woman was hard to shake.

'Mrs Arlington,' said Jen, changing tack. 'I apologize. Tell me, what do you think happened?'

The woman looked directly at her and spoke calmly, like a trained liar. 'I don't know. But I know that Lily Fairweather is crazy. Three months ago she was in a nuthouse.'

'Who told you that?'

The tiniest pause: 'I Googled her. Only this morning, because, well, all this has only just happened. And, Detective, she is a *felon*! She is wanted in Switzerland for suspected *murder*. Yes! Check it, if you don't believe me. She strangled a nurse, or suffocated her, I don't quite recall, and escaped from the hospital.'

Mrs Arlington seemed to collapse in tears.

'I'll check it right now,' said Jen. She whipped out of the room and was back in moments. 'Mrs Arlington,' she said. 'I can't find one damn thing to corroborate your story. Not one damn thing. Now maybe my search engine isn't as advanced as yours, but I doubt it. So what do you say? I don't like having my time wasted, I got enough to do.'

The woman looked genuinely surprised. Then Jen noticed a faint flush of scarlet creep into her face. What? *What?*

'I'm sorry,' said Mrs Arlington, standing up. 'I must have made a mistake. I probably . . . got her confused with someone else. But I don't trust her. I think she's dangerous. She's vanished, so has my son, what further evidence do you need?'

'OK,' said Jen. 'Thank you, Mrs Arlington. You've been helpful. Is there anything else you'd like to add?'

The woman looked down. 'I don't know if it's relevant. It's probably nothing, I'm sure . . . I don't see how . . . but we recently promoted Ben to a powerful position within our firm and it caused a rift with his sister, Ariel.'

Madison waited. But the woman had said all she wanted to say.

'You think your daughter has something to do with this?'

'I don't know. I'm sure not . . .'

'That's fine. Thank you.'

After Sofia Arlington swept away in her armour-plated Mercedes, Madison spoke to her colleague, Oskar, who'd been monitoring the exchange on screen.

'Something not quite right about Mama,' said Oskar, leaning back in his chair.

Madison perched on the desk. 'Yeah, I agree.'

Oskar scratched his head. 'We missed something, Jen. We missed something that was right there.'

Jen sighed. She stretched across Oskar's desk to see if the gaping Doritos packet contained anything but radioactive orange dust. Then she indicated the tape. 'It's not as if I miss my family or need to see them ever,' she said. 'Play it again.'

Homicide Department, later that same evening

Jen

'You tell Sofia that you can't find shit on the internet about Lily Fairweather. Now, *look at her face!*'

Jen squinted at the screen. 'Yes. She looked embarrassed.'

Oskar said, 'She actually says, "I must have made a mistake." You know, I think she *did* make a mistake, and I think she realized it. She realized she shouldn't have told you that story!'

'Why?'

'No goddamn idea.'

Jen watched as Oskar typed 'Switzerland escape hospital nurse murder wanted' into the search engine.

'OK!' she said, as the results came up. 'The story is true, look, but the name is . . . Bessie Edwards.'

Oskar wrinkled his nose.

'*Yes*,' said Jen. 'Lily and Bessie are both shortened versions of Elizabeth. Could they be the same person? Could Fairweather be a maiden name, or vice versa? And if Lily and Bessie *are* the same person, why doesn't Sofia Arlington want us to know that?'

'She's all up in this shit, isn't she?'

'She's got something to do with it, but it looks like Lily Fairweather is no angel. We need to find an address, go through her stuff, or we got nothing. Ah, shit, hang on. Detective Madison speaking, how may I help?'

Seconds later, Jen snapped shut her phone. 'That was Sofia Arlington. She'd like us to pay a visit. She and Frank just received a ransom note.'

Arlington Residence, early hours of 4 September 2009

Jen

A mess of huge black SUVs and powerful motorbikes jammed the street leading to the private road. Paparazzi leaned against the enormous vehicles, their long lenses slung over their shoulders. Jen counted three television vans and felt the buzz of a helicopter tickle her ears.

Jen rolled her eyes at Oskar. 'Mrs Arlington likes a chat.'

She and Oskar flashed their ID at the armed guard in the booth. Another guard stood up; he had a gun in his belt and was flanked by two German Shepherds. He indicated that she open her window. He peered in and made a phone call. Finally, the barrier was lifted and they drove through to a frenzy of clicks.

They drove to the end of the private road; to a vast gated entrance and a second guard booth. 'You wonder how the note was even delivered,' murmured Jen.

A uniformed housekeeper, eyes downcast, opened the doors and led them through a palatial hall.

A vast glittering chandelier hung from the high ceiling; the exquisite stone floor was partly covered by a beautiful Italian rug and lined with marble statues on pillars. The most prominent statue appeared to be of Mrs Arlington as a goddess, complete with flowing robes and tumbling marble locks. A smaller one, possibly of Mr Arlington, was positioned to its rear.

Jen could hear shouting even as they approached the white double doors.

'. . . did this *happen*? You got to protect the rock! You don't protect the rock, you lose *everything*! The cops don't deal on our level! If it's Castillo, I'll—'

'It's nothing to do with Castillo, and stay away from him, Frank, you—'

'Mr and Mrs Arlington, the police are here.'

Sofia, eyes red-rimmed, walked swiftly forward and shook hands. 'I'm sorry,' she muttered. 'We're upset.'

'We all want the same thing,' said Oskar, 'to get Ben back safely. So let's try to stay calm, and work together. First, I'd like to see the ransom note.'

Frank presented the note with shaking hands. It was printed on A5 paper and neatly typed, possibly from a PC. Jen gazed at it. 'Pay $10 million to see Ben – or pay again and again and again.' It was so neat. Were men this neat?

She looked at Sofia. 'How was this delivered?'

'It was dropped from a helicopter.'

Oskar raised an eyebrow a fraction.

'It's not that unusual,' said Sofia. 'There's a lot of air traffic. But this one was hovering. I thought it was going to land in the grounds.'

'What time was this?' said Jen.

'Just before I called you. Maybe eleven thirty?'

'You get a look?'

'It's dark. It was small. It wasn't military. It was really loud, but it was still a way away. The grounds are extensive. I could see its landing light. I sent Sterling, my right-hand man, to investigate.'

Jen nodded. 'We'll check with ATC. Where did he find the note?'

'He took a torch. He saw it jammed under one of the statues by the fountain.'

'OK. When it's light I'll take a look. You got cameras?'

'Only much nearer the house,' replied Sofia. Damn if that woman had an answer for everything!

Frank was pacing. A servant knocked and walked in with a tray. Frank put out a hand to take a coffee; shook his head, then beckoned her back, and took it. 'The money's not a problem,' he said. 'I can get the money. I can pay it. I want my son back.'

'Sir, I understand, but there is the argument that if we

pay the ransom, we lose our bargaining power. We can't stop you from paying it, but we have a day before the deadline to discover where they're hiding out. Did you hear or see the chopper, Mr Arlington?'

Frank shook his head. 'I was in the media room. It's soundproofed. It also faces the front of the house.'

Jen had the sense that Mrs Arlington was the organ grinder, and Mr Arlington was the monkey.

'Oskar, let me see that note again.' She gloved up, and Oskar handed her the note. She saw Sofia watched her closely. The kidnapper was demanding that the money be wired to an offshore account by 10 a.m. the following day.

'The kidnapper has a keen grasp of bank opening hours,' murmured Jen.

'Are you being funny?' said Sofia.

'I'm trying to assess what kind of a person has kidnapped your son,' replied Jen. 'We'll take this. I'll need to talk to you all further. But until then, I suggest you all get some sleep, if you can manage it.'

'I'll talk,' said Frank. 'I'll talk till I'm blue. But I want to pay the ransom.'

'Mr Arlington,' said Jen. 'Let's think on it, just for a few hours.'

Frank started to shake. 'To hell with you and thinking. It's my son, my money and I want to fucking pay. I have a feeling – a bad feeling. If I don't pay' – his voice cracked – 'someone's going to end up dead.'

Harry's house, that same morning

Harry

Harry missed sitting round the office chewing gum. He missed swirling the foul coffee around the bottom of the Styrofoam cup, and he missed unravelling the mysteries of why people did the terrible things they did. He missed his buddies. And yet, despite all this, he was still sitting at home glassy-eyed, in a T-shirt and sweatpants, with the physiotherapist's notes tucked away in his drawer.

It was a shame it hadn't worked out with Ariel. He wouldn't allow himself to think more deeply about it. He didn't miss her, and he resented the fact that her face, her voice, her laugh, seemed wedged inside his head, taunting him with her absence. There was also no point thinking about the sex, so why was he?

He should think about why he was glad it was over. The fact that she'd kept on at him to take charge of his life – rich coming from her. She'd been desperate to see her brother again but refused to admit it, and now the brother had gone missing.

To him it sounded like a publicity stunt from a power-hungry family who craved attention, but Harry had tried to call Ariel when he'd heard, just to check she wasn't freaking out. But she wasn't picking up her phone, at least not to him. He was well and truly dumped.

Anyway, he was trying to take charge of his life. He'd rung Jen, his old partner; he wanted an insider's view as to his career prospects. This had nothing to do with winning back Ariel, showing her that he could get it together. To his surprise, Jen had said she'd come round.

Bang! Bang! It amused him that Jen didn't seem to know the difference in knocking style between duty and social.

'You look like shit,' said Jen as she stepped inside. 'You forgotten what a razor looks like?'

She whipped the cigarette out of his mouth – he hadn't even lit it. 'Some people would be glad to have a life. Stop wasting yours.' She looked him up and down. 'We'll talk when you're showered and shaved.' She marched into the kitchen and poured herself a glass of water. 'Do it! I've been up all night and I'm about to go home for some sleep.'

When he had fulfilled every instruction, she nodded tersely and said, 'You're seeing Ariel Arlington, I hear?'

A small curl of annoyance began to unfold inside his stomach. 'Why do you ask?'

She shrugged. 'All this year that girl has made trouble, and I wondered if you were a part of that. What do you say, Harry?'

Now he understood the heavy knocks at the door. She was suspicious. He was offended that she thought their relationship had not been true.

He said, 'You ever heard of *Romeo and Juliet*?'

'Yeah, I have as a matter of fact,' she responded, getting to her feet. 'I didn't like that movie. It didn't end well.'

She gazed at him, silent. That deep steady quiet gaze made suspects speak. She had the air of a disapproving yet ultimately sympathetic parent. You wanted to please her.

'If you are thinking that Ariel had anything to do with Ben's disappearance, then you are wrong.'

'Ah, Harry,' she said. 'You know better than that. It ain't about what you think. It's about where the evidence takes you.'

She gave him that look again. And then she was gone.

Lulu's apartment, that same morning

Ariel

The only thing that Ariel could do to repay Lulu for her kindness was to clean the apartment. It was tidy, but you could tell that Lulu didn't have spare time for, say, dusting behind the sofa. Ariel wasn't exactly fabulous at cleaning, never having done it before, but she found scrubbing the bath oddly therapeutic. You didn't have to think – it turned out she wasn't so good at thinking – and it was such a relief.

Frank had been right not to promote her. She was a quitter. She had quit on Harry who, without doubt, loved her. No other man had ever gone through the newspaper before she read it, ripping out the articles on cruelty to animals or children. Of course he knew she should read those articles, but he didn't bully her to change. He accepted her, and her weaknesses.

Harry knew her, and when you didn't much like yourself, it was too painful to be with a person who saw you

363

as you were. It wasn't so much balm to the soul as caustic soda. And he was irritatingly correct about Ben. Of course she had wanted to attend his engagement party, even if it was to that awful woman Sunshine Beam.

'Oh,' said Ariel aloud, scratching at a mark on the bath. 'Sunshine is *far* too harsh for Ben. Why do so many lovely men choose such hard, horrible women?' It reminded her of Sofia and Frank.

But pride and embarrassment prevented her from making contact. She was a little screwed up, that was for sure. Her only response, when she met an obstacle within a relationship, was to cut off. She had done it with her father, then Ben, and now Harry. The circles were getting smaller. She had not turned on the television since the day of the engagement, and her phone lay in her bag, out of power. She needed to retreat to recover.

'I don't care,' she said to herself. 'If someone really needs me, then he'll come and find me. God, this is exhausting!'

Meanwhile, with peace, and solitude, perhaps she would gain strength. She curled up on the sofa, with the satisfaction of knowing that underneath it was now a dust-free zone, and closed her eyes.

Bzzzz.

Ariel started. She must have fallen asleep. It sounded as if there were a bee in the room. Then she realized it was the doorbell. It was tiny in here, but cosy as a nest and as cute as a doll's house, with Joe's scribbles pinned up on the fridge. It was adorable, in a way that the Arlingtons' vast mansion never had been.

Bzzzz.

Oh my God, Harry had come for her. She had visions of him sweeping her off her feet, and away, murmuring, 'I'll never let you go again.'

'One second,' she yelled, shoving a mint into her mouth and running her hands through her hair as she opened the door.

'Ariel Arlington?'

She froze.

'I'm Detective Madison, and this is Sergeant Robinson. We're investigating the disappearance of your brother, Ben—'

'Ben's disappeared? What do you mean? Where's he gone?'

'We were hoping you might be able to help us answer that question.'

The woman stared at her with an intensity that Ariel didn't like. The man's expression was kindly tolerant, as though he was looking at a child who had just thrown all her toys on the floor. But that meant she had done something *wrong* . . .

She had. Even though he was more deserving, she had made it plain that she resented Ben's success. It was hard to face him after that. When you have exposed the ugly inside of yourself to a person, you want them to drop off the face of the earth. No one likes to be reminded that they're a loser; and you hate that person for knowing your weakness. But she didn't hate Ben. She loved him.

'I had no idea he was missing. That's terrible. Where is he missing from? How?'

'Miss Arlington, we'd like you to come over to our place, so we can talk.'

'About what?'

The cops exchanged glances. 'This is your chance to tell your side of the story, Ariel.'

Her mind was a whirl. Why hadn't she picked up the phone to Ben? Maybe he'd called her because he was in trouble. Tears were running down her face, her legs felt hot and weak.

An image flashed into her mind. She had fallen over in the garden, aged six, and hurt herself. As she stood there, screaming her head off, Ben, only five, had led her inside where he had grabbed a towel and run it under cold water, then gently dabbed at her cuts. Their nanny had settled them in front of *Scooby Doo*; Ben had sat with his chubby little arm around her, staring at the television, and pressing the cold towel to her knees.

Where *was* he? Was it Castillo? Her heart thumped. 'Do you think Luke Castillo had something to do with this?' she said.

The female cop pursed her lips. 'We're following some leads,' she said. 'You know what a warrant is, Ariel?'

'Yes.'

'We got one of those and we checked out your apartment, and guess what we found?'

What they were telling her made no sense. She didn't even know who Lily Fairweather was, yet apparently she, Ariel and Ben had been sitting in her apartment drinking vodka from black crystal goblets!

As they drove to the station, Ariel stared out of the window in silence and disbelief. Ben wasn't too bothered about what people thought of him. But Ben had offended Luke Castillo and Luke Castillo was connected. Oh

God, *she* had offended Luke Castillo. It could be *her* fault.

Luke didn't realize that in his son she had found the one person on this earth who understood her. When people sneered at her, it made her stupid. But she was clever when she was with Harry because he believed in her. But of course Luke Castillo couldn't see this, would never imagine it to be true. He must assume it was yet one more affront from the Arlington family: Frank, Sofia, Ben and now Ariel. They had all taken something from him. She had no doubt that Luke had done this. He was setting her up.

'Detective, I swear I have not been in my apartment recently, and I don't know who that woman is, I *promise!*'

'She promises,' said the man to the woman.

They were mocking her. Oh, if only Harry were here, he would know what to do! But Harry wasn't here and she couldn't go crawling back to him now.

She would have to manage alone.

Arlington Residence, the morning of 5 September 2009

Sofia

Sofia came hurrying to the door, beating the maid to it. 'Officers,' she said. 'Is something wrong? Do you have any news?'

'Mrs Arlington,' said the woman. 'Is there somewhere more private we can talk?'

Sofia composed her face into a serious expression. She was wearing Donna Karan grey and flat shoes; the picture of piety. Inside she was jubilant, throwing petals in the air. They had taken the bait!

She gasped when they told her about Ariel. A single tear dropped. 'Oh, are you sure? Has she told you where he is? Oh, I can't believe it!'

The cops looked professionally sad and sorry. They didn't care. They just wanted to wrap up the case. Well, she had a few more surprises for them.

'Mrs Arlington,' said the female cop. 'In processing the scene, our CSI found three sets of fingerprints on glasses in your daughter's apartment. Those fingerprints were identified as belonging to Ariel, Ben and Lily Fairweather, OK?'

Sofia slowly nodded.

'We also found Ms Fairweather's sunglasses. They had prints, but there was nothing else, no DNA. Do you know what DNA is?'

'I think so,' replied Sofia prettily.

'OK, it's like a chemical identity particular to a person. Everyone on this earth has their unique DNA, and family members share strands in common.'

'Yes.'

'Well, here's our confusion. Three sets of fingerprints, and hairs: the DNA is male, OK, so we presume it's Ben's. To make sure, we take a toothbrush from his apartment, for comparison.'

'Yes, I think I understand.'

'So, we want to be thorough, Mrs Arlington, so we send the swabs to the crime lab for analysis. Our CSIs compare that DNA to the DNA contained in the saliva on Ben's glass. It's dried, but it's still there.'

'Oh dear,' said Sofia. 'This is quite technical. Chemistry was never my great strength.'

'Understood, Mrs Arlington, but I just want you to be clear on what we found here. OK, so it's a match. The hair and the saliva belong to the same person: Ben.'

'Are you sure?'

'DNA doesn't lie, ma'am.'

'So he was definitely there! In Ariel's apartment! So she is in this with Luke Castillo! Oh my God, how could she betray her own brother?'

'Well, see here, Mrs Arlington, this is what I'm getting to. We wanted to make sure that Ariel was actually *with* Ben and Lily – that someone wasn't using her apartment to frame her. I know that sounds ridiculous but you'd be surprised . . . so we compared the saliva on the third goblet to check that it was indeed Ariel's.'

Sofia had a vague sense of foreboding, but couldn't think why. Everything appeared to be going as planned. And maybe that was the reason. It was one thing to plot and make provision for the most dire emergency, but to have that emergency *occur* and to feel responsible for the consequences you had put in place to divert blame: it was difficult.

'And was it Ariel's saliva?' she breathed.

'Yes. We compared it to her toothbrush.'

Sofia covered her face with her hands and shook her head. The words 'How long do you think she'll get?' were at her lips, when the female cop cleared her throat.

'Ben is not your natural son, is he, Mrs Arlington? It

turns out', she added, before Sofia could say a word, 'that Lily Fairweather is his biological mother.'

Outside Fairview Mount Clinic, Las Vegas, that same morning

Harry

A long time ago, Harry had visited Sri Lanka. The taxi driver had stopped the car, after five minutes on the road, to pray at a shrine. Harry supposed that he was asking God to bless the journey. His trip to the HDU of Fairview Mount Clinic served a similar purpose.

His feet took him to where he needed to go. There was a lump in his throat and the word 'sorry' couldn't make it. And yet, in this cool, sanitized room, he realized that no apology was required. Instead, Harry stood at the foot of the bed where the thin, grey-haired man lay, covered in tubes, wired to machines, his head in bandages, his colostomy bag in view, and saluted his lieutenant.

Now, an hour later, he was still sitting in his car, blinking away the tears. He raked his hands through his hair, and breathed deeply. It was good. He had derived strength from the man who had always been his guide, and who had always believed in him. Jen and Oskar were a disappointment. But they were doing their job and he couldn't hold that against them. Jack would have said, 'Be the bigger man.'

He sipped the bitter coffee from the Fairview Mount cafeteria. He would have faith that the evidence would lead to the truth. Yeah, they'd all laugh about this later. Harry turned on the radio with a wry smile. The announcer's words took a while to reach his ears. He spluttered coffee over the dashboard, but she had already moved on from the arrest of Ariel Arlington on suspicion of false imprisonment to another segment, about the new bridge being built over the Hoover Dam.

Lulu's parents' house, that same morning

Lulu

> 'This is the way the ladies ride,
> *Trit, trot, trit, trot,*
> And this is the way the gentlemen ride,
> *Gallop a gallop a gallop away,*
> And this is the way the farmers ride,
> *Hobble-di-hoy, hobble-di-hoy,*
> And down, into a ditch!'

Joe squealed with laughter as Lulu bounced him high on her lap and then tipped him backwards until he was almost upside-down. 'Again,' he shouted, 'again!'

'Baby, this is the *last* time, OK?'

'OK,' said Joe, not meaning it.

Even the rhyme was Ben's, it was an old English

rhyme and Joe loved it. That man was in her head, in her soul: how could he have vanished? She couldn't stay still, she was on the edge of tears.

'Are you all right, honey?' said her mother, walking into the room with a cup of tea.

Lulu nodded silently. She could barely focus on Joe. The only thing stopping her from falling on the floor and screaming with despair was to say this rhyme, over and over again. Joe was just young enough not to notice the nuance of mood. As long as she kept reciting and bouncing, he was happy, and she could think.

She knew she was insignificant to the great Arlington Corporation, but she was important to Ben. Every time she recalled Sofia hissing in her face: 'You loved him, and you blew it!' a small, defiant voice in Lulu's head replied that this was only true if she had given up on Ben – or she could seize the chance to make it right.

She didn't believe any of the rumours. There was rubbish about Luke Castillo, even Arnold Ping, but Lulu was certain that neither man would gain by causing harm to Ben. If Ben had been concerned about Castillo or Ping, he would have told her. And knowing that gave Lulu faith – that even if she didn't realize it, Ben had equipped her with the information that would make her useful.

'One second, darling,' she said. 'Here, look at this.' She gave Joe his favourite book and then, when he threw it aside, she sighed and turned on the television. 'Don't think this is normal,' she said guiltily, 'because it's not. It's just for today!'

She beckoned her mother to come out of the room. 'I have to do something,' she said. 'I can't just sit here.'

'You go, darling,' said her mother. 'But don't for heaven's sake do anything reckless. We'll look after Joe.'

Ten minutes later, she was driving to the Arlington residence. She had at least four kinds of ID, and if she said she had information vital to the investigation, maybe they'd let her in. Ben was missing and she had to do *something*.

The Medici, early that evening

Frank

Frank had also heard the news, which was why he was currently being dunked in the murky water of the Medici's ugly ornamental fountain. One steroid-happy bouncer was holding him under by the scruff of his neck like a dog; another ape was pressing his knee hard enough on Frank's back to crack his spine.

He had driven his purple Lamborghini (a car that could be heard from the distance of several blocks) at the highest speed it was capable of (10 mph, as he was driving down the Strip on a Saturday evening) until he reached the Medici's front lawn. He roared up the ugly mosaic drive, his hand jammed on the horn.

Then he smashed through the fake plastic shrubs on to the fake plastic lawn, right into the curly neon 'MEDICI HOTEL & CASINO' sign, revving, reversing, revving, reversing. The sign now read 'DIC HOTEL & AS'.

It was Fight Weekend, and the match was about to begin.

The Medici lagged behind every other casino in terms of food, shops and marketing intelligence, but on a fight night, they kicked everyone's ass. The Roman Arena rivalled the Garden Arena at MGM; it had fourteen thousand seats to Kirk Kerkorian's fifteen and its décor was a little careworn, but its lean, mean atmosphere gave it the edge. The boxers, the promoters, the managers liked the Medici: it was coldly unrefined and put people in the mood for violence.

Tonight was party night at the Cat; it was party night everywhere, because a big fight brought in the serious gamblers. Frank's hosts would have snapped up the hottest ringside tickets at the Medici for their rich, hard-betting players, and secured tickets to the pre-match celebrity party. Frank could never stand the thought that he was making money for Luke, so he always told himself that Luke was making money for *him*. After the excitement of the fight, his players would return to the Cat in the mood to party. Even though Frank and Luke hated each other, a fight at the Medici benefited them both, and demanded collaboration.

Frank was an egotist, but tonight he was grateful for his team. He hadn't been able to deal with work since Ben had gone. He felt raw, as if his skin had been flayed off. He was not a figurehead. He ran his empire; his was the last word. He had tried to suffocate his terror about Ben by losing his mind in the business, but he couldn't hear what people were saying, let alone make a decision. His head felt wadded with cotton wool.

As they sensed his paralysis, his most trusted employees had smoothly, respectfully moved for him, like white blood cells fighting an infection. He was relieved: no one, not the media, not his enemies, not his guests or shareholders, would be able to claim that standards at his hotels had slipped. Not so much as a creased pillowcase or forgotten salt shaker or wilted lily would reflect that the Arlingtons' beloved son was missing, possibly dead, and his parents were destroyed.

The fact that company stock had dropped like a stone felt like a betrayal. He couldn't think about it.

As for Sunshine, to his surprise and disappointment, she had taken 'sick leave'. Sofia had told him the engagement was off, but he didn't believe her; young people these days were always off and on. All the same, he had expected her support. Perhaps it was simply too much for her; not only her fiancé, but her mother was missing. The police had grilled her, he knew, but she had given them nothing. The female officer had assured him they'd keep an eye. He'd known though, in his heart, that Sunshine was not involved. It was Luke Castillo. And Frank was going to get the truth out of that bastard if he died trying.

As he sat, slightly dazed, in his crumpled Lamborghini – it was an expensive protest – security swarmed and he yelled, 'Luke Castillo took my son, give me my son, give me my son—'

He got a punch in the face, and four burly men roughly hauled him away from the staring crowds. The warm-up fight was imminent and even though tickets had sold out months earlier, people were still desperate to be close to the action. The queue snaked from the door, a fat unwieldy line that spilled off the pavement. Hundreds lifted their cell phones and took photos, and that was just *fine*.

Frank didn't stop shouting and struggling as he was dragged through reception and thrown to the floor. Lying with his face pressed against the dirty red patterned carpet for ten minutes he was aware of orders being received. Then he heard heavy footsteps coming closer. He felt the vibrations through the floor, even as he heard the *click, click* of steel capped heels on marble. He guessed that Luke would not be pleased to have been dragged out of the pre-fight press conference.

A gun was now rested on his cranium, but by rolling his eyeballs so far into his head that they ached, Frank could see a pair of black Italian designer shoes, stretched to capacity, three inches from his face. He braced himself for a kick to the skull, but none came. Instead, the soft order: 'Let him go.'

Frank jumped up and screamed in Luke's face: '*Where is he, you son of a bitch?*'

Luke sighed. He was done up in a monkey suit for the fight. 'Frank, Frank, always so impetuous. Your problem, Arlington, is you never *think*. My guess is you're not a reader, are you, Frank? The written word is too slow and considered a medium for you. It's a shame, Frank. You learn so much from reading. I'm not talking about novels, Frank, novels are pap, invariably the product of a sick mind bled out on to a page. I'm talking about *facts* – official documents – those apparently dreary but so informative bureaucratic markers by which the State attempts to retain its feeble grasp on its citizens from birth to death . . .'

As Luke rambled on, a tiny flicker of doubt entered Frank's bruised head as to whether Castillo was the kidnapper. This was unfortunate, coming as it did *after* he had crashed his favourite car into the centrepiece of his rival's hotel. But Luke was a superb manipulator. He was probably talking shit.

'Let's talk in the arena,' said Luke. 'I like to be the first. I like to get comfortable.'

In a daze, Frank followed him past the vast aquarium of sharks where, every day, hotel patrons were treated to the sight of those prehistoric killing machines in an orgiastic feeding frenzy (dinner was fish, although there were rumours that these man-eaters were also fed snacks from higher up the food chain).

Breathing hard, Luke traipsed up the endless curling flights of stairs. 'Elevators are for fat people,' he wheezed.

Finally, they reached the roof and the entrance to the massive open-air arena. It was lazily modelled on the Colosseum except, as Luke had boasted, 'The Colosseum didn't have a retractable roof for the one day in the year it pisses rain.' Also, the seats were plastic, rather than stone. It was perfect for its purpose, because as Ariel might have said, it was tacky as hell. Ah God, *Ariel*. Frank's heart beat hard as he recalled the moment he'd heard the newsflash: *Ariel Arlington has been arrested on suspicion of unlawful imprisonment* . . . Well, he'd ordered his solicitors to post bail, whatever the figure. It was the least he could do.

Luke walked slowly down towards the front of the arena, and motioned that Frank should do the same. Security guards with sniffer dogs were walking up and down the aisles. Lights and microphones were being checked. Within minutes, the great black metal doors would be flung open, and fourteen thousand people would swarm in.

As if Luke could read the pain in Frank's eyes, he shook his head. 'Poor little Ariel,' he said between pants. 'She didn't do it, you know.'

'I KNOW SHE DIDN'T DO IT!' screamed Frank over his shoulder. '*You* did it.' He wiped the sweat from his forehead.

'Me?' boomed Luke. The sound of his voice echoed around the vast arena. He faced Frank and tapped his own chest. He looked amused. 'I can see why you might think I'm involved, because, certainly, no one hates your family more than I do. But I had nothing to do with it. I wouldn't risk my peace of mind, Frank, not on putting *you* in your place.'

Frank's voice was quiet with rage. 'My son is gone and my daughter is under arrest. Put yourself in my place.'

As a small blonde girl with big hair and bigger boobs showed Luke to his padded ringside seat, Frank considered falling to his knees and begging. But it would be the wrong gesture to a man like Luke. It would be the wrong gesture to any man, for who respected desperation?

Luke smiled. 'I couldn't, Frank. Your place is New York. Las Vegas is *my* place. You lack humility, Frank. You came to this town, and you trampled all over it.'

The faint thunder of excitement rose to a roar as the

doors of the arena opened and the noisy crowds swarmed in like a herd of velociraptors.

The aggressive thump of the music invaded Frank's head, squeezing his thoughts into a corner. The middleweight fight no one gave a toss about would be first on the card; the big fight wouldn't start for hours. Frank would get the information he needed and leave before a single punch was thrown and he was glad. There was so much violence in his head that he had no wish to witness any more.

He sat, listless, as Luke greeted his whales; fucking shady bunch, the lot of them. At least three of his own major players were there, and he was forced to slap on his public face and exchange chitchat. Of course, anyone with access to a television or the internet knew the situation, but he made it plain from his jovial address that gossip concerning his personal life was not relevant here. Frank felt choked by Luke's rich cologne; it mingled with the greasy smell of hot dogs, burgers and sweat, mutating into one overwhelming, supercharged stink.

'Hubris, Frank,' added Luke, dropping hard back into his seat. 'It's a Greek word. It means "head so far up your own ass you can't smell that you're waist deep in shit". Ben is a schmuck, he deserves to be punished.' He leaned forward as far as his stomach would allow. 'I don't like you, Frank. I've never liked you.' Luke paused to sip at a Diet Coke. 'But now I'm going to point you in the right direction.'

'Why?' croaked Frank. His body was beginning to ache.

Luke grinned. 'Because you're so stupid, Frank, I don't think the truth is ever going to penetrate your thick skull. So I'm going to help you solve your problem, and I'll tell you why: the truth isn't going to make you feel better, Frank. It's going to make you feel a hell of a lot worse.'

The howls and jeering and cheers of the crowd were loud and grating in his ear as the sleek, bronzed announcer verbally whipped them into a frenzy. 'The most anticipated match in the history of boxing!'

There were screams of excitement and terror as the two boxers swaggered into the arena, each screwing up his face like an angry gorilla and gesturing, surrounded by a bevy of scantily clad showgirls. It was a cross between ancient Rome and a game show. The trainers, cuts man, promoters, girlfriends, hung off the sides of the ropes; everyone talking, arguing, passionate; the stink of bodies intensifying. It was so primal that it made the hairs on the back of your neck bristle.

And yet, amid the furore, the concentration of energy and heat, Frank, trembling with rage, felt dizzy and weak. Luke's calm in the face of his accusations had knocked the puff out of him.

As the announcer roared, 'Are you rrrrrrrrrrrrrrready to ruuuuh-uuumble?!' Frank had the sensation that he wasn't ready at all.

Arlington Residence, earlier that day

Lulu

She couldn't get out of the house fast enough. She didn't know what she had heard but she knew it was crucial to Ben's disappearance. She had taken a cab to the Arlington Residence, shown her ID to the guard and grandly announced that she had information that exonerated Ariel. This was a lie as there was zero evidence, merely opinion, but security had let her through.

She had wanted to speak to Sofia, but it appeared that Sofia was talking to the police. Lulu had waited, feeling foolish, outside the sitting-room door, not wanting to knock. It was wrong to listen, but the voices were so loud, it was impossible not to hear. Especially when she had her ear pressed to the door.

'. . . compared your DNA swab to Ben's . . . compared Ben's DNA to Ariel's . . . no strands in common, proving that, by blood, Ben is unrelated to you and Ariel but . . .'

'He's adopted,' she heard Sofia blurt. 'But I had *no* idea that he was . . . She must have put her daughter up to it to get close to him! No wonder the girl called it off at the last minute, she . . .'

What? She couldn't hear everything, but she had heard enough. Ben was not Sofia's real son. Right then, Lulu knew she was in danger. She must creep out of the house undetected and tell someone, but *who*?

Holding her breath, she backed away from the door. OK, nice and quiet. She squeezed her eyes shut briefly, and thought of Joe, safe, sweet, her little wombat, she called him, because he was so cuddly and chunky, it would—

She screamed as someone gripped her arm. She stared into the cold eyes of Sterling, that creepy henchman of Sofia's. He had appeared from nowhere, silent as the grave.

'I was just going—'

'You're not *going*,' he said. She looked away from him.

The sitting-room doors burst open; Sofia and two police officers. 'What's going on?' said Sofia sharply. 'Lulu? What are you doing here?'

'Listening at doors,' said Sterling. 'And we all know that no good comes from listening at doors.'

Lulu's voice suddenly lost power. 'I just came to see if I could be of any help,' she croaked.

Sofia smiled. 'I'm sure you could, Lulu. Wait with Sterling until the police are done.'

The female police officer said, 'Who are you, Lulu?'

'I'm Ben's PA,' she replied.

The police officer raised an eyebrow. 'Ah yes. You allowed Ariel to stay in your apartment. We'll take a break now. Sofia, if you could arrange for the adoption documents to get to me at the station, asap, I'd appreciate that. We also need to speak to Frank. Any idea where we can find him?'

Sofia grimaced: 'I'm so sorry, but no, although I'll pass on the message as soon as I see him.'

Lulu could barely speak for terror. The cops were sauntering towards the grand front door, leaving her in this vast soulless house, with its labyrinth of basements and cellars, to her fate.

Why had Sofia lied? It was plain that she didn't want the police to repeat the adoption lie to Frank. She wanted *no one* to repeat the adoption lie. Lulu knew it was a lie because she and Ben had discussed adoption: she'd told him that when she had fallen pregnant with Baby Joe, a relative had suggested it. Lulu refused to consider it, and Ben had agreed that he couldn't understand how a woman could give up her own baby. If *he* had been adopted, Lulu was sure he would have told her then.

'Officer!' cried Lulu. 'Would you be able to give me a ride?'

The female cop smiled at Lulu in an unfriendly way. 'Sure,' she said. 'It would be good to hear your take on this.'

'Yes, of course, thank you.' Lulu bit back tears of relief as Sterling released his grip with regret. She walked out of the house on wobbly legs with her police guard.

Las Vegas, halfway up a mountain, noon

Lulu

Occasionally, the combined pressures of being a mother and a professional and a housekeeper while retaining the luxury of washing her face in the morning merged into a big custard pie splodge in her head and made her an idiot – like the time Ben and Joe were waiting for her in his black Mercedes SLK Roadster outside the store, and she'd gone to the wrong, near identical car, and stood there wondering why Ben was now ten years older, and why there were *two* children in the back . . .

But now, buzzing with adrenaline, her brain felt pin-sharp. She would wow the police with a finely honed argument as to why Ariel must be innocent.

The police were talking quietly. 'If anyone knows where they are, *she* does . . . She won't do anything until tonight. Too risky. Put a tail on her then . . . lead us to her . . .'

Lulu strained her ears, but the police stopped talking.

'So,' said the female officer. 'You're pretty friendly with Ariel?'

'A little,' said Lulu. 'We work together – or we did – and now and then, we'd go out together. Ariel is sweet and fun. I have a young son, and Ariel always teased me that I didn't get out enough. She did argue with Ben, but she regretted it and was hoping to make up with him. She had come to me sad about breaking up with her boyfriend and so I offered her my apartment. She didn't feel like going home; but I don't think there was any sinister reason, other than wanting some peace and quiet. I think she felt embarrassed about having fought with her brother, because they are actually very close—'

The female cop's cell phone rang. She signalled for Lulu to stop talking.

'Frank's posted bail.'

The cops exchanged glances, and Lulu's heart hammered. Did this mean that Ariel was *free*? Thank goodness.

'Lulu, thank you, you've been a help. We have your details, so we'll get in touch if we need to speak with you again.'

They dropped her off outside the high silver fence of a modern architectural 'triumph' as she had requested. It was halfway up a mountain and, according to its owner, often quoted in *Vegas* magazine, 'The most attractive feature on the real-estate listing was the entry, 'Community name: None'.

Lulu sighed, and rang the video entrance phone. This was not going to be fun, but she would be selfless in the accomplishment of her mission, which was to tell someone who could *do* something, who might *know* something that could help Ben. And, she was sorry to say, that person was Ben's fiancée: Sunshine Beam.

The official word was that Sunshine Beam had taken 'sick leave'. Lulu presumed she was too distraught to work. Unless she had checked into a clinic, she must be here. The elaborately wrought steel gates whirred open, and Lulu started uncertainly down the wide flagstone path.

'What do *you* want?' screeched Sunshine, suddenly appearing in the middle of the path. 'You've got a nerve, you little tart! Get off my property! Go!' She was swigging from a bottle and her eyes were glittery. Her hair was spiky with grease, and she was wearing old navy track pants. Oh God. Sunshine looked as if she might hit her, which, actually was fair enough.

'Oh, will you be quiet, Sunshine, for one minute!'

It appeared that she had stunned Sunshine into silence.

'I'm so sorry. I'm so sorry about Ben. You must be

frantic' – Lulu just stopped herself from blurting, '*I* am' – 'but I heard something. Sofia said it and I'm not sure, but I think it has something to do with why he's gone, and it might help find him.' Lulu sucked in her stomach and stood tall. 'I don't like you either, Sunshine, and I wouldn't disturb you unless I thought it was important.' Immediately, she felt unkind and added softly, 'You must be desperate to get him back.'

Sunshine opened her mouth, and then shut it again. 'What did you hear?' she said eventually.

Lulu stood on the path, in the midday heat, and told her.

Sunshine sat down suddenly on the manicured lawn. Lulu sat down too, and realized the grass was plastic. She was a little concerned for Sunshine's health. 'Are you OK?'

Sunshine's eyes were wide, and she flicked Lulu on the arm and said, 'Shush! I'm thinking!'

Lulu pursed her lips and said nothing. Then she jumped: Sunshine had burst out laughing. 'Oh my *God*, oh my GOD,' she shrieked, and before Lulu could lurch away, Sunshine had grabbed her and kissed her smack on the lips with fumy vodka breath.

'What? What?' she cried. 'Do you know where he is?' Lulu suddenly remembered that Ben was with Sunshine's *mother*. She had been so focused on finding Ben that she had forgotten. 'Do you know where your mother is?'

'Yes,' said Sunshine, grinning. She seemed quite mad with glee. 'Thank you, dear Lulu. You know, Ben was right. You really are a star.'

Lulu wanted to shake her. 'Please, Sunshine, where is he? Is he in danger? What does it mean?'

'I shouldn't think so,' said Sunshine. 'I should think that Ben is perfectly safe. And *I*, Sunshine Arlington, am – with the right team of lawyers, of course – a cool billion dollars richer!'

Lulu stared at her. Had she taken out some horrible insurance policy on Ben? She was already calling herself Sunshine Arlington. Had they married in secret? Oh *God*. Suddenly she felt so weary that she could have lain down on the hot pavement and fried to death in her sleep.

Then she remembered. Ariel's ex-boyfriend, Harry; he was a police officer. And he was Luke Castillo's son. But she couldn't believe that *he* was in on it – anyone who dated Ariel had to have a soft heart. Anyhow, she'd take the risk. He was her only chance. Lulu hazarded a look at Sunshine's car. It was low and fast-looking, and – yes! – the keys were inside it. As Sunshine staggered towards her mighty front door, waving her hand over her head in a drunken goodbye, Lulu crept towards the car. As she turned on the ignition, the silver gates whirred slowly open.

'*Hey!*' shouted Sunshine, reappearing at the vast front door.

'I'll bring it back later!' shouted Lulu. 'I promise! I'm a careful driver!'

'*Vrrrrrrrrrrrrrrrrrrrrrrrm*,' said the car, making Lulu squeak. As she backed at top speed out of the drive, Sunshine covered her eyes with her hand. But she didn't try and stop her. For some reason, Sunshine believed she was about to be one billion dollars richer. Presumably, then, she could buy as many low fast cars as she wished.

Arlington Residence, that evening

Frank

Luke's driver had given him a ride home.

Frank burst into the great blue nursery and sank to his knees on the soft carpet. The sound and fury of the fight had kept him operational. Now silence and stillness gave stage to his fears and he moaned aloud.

He staggered over to the grand carved oak cot and pulled the pale blue cellular blanket and cried into it. Oh, my boy . . . He was retching with the agony of loss. It smelled musty, and yet he could still recall the beautiful baby smell. He'd return from work and sniff Ben's hair. 'I adore him,' he'd say to Sofia, 'he's my little protégé.'

They had decided to preserve that magical time by keeping the nursery as it was. Now, holding a stale baby blanket, Frank realized their idea was a curse, the kind of thing people did for dead children.

Frank was strung out and exhausted, unable to cope with the torture of his imagination. These last nights, he'd been falling asleep listening to the radio. The mindless murmuring of the late-night presenters seeping into his skull was preferable to his own thoughts and the terrible wondering about Ben's fate.

He was sure now that Luke wasn't responsible. The man was a filthy liar but if he had done it, he would have found some way, however obscure, of letting Frank know. His ego would demand it.

Instead, he had tried to taunt Frank with rubbish about Sofia. Was the truth in their marriage certificate?

Luke had said, 'Look close to home. Actually, Frank, look *in* your home. Look in your *bed.*'

God knows, there was no love left. The disappearance of Ben, and the stress and pain, had ripped away the veneer of civility between them.

He'd followed police orders, and not paid the ransom. The deadline had passed, and nothing had happened – no word, no sign, no proof that Ben was alive – and Frank felt helpless and stupid and foolish, wondering if he'd made a terrible mistake. He should have paid the money in secret. If it was someone *else's* child, he would have made the transfer, but it was his child and he couldn't risk it.

He could feel his worn and beleaguered brain trying to scramble sense. *Official documents* . . . Of course: the key to Ben's disappearance was, according to Luke, there in an official document.

He had no idea where Sofia kept them.

He called Gloria-Beth and told her to check with his legal team. It took an agonizing twenty-five minutes for her to roust them out of their Fight Night parties and into their offices to search for the documents. But finally, he had a response, and it wasn't good. Mrs Arlington's legal team had retained the original documents. 'Send what you have,' he ordered grimly. As he leafed through them, the tremor in his fingers forced him to place the documents on his desk. But though he scrutinized them, even grabbing a magnifying glass, he couldn't see anything out of the ordinary. There was a birth certificate for each child, and for Sofia, and for himself. There was their marriage certificate. He swept the papers to the floor.

Something was missing. He needed to see the original documents. A call to Sofia's solicitor from his PA elicited the cool response: 'We only have copies. Mrs Arlington has retained the original documents.'

Then he knew that she was hiding something from him in one of those documents. Otherwise, the safest place for them would have been with her solicitors or the bank. He swallowed. The trouble was, Frank realized, that Sofia had taken over.

He couldn't check the security system at source, because she had peopled it with *her* men. He flicked through the surveillance images in his study; they weren't comprehensive, but he could see only staff. There was no sign of Sofia or Sterling. He had a little time before any one of her cold grey men reported back to the boss.

Frank was certain that whatever it was he needed was in the house. *Where?* He walked slowly, casually, to the master bedroom. Frank pulled open Sofia's bedside table drawers. He walked into her closet and opened her wardrobes. He stood on a ladder and lifted down hat boxes.

Nothing.

He hesitated, before lifting the mattress off the bed. Nothing. What mattered to his wife, apart from Ben? What really mattered?

Money.

Frank revved up his Maserati and roared downtown to their other, older, smaller property. Bijou was no longer called Bijou, it was called Ace Harry's. Ace Harry's was where Ariel had managed to pull in eighteen million dollars by putting music, booze and a bunch of horny kids in the pool area on a Sunday lunchtime and calling it: 'day life'. In her own sweet way she was a smart girl; he'd let her down. God, he'd failed his kids.

'Back in Black' blasted out from his car stereo. He turned it off. He needed silence. The air con chilled his hot forehead and goose pimples ran up his arms. He banged his fist on the steering wheel and howled with impatience, grateful for the tinted windows as he waited at the intersection. He stared hopelessly into the sea of tourists bumbling along in their pastel T-shirts, pink, yellow, pale blue, as if miraculously, Ben would emerge, warm and alive, from their mass.

Frank ditched his car, chucking the keys at the valet. He pulled his baseball cap down and summoned the Chief of Security – a guy he'd known for fifteen years, one of *his* fellows. He explained his requirements. The man nodded slowly, not daring to say 'no'. Silently, he ushered Frank down into the vault, through a series of metal doors and old-style key pads to the hard count room.

All the coins collected from the slot machines on the casino floor by the count crew ended up here. The money was transported on a cart to the vault area, and the final destination of every coin gambled away was this small concrete room. The walls were concrete; the floor was concrete. Inside the room were ten top-loading machines that counted and rolled coins. Each one could count up to three thousand coins and wrap up to forty rolls per minute.

But this was an old-style operation. They stopped short of cleaning the coins so the gals' white gloves stayed white. The crew wore uniforms and, following reports of a complaint about 'itchy eyes', Sofia had offered the crew the opportunity to wear respirators during their shift. Sofia didn't want anyone hitting them with a lawsuit, and the fine patina of nickel, copper and zinc dust that covered all surfaces at the end of every shift suggested that metal-dust pollution might be an issue.

And, as well as providing ear protectors for the crew, Sofia had ordered the receptors of the top-loading machine chute to be lined with velvet, to reduce the cacophony of metal hitting metal during the transfer of coins from the container.

Oh yes, Sofia appeared to be a model employer, but Frank knew why she took such care of her staff's health and welfare, way beyond what the unions demanded: she couldn't be arsed to deal with the bigger problems caused by the small neglects that came further down the line.

Ten years earlier, one senior catering hostess had gouged them for months of paid sick leave and then had the nerve to expect sympathy. 'Let me tell you why I'm depressed,' she'd said to Sofia.

'Or keep it to yourself?' Sofia had replied. 'I don't go that deep.'

It had emerged that the woman had had a miscarriage. This could not be legally blamed on the fact that her job involved a degree of heavy lifting and a lot of standing up, but after the woman finally quit with a lump sum, Sofia had become a health-and-safety zealot.

Frank leaned against the whitewashed corridors in the bowels of the building and inhaled the chalky smell of brickwork. That was Sofia's way, he realized: she appeared to take care of you, but in fact she was taking care of business. But now she was found out. He was moments away from uncovering her secret.

Frank's heart pounded high and fast. It was 1.29 a.m., the start of the first shift. The count crew would still be systematically removing paper and coin currency from each slot machine on the casino floor. He had plenty of time.

He stood for one minute before a man brought him a chair. But he was too agitated to sit. In moments, it was done. Noiselessly, the cameras focused on the hard count room lost power.

Frank watched as the security guards stationed along the corridor walked obediently away. Then he slipped into the hard count room, pressing shut the bullet-proof door behind him.

He raked his hand through his thick black hair, and a thousand reflections copied his movement. While the cameras had been switched off, the many mirrors in the room mocked him. He felt clownish, and rattled. He was so nervous he almost tripped over a rolling cart.

Where?

He knew instinctively, just as a man who sees for the

first time the woman he is going to marry and *knows*, that Sofia's secret was in here. Carefully, he pressed his hands along the walls. He trod every inch of the floor. He even checked the coin-counting machines for secret compartments.

Then he looked up.

The ceiling was suspended. There was 4 feet of space between the real ceiling and the suspension. Frank really wasn't sure why; heating and ventilation wasn't of great interest to him. He guessed it had something to do with fire regulations.

Frank dragged a rolling cart to the centre of the room and stood on top of it. This gave him just enough height to reach the air-conditioning vent. He pushed; it lifted away. He took a deep breath and fumbled in the darkness. It was furry, dusty, and he shuddered. He gritted his teeth, stretching as far as he could, and groped further. His fingers briefly brushed against cardboard. Grunting with effort, blinking the sweat from his eyes, he jammed his arm into the black as far as it would go and grabbed at the object. It was a thin manila folder.

He held it in his hand, suddenly terrified. He squeezed his eyes shut tight, and then, with clumsy grasp, he opened it.

But before his eyes could focus on the document, a powerful shove sent the cart spinning across the room. Frank fell backwards with a shout. His head smacked into the concrete wall and everything became night.

Hard count room, Ace Harry's, early morning, 6 September 2009

Sofia

As he lay on the ground, she cradled him.

'Oh my God, Frank.' She stroked his hair. She murmured softly in his ear, 'I love you, Frank. I did. I do.'

Briefly, he struggled to consciousness, choking, gasping for air. His last word took every last scrap of energy and will. 'Ben,' he said, splattering the front of her bustier with blood.

'Just a little money I'd put aside for myself,' she murmured, waving the folder, knowing that he would believe it. As Frank closed his eyes with a pained smile, she shoved Ben's original birth certificate into her bag. Bessie had called him Tyler. Her lip curled. She felt sick about Frank; she had heard the crack of his skull, but at least it would be quick. Knowing he was nearly gone, she whispered that the ambulance was on its way. It's OK, she lied, Ben was found; it was the woman, she was crazy, but he was fine, he was coming home to his daddy. She saw the question in Frank's eyes, and told him Ariel was innocent: the Arlington family was whole again. She felt his body relax.

'Our boy is safe, and our girl is innocent,' she said again, fiercely, and Frank's last thoughts as the world faded were that his wife had never been so curiously tender and that if his son was safe and his daughter was innocent then his greatest purpose in life had been achieved.

BOOK 4

Angel, mid-morning, 6 September 2009

Ben

Ben stared at the grubby floor of the Bunny Fluff Motel and wondered why Lily didn't care about dirt. He had to get out of here. He had done as much as she could expect. Sofia would have killed her at the hospital; he had fulfilled his duty.

So here they were, two strangers with nothing in common, hiding out in a godforsaken desert hole. He had a life to get back to – at least, he hoped he did. And Sofia must realize that it was too late to try to silence the woman she had paid to give her a son, now that the son knew the truth.

It was time to leave.

'Lily,' he said.

She winced. She'd wanted him to call her 'Mommy'.

'I need to go.'

'*Why?*' she cried. 'We've had so little time together! We're just getting to know each other after all these lost years.'

He bit back his response, which was that they

hadn't been lost; they'd been surrendered for cash.

'You'll be safe now, Lily. The truth is out. Everyone will know, and that in itself is protection.'

The woman was dissolving into tears; it horrified him. 'You can't go! Stay and look after me! I have no one else! She'll kill me anyway! She hates me.'

'My feeling is Sofia will be too busy with a lot of expensive lawyers trying to keep out of jail to commit any additional crimes. People need to know where I am – and I'm sure Sunshine is concerned about you. My father will be frantic. It's too unkind. I've already put my family and friends through too much – for *your* sake.'

He was desperate to escape from her cloying presence. He wanted to be back with people who mattered to him, who truly loved him, and whom he loved, who made him feel happy.

Lulu.

He was in love with her and he'd denied it because it was so . . . *impractical*. Meanwhile, the memory of that kiss had sustained him. But he could hardly bear to remember how, when she had confessed her feelings, he'd made her feel ashamed – when she was the one.

He was a moron. And now it might be too late. He had been so caught up with his own ego that he had ignored his heart. And yet the facts were there: when he was agitated, he turned to Lulu for comfort; when he was happy, he turned to Lulu to share. She was his best friend, he never tired of her company, and she was *hot*. She was absolutely gorgeous, and a beautiful person; the way she was with Joe touched him deeply. That little fellow was easy to love, but when he saw

400

Lulu with her child, he saw how a mother should be.

Ben glanced at Lily. She gazed at him hopefully. She was twisting her hair through her fingers, again and again, fast. She looked unhinged.

'What are you thinking?' she said.

He shrugged, and then took pity on her. 'I'm thinking about the woman I love,' he said, 'about how she fits into my world.' A smile crept across his face as he thought of Lulu. 'She can cope with anyone, and anything; a puffed-up casino operator or a waffling world leader. I guess I'm wondering if I can fit into *her* world. She thinks I don't appreciate what I have, and that annoys her. She thinks I fight against admitting how lucky I am.'

But he and Lulu valued the same things: personal relationships, loyalty and close family ties.

'Oh my *darling*,' cried Lily. 'Of course I can fit into your world! Oh baby, you are so sweet!'

Ben stared at her aghast. 'I'm sorry, Lily. But I wasn't talking about you. I meant the woman I want to *marry*.'

'Sunshine!' spat Lily. 'That bitch!'

His feelings for Sunshine had melted away, leaving a residue of embarrassment. There was a new clarity. He could see now how Sunshine took after her blood mother: Sofia. They were two of a kind, hard, cold, out for what they could get at the expense of whoever had the misfortune to stand in their way. He had been blinded by her beauty and confidence. Success was attractive; it masked a lot of ugliness. Frank had a saying, trotted out every time a business rival opened a new, glittering hotel: 'It's not the hen that cackles most that lays the largest egg.'

Sunshine made a lot of noise, but she was an empty shell.

'Sunshine isn't so bad,' said Ben. 'She's just ambitious. But no, it's over between Sunshine and me.'

'So who's the lucky lady?' sneered Lily.

'Lily,' said Ben. 'You have no right to be bitter. My family are the people who are there for me. You weren't there.'

Lily lit another cigarette. 'You're nothing like your father,' she said. She laughed.

'My father is Frank,' said Ben.

Ah, God. Frank. The knowledge would destroy him. But, thought Ben fiercely, in every fibre of his being he was Frank's son, in spirit, if not in blood; and Ben looked forward to telling him so to his face. Ben felt a sweep of gratitude for all that Frank had given him: the man had a heart full of love. There was nothing more important.

'You have a brother,' said Lily wildly, 'and a sister! Sam and Marylou! Don't you want to meet them?'

Ben shook his head. 'I'm sorry, Lily. But you don't understand. Ariel is my sister.'

The first thing Ben would do on his return was to find Ariel and ask her if she wanted in on his Macau venture. No, no. The first thing he would do was to find Ariel and tell her he loved her. And when he was satisfied that he and Ariel were good again, he would seek out Lulu to apologize – and tell her he loved *her*.

'I suppose it's about money,' said Lily. 'You don't want to be mine because I can't make you rich.'

Ben sighed. 'Believe that if you wish.'

It had occurred to him, in a sweet irony, how he had

often said that he would not take up his inheritance. Now, perhaps, if he was proven to be the son of *other* parents, legally, he might not be able to claim the inheritance regardless. It appealed to him, that cosmic joke. He had no fear – not now, not any more.

Lily sniffed and wiped her nose on the back of her hand. 'Sofia is *evil*. Don't you want to escape from that?'

Ben shook his head. 'I know it's painful, but the truth is, Lily, I don't need you. All you have told me only makes me see how *happy* I am.'

The shock, grief, anger: all were wounds that he could recover from. He was stronger, better for his scars; he was filled with a crazy optimism, for at last he saw his future, and freedom stretching ahead. He knew what, and who, he wanted, and very little stood in his way. Even if the venture with Charlie were to come to nothing, it would not be a reason for despair. If Arnold Ping proved to be too much trouble, Ben would have no problem turning his back on Macau.

He sat on the little tin chair at the chipped Formica table as the overhead fan noisily and pointlessly stirred the hot air. He'd fly the plane out of here, report to the police, clear up the whole damn mystery. Lily hadn't bothered to remove the radio; you couldn't get reception anyway – he had tried. But he guessed the furore would be citywide – nationwide even, depending on how hysterically Sofia had decided to act. With some disbelief, he realized he didn't hate Sofia. She had loved him as much as she could love anyone.

He saw, even now, that, in Sofia's fractured, imperfect way, she loved him the most. He didn't know if he forgave her. Forgiveness was, he sensed, not a single conscious act but a slow and involuntary ebbing away of anger over time.

'You're not leaving me,' said Lily. There was a new harsh edge to her voice, that made him look up. With trembling hands, she was pointing a gun at him.

He stared at her, incredulous.

She reddened, a flash of irritation passed across her face. 'I can't . . .' she said in a husk of a voice. 'I can't lose you again.'

He stood up and said coldly, 'You just did.'

Harry's house, early that same morning

Ariel

'You're my hero,' she blurted when he opened the door. 'I'm so sorry I stormed out. I just wanted you to know that. It's, it's not too early, is it?'

Instead of laughing in her face, he pulled her inside, and she saw, to her surprise, that her recluse of an ex-boyfriend was dressed to go out.

'When did you get out? Did anyone see you come here?' said Harry. He looked and sounded different. It wasn't only that he was wearing a pressed T-shirt and fresh jeans. She could see it in his stance – it was a little more upright, proud.

Bones, trotting out from the kitchen, his claws

404

click-clacking on the stone floor, barked with joy and hurled himself at her. She picked him up, even though he weighed a ton, and kissed him.

'No,' she said. 'Now listen, Harry. I need to say what I have to say.' She put Bones down, and smiled though her knees were shaking. She was terrified Harry would tell her to get lost. Men liked women who were mean and cool, but she couldn't be like that. She was tired of playing games. She had already lost him, and her dignity: there was nothing left to fear.

'I like', she announced, 'that everything about you is *true*. You face situations that most people go out of their way to avoid. That is amazing to me. I admire your strength; I am in awe. I wanted to say I am sorry. I was wrong to try and push you, hurry you along to recover after your lieutenant was shot.' She blushed. 'And you were right about Ben.' She felt as if she might start to cry, but she resisted. 'I should have made up with him. And now he could be dead in a ditch.'

Harry gazed at her for a second. Then he stepped forward and swept her into a kiss; a long, lingering delicious kiss. 'Don't think for a moment that I let you go,' he said, gently tracing the line of her mouth. 'I was always coming back for you.' He smiled. 'You just beat me to it.'

Upon her release, she had gone home and slept for twelve hours. Then she had taken a short, cool bath, scrambled into clean clothes, and driven straight to him. It suddenly seemed ridiculous to be anywhere else.

Now she smiled, basking in the feel of his arms around her. 'Sitting in a police cell for twenty-four hours sharpens the mind. Thank goodness for Dad. He paid to bail me out. I'll work to pay him back. I owe him so much. I've been so bloody ungrateful.' Now she *was* going to cry. 'I guess he's forgiven me for being such a cow. I feel . . . different now. As if I understand a whole lot more. I need to thank him and say I'm sorry.'

'Oh baby,' murmured Harry. 'I didn't mean any of those things I said. I love you so much. You're my girl and you always will be.' He hugged her tight – almost too tight. Immediately, a curl of fear began to unravel inside her.

'What is it, Harry?' she said, pulling away.

He ran a hand through his hair. For a second he looked . . . she could only describe it as heartbroken.

'What?' she said. 'What's happened?'

He hung his head. 'Ariel,' he said. 'I need to explain. I knew you were under suspicion regarding Ben's disappearance, and I heard that you'd been arrested. But I did nothing about it.'

She couldn't wait to absolve him from guilt. 'Oh darling, don't worry! It wasn't your call! I was fine! I managed on my own! I saw it was time for me to read the newspaper with no holes cut out! And, Harry, what could you have done anyway? We'd split up—'

He shook his head impatiently. 'No, Ariel, it wasn't that. Of course I would have done anything, everything in my power to get you out of there – had I thought it was the smart thing to do. But . . .' He stopped. He stroked her cheek. She trembled. 'Someone was setting you up, trying to frame you for Ben's kidnap. I figured that as long as you were locked up, then everyone

406

involved in this bizarre situation was *safe*. Because the real culprit wouldn't harm anyone else, do anything, change anything significant, if you were behind bars, because then your innocence would be irrefutable.'

'OK,' she breathed. 'But I've been out since yesterday.'

Harry gripped her shoulders. 'I'm sorry, Ariel,' he said. 'And I wish I had known because then maybe I could have done something to prevent this.'

'Prevent what? Harry, what on earth are you going on about? I don't understand!'

He shook his head. 'I've got bad, really bad news. It's Frank. I'm so sorry to tell you, Ariel, but he's dead.'

She didn't believe him. It was impossible. Frank was so . . . alive. She stared at him, mystified. 'He can't be, Harry,' she said in a small voice. 'He just paid bail. How could he be?'

'It came through just now, on the police band. It's definitely him. And it sounds as though . . . he was killed.'

'Oh God, Harry.' As she sobbed into his shirt, he told her what he knew. 'How? Why? What does it mean?' she cried. 'Who did it?'

'He was found by the security guard. I don't know the details, but I think he bled out from a head injury. He had a fall. It looked like an accident, but it's too convenient, too much of a coincidence. I'm guessing it was the same person who was behind Ben's kidnap, but I don't know.'

She sank to the floor and howled as he rocked her and stroked her hair. 'I'm going to look after you, Ariel,' he said softly. 'I am going to look after you, for ever, like your dad would have wanted.'

She nodded, unable to speak. Bones rested a paw on her leg.

Then she drew herself up, and dried her eyes. She hugged him and whispered, 'I love you, Harry. But from now on, I am going to look after myself.'

He looked at her, alarmed. 'Don't you want to be with me?'

She stroked his face. 'Of course, darling Harry, I want you to be mine. But I don't want you to feel responsible for me, like a *child*. I've never looked after myself and I need to learn.'

'Ariel, all I mean is that we'll look after each other.' He frowned. 'And, starting right now, you aren't safe, and you're going to be in danger until your brother is located and we all find out what the hell this is all about.'

She nodded, her heart pounding. She was in shock, she supposed; she wasn't allowing herself to feel the horror of her dad's death – *death*. The word, the idea of it, in conjunction with her father, so vital, so alive, so thrilled to be part of the world, was outrageous and obscene.

'We've got to get out of here,' he said. 'This is the first place they'll look, whoever *they* are.'

'Where will we go?' she said. Her mind was blank. It took a moment to realize that he had just shoved a gun into his belt. Oh God, it was serious.

And then, *bang! Bang!* She jumped in fright. Harry put his hand over her mouth to stop her from making a sound. Someone was hammering at the door.

Leaving Fremont Street, early the same morning

Sofia

She slunk away from the crime scene; how fortunate that Frank had asked for the security cameras to be turned off. But she couldn't revel in good luck as she usually did. She felt flat, sick and sad. It was a terrible thing to take a life. In war, you were fighting for a greater cause. In war, you had to justify it, or you couldn't *live*. But to kill innocent people because you were caught in a trap of your own making: it was ugly.

Twelve years earlier, she had ordered the execution of Hank Edwards in a fit of rage. Bessie had been careless, flaunted her affair with the lawyer from work; she had not considered the consequences of her husband discovering her disloyalty. Hank Edwards, drunk on bitterness and cheap malt, had grandly demanded a paternity test, to see if his youngest daughter had been fathered by him, or his wife's boss.

Bessie had called the emergency number in a panic. After thirteen years of silence, it had been a considerable shock. But Sterling had been his usual efficient self.

At the time, Sofia had believed she had no choice. Hank would have discovered the child was *not* his, and she had no way of knowing how far he would go to in search of the truth. He might beat it out of Bessie. And then there was always the chance that Hank *knew* someone who knew someone. Sofia understood a little of the sly, sinister ways of government; who was to say that her

ot recorded on some secret database, ready to
al her darkest secrets and destroy her in one
st computer printout?

After Hank had been dealt with, Sofia had become
slack. She no longer read the surveillance reports and,
after two years, had stopped commissioning them. They
felt redundant, not to mention incriminating. She wanted
to move away, forget, and so she had madly, foolishly,
stopped watching Bessie; she had left her to her own
devices, thinking she had been taught a harsh lesson and
would not deviate again.

The fact that Ben was not Sofia's biological child was
anathema to her. *This* was the reason that she had
stopped monitoring Bessie and Casey Edwards, because
Casey Edwards was the embodiment of her damaged
psyche. Casey Edwards forced Sofia to face what she
physically and psychologically couldn't bear to: that
she had committed a sin, many sins, in order to fulfil her
wish – *the wish*.

She had been so reckless. She hadn't expected to love
Ben as much as she did. So when Hank had threatened to
destroy her idyll, she had given the order that ended his
life. Luke Castillo, all her love for him distilled into hate,
had made a handy scapegoat. How lucky that Hank had
owed him money. Back then, she had been cock-a-hoop,
as her mother would have said. Now she was wretched.
It had all fallen apart.

Frank would never know the truth, which was some
small comfort. His peace of mind, and his will, would
remain intact. And yet, over the years, she had changed.
When Sofia had begun this, she was fixated on power

and status, on reigning supreme, on making her lover rue the day he had replaced her and married another woman. Love – she had been fond of Frank – was a small and sorry part of it.

Now she was the de facto ruler of Arlington Corp. She had more money and status than she could possibly wish for. And that was the crux of it. Those two desirables were no longer what she craved. In excess, they became like any other commodity: worthless. The catalyst had become the end in itself. The baby boy, who had been so dearly bought, and the route to happiness, was what she wanted now. She loved him beyond words and flesh and blood had little to do with it. She and Bessie were fighting over the same prize. But Sofia knew that it was impossible to win.

As she crept out of Ace Harry's unseen, she was almost ready to give herself up; to admit defeat. Will you quit, Sofia, her mind asked in amazement, will you quit and have it all be for nothing? It was this thought, and the realization that, deflated and wretched as she was, she couldn't bear the idea of Bessie's gloating triumph, that steeled her resolve.

Whatever it took, she would find her son, and with him, Bessie, the pretender to her maternal throne. The hunt was no longer about the secret which, despite her best efforts, could no longer be preserved. A shared secret is like a boiled egg; its original form can never be recovered. She was beyond caring. With Frank dead, the secret hardly mattered. Now, her priorities were morally irreproachable. She would find Ben and beg him to pardon her. Once she had his forgiveness, or even his understanding, little else mattered. She would face her fate, whatever it might be, with fortitude and calm.

Of course, thought Sofia, grappling the gun out of her glove compartment and relishing the weight of it in her hand – ah, old friend – fortitude and calm would descend upon her like snowflakes, once she had pressed that barrel to Bessie's chest, squeezed the trigger and watched that woman's heart bleed out on to the desert sand.

Harry's house, a few minutes later

Lulu

After leaving Sunshine, Lulu had moved her parents and Joe into a hotel. Her mother and father had been most reluctant. The long and arduous act of persuasion had prevented her reaching Harry and Ariel until now, but Lulu couldn't regret it. She needed to be certain that her family was safe from Sofia. They were her life, and Ben would not want her to risk her life for his sake. Now she prayed that the delay would not prove fatal to *him*. She knew where Harry lived – Ben had sent his sister letters to this address. However she had been a little stunned to knock on the door and find it answered by a man with a gun in his hand. But, it was understandable. Anyone would be jittery in Ariel's situation, and Harry adored her, it was plain. The flicker of envy, to be loved like that, subsided with a sense of shame. Ariel had just heard that her beloved father had been killed, and the unknown enemy was out to get her. Lulu could hardly begrudge her a sweet boyfriend.

She felt shaky, unnerved to hear of Frank's murder. 'I'm so sorry, Ariel, I'm so sorry. I can't believe it. He is – he was a wonderful man.'

'Ariel, Lulu, this may sound harsh but we are going to have to do our grieving later. We need to clear out of here.'

'Should we go to the police?' Lulu blushed. 'I mean, the other police?'

Harry and Ariel shook their heads. 'No. They're already half convinced of Ariel's guilt, and someone is trying to pin this on her. Now Frank is dead there's a chance they'll want to take her in again for further questioning. Whoever is behind this is determined; they must have a lot to lose. And the only way we can guarantee Ariel's freedom is to find out who the hell is doing this and why.'

'I don't know *who* is doing this,' said Lulu, 'but I have certainly heard some strange things in the last twenty-four hours. I'm sure they're relevant but I don't know how.'

'Great,' said Harry. 'Let's move.'

'Move where?' said Ariel.

'Anywhere but here.'

Lulu spoke up. 'We could go to my parents' house?'

'Isn't that too obvious?' asked Ariel.

'OK,' said Harry, 'I know another place. Let's hustle!'

413

The three of them hurried out of the house, with Bones running behind, and Lulu gestured towards Sunshine's car. Lulu had always thought tinted windows were pretentious but now she was glad of them. Harry raised an eyebrow but otherwise didn't comment. He and Ariel jumped into the back seat. Harry gave directions, and Lulu drove. Ten minutes later, they pulled up outside a smart gated community. Harry spoke into the entry phone, and the gates opened. 'We're going to Mabel's house.'

He grinned, and Lulu realized it was the first time she had seen him smile.

'Mabel is my old landlady,' added Harry. 'I lodged with her for three years, after graduation. She's Spanish, very correct. OCD neat. She may seem a little disapproving, but she has a good heart. As I recall she was always spoiling the little kids next door with liquor chocolates and making them sick.'

Mabel was at least seventy, with a fierce tan and burgundy hair. She opened the door with a cold expression that immediately melted away on seeing Harry. She leaned an inch forward and allowed Harry to kiss her. She wore smart black slacks and a pressed white-and-blue-striped open-necked shirt. Harry murmured in her ear.

'The dog', said Mabel, 'can play in the yard.'

She nodded stiffly to Lulu and Ariel and showed them into an immaculate sitting room. The white crocheted tablecloth, the old piano and grandfather clock, the mantel full of carefully arranged bone-china animal figurines, the yellowed photograph of a young man in his army uniform: it all gave Lulu a pang.

'Don't knock anything,' she said briskly and shut the door.

'OK,' said Harry. 'Lulu, what do you know?'

Lulu glanced nervously at Ariel. 'This is awkward,' she said.

Ariel shook her head. 'Don't worry about me,' she said firmly. 'Right now, honey, I am entirely *goal-orientated*. I'll do whatever it takes to find Ben – and get justice for my dad.' Her voice trembled, and then recovered. 'Hit me with whatever you like. Nothing is going to hurt or surprise me.'

Oh dear. People always said that and then Lulu would blab out something tactless, and their promise turned out to be a lie.

'Well then,' she said slowly. 'I overheard the police telling Sofia that this supposed evidence was found in your apartment. They found fingerprints belonging to Ben, yourself, and Lily Fairweather—'

'That's right,' said Ariel. 'I didn't even know who Lily Fairweather was, but the police tell me she's Sunshine's mother, the woman who disappeared with Ben.'

'So Sunshine changed her name from Fairweather to Beam?' said Harry. 'Hardly seems worth the effort.'

Lulu snorted. 'No, she changed it from *Edwards* to Beam. Fairweather is Lily's maiden name. I had to go through this whole rigmarole to track down her mother for the engagement party – and, well, Lily Fairweather didn't seem to exist. So I spoke to a girl I know at the Medici, and she spoke to HR – well, she didn't speak to them, but she found an old file – and Sunshine's old name is Casey Edwards. I found an Edwards, a Bessie

Edwards, that seemed to fit, but obviously, she doesn't *call* herself that so I addressed the envelope to—'

'Edwards?' said Harry. 'The family name is *Edwards*?'

'Yes, although when I went to Sunshine's house yesterday, to try and see if *she* could help – you'd think she might want to help find her fiancé if not her mother – I found she'd changed her name again. She was calling herself Sunshine *Arlington*. You know' – Lulu prayed that her voice sounded smooth and unruffled – 'maybe Sunshine and Ben have already married in secret. Could that have something to do with this? Sunshine also seemed to think she was a lot richer, suddenly. You don't think she's hoping he *won't* come back? Oh my God, maybe she and her mother were in this together? Sunshine marries Ben, the mother does away with him, and then Sunshine claims his inheritance!'

'It's . . . possible,' said Harry. 'What else? Was there anything else?'

'Yes,' said Lulu. 'There was.' She paused. 'I'm sorry, Ariel, but the DNA from your apartment showed that Ben is – of course he is your brother – but he's not your *genetic* brother. When the police put this to your mother, she said he was . . . adopted. I think they told her something else, but I couldn't hear that bit. But I got the feeling she was lying her head off.'

'Oh my God.' Ariel burst into tears.

Lulu sighed. 'Sorry, Ariel, I didn't mean to upset you.'

Ariel sobbed into her hands while Harry patted her back. 'It's not your fault, Lulu,' she gulped. Then she pinched the bridge of her nose; sat up; dried her eyes. 'I'm sorry,' she said. 'I feel like my family, my life is

416

disintegrating. But if Ben is not my natural brother, then he *must* be adopted.'

'Or Sofia had an affair.'

Ariel wrinkled her nose. 'But . . . *how*? It would have to have been . . . She had me pretty much nine months after they met, and then Ben, almost directly after that. We worked it out once that she was only non-pregnant for about two or three months. Do women have affairs right after they've given birth?'

'*Edwards*,' said Harry. 'Lulu, was Sunshine's father at the engagement party?'

'Oh no,' said Lulu. 'No, sadly, he died. Hank Edwards died of a heart attack more than ten years ago.'

'No,' said Harry. 'Hank Edwards did *not* die of a heart attack. Hank Edwards was murdered. He was shot, execution-style, in the back of the head. Luke, my father, came under suspicion because the guy owed him money, but they never found out who did it. The case intrigued me – it just got me. It still gets me. *Why?* His wife at the time . . . Bessie, that was it – Lily, that is – kept gabbling on to the press until we all suspected that she was somehow involved. But we couldn't prove a thing. There was no physical evidence to link her to the crime. But now it strikes me that Bessie Edwards seems to attract trouble.' He paused. 'Ariel, are you *sure* you never met her?'

Ariel shook her head. 'No. I don't know how her fingerprints got to be in my apartment. The awful thing, though, was that the police showed me a photo of the vodka we were supposed to have been drinking, and the goblets, and they said, "Do you recognize these cups?" and I said, "Yes," because I did recognize them!

They're the black crystal goblets from the VIP poker lounge at the Cat. But they didn't want to listen to that bit, they just wanted me to admit to recognizing them.'

Harry cleared his throat. 'So, these are the facts. We have two husbands, murdered. We have Ben, revealed as *not* Frank or Sofia's son by birth. Sofia knows this, Frank presumably doesn't—'

'Daddy would *die* – I mean . . . It would have killed Daddy to know that Ben wasn't his. He would divorce Sofia, strip her of everything. He idolized Ben. Oh God, do you think . . . ?'

'I do think,' said Harry. 'I'm afraid I think Sofia killed him to prevent him finding out. She is up to her neck in this. *She* planted the evidence in your apartment—'

'But why is Bessie Edwards involved?' said Lulu. 'What reason would she have to kill her husband, or to have him killed? And why would she take Ben?'

'Wait,' said Ariel. 'I see it . . . oh good God. I see it. Lulu, you, you don't know Sunshine's date of birth, do you?'

'I do, as a matter of fact. She was born late at night on 20 August 1984. I only know it because Ben was born the day after: early morning, 21 August 1984. She was trying to bully Ben into having a "joint fiftieth birthday" this year, and he thought it was naff!'

'Jesus,' said Ariel. 'It's there. It's all there. Sunshine called herself Sunshine Arlington, right? That isn't because she married Ben in secret, it's because she realized the truth. She is my *sister*!'

'Of course,' said Harry soberly. He stared at her. 'Clever you, you figured it out. Sofia and Bessie swapped their babies. And that must have been how Bessie came into all that money. We couldn't figure it out. *Sofia*. But why would Sofia do such a thing?'

Ariel smiled sadly. 'You're looking at why. Frank didn't want another girl. Girls, what are they good for? He wanted a little boy, a baby casino operator, and Sofia knew it.' She shuddered. 'Sunshine is my *sister* . . . Ugh, it's like I'm her . . . *ghost image*.'

Harry looked at Ariel sharply. 'She can't hold a candle to you.' He paused and said, more softly, 'A relationship only means what you want it to mean, and the truth is, in here' – he gently touched her chest – 'Ben is yours; Sunshine is not.'

Lulu clapped her hands. 'So now we know the why,' she said. 'But . . .' she added slowly, 'we still don't know the *where*.'

A quiet knock at the door made them all jump. 'Yes?' said Harry. Lulu's heart pounded; maybe Mabel had slyly called the police? But no, here she was, with an awkward smile, carrying a flower-print tray, heavy with gold-leaf-tipped cups and saucers, a fancy teapot and a lemon cake that looked dense enough to break a window.

'Thank you, Mrs García,' said Harry meekly. 'Ah, your delicious lemon cake.'

A faint colour suffused Mrs García's leathery cheeks. She replied, 'The dog is happy. He found a ball to chew.'

'Ladykiller,' said Ariel, with a weak smile when Mabel had gently closed the door. 'Lulu? What is it?'

Lulu was staring after Mabel. She looked at Harry. 'I think', she said, 'I may know where Lily is hiding.'

An upscale suburb in Las Vegas, minutes later

Harry

'I can't see that she'd be anywhere else,' shouted Harry over the roar of the engine. Lulu, Ariel's friend, would have made a good detective, he thought.

'*You* chose to come here,' she'd said, nodding at Mabel's sitting room. 'A place you once lived, where you were happy. Maybe Lily would do the same? Go somewhere she felt happy, or safe?'

Harry had snapped his fingers. 'Yes,' he'd said. '*Yes*. That's it.'

He remembered Hank Edwards's case file. In the course of his investigation, he'd discovered a lot about Hank's history. At the time of death, he and his wife had been living in an enormous gaudy mansion in a loose-lipped tight-assed suburb of Las Vegas: gossipy neighbours with snooty attitudes; Harry's worst nightmare, but, apparently, Bessie Edwards's dream.

He had the information on his laptop, at home. He'd parked the car a cautious distance from the house, made sure the entrance wasn't being watched, and then crept in, and grabbed it. He looked up Bessie's address on his laptop back in the car. They left the car in an adjacent street and approached the mansion on foot.

'Are we sure about this?' murmured Ariel. 'I can't imagine that the current owner would be too happy.'

'We can assume Bessie's armed,' said Harry. 'Then no one but her has a choice. There could be a bunch of people hostage in there.'

Lulu said, 'I don't think Ben went with her because she had a gun. I think he did it to protect his family.'

Harry didn't want to put Lulu and Ariel at risk. 'You need to stay back, right back,' he said. Reluctantly, Lulu and Ariel retreated. 'More,' said Harry, and they shuffled a few steps further back. 'Go and wait with Bones in the car!'

They didn't move and he sighed and sauntered a little closer to the property. Suddenly, to his surprise, the front door of the house swung open, and out trotted a smartly dressed woman with two immaculate children in tow. The girl was dressed in ballet gear and singing 'I am sixteen, going on seventeen'. The mother was speaking into her cell: 'Haddock, Matilda, no, monkfish is far too *fleshy*.' The boy was walking with blind confidence down the steps while jabbing frenziedly at his Nintendo. Hastily, Harry holstered his gun and did an about turn. They trooped back to the car, disconsolate.

And then he remembered. Before the Edwards had lived in the mansion, long before, Hank had been arrested for being drunk and disorderly at a smart casino. And his address had been some crappy mobile home at the arse end of nowhere. Cherub? *Angel!* A tiny, remote cluster of tin-can houses plonked in the desert, not too far from Area 51. It had intrigued Harry at the time. Why would a family move *there*?

It expressed a desire to escape humanity, because while the Edwardses had no money, there were cheap trailer parks dotted all around. Solitude was definitely a preference. And Harry understood it. He recognized that urge: to run from all that hemmed you in. Bessie had sold a child for money; money was everything to her. But when she was poverty-stricken, she had chosen to live in that place. Oddly, it made sense; she must have felt safe there, because only the eccentric, socially curious would choose to live in a spot like that. There Bessie was far from the malicious gaze of the brittle middle classes gloating over one of their own fallen on hard times.

Harry opened the door for Ariel and Lulu. He said, 'We need to head for Area 51.'

The fast low car was tested to its fullest capacity; they sped along Highway 375 in a yellow cloud of dust. He felt alive, he had joy in his heart, he had his girl, he had a mission; he had purpose. Life, he felt, had the capacity to be good again.

'What is our plan?' said Ariel. There was a new strength to her voice. She was in shock, no doubt, but she was remarkable. To have absorbed, or at least heard, what she had heard today would have shattered some minds, but she was tough. He felt a beam of pride. That was his girl: when she was down to the wire, she was as tough as old boots.

'We have two choices. Either way, we keep it simple,' said Harry. 'First, you keep out of sight; we don't want to aggravate her. I knock, tell Bessie it's Las Vegas Police, the show's over, and to come out with her hands where I can see them.'

'She's desperate, Harry. And she's mad. She might try and shoot you – or Ben. What's the other plan?'

'I kick down the door, take her by surprise. Or, maybe, I just open it. I doubt it's locked. There's nowhere for Ben to escape to. We might have to walk for a bit. Or she'll hear the engine.'

'I like it,' said Lulu. She smiled, feebly, and squeezed Ariel's hand. 'I like it when a plan comes together. Oh God, Bones has really chewed the seat material!'

Lulu was right. Once you ordered your thoughts, you could relax a little. Harry felt better now; he felt in control. Harry glanced in his wing mirror. He started, and looked again. Not so far behind them was a large dark blue van, racing along at such a speed that at every bump its wheels seemed to lift off the ground.

'Ah, crap,' he said. 'We're being followed.'

En route for Angel, that same morning

Sofia

'Go *faster*!' she shrieked, gripping the steering wheel until her knuckles turned white. Her mood was poison. It was hard to be anonymous when you were Sofia Arlington, but she had managed it. The Metro were years behind – that female cop and her pal were on her tail but their car wasn't as fast as hers.

Sofia had slipped into one of the security vans used by Ace Harry's and sped home to dispose of her blood-soaked clothes. It was inevitable that the police, slow-witted as they were, would put her under surveillance. No doubt they liked her for Frank's demise, and if she wanted to add the murder of Bessie Edwards to her résumé, she needed to get a move on.

It had been an unwelcome surprise to find Sunshine Beam lolling on her doorstep. This visit was plainly the climax of a massive drinking binge for the girl could hardly stand. 'Apparently, nurture was as powerful as nature. Where the hell have you been? I've been here all night!' she slurred. 'But I've forgotten my manners. Hello, Mommy dear!'

The girl had actually expected, because she was 'blood' as she phrased it, to collect on Ben's inheritance. It had made Sofia's own blood run cold in her veins. But, outwardly, she had dismissed the suggestion as ludicrous. She told the girl she would be laughed out of court and then drummed out of Vegas.

The girl had spat, 'Luke Castillo will have me back, *and* he has a whole room of lawyers.'

Sofia had wanted to throttle her, so acute was the spike of envy. 'Oh darling,' she'd said witheringly, 'a whole room? *I* have a whole floor of lawyers. Run off and make do with a whale. Trey Millington pants after you like a dog. He has made a ridiculous fortune from mechanically recovered meat and I have no doubt you'll be very happy. Now go. How glad I am to have twice escaped having you as a daughter.'

'You are a bad loser,' the girl had said, laughing.

Sofia had slapped her across the face and shouted, 'I *never* lose!'

'You've lost everything,' the girl had said, staggering down the path, garrulous with drink. 'But it's your own fault. You gave it away, and now you can't even get it back. *I* know where Bessie has taken Ben. Even Lulu knows. In fact she took off in my Lamborghini and I'll bet she's already headed over there. Only *you* don't know, and it's because you are too arrogant to understand people. Empathy is the trump card of the narcissist, Mother. I understand Bessie even though I hate her. You hate her, so you don't bother to understand her – and so everything she does surprises you.'

Sofia had trembled with rage. 'Shut up,' she'd hissed. 'Shut up!'

But it was true. One of her many blunders had been to assume that Luke was responsible for Bessie tracking her down and to rashly reveal everything to him.

In fact, there had been no dastardly plan, no puppet master pulling the strings. Sofia's perfect life had unravelled because of sheer maternal desperation; the wish, the craving at molecular level of Bessie to reclaim her son, to wade back through time to a quarter of a century earlier; and to have said *no*.

Now, picking with clammy calm through various, mundane possibilities, she guessed that Bessie had spent endless maudlin hours poring over rich lists and birth dates until she chanced upon the likeliest candidate. Or had she hired someone? A professional investigator! Sofia's blood boiled. It should be illegal.

The pious simplicity of Bessie Edwards's dream made Sofia feel sick. No, she hadn't the first idea where the bitch was hiding out with her son – *her, Sofia's son* – but Lulu knew, and she was driving Sunshine's car.

Sofia had barged past her daughter – only a twinge of regret, the flicker of acknowledgement that in another life, she and Sunshine would have been close – and jumped into the blue van. She had sped around the city, barked orders to Sterling to have his men on the lookout for a red Lamborghini with the licence plate *HOT 1*.

Sterling was well connected: the car's location was relayed to her fifteen minutes later. And now she was in pursuit. Lulu, so hopelessly devoted to Ben, would lead Sofia to him – and to Bessie. And then: *payback*.

Angel, mid-morning

Harry

Harry rammed his foot on the accelerator; so much for creeping up on Bessie. Now it was a question of who got to Ben first. He was nervous. His shoulder ached but today it was because he had actually started his physiotherapy. Still, he wasn't sure about his ability to defend himself or others in a gun fight. Bessie wasn't trained to use a firearm, but according to Ariel, Sofia was ex-military.

'You women should stay in the car,' he said, knowing that he was wasting his breath. 'I ask for selfish reasons.'

They had passed alfalfa fields half an hour back, but now, zooming along Highway 375, there was nothing but rocky desert, unforgiving arid mountain range and endless indeterminate scrub and sand. In the distance, he thought he saw it: the tiny cluster of mobile homes; silver metal glinting in the sunlight. It was here that Bessie had lived for two years. He realized now what she had done on receipt of Sofia's monstrous payment for services rendered. She had bought her ugly grandiose pillared mansion but, ever mindful that poverty could always strike, she had retained ownership of that miserable little trailer and at some point turned it into an investment.

The Bunny Fluff Motel had quite the reputation, although for IRS purposes it was a 'beauty parlour'. Only two girls worked at a time – there wasn't room for more – but, by all accounts, the staff were talented. Harry would go so far as to say, along with Area 51, Bunny Fluff had put Angel on the map.

'My mother has very little to lose now,' said Ariel.

It was true, and it made Sofia more dangerous than ever.

'Nor does Bessie,' whispered Lulu.

Harry always had a plan but, as they hurtled towards their mission, his mind was suddenly, terrifyingly blank. He needed to subdue two women, both of whom were armed. Ben might be injured, unconscious, or worse. There was a serious possibility that this 'rescue operation' could end badly. He hadn't voiced these thoughts to either Lulu or Ariel. He didn't want to jinx the battle before it had even begun. You had to believe you could win, or you were doomed.

He screeched the car to a halt, outside the Bunny Fluff trailer, and leaped out, his gun trained on the door, his heart pounding.

Behind him the blue van skidded to a stop. Sofia, eyes wild, jumped down and started to run towards him.

The tin door of the Bunny Fluff Motel burst open.

Angel, mid-morning

Ben

Apparently, if someone meant to shoot you, they shot you; if they discussed shooting you, it was likely they wouldn't. Armchair wisdom wasn't as comfortable when there was actually a fine chance of getting your head blown off. Lily's face was chalk-white; the fake tan had faded. She smoked compulsively, and drank coffee after coffee; she was as snappy as hell.

'Don't say that,' she muttered, pushing her hair from her eyes, 'I haven't lost you. I've found you, baby, I *found* you. It took me all this time, but I did it, and you can't go. I won't let you. If I can't have you—'

The roar of powerful car engines cut into the silence. The peace here was certainly intermittent, with the ear-splitting zoom of jets flying low enough to skim the rooftops, but this was unusual.

Bessie had the drapes drawn, but now she pulled one open with a shaking hand, keeping the gun trained on him as she did. Ben looked also and he saw, with shock, that it was one of Sunshine's cars.

Relief flooded every sense: surprise; gratitude that she would come to his aid, having sworn that the relation-ship was over – maybe he had misjudged her; and then a curious flat sensation of disappointment, a feeling of dread in the pit of his stomach, that now he would be obliged out of duty, to marry her, a woman he no longer loved.

'Oh Jesus,' Bessie was muttering, 'he's a cop, I know it,

I can sniff out a cop a mile off.' She turned on Ben, bristling with accusation: 'How did you do it? How does he know you are HERE?'

He looked again. There was no sign of Sunshine, but a tall, hard-looking guy who was moving forward with a cool determination. Who *was* it?

Bessie's voice rose to a scream as another vehicle all but flew into sight. Bizarrely, it was Ace Harry's party bus. His heart leaped: Frank? No, ah, it was *Sofia*.

'Fuck,' screamed Bessie, and then, as he stood up, she clutched her head as if it hurt. 'Sit down, Ben. I am warning you: *Sit!*'

He might have obeyed her, because bravado meant very little when you were drowning in a pool of your arterial blood, when, out of the corner of his eye, he saw another person exit the red Lamborghini. Lulu, his darling Lulu, started to run towards the trailer, even as the tall guy yelled a warning.

'Lulu!' cried Ben. 'Don't!'

'*Lulu!*' shrieked Bessie. 'So *that's* the little bitch who's keeping you from me!'

'No!' he shouted, in a voice he had never heard before. It rang with pure, distilled fear. As she aimed the gun, he lunged at her as if her bullets couldn't hurt him. But even as he yanked the weapon from her grasp, he heard the shot – and the scream.

Angel, moments later

Ariel

For her whole life, Ariel had suffered being second best. No one cared because she had so many advantages. Certainly, it was true that if she had wanted that sort of existence, it was there for her: the Paris Hilton world, where she was mistress of her own pink empire, chief purveyor of perfumes, handbags, dog dresses, shoes, lipsticks, nail polish, novels . . . But Ariel had rejected that particular pathway, because she wasn't clever like that and she didn't like to be stared at.

Ariel was good, sweet-natured, serious – as Frank always told anyone who would listen – and so she had buried her anger, repressed every undesirable emotion, even though her mother's lack of respect and love had damaged her, crushed her self-esteem and made her doubt herself.

Sofia would have preferred it had Ariel snatched every tatty opportunity afforded to her by her family's status and wealth. And she had made her opinions painfully known. She was openly disrespectful to her daughter, borderline rude, and Ariel had borne it all, patiently and silently, until that terrible evening at the Grand Opening when she had exploded with humiliation and clawed at her father's face like a cat.

And yet, poor Frank, her dear, well-meaning father, had been a scapegoat. Sofia Arlington was the real subject of her fury but Ariel had always been too frightened, too meek to stand up to her. But now, she saw, that of course Sofia had been the one who had placed those goblets in her apartment. Sofia had set her up to take the hit for her own evil deeds – and now, those years of bottled-up rage burst forth like lava from a long-dormant volcano. Ariel crept silently from the red car and sprang at Sofia.

'How could you kill Daddy?' she screamed. 'How could you?'

Ariel's hand balled into a fist and she swung at her mother. Throwing her entire bodyweight into the punch, she launched a mighty left hook to Sofia's right cheek and, in what seemed like slow motion, her mother jerked forward and fell, dropping her weapon.

Ariel heard and felt the crack of bone. She had fractured Sofia's jaw and, from the pain of it, running up her arm in hot, faint-making waves, she had broken her own hand. Ariel started to scream, but not from the pain.

She was screaming at the gunshot that had exploded without warning, from the trailer – and at the sight of Lulu, sprawled on the ground.

Angel, seconds later

Ben

As he ran out of the trailer, the primal rage in Ariel's voice told him it was true. Frank was dead and Sofia had killed him. The sickening truth passed through him like a ghost, dragging cold fingernails across his heart.

The breath left him; the strength went out of his legs, and he fell to his knees in the dirt, cradling Lulu. The blood – he tried to stem the blood that seemed to be seeping from her neck. Oh Jesus. The tears started to creep from his eyes as he held her to him. It would be too cruel, he couldn't lose her too. 'Oh please, Lulu, I love you, oh baby, wake up, ah God, please, baby, wake up, I love you so much, I'll do anything—'

There was no response; only limp silence.

He moaned aloud. He didn't care any more. Sofia lay unconscious and a slew of police cars wailed and screeched to a halt around them. But it was all too late.

Crack! A second gunshot sounded like thunder, and the Bunny Fluff trailer shook. There was a splat, and the plastic window dripped red with blood and brain matter. Ben closed his eyes, shuddering. 'Oh my God,' he heard Ariel – his angel sister – gasp. 'Dear God.' And he saw the tall guy run to her and hold her. Ah, the cop, Harry Castillo.

As for his biological mother, he felt sick but he couldn't be sorry: Lily Fairweather was author of her own downfall and she had chosen to end her life. How could he pity her or believe in her professed love when she had shot his darling Lulu out of jealousy and spite? Bessie had finally succeeded in ruining his life.

She had made the pact with the devil: Sofia. Ben's fist clenched. Sofia had robbed him of the man who had so tenderly raised him, and she had driven Bessie to the depths of hell. Now, beautiful innocent Lulu was gone, and it was Sofia's fault. Ben felt choked by his anger. He half rose to storm back into the trailer and prise the gun from the still warm hand of Lily Fairweather and shoot Sofia dead.

'I can't do it,' he said, aloud. Revenging Lulu's death was a luxury. It was more important to be there for Joe.

'What?' whispered a voice croakily, and then, as he stared in joyous disbelief: 'You just said you'd do anything, and you've already changed your mind?'

'Thank God,' he whispered into Lulu's hair. 'Thank God you're OK.'

'It got my shoulder,' she murmured. 'It damn well hurts.'

He gently cradled her, kissing her fiercely on the hot desert floor. 'My darling,' he said, 'my darling Lulu, I am never going to let you go again. I love you so much.'

A second convoy of black and whites, their sirens screaming, skidded to a halt, the ambulance close behind. He saw Harry speaking to the other cops – a man and a woman. They seemed to know each other. He saw Sofia cuffed as she woozily came round. He saw her hauled into an ambulance under armed guard.

'Wait,' she screamed when she saw him. 'Wait! I didn't tell Frank! He never knew!'

Ariel hurried over to them, and Ben hugged her. He signalled for the medics to attend to her hand and Lulu's shoulder. 'Ariel,' he said. 'You are a star, and you will always be my favourite sister.' He smiled, but his eyes searched hers for an answer. She stood on tiptoe and kissed him tenderly on the cheek. 'And you', she said, 'will always be my favourite brother, my dearest Ben.'

She held him tight. The sadness squeezed his heart

until he thought it might burst. He closed his eyes against the ferocity of the pain and Ariel rested her head on his chest.

'We'll make Daddy proud,' whispered Ariel.

He lifted her chin and told her, 'He already was.'

At last, he and Ariel slowly walked over to Sofia. He wanted to look her in the eye. She stared back.

'I'm sorry about Frank,' she mumbled, grimacing over the pain of her jaw. 'Truly I am. But I cannot regret anything else.'

Ben gazed down at her. She was beneath contempt. 'Ah,' he said. 'But you should, Sofia. The truth is, Frank loved you. He always did. That was why he married you. It wasn't because you gave him a son – it was nothing to do with me at all. Simply, it was because you "enchanted" him.'

Sofia's face was a mask of horror. Slowly she shook her head. 'Don't be ridiculous,' she said through gritted teeth.

'He told me,' said Ben. 'Dad led with his heart, always. When I told him I was engaged to Sunshine, he couldn't hide his disappointment. He said: "Son, don't ever marry to further your business interests. You gotta marry the girl you'd wish for on a desert island, like I did!"'

Sofia choked. She turned away abruptly, walked three steps and then collapsed. Two burly police officers grabbed her as she fell and hauled her to the ambulance. Her wrenching sobs cut into the silence.

As they closed the doors, Ben walked, and then ran towards the girl he had wished for while stranded in the desert.

434

Epilogue

Lulu

Lulu watched Tallulah Castillo (two and a half), and James Arlington (two) jostle over possession of a pink ride-on tricycle and then squeeze into it together. Bones ran around them wagging his tail.

Lulu and Ariel exchanged glances and smiled.

As long as love existed, so would grief, and yet, even in the most harsh and unpromising of circumstances, it was possible for good to triumph over bad. Time washed away old sins, and even in sorrow, comfort could be found by those with the resolve to seek it out.

When Frank Arlington's will was read, it became clear that Frank had changed his mind about the inability of a mere female to operate a casino. He had requested that Ariel be appointed to the board. In the event, she had decided not to accept, agreeing only to take up a more junior position when Ben agreed to put his Macau venture on hold and help her to reshape the Arlington Corporation.

'Daddy!' roared Joe as Ben swam to the edge of the pool. 'I want to jump off your shoulders!'

Lulu's heart still swelled every time she saw them together.

'*My* daddy!' cried Tallulah as Harry walked towards the barbeque, whistling, with a tray full of raw sausages. '*My* daddy is a police who rescues people and he is going to burn some sausages for us to eat!'

It amazed Lulu that only four years earlier, at the Grand Opening of the Cat, Ben had told her that if she never gave up, she would get what she wanted. Or at least, she had thought he'd said so at the time. She had held fast to that unlikely belief, and even if her hopes had come to nothing, she could not have regretted her wish. In the hardest of times, what else did you have to sustain you?

She had another wish, for the little ones now (she and Ben had learned to be both ambitious and modest in their aspirations) and it was this: wish only to be happy, and never regret your dreams.

And so, in the light of their parents' love, the babies of Ben and Lulu, Harry and Ariel fought together and played, and around them swirled the hot sands of Turtle Egg Island, earth ground to dust by water and wind over millions of years. The human race, thought Lulu, was a small, brief dot in time, a force for both good and evil, but mostly, she was certain, for good.

Betrayal

By Sasha Blake

MONEY

Emily Kent is the daughter of one of the most powerful women on the planet. Her mother and billionaire father have laid the world at her feet – it's not enough. Emily is determined to make her *own* luck.

LUST

Claudia Kent is Emily's step-sister – all she craves is love. Desperate to escape the misery of her past, she meets the man of her dreams. Or so she imagines . . .

VENGEANCE

Nathan Kent is the son of no one. Adopted, and then discarded by the one family who could have loved him, he has only one goal in life – to get his revenge.

GREED

As disgraced tycoon Jack Kent and his wife Innocence fight for supremacy over their vast empire, family ties are flung aside – no one will stand in the way of their obsession with money, sex and power.

9780553819151